VOK

Jason Kucharik

Luke,

Thanks for the support! Hope you enjoy the book :)

Copyright 2016 Jason Kucharik
Published by Jason Kucharik

ISBN-13: 978-1533392312
ISBN-10: 1533392315

Table of Contents

Dedication

Acknowledgements

Chapter One: A Bullshit Mission	1
Chapter Two: Surfacing	23
Chapter Three: Extraction	37
Chapter Four: The Devil is in the Details	49
Chapter Five: Scratching the Itch	63
Chapter Six: Abomination	71
Chapter Seven: Down the Rabbit Hole	87
Chapter Eight: Rebirth	95
Chapter Nine: Blood is Thicker Than…	103
Chapter Ten: Lightning Never Strikes Twice	113
Chapter Eleven: Push Back	123
Chapter Twelve: Starting from Scratch	141
Chapter Thirteen: Employing Assets	153
Chapter Fourteen: Muscle Memory	167
Chapter Fifteen: The Dark Castle	177
Chapter Sixteen: First Mission	187
Chapter Seventeen: Wake Up Call	197
Chapter Eighteen: A Glittery Mission	209
Chapter Nineteen: Blind Bet	219
Chapter Twenty: Hurry Up and Wait	229

Chapter Twenty-One: The Never-Ending Day	239
Chapter Twenty-Two: Mini My Ass	249
Chapter Twenty-Three: Realization	257
Chapter Twenty-Four: Stressed	263
Chapter Twenty-Five: Sacrifice	271
Chapter Twenty-Six: Ramifications	277
Chapter Twenty-Seven: Déjà Vu	287
Chapter Twenty-Eight: The Outer Shores	297
Chapter Twenty-Nine: The Unexpected Visit	305
Chapter Thirty: Delayed Vengeance	313
Chapter Thirty-One: Welcome to the Party	321
Chapter Thirty-Two: Blink	331
Chapter Thirty-Three: Damn Arrow	337
Chapter Thirty-Four: Catch	347
Chapter Thirty-Five: Infiltration	357
Chapter Thirty-Six: Just Keep Moving	367
Chapter Thirty-Seven: Dropping In	377
Chapter Thirty-Eight: The Challenge	385
Chapter Thirty-Nine: The Pain of Irony	393
Chapter Forty: Successful Failure	403
Chapter Forty-One: The One Who Returns	417
Chapter Forty-Two: The Mess	425
Chapter Forty-Three: Hello Boys	439
Chapter Forty-Four: The Forgotten Planet	455

Chapter Forty-Five: How Romantic	461
Chapter Forty-Six: Prerequisite Bullshit	475
Chapter Forty-Seven: The Final Mission	483
Chapter Forty-Eight: The Firestorm	495
Chapter Forty-Nine: The Fall	505
Epilogue: The Myth	521
About the Author	525

Dedication

This book is a dedication to my parents. It's a dedication to the all the hard work, discipline, focus, and passion that was instilled in me and subsequently required to make this book possible. It's a dedication to their continued support for nearly thirty years, while I switched from one focus to the next, unsure of what I wanted to accomplish in my life. It's a dedication to the man I am today, because of the blood, sweat, tears, money and most importantly love, that they never stopped pouring from their souls to ensure that I would become a man that they'd be proud to unleash upon the world. I hope that whatever I do, wherever I go, or whoever I become, that I continue to feed their pride. Thank you for making this possible.

With love, Jason

Acknowledgements

First and foremost, I would like to take the time to thank my editor, Stacey Kucharik of Polished Print. For all your guidance, direction, and patience along the way. A very large part of who I've become as a writer is a direct result of your continued guidance and insight. I don't know where I'd be with my writing if it wasn't for you, but I can guarantee that no one would be reading this right now. I cannot even begin to express my thanks, and I look forward to working with you for many years to come. Secondly, I would like to thank all of my early beta readers, certainly not the least of which is my uncle, Frank Kucharik. You were one of the first people to read my work and take the time to make a ton of grammatical corrections as well as offer insight to the storyline and characters. To this day, whenever I post new work, I can't wait to hear what you think. Directly behind him would be my aunt, Nancy Kucharik, my mother, Karen Kucharik, my father, Jim Kucharik, and my sisters Becky Confer and Rachael Bowers. All of you pushed me to continue the story and were always available to help me shape ideas as I often hastily explained what I had in mind for this fictional universe. Next, I'd like to thank my good friend and fellow writer, Taran Matharu. You paved the way on Wattpad and your insight into the publishing industry has been invaluable, not to mention your honesty and friendship. Congratulations on all of your success, and I can't wait to catch up. Number three, eh? Challenge accepted. Thank you, Stephen Landry. Not only for posing one of the inciting questions that led to this book, but for your friendship, support, and late night chats about Science Fiction and various authorial ideas. You're one hell of a talented guy, and look forward to your success. Peter Hackshaw, you cheeky bastard! You came into the fold last, but definitely made up for lost time with your creativity, passion and, at times, sickly amazing skills as a storyteller. I appreciate your friendship, honesty, and creativity. I have no doubt that your work will take off. Miguel Santoyo and Luca Gonzales. You guys are awesome. Thank you for your undying friendship and always being there when I needed to talk. Just by being the men you are, you pushed me to be a better person and author and I love you for that. James Jones, Jr. Thank you for making me understand that sometimes you need to stop trying to fix what's broken and instead create something new. San Diego led directly to writing and you are an integral part of that. Chris Godsoe, Mary Fan, Terry Hill, Scott McCoskey. and David Stegora. Not only are you all immensely talented individuals, but I'm proud to call every last one of you friends, despite the odd nature of us connecting and getting to know each other. You've all helped in more ways than you know, and I'm forever grateful. Tyler Thull. The cover you created put a face to VOK. Your skills and direction while developing the cover led to an image that I didn't directly envision, but love nonetheless. I can't wait to see what you'll produce for me in the future. Last but not least, I'd like to thank not only the entire staff at Wattpad, but all of my readers on Wattpad as well, especially my early readers that have been so vocal since the beginning. There are too many to name for fear that I may miss a few, but you know who you are. If it wasn't for your constant support and help in shaping VOK as I wrote it, this book wouldn't exist. You're all amazing and honestly a huge reason as to why not only VOK happened, but why it happened so quickly, though I'm sure it didn't seem too quick! Your feedback was invaluable throughout the writing process and I look forward to posting more work for everyone to read. Thank you for being so interested and keeping me on track! To everyone mentioned above, and all of my friends and family, I love you from the bottom of my heart.

Chapter 1: A Bullshit Mission

Dec 25th 2467 1:30 pm Earth Time

There are a lot of things in this world (and a great many others for that matter) that I never expect to see. Whales, for one. Rumor has it that they died out centuries ago. I can't even imagine what it would be like to see a beast that large swimming seamlessly through the ocean. Of course, in all fairness, the oceans of Earth were a lot deeper back then.

Humans, most definitely. It's odd, seeing as they've been the foundation of our society and lifestyles since we discovered their existence, but still, I don't think I'll be seeing any humans in my lifetime. At least not a proper human. I heard that the last of them are reserved for royalty, if there *are* any left at this point. Though Bill and I have been to The Outer Shores and haven't even seen them there, so I highly doubt it. Let's see what else...

As I rack my brain for more things that I'll probably never have the chance to see, Bill pulls off his pack, swings it around his shoulder to his chest and pulls out an IV spout. Before I can yell at him for being so incredibly stupid he swings it up over his head and jams it into the bark of the tree behind him.

"Are you a fucking idiot?" I growl through my teeth knowing full well the answer.

Looking at me with those eager, thirsty eyes, he leans back against the tree turning his attention to the spout as a thick blood-red liquid starts to drip into his open mouth. It's lazy for me to call it blood-red seeing as it *is* blood in some loose sense of the word, but I'm too exhausted to use proper syntax at the moment. Rumor has it that for years after the Bloodwar of 2106, our top scientists poked and prodded, experimented and spliced the humans into horrific abominations. Sometime after that—no one truly knows when—the Picea Hemofilia, more commonly known as lifeblood tree, was born. A basic tree spliced with human DNA, it almost resembles a naturalistic version of bio-computers. These trees are living, breathing, twisted versions of what humans once were and honestly their greatest contribution to our species, even if it is, by all accounts and purposes, totally fucked up. You won't find any sympathy from our people though. My company commander always says, "Maybe if they stopped fighting each other for ridiculous beliefs and just evolved they would have survived." But they didn't. They nearly tore each other apart before we got there. We were just the cleanup crew.

"Okay, you know why we're out here, why would you even think to risk that?" I ask Bill knowing full well the answer.

"I'm hungry," he gurgles out between sips. The blood is flowing more consistently now.

He's hungry, of course he is. Fuck. If I had a single blood coin for every time I got into a situation because Bill was *hungry*. Although to be fair, the only reason it's much more dangerous on this mission is because we're supposedly hunting a legion of Thyr and they can smell fresh blood from miles away. Which comes full circle to my original thought. I never thought there could come a day that I would see a Thyr, let alone a legion of them. From what I understand, they weren't around when humans lived freely in these lands, but they were foretold by some prophet of men called J.R.R. The prophet warned of past times when the Thyr, or as he called them, Orcs, ruled the lands and tried to take control of the one ring.

They were smaller in his prophecy, the size of humans, and I have no idea how a simple ring could be an object of power. It seems unlikely to me, but then again, I'm sure we seemed unlikely to the humans before we showed up.

There was another time that they popped up in our own personal history. The uprising of 2252. Unfortunately, Bill and I were stuck out in The Outer Shores on some shit detail when it all went down. While the intel on this current mission is supposedly rock solid, I have my doubts. I know the Alphas who led the tide against the uprising, and believe me when I say, they crushed those bastards out of existence. Still, the universe is a frighteningly large place, and I've come to learn that anything is possible, no matter how unlikely.

The other thing that makes this operation more dangerous than usual is the frequent reports of Mini Ks scouring the area. Now Mini Ks were supposedly foretold in another human prophesy, but not in writing. From what I was told, this one was in visual form, a sort of glass-like surface that allowed people to view the future as it would come to pass. This particular prophecy was told by a man named Del Toro. He was much further off from the truth than J.R.R. There are beasts that exist, as he described them in the stunning blue imagery that his prophecy was shown, but they are much smaller in size. The infants are closer to that of an extinct moose if you will, the adults about twice that size. More than big enough to cause some damage if they come rummaging through the battlefield as they often do, making a great bloody mess of things as they go along. The creatures in his prophecy were called Kiaju. Stupid name, I have no idea what it means. Stupid or not though, it didn't stop the soldiers from naming the actual creatures after them. Mini K, seeing as they're smaller. Small enough to hitch a ride on one of our larger cargo freighters and get off on Earth. Our sensors don't pick them up because they're genetic structure was completely different than anything we had come across at that point. The sensors were updated after that mishap. They populated quickly, being able to carry two litters at once, much like the mythical rabbit. Mini K, real fucking original. Only a jackass uses the term Mini K.

"Put the damn IV away and keep on the lookout for Mini Ks." Yes, I just called myself a jackass. "We've had reports of them in the area and I for one don't want to get trampled to death. You remember that snatch and grab on that planet...what the hell was it called? The one with the blue ferns?"

"Shit, how could I forget? Ten days of waiting, just to avoid getting trampled by spending hours in that tight crater you made with a directional grenade. What a pain in the ass that was."

"Exactly, I'd prefer not to go through that again."

"Yeah well, we're on this damn peak, it's not like they're going to trample us up here." Bill has a tendency to approach missions in a more straightforward manner. He deals with problems as they're presented, even though it goes against our training. He says it allows him to be more flexible in the field. I prefer to look at every possible angle and be prepared for whatever might come. As much as I'd prefer him to think more like me, his mindset does allow for a different perspective and together we're able to cover all our bases.

"And..."

"And if we're forced off the peak the ground around us is a perfect stomping ground for those monstrous assholes," He answers in a mocking voice while bouncing his head from side to side. "If you ask me, this is a bullshit assignment," Bill mutters as he begrudgingly stuffs his IV back into his pack. He pulls out a few snack-size bags to catch the excess blood flowing out of the small hole in the bark.

"Funny, I didn't ask you. Just like the last fifteen times you said that." I shoot back. "This is not a bullshit assignment, the High Order believes that Thyr may be back in the area and they want to make sure that they aren't trying to take back Earth. There have been more than a few communications disruptions over the past couple of months. Classic Thyr guerrilla tactics." I wonder where that term came from...guerrilla tactics.

"'Classic Thyr guerrilla tactics'," he mocks, "Get that from your overly boring, extensive research did you? This is a bullshit assignment and you know it. Nobody has seen a Thyr in over a century and it's been over two since a legion was seen. Not since the uprising of 2252 and there's no evidence that they held the Earth for more than a few years before we discovered and then enslaved them in that year. We are assets, extremely skilled assets, who could be put to better use in other parts of the galaxy in more pivotal portions of the war against The Plague."

"There's also no evidence that the Thyr who fought in the uprising comprised the whole species shit head. Ever think that there were other colonies out there? And what about Vali's intel?" I ask. That shuts him up. Bill knows as well as I do that regardless of what bullshit intel the High Order feeds us, Vali knows his shit. Through and through, he's been there to provide the quality intel that we so desperately need on ops. Vali is an...information broker of sorts. We've worked with him for centuries.

He is right about us being better put to use though. As Alphas we are the best that the Red Military has to offer, but I don't like making a habit of confirming Bill's points. The plague, by the way, is a genetic mistake from our High Scientists. Not everything they do is as beneficial as the lifeblood trees. They attempted to take a viral approach on curbing 'the appetite' of our people, Hemosapiens, also known as Hemos, but it only made things worse for the subjects who volunteered. Then when they tried to tweak the virus and fix their mistakes, it made things much worse. The test subjects essentially turned into rabid, bloodthirsty, uncontrollable versions of themselves. They couldn't help but tear everything apart and feast on whatever was before them. At first we had just assumed that they were mindless creatures that needed to be put down. Then they started to organize. They continued to feed but also selected certain people to infect and turn, always the strongest, always the smartest. They are evolving as a mutant species and becoming more intelligent by the day, all while gaining more control over their feeding habits. This doesn't hinder their ruthless, violent behavior though we can keep hoping as useless as it is.

"Of course maybe," I bring my pointer finger up to my lips and tap them sarcastically, "just maybe, we wouldn't have gotten this assignment if you hadn't told a High Priestess that she could *suck you bone dry any day.*" I say the last part of that sentence in my best Bill-voice.

I'll give him credit for trying to contain his laughter, but not for the weak explanation. "That's," he chuckles, "that's not my fault!" Another giggle escapes his lips. "I didn't know she was a High Priestess, and to be fair, did you see her?"

"Oh yes, I saw her...and I saw the face she made after you said that, right before I put my hand over my own face in disgust. In fact, I saw everyone's around her too as I'm pretty sure most of the patrons in the ballroom heard your loud, crude ass. We're in a war with savage beasts who can't control their thirst...a little discretion in your choice of sleazy pick-up lines might be wise. And, might I add, who you deliver them to."

Bill doesn't respond. He just smiles and pulls up his rifle to scan the area muttering, "She's no Blaze though." under his breath as he does.

"What's that?" I shoot back.

"Oh nothing, you do you, or you know, her," he chuckles.

I sigh. "What ever happened to 'not my place'?"

He shifts slightly to get into a more comfortable position while keeping an eye down the barrel of the rifle. "Well you know, that was before I knew you loved her."

Great, I've barely admitted that to myself let alone her. I'm better off avoiding the topic all together. "And now you know, so now I can look forward to more sarcastic comments and prodding questions?"

"Yeah well," he smirks.

Typical Bill. Luckily, he doesn't say anything else and seems to be momentarily content on doing his job without talking. I find myself thinking back on the humans and how little proof there is on their history. The problem is that all humanistic forms of written, auditory, or visual communication from before the Bloodwar of 2106 were banned and subsequently destroyed by the High Order. That's why a lot of the fact and myths we know today are surrounded by muddied water. Hell, I had some recruit tell me just the other day that he heard from a classmate in Impulse Control 101 that humans used to just give their politicians millions upon millions of dollars to travel the country and talk about themselves. I don't know how much a dollar was worth to the humans, but I imagine it's close to our denomination of blood coins. I could retire from the military and live out the next five centuries traveling the universe on that kind of money. To make matters worse, he said the humans would then choose the most popular one to lead them.

What insanity! Here's a shit-ton of money, go become popular and we'll award you the opportunity to rule over society. They didn't base it off of intellect or military prowess. I mean, if our leaders did their jobs out of greed for money instead of the honor to serve their people and create the strongest society they could...well, no wonder the humans didn't last that long. Don't get me wrong, there are a few leaders in the Red Military that need to be reminded of this fact, but nowhere near to the extent where it hurts our race overall. Though I was also told they had an obsession with fried dirty animal fat and worshipping prophecies to the point of not actually living their lives, so who knows? My point is, there's a lot of crazy theories out there and no proof to support them. The most laughable one suggests we're descended from them. Really? Come on people, really? We look the same externally and may have some similar base DNA codes, but there's no way they came first, we've been around for millennia and are far more advanced.

    I should probably get to the mission at hand, though it's not like I can't multitask, this is boring as hell. I pull my rifle up to scan the valley below. Still no sighting of Mini Ks in the area and no signs of Thyr either. We're on a peak, Frary peak (once again, no idea why it was called that or what it meant) with several lifeblood trees for cover/food, overlooking a massive crater that at one time was called the Great Salt Lake. It isn't a lake anymore, there's barely any water left. Mostly just a valley of dried rock and sand. The communications arrays that have been going down are all along the far edge of the valley in front of us. High Order Intelligence groups suggested that the Thyr have survived and regrouped in the west and are crossing the Salt Flats and then the Great Salt Valley to set up a base camp in the forested ridges behind us. When I asked to see the thermal scans of the area I was denied access. Something's going on.

Yet, there isn't anything out here and the forest behind us aren't even that big. Maybe that's why the Thyr wanted them. We wouldn't suspect a base of operations for a woodland dwelling species in the middle of a mostly-desert. The fact that the wooded area behind us thrived remains a mystery. Earth's ecosystem was never fully mapped and understood by our people and no matter how much we bombarded, irradiated, and tampered with the plant life, that one section behind me continues to receives rain and grow. The damn lake dried up but the trees are fine. Go figure. It's not unheard of; there are areas like that all over Earth and those are the areas that we fear. Those are the areas where it's easy for the Thyr to hide and scheme and grow.

Thyr aren't as dumb as they seem either. They may be large and brutish, use only blunt weapons or swords, but it's not because they're stupid. They've mastered space travel and light speed just like we have, but they're bound by old ways. The Thyr believe in honor in battle above all else. Any weapon to be used that doesn't become lethal due to the Thyr's own muscle is considered dishonorable. Guns, lasers, bombs, all out. Swords, axes, hammers, bows, these are the weapons they fight with. It's said that when the Thyr first returned, a group of Hemo Beta soldiers underestimated the large opponents due to their choice of weapons and battle style. In turn those soldiers, or what was left of them, became a bloody message that was delivered to High Command. Our tactics were altered after that. See a pattern?

Thyr are big, nearly twice the height of us, muscular, fast, and will fight to the last breath. I could take the arm off of one of them a thousand yards away with my laser rifle and he would still run up and cut my head off given the chance. They carry phosphate powder on them at all times. Should a wound become too bad, they smear it across the skin and immediately fuse the flesh together to stop the bleeding and keep fighting. They feel pain, but it doesn't faze them. Decades of training their soldiers to ignore pain, or welcome it, has made them into near perfect soldiers. By the High Order, we're screwed if they ever lose their honor and pick up normal weapons. They don't need much sleep and there is absolutely no questioning of orders among the ranks. With their strength and size they can set up camp for a legion in a few hours from nothing other than the materials of the forest or by burrowing a cave system into the earth. Once the camp is set up, autonomic sentinels fly in their communications and recon equipment. They are extremely efficient, thus making them extremely dangerous.

    All said and done, the Thyr may seem undefeatable, but this only exemplifies how lethal we, as Alphas, are in turn. They are fast, but we are faster; they are intelligent, but we rank as geniuses; they are efficient, but we are damn near perfect; they're bred to fight, but we're bred to survive. Our endurance is what really gives us the edge though. We can fight for days at a time without stopping, slaughtering everything in our path. Give us scattered moments of rest and a supply of fresh blood and that turns into weeks. Our rifles, side arms, Ka, electrostatic exo-skeletons, recon equipment, and jump gear, allow us to tear them apart one by one and if need be, move faster than they can hope to keep up. We may have never seen a Thyr in person, but virtual training has made us surgeons of destruction. We know exactly what to expect and how to fight them. High Intelligence suggests that there could be up five thousand Thyr here, enough to comprise a full legion. If that's true, it would be more than we could handle alone, but given our equipment and skills we could separate them and cripple that legion to the point of being utterly useless in a few days. That isn't our mission though. Our mission is to gain intelligence on the surrounding area, nothing more. Engage only if we are engaged first.

Bill's finally content with doing his job so I raise my rifle as well and scan the valley below. Something's off. There's no movement, which was normal considering the lack of wildlife in the valley below, but...we're missing something. As I try to figure out what has me so spooked, warm, moist air rolls over my back, followed by an ever so faint, rumble from our rear.

"CONTACT!" Bill screams and the whooshing sound of a large metal hammer closes on my position. I roll to the left away from Bill. Lying on my back I look up to see a massive Thyr hunched over, hands gripping the hammer that just split the rock I was kneeling on. Bill pulls his side arm and fires a laser into the beast blowing its kneecap all over the ground. The Thyr topples down onto its hammer and grits its teeth at me with a deep low growl. His head explodes. I wipe the dark blood from my visor to see the barrel of Bill's primary rifle through the massive hole in the Thyr's head. Lucky for me laser rounds explode on impact. One of the many beneficial experiments of the High Scientists that actually worked...most of the time. It cuts down friendly fire in the field by ninety-five percent. It's not perfect, but hell, I'll take it.

"How the fuck did he get the drop on us?" Bill yells. His frustration is more about competition than anything else. We're better than them, even with all our fucking around, this shouldn't have happened.

"A testament to their eyesight and our ignorance." I reply calmly.

"The Thyr don't have recon teams!" He's pissed and ready for blood. I'm pretty sure I know what's coming, and I'm glad that Bill is amped up. I have a feeling he's gonna need that fire, the Nox-Ira. Every Alpha has their own Nox-Ira, in fact, it's one of the ways our people are able to distinguish soldiers who are qualified to become Alphas. The Nox-Ira is a separate personality that takes over when the bloodlust becomes too great, an inner demon of sorts that ignores pain and fear while embracing rage.

"That we know of," I note quietly staring at the drop behind us. Bill takes the hint and shuts his mouth as I rise to my feet and inch my way toward the drop off. I slink to my belly and crawl to the edge, peeking my head just far enough over to observe the cliff below. A massive sword flies past my head and into the air above me. The rock face is riddled with Thyr all climbing at an increased rate at the sight of my face, which serves as a confirmation that we killed their sentry. The blade comes back down and lands an inch from my head, sticking into the ground. I actually forgot about that for a second.

"Well hello, Sally." Bill says from behind me. I jump to my feet and run over to his position in front of the other drop off. "How many?" he asks eagerly.

"Too many to fight in this location. Launch," I order.

"Aw, come on...," he starts to protest as another large blade pierces the lifeblood tree next to us, causing blood to spray out in every direction. We turn to see another Thyr crouching down in attack position. He lets out an ear-piercing, deep roar that echoes through the valley below.

"LAUNCH!" I shout, and a second later we're in the air. Now, due to our natural strength, we're fast on our own, but our recon suits are one of the main reasons that we're such a force to be reckoned with on the battlefield. They're light, and shrink onto our bodies like a second skin that increases our strength and speed. Science aside, the outcome is us being able to run at top speeds of one hundred miles per hour in ideal conditions and launch ourselves up to a mile and a half depending on the base strength of the soldier. I can launch just shy of a mile and a half and Bill is never far behind.

As we fly through the air there's still something about the valley below that's bothering me, something that doesn't quite add up. Upon landing, I become painfully aware of what it is. I touch down first, dust and sand flying out in every direction as I do and Bill touches down a second later. We're surround by Thyr and they're all glaring with hatred, lips peeling back to reveal their razor-sharp teeth.

"Launch!" I shout again and we're in the air before any of them can swing an axe.

"They're using cloaking tech!" Bill hollers through the comms.

"Bill, sophisticated technology. Inside voices." As I've told him a million times before on ops, I don't need him screaming in my ear. "Yes, they are. Which is why we couldn't see the legion and didn't know that they had circled around us."

"Sorry. Well, there are no reports of them ever using cloaking tech, it doesn't line up with their honor or whatever."

"Yeah well, there's a ton of unreported shit in the universe. Nobody has seen a force this size in two centuries. I'm guessing they're desperate. Even the most honorable will turn to different means when their species is about to be wiped out. We're just here to gain intel, looks like we just did."

We land a little over a mile away from our last position. Based on how far away they are, we must have been near the rear the first time we touched down. The cloaking has been disabled now and we can see the entire legion. They want to make their presence known. Doesn't matter if they think it's just us, or a larger force, they're ready to fight.

We turn away from main mass to look at our exit options, but it isn't looking good. There's another group of fifty Thyr, now in front of us, bringing up the rear. Huh, scouting parties at the front and the back. That's different. More intel.

"Uh, these guys are charging. What are we doing?" Bill's right, the group of fifty to the rear started closing on us, but as long as the legion stands its ground we'll be okay. We could try to make an exit to the left or right, but where's the fun in that? Bill and I have been training our whole lives to fight the Thyr, and I'm not about to throw away this shot at a 'live fire' exercise to see what they're really capable of.

"Rifle, and call out." Bill and I have been operating together long enough that he knows those four simple words mean more than they project. Head shots are standard, well, when it comes to species who have heads that is. Call out means we'll tell each other the basic stats of each shot, it helps with situational awareness. Thyr are fast and I want to take them down before they close the gap. Our rifles can be set up for distance sniping or close quarters, but generally speaking we have a tendency to sling the rifle and switch to side arms at close quarters. We both take a knee to get into a more stable firing position and begin to drop Thyrs as they advance.

"A hundred and fifty yards." Bill pauses.

There's a brief moment, before an op gets crazy, before that first shot is fired, that I focus on the world around me. All the little changes in sound, atmosphere, every little idiosyncrasy that my body can register, in whatever means possible. I sense it all at an increased and amplified rate. It's my Nox-Ira; he wants come out and play. He doesn't take prisoners or make mistakes. He is an unrelenting machine, made for one purpose. To kill.

Every grain of sand that kicks up from the oncoming Thyr I see. Every little gust of wind I feel. Each massive foot that makes landfall I hear. There's a small sensation of heat to my right, it's

Bill's barrel priming as he squeezes the trigger on his rifle. Then, as is typical, time falls back into place as it should and I'm in it.

"Down," Bill fired his first shot. "Whoooo! Holy shit did you see that!"

I did. Nothing could make me feel better about our current situation then seeing that head explode into a cloud of black mist.

"Bill..."

"I mean fuck man, I've never seen a Thyr head explode before. *That* was awesome."

I call off my own as well, "One ten, down. You just shot one in the head on the peak. One thirty-five, down."

He chuckles, "Yeah man, but that was close quarters, made a clean hole. Two hundred, down. This thing fucking exploded."

"Focus," I remind. Bill can get excited when it comes to killing. This situation could easily go south, especially with the legion behind us.

"Yeah yeah," he placates. "One twenty five, one fifteen down. By the way, they're picking up speed."

"Switch to burst." Burst mode on our rifles allow us to scope a target, lock on, then move to the next. We can acquire up to three targets before firing and the lasers would find their own way.

"One two five, one three oh, one three oh. Three down." Bill calls off.

"One ten, one-oh-five, one. Three down." As they close the gap, I can see the rear proximity sensor in my optics flashing.

"Oh, shit just got interesting," Bill says. He's right, the legion is sending out another squad of Thyr from behind us. Some straight to us, then a group to the left, and one to the right. They're planning on trapping us. We could just launch over them and escape, but I won't lie, I'm really interested in seeing what they can do.

"I see 'em," I say.

"Escape plan would be nice...sir." Bill only calls me sir when he's nervous. To be fair, there's good reason to be, but it's my job to remove that reason and replace fear with fire.

"Shoulder primary and move to secondary and Ka, launch forward and bring the fight to them, we'll tear our way out of this mess. Bill...," I pause, glancing to my right, waiting for him to look at me. "Let's remind these fuckers why they hide."

A deep satisfaction crawls its way across Bill's face in the form of a wide, grim smile before he launches into the air toward the rear scouting party. I follow right behind him. The second we're in the air, we toss our rifles over our shoulders. Nanotechnology allows them to snap to our bodies, if we ever lose them in battle, they come back on their own. If we toss them over our shoulders, they contract into a compact little package and latch onto the back of our suits.

Like finely calibrated machines, we pull out our side arms in unison and prepare to land. Bill blows a Thyr's head off before landing on its shoulders and riding the body to the ground. He's always loved theatrics on the battle field. This only incites the rage of the other Thyr, something that will definitely benefit us in the fight. Enraged Thyr are said to be more likely to make mistakes.

"Count 'em off!" I yell to Bill.

"Gladly!" he replies. "One down!" He moves to the next closest Thyr and dodges a sword, whipping out his Ka, or close contact blade, to sweep the back of the creature's legs while moving past it. The Thyr drops to the ground as Bill slides on his knees behind it. He rotates away from the downed Thyr, and back up on his feet to shove the pistol against another Thyr's chest, blowing a hole where its heart should be. If that's not enough, with a flick of the wrist, the Ka slices open its throat. Bill rotates back to avoid the newly created corpse as it falls forward, and he presses the pistol to the back of the first Thyr's head. Boom. "Two and three, both down!" he calls out.

Our Ka is thin compared to the Thyr's massive swords. The hilts are custom and just big enough to encompass the user's hand, there's no guard and the blade itself is only three inches wide and less than an eighth of an inch thick, ending in a squared off edge three and a half feet away from the hilt. It's small, but nearly unbreakable and easy to move around at quick speeds. The best part is that we can eject the blade out, breaking it into pieces connected by nanowire, creating a ten-foot long, razor sharp whip that will slice through anything unfortunate enough to get caught in its path.

"Four, five!" I yell back taking down two coming up from my rear. There's dual purpose to counting off our kills. One is that it's easy and helpful to keep up situational awareness. We've been trained to do complex mathematical equations on the fly, so counting off our kills in order to know how many are left is simple. The second reason is to taunt the enemy. Throw them off balance, make them realize how quickly we're taking them down. Of course, who knows if it works against an enemy as ruthless as the Thyr. Five down, plus the eleven we took out before launching the second time, thirty-four to go, more than doable.

We continue killing and counting off. As long as I hear Bill shout out a subsequent number I know everything's okay, there's no reason to check. We hack and slash, fire off rounds with our side arm when possible, sometimes headshots and sometimes just shots to give us that extra precious second to react. Bill does a mini vertical launch once to gain some perspective, but for the most part we keep the fighting close to the ground. With their size, it's difficult for the Thyr to match our speed.

"Thirty-four!" Bill shouts. It's done, we took out the entire rear recon squad and in doing so cleared a path of escape. "That it?" he exclaims jubilantly, laughing as he does. "Okay, Blaze was right, they are stronger than the practice drones, but come on, gimme a challenge, am I right?

"How about a legion?" The groups that broke off from the legion are still advancing with the closest one only a hundred yards away. I'm willing to bet they wouldn't hesitate to turn around the whole legion if we kept taking them out. While this nice little battle has solidified my confidence in our ability to kick their collective ass, it's not our mission. We need to report back.

"We need to launch again. Follow my lead." I take off without allowing him to reply. He follows without hesitation. Now, I'm not in the Patriarch, our Fleet Command ship that's sitting just outside the Earth's atmosphere, but I know exactly what's going on. The funny thing about our feed systems is they're a two-way street. The High Scientists don't tell you that, but the information is streamed directly from your visor in case anything goes wrong in the field. That way they don't lose the data, but they only have video feeds from the gear built into our helmets. There are rumors that they used to have a way to record subconscious brain waves and other information but it caused too many problems and got nixed pretty quickly. At the very least, that story lines up with the High Scientist's process. It leads to theory that if something can send information out, then you could find a way to push information in, and with all the cameras on the Patriarch, well… it isn't just a theory, it's fact. Vali, our information broker and well…hacker, built us a back door. Direct access to all feeds from the Patriarch. I can't review saved data at all, just see live feeds, but it helps occasionally. Honestly, I don't really use it that often. We land and launch again.

"Captain Otto, come in. This is Blood Pack Alpha Recon Team Delta, Alpha, Echo operating in the..." I don't even get to finish the transmission.

"Get on with it, Lieutenant, we don't have time for pleasantries."

"Yes, sir. Thyr existence confirmed, one legion seen moving west of Old Salt Lake into forested region."

"Any engagements?"

He has access to sophisticated imagery and is no doubt watching our every move, why even ask? "Yes, sir. One killed at surveillance position, fifty killed during escape."

"They got the drop on you, Lieutenant?"

"There's new intel we need to..."

"Never mind. I'll review your visor feeds. Hold on, Lieutenant." He's reviewing retrieval options with his second in command. An urgent message comes through the comm channel on the bridge. The Captain is told that they are being called into the dark quadrant of the Red Galaxy to combat the plague. *Jump immediately, plague soldiers getting too close to High Command*, is the phrase used. He's going to leave us. Still, there's a little quiver in his upper lip. It happens when he gets frustrated or struggles with an order. I feel a little better knowing that he struggles with leaving us here.

"Okay, here's the deal Lieutenant, we're being pulled back to the Red Galaxy. Sending AR drop ships in T minus two minutes.

Get to them ASAP and find your way back to the recon outpost on the outskirts of the Milky Way. Understand?"

I sigh, this sucks. "Yes, sir."

"Is there a fucking problem with that order, Lieutenant?" He's stressed, I don't need to see his face to know that. We're both pressed about whether or not this mission was worth our time given how fast the Plaguers are spreading. I'd image that while we gained some pretty critical information about the Thyr, the captain isn't too happy about the fact that we were right.

"No, sir. See you soon, good luck."

"You too, soldier. Make it back in one piece."

That's the captain's way of telling me he cares. Both Bill and I are pretty damn close with the man, but he can't show that to the rest of the command deck.

We land and I shoot a look at Bill and launch again. "Fucking, AR drop." he whines. I'm just happy he didn't interrupt the captain. Bill has no problem spouting off against the brass, but he probably heard the frustration in the captain's voice and decided against it. Maybe Bill's evolving, what a weird thought.

"Yeah." AR drop ship. The AR stands for Autonomous Retrieval. They're robotically piloted ships that hone in on our location, read the topography and life in the surrounding area, and land in a spot that it deems safe. The problem with that is, it doesn't always work. *This* is a High Scientist fuck-up. Something they need to fix, but never get around to. These damn things could land in the middle of the Thyr legion with how reliable they are. We land and stop. I turn around and use my optics to search for any Thyr that may be following our trail. Nothing. They've fallen back to the legion. Probably after finding fifty bodies scattered across the ground.

"But hey we were right," Bill says. "They should have put us on the Plaguers."

I turn from Bill and pull up my nav computer. "I don't know about that. A Legion of Thyr changes things, especially if they're using cloaking tech. It means they're more comfortable or willing to use technology where they normally wouldn't and that's not good. They haven't been seen since 2252 and now there's a legion *and* they're using cloaking tech? I don't like it. Add to that the Patriarch suddenly getting pulled back to the Red Galaxy like this to combat the Plaguers. So suddenly that they can't wait for us."

Bill doesn't say anything. I lock in on the AR's signals and pull up a holographic map of the area. "Either way we need to get out of here. A war with two fronts is going to get fucking crazy real quick."

Chapter 2: Surfacing

Feb 28th 2014 11:52pm

"Daemon," Aden says sitting next to me on the cold, hard, concrete sidewalk. He sounds so far away, his voice echoing in the salty, stale air.

"Daemon," he says again. I turn my head partially toward him. "Is this even going to work?" he asks in a shaky tone.

"I don't know," I sigh, exhaling loud and long. Tightening my grip around the small metal rings in my hand, I playfully tug at them, watching the wires they're attached to glitter in the moonlight while bouncing up and down. "All I know is that everything was so much simpler a few weeks ago."

And it was.

I think back to when this all started. Two weeks ago I was finishing up a three day backpacking trip through Cleveland National Forest just east of San Diego. It's something I had been doing for a few years. It allowed me to disconnect from everything and just be. Some people deal with life by working out or watching movies, others by reading books or writing their feelings down, maybe listening to music. That was all well and good for them, but none of it worked for me. I just need to be away from everything, in the silence, in the dark.

After high school I bounced around between jobs here and there, not really sure of what I was going to do with my life. Big surprise, real original, right? I was stuck in the world wondering what it all meant, swimming in a sea of confusion just like everyone else. There wasn't really anything that I enjoyed enough to make into a career, but to be honest I hadn't really searched that much either. I floated through high school and just did what I needed to do.

I was smart, probably too smart for my own good, and maybe that was the problem. No motivation in school, I wasn't challenged at all, and in turn it made me lazy. I don't blame anyone for it. Lord knows my parents gave me plenty of options to branch out as I grew up. Baseball, soccer, basketball, I was never forced into anything, but if I expressed an interest, they signed me up and I finished the year. No half-assing it. Still, there was no real motivation that took hold. Classes and tests came easily, as long as there was some passing interest and I left my ears open enough to learn. I got good grades and tested in the one thirties on an IQ test that our school offered. I was never snide about it, but the school made a point to tell me I was smart. Smart enough to make something of myself.

But, I didn't. Just like high school, passing interest and general concern for my surroundings allowed me to be good at any job I decided to try out. I was usually pushed along by my managers, told I could 'take their job in no time', but I didn't. I just took that as a sign that it was time to move on. Ten jobs in two years and I learned a lot. After a while my parents started to drop comments about my direction in life, or lack thereof. They offered up more stories about kids my age who were doing amazing things with their life. Poli-Sci graduates writing speeches for some supposedly important politician, journalism majors doing summer internships at CNN or the like, or the always popular high school jock turned caring physician. I had to do something. My parents were great, they loved me, and they didn't want to just come out and say 'do something!', but their stories took hold. I did need to do something.

So I joined the military. Nothing crazy, I didn't plan ahead for a career as a government employee traipsing around all corners of the earth with an eighty-pound pack. I joined the National Guard, figured it'd be easy enough. It was more of a challenge than I expected, though.

There was structure I wasn't used to, physical requirements I wasn't fond of, and—regardless of what the comforting videos showed on the recruitment sites of understanding boot camp officers—always someone screaming in my face. Looking back it was good, it did end up giving me some direction.

The physical stuff came easier and basic training got me into more outdoor activities that I would've never tried otherwise. I was unenthusiastic about life before I started, so I picked some bullshit, mickey-mouse military occupation, like warehouse warden or something like that followed by four other mediocre picks. It turned out there's some small print in the contract you sign stating that MOS selection choices are just preferences. I didn't get any of the jobs I picked. Instead the powers that be, and by that I mean whoever finalizes the career selection, decided that military intelligence would be a good fit given my state testing and ASVAB scores. As much as I was annoyed at first, they were right. I'm analytical when I need to be and the structure and forced military drive focused my mind. I was finally great at something.

It's all secrets in a sealed file somewhere, but I *was* great at my job. Four years of service, two off and another two of reactivated service and I was done. It may not have seemed like much to some people, but for a small town kid from the east coast, it felt like a lifetime. There wasn't much else I wanted to do in the military, it gave me some direction and taught me how to enjoy life.

My passion for outdoor survival grew, which will happen when your job consists of sitting at a computer all day, and I started backpacking. I had some money set aside so I traveled for a bit, then finally settled in San Diego. There was so much to experience and some great hiking and backpacking land really close to the city. Military money ran out and I needed a job, so I looked into the National Parks service. They only open up for hiring once every three years and it just so happened to be one of those years. My military service granted me a little nudge above the other candidates and I became a Park Ranger.

There wasn't much to the job, mostly driving around in a truck and occasionally yelling at some misguided teens fooling around in the woods or doing stupid shit, but it got me outside. It afforded me the chance to spend time in nature, get decent pay, and just settle down to enjoy the simpler parts of life. I was content. No, I was happy.

Aden, my little brother by a few years, came out to visit me for my thirtieth birthday five years ago and, in keeping with his consistent spirit of nonchalance, ended up staying for good. Still finding his way in the world, he took various jobs in the service industry and caused trouble in his free time, but he was a good kid. Genuine, kind, albeit sarcastic as hell, but a good kid.

He always worried when I went backpacking into the woods alone, and spent months convincing me to carry a phone. If I had my way, I'd pretty much stay away from technology at all costs. Work made me carry a basic rugged phone with walkie talkie capabilities, but other than that I never carried one. Eventually Aden won the argument and carrying an emergency phone became standard operating procedure, as did turning it off, and him scolding me for it. He always tried to check in on me. I would just tell him that the battery wouldn't last the two or three days I was out, so he bought me an extra battery pack to solve the problem.

No excuses. It was all a joke in my book, what was really going to happen that I'd need to call him? People lived for thousands of years without cell phones, I didn't see any harm in going out into the woods with plenty of survivalist supplies and advanced camping gear without a form of communication. I wasn't in the Middle East for Christ's sake, I was in San Diego.

Even though I don't like to get into the habit of saying my brother's right, he was. Snake bites, cougar attacks, heat stroke, there's plenty of things that can go wrong when you're backpacking alone in San Diego, but I never thought they'd happen to me. So why, oh why in the world, would I even think that something as ridiculous as the city coming under attack from undocumented enemy soldiers could be a concern?

I was Intelligence, I knew a great deal more than I cared to about the countries that hated America and of what they were capable. While I didn't retain everything, I knew a continental attack was extremely unlikely. One primary skillset that I retained was the ability to hold and release details at will. Military Intelligence taught me that; make space for the things that mattered and let the rest go, it was white noise.

That day will forever be seared in my mind, and something tells me it'll be the last time I ever hiked for fun. For days, nearly every waking hour, I replayed the events in my head like a movie, trying to make sense of what happened.

I hiked ten miles back to my car and once out of the woods I swung my bag onto the bed of my truck and pulled my emergency phone out of my pack to check for messages. The first battery died (probably the first night) and I didn't care to put the other one in. I figured I'd shoot my brother a text before leaving so he could stop worrying.

As I switched on the phone, it blew up with an array of notification sounds, one after the other for what seemed like a half hour. Thirty missed calls, twenty voicemails, and seventy-five text messages.

Where are you?

Answer your phone.

I need to talk to you!

It's getting crazy over here!

All hell is breaking loose!

The messages went on. Looking back in the direction of the city, I had seen smoke rising to the sky since yesterday, I just assumed it was brush fires. It was dry season after all, and California had become increasingly arid over the last few years.

I immediately tried calling Aden, but the call wouldn't connect. I kept getting the same *We're Sorry...* message over and over. It didn't stop me from trying though, the messages came through, stuck in the system or not, it had to still be working. Pushing my gear into the bed of my truck, I slammed the gate shut and stuck the phone onto my steering wheel with the Velcro I had glued to the both of them and kept calling. I'd never driven so fast in my life. Call after call produced busy signals, while text messages just simply wouldn't go through.

As I came around the base of the mountain out of the National Forest I could see more smoke rising from various points of the city. What the hell was going on? Was it a terrorist attack? Even though my mind was racing with horrible possibilities, asking questions was useless. I needed to get back to our house as soon as possible.

Driving on I-8 toward San Diego the city looked dead. No movement, in the streets or highways. I drove past traffic light after traffic light, no comforting glow to suggest what my subsequent actions should be. I think that was the most nerve racking of all. The streets could be empty, smoke rising in the distance, but someone made the decision to cut basic power. If this was just a power outage, there'd be more movement, any movement. SoCal lost power for twenty-four hours the year prior and people were everywhere outside. Driving around, playing in the street, riding bikes, walking, anything to get their minds off the fact that they couldn't watch TV. I don't know if this is the work of terrorists, an invading nation, or something else, but the no power thing pushed me over the edge. I was no longer worried, I was downright frightened.

After making a sharp right turn and driving past another dead traffic light, my eye caught two military helicopters in the distance. They were circling the city near the beach. Luckily our house was in Lakeside, northeast of downtown by about twenty minutes. The landscape was more of what we were used to on the east coast, land, trees, wildlife, but still only a short drive away from downtown and the beach or the National Parks.

Five minutes after getting off of the 8, I pulled up our street. There was still no activity, but I would occasionally catch a person here or there peeking out from behind their window curtains. Luckily, Aden's truck was still in our driveway and as I drove up to the house he came running out the front door.

"Daemon!" he yelled, barreling into me with open arms.

"What the hell is going on?" After a second of hugging, I pushed back to look at his face.

"They don't know, they just starting killing people. Downtown is totally locked down."

"Who started killing people? Terrorists?"

"Come on, come inside," he said nervously pulling me by the arm. Aden looked worried. It looked as though he wasn't sure how to explain the situation.

The house was a mess, no surprise there, he didn't even keep it clean when I was home, let alone when I was gone. Our living room was right inside the door, TV to the right and couch to the left. He sat down in the recliner and motioned for me to sit on the couch in front of the TV. Our house still had power. I could hear the generator running in the back yard, and smell the gas fumes seeping in from the rear window. Aden must have spilled some while filling it up. In all honesty, I'm surprised he was able to get it working. He's not the most, self-sufficient person I know.

"Sit, I'll show you." He turned on the large flat screen TV with the remote. The TV was Aden's, I didn't have much use for it. "I started to Tivo all this shit when it went down yesterday morning, figured it be easier than explaining it to you." He pulled up the recently recorded list and moved up to a news recording dated this morning.

"It's unclear as to what the man is doing on the beach, but he's certainly started to gather a crowd of curious onlookers." A male reporter showed up on the screen, short black hair, mid-forties, standing on the sidewalk in front of the sand on Ocean Beach.

Aden pointed at the TV. "He just came out of nowhere, just walked out of the waves they say." I didn't turn to acknowledge my brother, my eyes were fixed on the TV and the large muscular man dressed in Spartan-war-gear on the beach.

The reporter continued speaking on the left of the screen as the right of the screen showed the man in the background. "A little over an hour ago San Diego residents started to crowd around a small section of Ocean Beach where a man, wearing full Spartan-war-gear just like what was worn by actors in the hit movie "300", supposedly walked out of the water and onto the beach. Some bystanders have speculated as to whether or not the soldier, dressed in a red cape, sandals, metal helmet, shield, spear, and a short sword attached to a belt of his leather looking speedo, is part of some kind of viral advertising campaign for the sequel, which is set to be released later this summer. After exiting the water, the seven-foot tall, muscular soldier walked some thirty feet onto the dry sand and stood at attention. He has not moved since exiting the water and more people continue to congregate in the area as they come out for their morning activities."

They were indeed starting to gather. In the background I could see people on their morning runs and dog walks stopping to see what all the commotion was then just staring in awe at the massive man. His forearms alone looked like they were the size of my thighs, and dried salt from the sea water made his abs glistened in the morning sun.

"What the hell is this?" I asked, turning to Aden.

"Watch, watch!" he motioned quickly toward the TV.

The soldier reached around and pulled the large metal shield off of his back. The video shook as the camera man motioned for the reporter to turn around. "It looks like the soldier is moving. He's armed his shield, pulled out his sword, and crouched down into an attack position." The soldier, his eyes void of emotions, glared forward looking like a larger-than-life statue. Some curious young man in wife beater shirt with khaki shorts and sandals moved forward from the crowd surrounding the soldier and walked directly in front of him. The young man looked like a midget compared to the soldier.

"Oh, it looks like someone has become curious enough to try and talk to the actor," the reporter said, glancing back at the camera as he did.

That's when all hell broke loose.

Emotionless and without warning, the soldier brought his short sword down onto the young man's left clavicle with such force that the blade wedged halfway into his lung, it's tip sticking out of the man's back, perpendicular to his waist. The swing happened with such speed and precision it was over in a fraction of a second, so fast that the movement was blurred on camera. A few seconds later, everyone in the crowd realized that this wasn't a publicity stunt as the soldier pulled his sword from the man and blood shot everywhere. People started screaming and running. The news reporter looked back at the camera and rolled his finger at the cameraman to suggest that he should keep filming.

The soldier started attacking more people around him, cutting off arms and legs with ease due to his size and strength. In all the chaos a young woman tried to run behind the soldier, but he dropped the shield, snapped his arm out, and caught her by the face with his massive palm. With a flick of his wrist, I heard a faint snapping sound on the video as she fell lifelessly to the ground. The camera crew scrambled and the video was hard to make out, but the reporter was trying to get a better angle on the action. He ran to the steps of the pier on the left and the cameraman followed close behind catching flashed shots of the carnage as he did.

As he stabilized the camera on the rail of the pier, the soldier, roughly fifty feet away and twenty feet below, met with two police officers who ran onto the beach from the street to the right. They were screaming at the soldier, guns drawn on the approach. The soldier continued moving fluidly through the chaos swiping his blade and shield at the frantic people on the beach.

Both police fired, emptying their clips at the muscular death machine. Some of the bullets bounced off of the shield, others made contact with the soldier who finally turned his attention to the police. At least five bullets tore into the soldier's skin but it didn't faze him at all. There was no blood either, just small dark holes in his skin where the rounds made contact. This was the first time in the video that I had seen the soldier convey any kind of emotion and, unfortunately for the policemen, it was rage.

    He charged the police with his shield forward and his sword at his side as they attempted to reload their pistols in shock. The shield made contact with one officer, knocking him back into the air ten feet. The other officer pulled out his Taser gun and fired it at the soldier's face. The prongs stuck into his cheek and crackled as the officer held down the trigger. The soldier reached up and pulled the prongs out, then shoved them into the top of the officer's head through his hat. The officer seized before falling to the ground and the soldier kneeled down ramming his short sword through the man's chest to finish the job.

    The camera shuddered and then turned to the reporter whose body was draped over the railing of the pier with a spear sticking out of his back. The camera lowered a bit to reveal the spear sticking through the cameraman's stomach as well, then fell to the sand below. The video feed flickered as it showed another soldier, just as big and dressed exactly the same, pull his spear out of the cameraman's back above. Then the recording stopped.

    That day was two weeks ago today.

    Stay in your homes, they continually said on the TV and radio. Stay in your homes my ass. We waited for two more days for updates that never came. It was only a matter of time before *'stay in your homes'* became a repetitive reminder of what these terrorists had done to our lives. We were living in constant fear without the ability to do anything about it. Aden and I had no intention of waiting for someone to save us; we weren't going to sit around and become victims crippled by fear. I started to dig around with some old contacts from the military and it didn't take more than a few hours to figure out that they were oblivious to what was going on other than knowing that subsequent attacks happened at night. They always came out of the water at night after that first day. Midnight, like clockwork every night. We thought it was some kind of fear tactic, the first day they showed us what they're capable of, but after that they just came in the night to kill, crippling the city with fear. That's when my brother and I took to the streets to get our own intel.

We still don't know what the hell is going on, but we've figured out a few things about them. We don't know why they are here or what they want other than carnage, and we don't know how they can breathe underwater, but we do know that they can be killed.

"Daemon," Aden says quietly shaking my arm. He knows I'm prone to trailing off in my head sometimes. "I think they're coming."

I tighten the grip on the metal rings in both hands and glance down at the screen of my smartphone. It's currently tapped into five different HD wireless cameras that we had set up on the surrounding buildings and pier at the end of Newport Avenue in Ocean beach. They're all pointing toward the water. Visibility isn't fantastic, but the soldiers are big enough for us to pick out. We're crouched down, our backs against a short concrete wall that separates the sidewalk from the beach. The water is about two hundred feet behind us.

Staring at my phone with such intensity that I fear I'll crack the screen, a figure breaks the reflection of the moonlight on the surface of the water. Then another, and another, followed by twelve more making fifteen in total. This fits with our theory. They add a soldier to the group each night. We haven't been able to surveil the beach every night since the first incident, hell we didn't even know it was continuing until large amounts of people started dying each night, but it fits. Two the first day to make a statement, and now fourteen days later, fifteen in total. There were fourteen last night, and ten of them five days ago. Once we started to see that the number of dead was growing exponentially each night and the wounds were consistent with the kills from that first day, we knew it had to be them.

    I tap the earpiece of my comm unit. "Okay everyone, we've got fifteen total just like we predicted. Remember, when the count reaches zero, close your eyes, plug your ears, and pull. Give it five seconds, then get off your asses and get some revenge. Back of the neck where the spinal cord meets the brain stem. Signal understood?" I look down the wall to see fifty men meet my thumbs up with their own.

    Aden leans over and whispers to me, "This should be fun."

    I put my finger up to my lips and he presses his back to the wall and grips the rings in his hand tighter, tensing the wires they're attached to.

    We had learned over the last few weeks, through painful experience, that these soldiers aren't only bigger, stronger, and faster than us, but their senses are more attuned to their surroundings. They can hear the smallest noise over great distances and have fantastic eyesight. They also seem to be able to pick out faint smells whether it be body sweat or deodorant. We had the upper hand near the beach, the waves messed with their hearing, and we all rolled in sand from head to toes to cover our scent. The only thing left was sight, and we're about to take care of that as well.

Aden points to the phone and I can see the soldiers approaching our mark. I tap my comm unit sending a computerized ten second countdown to each of the men's earpieces. Looking down the line, I can see all of them tightening their grips on the small metal rings with one hand and covering their eyes with the other. They all have their earplugs in place as well.

The countdown reaches one and we all violently pull the metal rings as hard as we can. Dozens of flash bang grenades ring out in succession along the concrete brick wall. This is the first time we hear a soldier cry out in pain. It's a high pitch screech, followed by a deep low growl that makes me think we're going to be facing bears once we jump the wall. Everyone down the line is struck still by fear.

I turn to them and shout, "Now!" into the comm unit. Their anger is reinvigorated. That 'now' has come to represent the fiery revenge that is sitting deep in our guts. That 'now' represents the family members and friends that we lost over the last two weeks. That 'now' represents 10,400 people of this great city dead, because these bastards all claim one hundred lives a piece, each night they attack our city. I jump over the wall, sword in hand, to remind these vile fifteen murderers that this is our city and I will do whatever it takes to defend it.

Chapter 3: Extraction

Dec 25th 2467 2:30 pm Earth time

    It's funny how Bill's mind works. I've been partnered with him for a long time. Long enough to know every little physical tick that he's come to display. He's always hungry, it doesn't matter what we're doing; mission, training, guarding an embassy ballroom, whatever. When he's nervous though, which is rare, the hunger disappears and it's replaced by a simple bouncing of the knee. Bill and I are kneeling down on the edge of a small section of forest a hundred miles north of our last position near the dried up Salt Lake. It's the entrance to a much larger section of growth called Sawtooth, which baffles me as much as the forested area to the east of the Salt Lake. With everything that's happened to the surface of this planet, everything that we did, how are these forests still thriving?

    "You really think the Thyr pose a threat?" Bill asks nervously, leg bouncing up and down. "I mean come on, we took down fifty like they were nothing."

    The thought of fighting two major forces in an all-out war has been festering in his head. We've been at war with the Plaguers for years now, and for the first time in centuries, our people are on the defensive. That's not only disconcerting, but pretty damn frustrating. Don't get me wrong, we excel at war, but we're almost always on the offensive. It's extremely rare that species challenge us, and even when they do, it's more for pride than anything else. The Plaguers have certainly become a problem on their own, and there's no question we're at war. The Thyr could be just as big of a problem, depending on their numbers. The fact that both of them may be targeting us at once is a scary thought. Two wars across the universe leaves a lot of room for tactical error.

Bill either doesn't want to know the answer, or just doesn't care to think of it anymore. Before I answer, he asks, "Where are they?" He is of course talking about the stupid ass AP dropships that are supposed to get us off of this godforsaken rock and a safe distance away from the legion of Thyr that we just escaped.

"Well," I say exhaling with disappointment, "they did not land together." Bill scoffs. "I have one tracking roughly forty miles north of our position." I sigh at the small flexible nav computer that's built into my suit's VOK unit, a bio-computer that pairs with my suit and neural implant. "And the other a hundred and sixty miles north of that."

Bill shakes his head, and his leg stops bouncing. "Fucking AP drops. So one of us is humping it alone an extra hundred and sixty miles."

"No," I set my hand on his shoulder. "I'm humping it an extra hundred and sixty miles."

In a flat tone he says, "Oh, wait, no, let me go..."

"Ha ha, little shit," I chuckle. "You could at least try to care."

"Oh, I care," he counters. "Care about walking and or launching an extra hundred and sixty miles. Fuck that."

I shove him and start walking toward the first AP signal. "You know you'll just be sitting at the Milky Way outpost until I get up there right? They're not going to let you leave without me."

"Yeah, but fresh blood dude," I nod, of course. "There's a new cantina on the outpost and I don't care what Alexander says, Blood Trees never come close to draft."

This is very true, they don't. "All right look, I'll take point to the first ship, you'll exfil, and then I'll hump it to the second pod and meet you at the recon outpost. Understood?"

"Shit yeah, man let's do it. I want some dinner."

"Good to see you're not stewing about the Thyr anymore." I stop walking and scan the forest in front of us.

"Food trumps impending doom and death."

"Yeah, ha ha. Well, we shouldn't have a problem getting through here, it's not too dense and we can make interval jumps to cover more ground. It's unlikely that we'll encounter any more resistance, we just have to keep an eye out for Mini K."

"*Mini K,*" Bill repeats under his breath shaking his head. "You've got a hard-on for those little assholes. When's the last time they were seen on Earth?"

"When's the last time you pulled your head out of your ass long enough to use it?"

"Touché. But seriously. When?"

"We were here numb nuts. That joke of a mission in Forks, they streamed by the bottom of our slip on the way in."

"Oh, yeah. Still don't think we'll see 'em."

"Look, we're here to do a job and right now that entails getting the fuck out of here. I don't plan on sticking around, getting trampled, or getting stuck on this hell hole of a planet while the rest of our people jump back to the Red Galaxy. So do me a favor, cut the shit and let's just get moving." I stare at Bill for another second making sure everything sinks in and he realizes that I don't feel like putting up with his attitude right now. I snap up my eyebrows and tilt my head to the side as confirmation.

"Well, let's get moving," he says mockingly and steps to the side motioning me forward with one arm.

Bill's a great guy, he's a brother to me and there's no one else I'd rather have watching my back, but his attitude can get trying at times. There have been studies done with our people and the effects of living such extended lives. They don't feel extended to us, it's just living life, but as we reached out into different solar systems and interacted with other life forms we quickly realized how abnormal our species was. Most creatures we've encountered live less than a hundred years. Hell, humans would reach that if they were lucky and lived a clean life, but that's a fraction of what we live, a blink of an eye really.

I walk past Bill, patting him on the shoulder once more and start making my way into the forest. I'm curious as to what this area looked like before we scorched the planet. There is a lot of dry dirt and sand on the ground, barely any smaller plant life, but somehow the trees thrived. Healthy bark with moss growing on the side and pine needles jutting out of the branches. Most of them have pine needles, but every now and then we see ones with wide green leaves that occasionally float back and forth to the ground as we walk by. I'm looking down at my feet while walking and the dry earth is flying out from underneath my boot with every step I take. It's so lifeless here, minus the trees.

"How do you think the trees survive?" Bill asks from behind me. You work with someone long enough and you tend to think alike. I lift my arm and turn my attention to my VOK unit ignoring Bill's question.

"The trees are a little thick here to jump, but we're making decent time," I say dropping my arm back down to my side, scanning the trees ahead as we walk.

"Oh, ok. Yeah, you weren't just thinking about the trees like me. That's fine just ignore me," Bill says snidely. Here we go.

"Yes fine, I was thinking about the trees. But what does it matter?" Bill doesn't respond, which isn't normal. I always expect him to shoot back some kind of sarcastic quip when he knows we're thinking the same thing. I try to brush it off, but no longer hear his boots against the dry earth. Turning around, I see him crouched down on the ground examining the dirt.

"No seriously." he maintains. "This planet is dead, yet there are locations all over the place like this where the trees are alive and nothing else can survive." I look down at him and think for a moment.

"Not nothing," I respond, causing him to look up at me questioningly. "The Thyr and, well, the Mini K for that matter." He looks back to the ground and rolls the dirt around in his hand for a moment before picking up a handful and letting it drain onto the ground through his fingers.

"What are we missing?" he asks, looking back up at me.

Fine, I'll bite. "What do you mean?"

He glances off to the side. "Well, from what we know of our own history, we find Earth, for one reason or another, we wipe out the humans."

"High Order claims they attacked."

"Right yeah, High Order claims they attacked us after we found them, which may or may not be the case. At any rate, we find Earth, destroy the humans, scorch the planet, and leave. The

Thyr, who come from a forested homeland, take refuge here? It doesn't make sense, and if we burned the planet where did the trees come from? How did they start growing again?"

He had a point. This is becoming a habit more recently. It feels weird, I don't like it. "Oh! Ok, well, maybe the Thyr brought plants with them."

"Even if that's true, look at the soil. It's dead, just like the rest of the planet, how are these trees even here?"

"What about our Blood Trees? They survive in this soil."

"No, they were genetically engineered to thrive in bad conditions."

"Look it's weird, I'll admit that, but the Thyr could have engineered their own trees as well. It's not our concern. Let's just get to the dropships and get the hell out of here." I turn to start walking again, but out of the corner of my eye I can see that Bill isn't getting up and I stop. "Bill."

"This *is* our concern. Don't you see this is all connected to the Thyr? An hour ago we didn't even know they still existed and now there's a legion of them here that just pops up out of the blue? They have cloaking tech! They've never in any known history used or have showed any interest in developing cloaking tech. Something stinks, something is going on here. They hide in forests and forests now thrive on a dead planet."

I turn back around to face him, walk right up and look down at him crouched in the dirt. "You're not saying what I think you're saying, are you?" Bill tosses the rest of the dirt from his hand and wipes it on his leg as he stands up. "We *are* here to collect intel," he proposes.

"Not more than ten minutes ago you were complaining about getting back to the outpost so you could eat. Now you want to stay and investigate?" I continue to stare while trying to read what's going on in that thick head of his. He stares back and then shrugs. "You, you're unbelievable! Would you just pick a damn position and stick with it?"

He smiles. "Where's the fun in that?" Something does stink about all of this. The timing of our mission, the suspect past of our people, the burning of all humanistic forms of history. Something's going on and it's all tied together somehow. Our past, the humans, the Thyr, the Earth, possibly even the Mini K and the plague. Nothing good will come out of trying to reveal what it is, but as our Combat Spec Officer Red 'The Blade' Orion said in training, you can't draw blood without first knowing who to cut. Red was old school, wore a red cape and small leather piece of armor that barely covered his midsection. He fought in sandals that tied around his ankles and wore braces on his shins and forearms. The only reason that we're so proficient with our Ka is because of Red's training. Supposedly he was one of the most influential soldiers in the Bloodwar, or at least that's what he tells people. I haven't heard any of the older officers argue the fact and honestly Bill and I have more reason to believe him than most.

A little over three centuries ago a mission of ours went belly up. It wasn't a normal mission mind you. The High Order was looking to rebuild the Alpha training program from the ground up and wanted the two most experienced soldiers in the field to help with that. Enter us. We ran mock missions for months, created from some of the most difficult situations we'd been in, and then they decided to kick the program up a notch. They wanted to know exactly how far they could push a trainee before they broke. We were put into a captivity and torture simulation for five years. Alphas do not fail; they find a solution or they die trying. We spent five years looking for an escape to a situation that didn't have one and the torture continued until the point of extensive brain damage which resulted in permanent amnesia.

    We were no strangers to starting over—Alpha's memories are wiped when they're selected for active duty—but retraining us would take time even with the new program. Killing us however, would set an example. The Red Military didn't tolerate failure, not at our level and even though the whole situation was simulated, it would very clearly define the stakes for any future trainees. Our two best and brightest failed in a simulation and were killed, what do you think will happen if you fail a real mission? Can't say that I blame the High Order, we knew the stakes of being an Alpha when we joined. It's just the stakes of war, greater good and all. If our death meant that others would survive in the future, then so be it. The brass slated us for summary execution, but Red called in a few favors and Captain Otto stood by him. They made sure that we had a second chance when it seemed like the whole universe was working against us. We're both indebted to them in a way that can never be repaid.

    So between the preliminary Alpha wipe, then the five years of torture and brain damage, we don't remember anything about our families. Even though we don't talk about it, Bill and I both see eye to eye when it comes to Red. The man's like a father to us, and the captain is a close second.

    "Thinking about Red?" Bill asks.

    "Stop that! I hate it when you do that." Pushing Bill away from me, he laughs while stumbling backward before regaining his footing. I shake my head. "Damn it." Now the questions are eating at me as well. He always pulls me into his over anxious way of thinking. I raise my hand and point a finger into the air, signifying a one and push it toward Bill. "One hour. That's it. Then we get to the dropships and get off this damn rock. Dual front war, remember?"

"Single front with dual seemingly imminent," he corrects. I wave him off.

Bill smiles widely and hops up and down in place a few times out of glee for winning me over. It's all about the game for him, questions need answering and he loves being the one to find out the answer before anyone else even asks the question. It's going to get him killed some day. Hell, it'll probably get both of us killed.

"So, where do we start?" I ask.

Bill brings a hand up to his face, caresses his chin and squints his eyes as if he's thinking hard about something. "How about," he turns around, taking the same hand and swinging it out as he prepares to point at something. "There." Pointing to a large open patch of dirt twenty meters to our left, he runs over with bounce in his step, then stands on it proudly placing his arms on his hips.

I follow behind a little slower and less enthusiastically about a random patch of dirt in the middle of the woods. He stands there for a second then gently thrusts his head in my direction raising his eyebrows. By the blood of my kin, he's actually going to make me say it. He tilts his head and looks up at the sky waiting for me to egg him on.

"Okay Bill, what's so special about this spot?"

"Glad you asked, LT!" He snaps up, releasing his waist and points to the dirt with both hands flat and parallel to each other in front of his thighs. "There's something under here." Bill doesn't try to make a fool of me unless he has something. I look down at the dirt and tap my temple, switching the ocular shields in my eyes to thermal vision. Everything around us is bright to dark blue due to its cool nature, but the patch of dirt that Bill is standing on is glowing red.

"You son of a bitch," I mutter under my breath.

"I saw you looking at the dirt when we were walking and figured the trees were bothering you just as much as me, so I switched to thermal and started scanning the forest as we moved. What do you think it is?" The game. I can hear it in his voice. It's taking over. Honestly I'm not sure that I want to know, but there's no way that we're leaving here without checking it out first. Curiosity is one thing that Bill and I have in common, we need to scratch that itch even if it's just a dull feeling in the back of our head that we can't place our finger on. It's why we work so well together. It's also why we find intel that other recon teams don't.

"If I had to take a guess?" I'm looking at the size of the red square beneath his feet. "I'd say it's an entrance hatch to an underground facility."

"My thoughts exactly, LT. Question is, whose facility? It doesn't exactly scream Thyr, and we never had facilities on Earth that I'm aware of."

"Me neither," I whisper still studying the 'hatch' through my thermal vision, and thinking about what could be underneath it.

"Right, so...who does it belong to?" He asks as a means to fuel the itch. Any other team would have humped it to the exfil point. Any other team wouldn't have used their thermal vision to scan a forest on a dead world and if they had; if they had happened to catch this out of the corner of their eye, they would have left it be. Not us though. We had to ask the questions that shouldn't even be thought of.

"Wanna open it?" Bill asked excitedly. I tap my temple again to switch the thermal vision off and look up at Bill who's smiling eagerly. Exhaling loudly, I reach forward and grab Bill by the arm, pulling him back so we can open the supposed hatch.

"Shit," I pull out my sidearm and step back a few feet, while Bill follows in unison. Lifting my side arm, I switch to a physical manipulation field, then set the ultrasound adjuster to ten and the effective range to a wide six-by-ten feet. Normally that's good enough to shove a Thyr back about fifteen feet, so it should be enough force to push the dirt covering the hatch out of the way.

Looking up at Bill next to me I ask, "Sure you want to check this out?"

"No," he says calmly, then looks back at the dirt in front of us. I look back down and slowly squeeze the trigger of my sidearm.

"Wait!" Bill shouts. With how quickly he spits the phrase out, I nearly jump out of my own skin and turn to glare angrily at him. "Wanna take bets on what's down there?" he asks, smiling at the dirt. I scoff and turn my head back into position.

"Fifty blood coins it's Thyr," I say dryly.

"Deal."

I question what we're doing one last time and squeeze the trigger before losing my nerve. The dull sound of my sidearm bounces off the surrounding trees as dirt and sand fly up out of the ground in front of us. As the dry dirt settles, I see the outline of a hole that's roughly a foot deep, six feet wide, and nine feet long. More dirt settles and as visibility increases a dark shadow in the center of the hole slowly transforms into a black metal panel with studs around the edges and a square handle on the right.

"Well shit LT, we found a door," Bill says with some satisfaction. "Mind if I open it?"

I holster my sidearm and take a second to look over the panel, then quickly scan the forest around us. Somewhat satisfied, I reach over my shoulder and pull the compressed rifle from my back. While I don't fully understand the nanomechanics of our gear, I've always been impressed by its speed and responsive nature. It takes a second for me to remove the rifle from my back, but it's already fully extended when I rest it in front of my chest. Pressing my middle and trigger finger just below the scope activates assault mode. The barrel separates halfway and the nanomachines that make up the rifle peel backward over the body, building a more agile design with a compensator around the shorter barrel. The stock reduces in length and develops into a bulkier design which stays tucked between my shoulder and chest for greater stability. Finally, the optics break down from a magnified long-distance scope to a close quarters red sight with built-in density calculations and thermal detection. Bill moves behind me, pulls out his sidearm, then points it at the center section of the panel. He bends over and grabs the handle with his other hand. I press the rifle's stock against my shoulder and point the barrel down at the door then nod once quickly and sharply.

Bill rips open the door and a wave of hot, moist air explodes out of the opening as he does. I stay focused on the entrance as the intuitive glass on my helmet compensates for the temperature differences and moisture, preventing a buildup of fog. As the air clears, I continue to focus on the entrance and wait for something, anything to leap out at us. Nothing but air. I can see weathered stairs leading down into the humid darkness. I glance over at Bill still pointing his sidearm straight down the steps. He glances at me and nods, then taps the side of his visor twice, switching it to thermal night. I remove my hand from the trigger of my rifle and do the same. We step into the darkness.

Chapter 4: The Devil is in the Details

Feb 28th 2014 12:04am

    It's not pretty, but we got the job done. Fifteen lumbering murderers now lay face down in the sand of Ocean Beach. We lost a few men in the process and that's a tragedy, but considering the last two weeks of bloodshed, it could've been a lot worse. There's no way for us to tell how many more of these monsters are hidden under the waves, but we know how to fight back and the next time one of them comes out of the water there'll be a message waiting. Not a declaration of intent or a letter stapled to a telephone pole, but a message painted in blood. It's fitting seeing as that's the only way they've chosen to communicate with us so far.

    "Sergeant Athano. Report." The Marine captain's voice is screeching through my earpiece due to his sheer volume and shrill tone.

    "I'm not a sergeant anymore," I simply respond. The military doesn't know what's going on any more than we do. In fact, because of the procedures they have to follow, we've actually gained more intelligence over the last few weeks then they have. Granted this isn't totally due to our own diligence, we owe Red most of the credit for the quick progress we've made.

    Red is a tall, muscular, seemingly all-knowing brute of a man who wears a shemagh over his face at all times to maintain his anonymity. He appeared out of the darkness the first night that Aden and I left the house in an attempt to gain intel after the repeating message of the emergency broadcast system. Despite the fact that I never really left the government's all-seeing eye, Red seems to have penchant for staying hidden. While he never has a problem getting around their surveillance, Aden and I were a different matter. Once we popped up on a few of their security feeds downtown, the military decided to make contact. At first it was to stop us from operating in an area that was held under military control, but then they started losing men while we continued to make contact and survive. Their puffed-up chests started to deflate and their communications quickly changed from 'cease and desist' to 'please help us'.

"I don't give a fuck what you *think* you are Sergeant Athano! You're currently under military command. Now report!" Of course that doesn't mean that any of the men in the field are happy with that, Captain Hoffman most of all.

"Oh, go pound sand," I say under my voice yanking the device out of my ear and letting it dangle near my chest on its chord. Aden pulls a machete out the back of a dead soldier's neck and looks up to me as he's catching his breath.

"Captain Asshole I presume?" He smirks standing up straight and resting the back of the blade on his shoulder.

"I can hear that, son!"

"Ah!" Startled, Aden jumps back pulling the device out of his ear and laughs as it bounces off his chest. The captain continues to scream through the earpiece causing the small speaker to hiss and buzz. Aden has less patience than I do and doesn't hesitate to rotate the blade down and slice the thin wire causing the earpiece to fall quietly onto the beach. He stomps on it with his left foot a few times for theatrics, twisting it deep into the sand with the front of his boot toward the end of his tirade.

Seconds pass and now my earpiece is hissing and buzzing again with the captain's angry shrill voice. I shake my head and run fingers up the inside of my eye sockets and massage my forehead before reaching down and putting the earpiece back into my ear. I may have more patience than Aden, but it doesn't mean that I plan on listening to the captain's scolding.

"CAPTAIN HOFFMAN!" I yell loudly and authoritatively. Aden glances at me and brings both his palms up to make this gesture that just screams *oh, big man*. I can hear him saying it sarcastically in my head even though he keeps his mouth shut. My attention to Aden gives the captain a few precious seconds to shut his damn mouth. I don't think he was expecting me to yell at him.

"Thank you. Now listen carefully because I'm only going to say this once, and I'll say it really slowly and make sure it's simple enough for you to understand. I don't...have a...commanding officer. Now you, you have a commanding officer. I know this because he approached me when you didn't make any progress. He approached me because you were continually failing at the job the government pays you to do. The job they expect you to be good at. I, however, was making headway out of sheer curiosity." And maybe a little help from the lumbering man who walks around dressed like a he's robbing a liquor store in the Middle East, but I digress. "*Your* CO thinks I can do your job better than you. So, if you're interested in a report, you have to start asking nicely, otherwise take it up with him."

There's silence on the other end and Aden is snickering as he walks away to check on the rest of our men. The silence continues while the snickering turns into full blown laughter as I hear Aden say to himself, "ask nicely" and exhale before continuing to chuckle.

While clearing his throat Captain Hoffman makes it apparent that he's speaking through clenched teeth. "I...would like a report, sir." I smile to myself and hold back from laughing. It's difficult, but I manage.

"I would like a report, sir, what?" I ask.

Hoffman exhales, "Please." I can just feel those teeth grinding through the headset as he speaks. Luckily the government offers a decent dental plan.

"See, now how hard was that, sir?" I ask in a cheery tone. Hoffman scoffs. "Fifteen soldiers came out of the water as we predicted and fifteen are dead. We've lost five of our own in the fight, they never had a chance. Some of the soldiers recovered sooner than we thought and caught our guys off guard. At least the bastards gave them a quick death, although the circumstances didn't really allow for choice.

"And it seems," I look over at Aden who's holding up nine fingers at me from thirty feet away, "nine of our men are wounded, not critical, broken ribs, twisted ankles, that sort of stuff, but they do need medical attention. The flashbangs worked, as did the machetes, or blades, if you prefer."

"As much as it pains me to say this," Hoffman pauses, "great work, soldier."

Pains you, nice choice of words, Captain Asshole. It must be real painful sitting behind a monitor watching us fight. I stifle the coming rage and instead say, "I'm not a soldier anymore," in a sing song voice, but he ignores me.

"A medical and coroner team will be dispatched to your position. We will also be sending a separate crew to collect the enemy bodies. We'll want to crack a few of them open and see what makes them tick."

Rushing, I spit out, "I don't see that being possible, sir," as quickly as I can.

"Well, why the hell not?" he yells at me over the comms.

I'm not necessarily listening to him at this point. I'm too busy running over to Aden who's standing in the sand looking dumbfounded as the dead bodies of the soldiers begin to slide toward the ocean.

"Sergeant!" Hoffman screams through the earpiece.

"I'm not a fucking sergeant and look at the damn cameras for Christ's sake!" I could think of a few things to make this whole situation even weirder than it already is, and even though self-navigating dead bodies isn't the first thing to jump into my mind, it sure as hell does the trick. The cadavers start sliding slowly at first, but pick up speed quickly. I run in front of Aden and leap face first into the sand, locking my hand around one of the cold dead wrists. It doesn't matter, the body continues to move as if its feet are attached to a chain and being pulled back under the water by a hydraulic winch. Sand shoots up all around me as I'm dragged across the beach on my stomach making it difficult to see anything. Just before we reach the water I let go in futile disappointment. In less than fifteen seconds all the bodies disappear under the cold, black waves and sink back into the abyss.

I can hear Aden trudging up behind me in the sand. "Goddamn it!" I scream, punching the coarse sand with my fist.

"What the...what the hell just happened?" Aden asks in shock staring out at the waves. I roll over on my back to see a few of the others coming up behind him to stare in shock. I want to answer, but I've got nothing. Since day one of this weird infestation it's been nothing but one surprise after another and it just seems like we can never get ahead, regardless of any help we get. Taking a deep breath, the world around me begins to settle and I can suddenly hear Captain Hoffman going crazy in my earpiece again. I'm just going to respond without listening to whatever the hell he's rambling about.

"The bodies are gone. They were dragged back into the ocean."

"By what?"

"Nothing we could see."

"I'm sending..." And now I'm done. I rip out the earpiece and the rest of the communicator and toss it into the sand. I sit up and pause for a second before getting back on my feet.

"What now?" Aden asks while I stare down at the grooves in the sand. I shake my head without looking back at him. "What about Red?" he asks insistently. "Maybe he could help shed some light on this whole weird ass situation."

Raising my head, I finally look up at Aden and nod slightly. I walk toward him and lightly touch his shoulder, stopping for a second as I pass. "Yeah, but we've gotta find the bastard first." Red isn't somebody you just call, or go visit at the drop of the hat. He has this odd knack of showing up when we need him, other than that, there's not much to go on. No phone number or address, no way of communicating with him at all actually. He just appears.

Ever since he slipped out of the darkness without a sound nearly two weeks ago, he's given me this uneasy feeling, this crawling of the skin that only breeds distrust. I don't like the fact that he talks in riddles and I have no idea how he knows so much, or why he started feeding us information. He knows about their strength, their heightened senses, and he's the reason we knew where to stab the bastards for a kill. Every time we talk I'm on edge. I keep both eyes on Red, one hand on a blade, and one on a gun. It doesn't help that he's damn near seven feet tall. His knowledge, size, and sudden appearance with these soldiers makes me leery, and I don't like the fact that he hasn't revealed his connection to them yet.

While we need information about what's going on here, as it's very likely that there are more of these soldiers and they're watching us, all I want to do right now is take a shower. I'm covered in sea water, sand, sweat, and blood, am tired and frustrated, and I won't be able to think worth a damn unless I clean up and change into something dry. As is custom with the last few weeks though, I'm sure the night has other plans.

Aden and I walk over to the public showers to rinse off quickly before heading home to recharge. Hoffman's teams will be here any second and I have no intention of dealing with them tonight. I trust our team to share the details of our brief encounter; they're good men. Leaning against the cool, steel pipe, I close my eyes, and yank on the chain attached to the shower head but no water comes out.

"I believe the water has been diverted for emergency efforts." A smooth, low voice says from behind me. It's almost hard to hear, but has a certain sense of calm assurance as it floats across the late night air.

"Red," I reply quietly, tapping the loose chain against the pipe under my forehead. I'm frustrated with everything at the moment, the least of which isn't Red's secrecy. "Fucking figures." I turn around to see Red lumbering over to Aden on the concrete pathway next to the showers. Letting my body fall back against the metal pipe with a thud, I use it to prop myself up since I'm almost too tired to stand at this point. For how soothing Red's voice is, even in its low tone, you'd never pair it with how large of a man he is. He approaches with arms folded behind his back and is dressed the same as always. Flat black boots, dark blue jeans, and a plain black cotton sweater with a black and dark grey checkered shemagh wrapped around his head and mouth, the excess of which runs down his shoulder and back. He always has that damn shemagh on. Also, his eyes are dark red. Not maroon, not red, I want to say auburn, but there's less brown and more red, almost like dried blood. A chill runs down my spine every time I look at them.

"Daemon. You were worried, but judging from the scene on the beach my information worked out for you and your men."

"Not for the ones that died."

"Still, fifteen soldiers less in this world. How many future innocents did you save tonight?"

"Let me ask you a question, Red." I can see Aden shaking his head lightly as he walks over to stand next to me. We both already know how this is going to go.

"You know I don't answer questions. I merely provide useful information when it is needed."

His response doesn't stop me from asking. "You show up out of the blue two weeks ago, looking about the same size as those bastards we just killed, know how to fight them, and don't tell us anything about yourself. Who are you? Why should we trust you?"

"Tell me Daemon, why do you ask questions you know the answer to?"

I'm not sure who's worse to deal with, Red or Hoffman. At least Hoffman doesn't talk in riddles. "Fine, yes we trust you because of the critical information you've given us so far, but..."

Red cuts me off. He never cuts me off. "That is not the question to which I was referring." I glance at Aden whose mouth is half open and then back to Red who's looking down at us calmly.

He wants me to say it, but I'm not sure that I can. On one hand, I'm not sure that I want to believe it, given what's happening, because it will change everything if it's true. On the other hand, accepting it may make him trust us more and that will hopefully mean more information. Information which we sorely need.

"You're one of them." It feels like the words tumble of my mouth as if someone's punching me in the stomach. I'm amazed they found their proper place when crossing my lips. Red nods once, no emotion in his eyes, no creases in his cheeks to hint that he might be smiling at my newly formed revelation. "Why didn't you..."

Red moves his left hand up from behind his back and holds out his pointer finger in front of his chest. "I do not answer questions." He *doesn't* answer questions. I'm frustrated about how he chooses to communicate with us, but then it hits me. Maybe it's not his choice. I push myself up off of the pipe and walk past Red running the events of tonight through my head. We killed the soldiers on the beach, they were dead, that was confirmed, and then the bodies got sucked back into the ocean without being attached to anything. Clearly something or someone can manipulate these things from a distance. Maybe it's more than just physical manipulation at work here. I shake my head and turn around to look at Red whose calm gaze is following me as I pace around. He knows that my mind is racing and he trusts that I'll find the answer. Aden, meanwhile, is trying his best to keep up.

"You *can't* answer questions." I say while looking up at his emotionless eyes.

Aden is still lost. "What do you mean he can't answer questions?" he asks. I move closer to Red, within inches of his chest and stare up at his dark red eyes. He nods ever so slightly at me. I move past him over to Aden.

"Think about it. Those soldiers we killed on the beach..."

"Yeah dead, we checked."

"Exactly, and yet somehow something or someone pulled them back into the ocean, *without* having anything attached to their bodies."

"That we could see."

"Right, yeah no, that we could see. Meaning something is able to...physically manipulate them from a distance."

Aden pauses for a moment, letting it all sink in. "What, like remote control?"

"That might be a crude way of explaining it but sure, yeah. Remote control. Or magic, or telepathy, call it whatever you want, but the dead didn't slide through sand on their own."

"Well, to be fair, up until two weeks ago, supersized Greek soldiers didn't come out of the ocean at night and slaughter thousands of people in their sleep either, so..."

"Eh, touché."

Aden and I tend to snowball when it comes to bouncing ideas off of each other, and we forget that Red is still standing behind us. He clears his throat to remind us.

"Right." I spin around to face Red. "So you can't answer questions, but you offer up information as we need it. Can you confirm or deny ideas that we guess?" Red just stares back at me.

"That's a question." Aden chimes in.

"Damn it. Okay, let's uh..." I turn back and grab Aden by the shoulders and shove him next to Red so I can see them both at once.

"What the…"

"Okay, Aden."

"Yeeess?"

"The soldiers could be killed by stabbing them in the back of the necks where the brain meets the spine, correct?"

"Well, yeah. You were there, why are you…"

"Just bear with me for a second, okay?" Aden shrugs and glances down at the ground then back up at me tired and annoyed.

"Yes."

"But there was hardly any blood when we stabbed them, I mean there was a little, but not what you'd expect from ramming a sword through someone, right? When the cops shot them in the news video they didn't bleed at all, right?"

Aden's eyes look up to the sky as he thinks back to the recording. "No. No they didn't."

I glance up at Red and it looks like his left eyebrow is slightly elevated. I think I'm getting somewhere. "Red is smaller than the others."

Aden turns around and looks at Red with bewilderment. "Red is not small, his arms are huge, and he's got to be at least seven feet tall."

"No Aden, not to us. Think back to those men, their size, their muscles, think about how big they actually were." Aden really thinks about it. He turns around and looks Red up and down, then walks behind him, reaches up and touches the back of his neck. Red doesn't move, doesn't blink; he's just staring at me with a slightly raised eyebrow.

"The back of his neck is tight. Like, muscular tight." Now I'm waiting for Aden to explain. "When I pulled my blade out of the last soldier I stabbed, the back of his neck was almost, soft. Like squishy. It wasn't tight like Red's even though he looked more muscular."

It's all coming together, and even though Red can't tell us, we have every intention of figuring it out. I think on it for another minute because I don't know if what I'm thinking actually makes sense.

"It's fake." I mutter under my breath. I look up at Aden and he's waiting for me to continue. "It's fake, the skin. They're not actually that big. Their skin is fake, some kind of protective suit, and that's why they didn't bleed when the police shot them, like Kevlar or something. But every suit needs a seam, a weak spot, and that's why Red told us to stab them in the back of their necks."

I look up at Red and his eyebrow is fully cocked in approval. Aden turns around to confirm Red's gaze with his own eyes. "Son of a bitch," he says under his breath staring back down at the sand. "It's a scare tactic. They want us to think they can't die, then they come up during the night and raid the city. It's terrorism at its worst."

I turn away from them for a moment and rub my chin. "Yeah, but by whom? Who the hell are they?"

"Well that's the question of the year, isn't it? Followed by how long have they been here?" Aden asks.

"Confirm," Red says in a hushed tone. We both turn around to see his head down, touching his ear through the shemagh with two fingers.

"Uh, what's going on?" Aden asks nervously moving closer to me. Red's head snaps back up to us.

"Execute," Red says staring at us with those cold dead eyes, his voice clear and concise.

Shit.

Chapter 5: Scratching the Itch

Dec 25th 2467 2:55 pm Earth time

Bill slowly makes his way down the narrow staircase into the darkness below. I'll give him this; for all his antics and joking around, he's a professional when it comes time to do the job. The light from his sidearm is illuminated by the moist stone stairs beneath our feet, but it's unclear how far down they go. I'm continually glancing behind me to make sure we don't get attacked from the rear. I closed the large metal door after we entered, but you never know. Our cautious nature is what's kept us alive all these years.

"Assessment?" I ask softly as we keep moving.

"Despite the size of the entrance, the stairs and tunnel suggest that the corridor was made by a smaller form of life. It's likely that this was built by humans. Way too small for Thyr, and there's nothing to suggest that our people built this."

"Read out from below?" I ask while glancing behind at the entranceway again. Still sealed, no signs of movement or life.

"Bottom of the steps is roughly fifteen hundred feet below us. Heat signatures suggest that there's tech down there, a lot. Too hot to distinguish life forms."

"Nothing from behind, no signs of any kind of security features either."

"Well, it *was* buried under the ground, LT." Professional or not, sooner or later the wise cracking always comes through.

I tap Bill on the shoulder. "Proceed with extreme caution. Deadly force authorized, do not hesitate."

Bill stops in the middle of the staircase and I almost trip over him. He turns around and looks me in the eye, but keeps his voice hushed. "All evidence points to this being a human installation. Human. You know...the species that died out hundreds of years ago?"

"What's your point, Sergeant?"

"PMF on our sidearm is more than enough to subdue a human combatant. Thyr can't fit down here. What if they didn't die out? We gonna finish them off without asking any questions?"

It's all about the game. Bill isn't really concerned about taking out the last of the humans—we've been integral in snuffing out several other speciess already—but he knows if there are some people left down this hole it could be quite a story as to how they survived. There's no way he could deal with not knowing.

"And what if it's something else, Bill, something more dangerous?"

"What are the odds of that?"

"Today? Pretty damn likely."

"Point taken."

I sigh. "Fine, switch to PMF, but I don't like this. Keep your eyes open and don't hesitate to go lethal if need be." Bill smiles in yet another accomplishment of making me change my mind, then turns and starts moving back down the steps.

As we reach the last few steps, the opening before us expands into a large room with odd looking tubes on the left wall and ancient computer terminals to the right. All of the equipment is covered in spider webs and dust, presumably from the crumbling roof of the cave. Bill motions to the right and continues forward with his sidearm at the ready. I move to the right and keep my eyes open while scanning the rest of the room. The end of it is dimly lit, but my sensor aren't picking up any signs of life other than the old tech.

"Clear," I say in a normal tone over the comms.

"Clear," Bill responds. "How is all this shit still running? Even the lights are on. It looks like no one has been here in ages."

I walk past Bill and begin tapping away at a touch screen perpendicular to what looks likes two large pods affixed to the wall. "Holy shit."

"What?"

"These pods are Hemo tech." Bill walks up to the pod and runs his hand down the rounded clear door that is propped open at a ninety-degree angle to the wall.

"The room is so tight, the entranceway, so small...what the hell is Hemo tech doing down here? What about the rest of it?" he asks, moving over to the pod on his left. The frame to the second pod is mangled and the clear security glass that used to serve as a door is scattered across the floor in front of it in pieces. He leans down and starts examining the pieces on the floor.

He's right, the ceiling is just barely tall enough to accommodate us without ducking down. I tap away at the touch screen trying to pull up some more information.

"This is a mixture of tech, some of it Hemo, and some of it looks..." Bill stops playing with the glass on the floor and looks up at me worried, knowing that there's not much that cause me to pause. "It looks human."

"How is it still running?" Bill stands up and walks next to me at the terminal.

"I don't know, this tech is so old." I had read theories of Thyr finding a way to steal energy from the sun, or even the earth itself. No clue how it works, but I'm sure it's possible.

Bill turns back to the pods and speaks over his shoulder at me. "Does it say anything about these? They look too big for humans. The tops of them are carved into the rock ceiling."

I tap through a few more screens. "Uh, it looks like they're some kind of...transfusion machines?" *What the hell is a transfusion machine?*

"What the hell is a transfusion machine?" Bill asks on cue, turning back around to look at the screen.

"I have no clue." I say under my breath trying to find more information in the terminal. "Hold on, let me see if V can tell us anything...huh."

"What?" Bill asks.

"I can't connect with V's signal." I glance around the room at all the ancient, odd mixture of equipment. I guess it's possible that something in here is causing inference or blocking the signal but it seems extremely unlikely. I also notice that our visor feeds are no longer transmitting information back to the Patriarch, but are still recording to local storage. That's actually comforting to know, depending on what's down here, we may have to have Vali delete some of the videos. Looking back at the console, I find something useful. A log in the form of a small icon that's continually replaying a clip of the contained video on the bottom of the screen.

"That's weird," Bill says.

"Here," pointing to the screen, I tap the icon so it'll play. The icon expands, taking over the whole display. It doesn't look like the recording feature was activated on purpose. There's a small female rushing around in front of the camera grabbing supplies. She must be human though, different features, way too small to be a Hemo. Behind her, there's a much larger male with his back to the camera, he looks to be Hemo, but it's hard to tell due to the quality of the video. He's crouching down over what looks like two smaller males, also possibly human. The males on the floor are both missing limbs and are a bloody mess. There's blood everywhere, including the woman's clothes and hands, as well as the Hemo's hands. The woman is frantically passing supplies to the Hemo who's reaching behind his back to grab them while staying focused on the men.

"Injured humans being helped by a Hemo?" Bill asks shaking his head. Something slams on the console in the video and the file ends. There's a date flashing on the screen as the video shrinks back down into a moving file icon on the user interface. "Did you see that date?"

I did indeed. "Yeah, 2014. Almost a hundred years prior to the Blood War." I shake my head. "There's no record of us being on Earth prior to the Blood War."

Bill taps the side of his visor and points down at the screen. "There is now. Play it again."

Grabbing Bill by the shoulders, I force him to face me. "We have to be careful. We don't know what we've found. We need proof that this is real. There's a reason our people destroyed humanistic data prior to the Blood War."

"Exactly," he exclaims. "Our people have been lied to for hundreds of years. We have proof! We can't just let it sit here in a stone tomb under the surface of the Earth." Bill tries to avoid politics as best he can, and with good reason. The downside to that approach on life is that he doesn't fully understand how dangerous the High Order can be. If this tech and recording is legitimate, we could get killed just for knowing about it, no matter why it was buried.

"Bill, this is the type of information that gets people killed. You think the High Order omitted this information from our history lightly? There's a reason they did, and they won't let an Alpha team stand in the way of manipulating our entire species."

Bill lets the information sink in for a second and tries to understand the gravity of our situation. "We can't just ignore it."

He's right, no matter how much I regret admitting it. "I know. But we have to be careful about this. Our visors may only be recording to local storage, but we still have to get V to wipe the info before someone sees it."

"Okay, what then?" he asks.

I don't have an answer for him. I brought tech with me that doesn't belong to the High Order, I always do. I've been in the game long enough to know that they can't be trusted, but I could have never imagined we'd find something this sensitive. "I've got tech we could use, but even then I don't trust it. What if it gets in the wrong hands?" We can't trust tech, and our own minds aren't viable proof, so what's left?

"Are there any more files?" Bill asks pointing back at the terminal. I swipe the screen and another video icon appears at the bottom.

"It looks like it's just another accidental recording. Think the others were deleted on purpose?"

Bill shrugs. "Hell, who knows if there were others to begin with. Tap the icon though, let's see if there's anything useful in this one." I tap the icon, and the video expands to encompass the screen and begins playing from the beginning of the recording. The video is partially blocked by the back of the woman we saw earlier, you can tell by the same color of her dull green outfit and brown hair. Her hair was up before, but it came undone and is now laying just below her shoulders.

"Is this going to work?" she asks sounding overwhelmed by stress and folding her arms in front of her chest. The taller male who was crouched down by the injured men is now standing in front of the transfusion pods. The video is a little clearer this time, he's definitely a Hemo. He's leaning on the pod with his hand against the glass door, and his face is blocked by his outstretched arm.

His deep voice sounds exhausted and somehow calming, "I don't know. It's only a theory."

That voice. It sounds so familiar and yet so foreign. I keep watching, just hoping he'll turn around and face the camera.

"It has never been tried before. There have been theories over the years, but they were never tried in actuality. Even if they survive, it will take decades. Our blood is like poison to you, like mixing the wrong blood type, but worse." So the men were human as well. What was a Hemo doing working with humans almost a hundred years before the Bloodwar? The woman lets her hands down and sets them behind her back. She must have bumped something on the terminal because the video goes black, flashing the same date with some other numbers behind it before shrinking back down to an icon on the screen.

We're both standing still, staring at the screen trying to make sense of what we just heard, dissecting the words and information from the video in our heads. "Did that voice sound familiar to you?" I ask Bill. He creases his eyebrows and nods. "I'm gonna play that again."

I play the video another five times as we hone in on the Hemo's voice, searching for some indication as to who it is. We know that voice, there's something in it, the calmness, and the deep smoothness of its tone. We both figure it out at the same time.

"Holy shit," Bill squeezes out as I say, "By the High Order." We turn and stare at each other blankly for a moment before I access a previous file from the nav computer on the back of my hand. An audio clip starts playing and Red's voice fills our comms system.

"That's Red." I say weakly, almost unable to support the words.

Looks like we found our proof.

Chapter 6: Abomination

May 1st 2014 10:01pm

"Hey, Kelly," I yell through the headset. She glances back in acknowledgement before returning her attention to the flight controls. "Aden thinks this is a bad idea."

She chuckles.

"No, no that's not what I said," Aden protests through his own headset next to me. "I just don't think this is the best idea. I think there are other ideas that are less likely to get us killed."

"What's the deal?" Kelly asks him. "It's not like you to get spooked before a mission. Where's that sarcastic wit? I look forward to it." Aden glances at me and smirks. He's got a huge crush on Kelly. There's no way he'll never admit it and if we lived a normal life, he'd probably ask her out, but we don't. Still, "normal life" isn't just something we can forget, even if we want to. Kelly likes Aden just as much as he likes her, even if my dense little brother can't pick up on the cues. I know, she knows I know, and Aden is left clueless and in the dark. That's normal life breaking through our abysmal reality, the reality that keeps me from pushing him forward. I want to tell him. I want to taunt him. I want to be the voice of reason when he enviably picks that horrible first-date outfit, but I also know that we live each day with the overwhelming odds that we will likely die at any moment. *That's* what holds me back. Everything's changed since we fought back and killed the soldiers at the beach two months ago.

"I'd feel better if we were in contact with Red. He touch base yet?" Aden asks.

I shake my head. "Not yet, but he's aware of the mission. He's never let us down before, I'm sure he'll make contact." God, I hope he does.

It's amazing how much faith we've put into Red over the last few months. Hell, we thought he was going to slaughter us on the beach that one night. Given all the trouble those ocean soldiers had put into terrorizing us, it wasn't out of the question. Befriend the enemy just to fuck with them, further fueling the terror.

Aden and I reacted, well, over reacted immediately. After a very quick look at each other, we both reached for our machetes and attacked. We thought those bastards on the beach were fast, but Red, goddamn, he was like lighting. Before I knew what happened, we were on the ground and Red was towering over us. Aden was groaning and my head felt like shit. I didn't even see him hit me. Red tossed the machetes into the sand and looked down at us.

"What the hell?" Aden shouted.

"I am sorry. I did not mean to harm you. You mistook my use of the word execute."

I slowly shook my head in disbelief and smacked Aden. "He just answered a question."

"Yes," Red responded. "It is safe for us to communicate openly now."

Red broke it all down after that. I won't lie, I didn't understand half of what he was saying. General gist was that all of the surface soldiers were injected with some type of experimental neural tracking implant. The signal recording had limited space and therefore only kicked in when the soldier answered a question. Red was in contact with some inside asset. I never met the asset, we never got a name. In fact, I didn't even know the asset's gender. Red always used neutral terms when describing him…her…it. This is the kind of stuff that made me nervous. So the asset, was working on permanently disabling the signal and creating a fake one to take its place. That night was when he became successful. On top of that, the Spartan-like suits used to scare us were laced with some kind of metallic substance. Not only was it interwoven with Kevlar to help with high velocity puncture resistance, but it allowed them to pull the bodies back to their forward operating base under the ocean. Obviously we'd analyze every inch of those bodies and the surrounding tech given the chance. They wanted to make sure that would never happen.

"We're coming in on the drop, guys," Kelly yells through the comms breaking my concentration. "Remember, this is a recon mission. Hoffman is sending you two in alone to gather intel. Keep in contact and be sure to get as much detail as you can before pulling out and calling for exfil." We both give Kelly a thumbs up and check our gear.

San Diego has been under martial law since the original attack. Most of the civilians were moved out of the area for obvious reasons, but a skeleton crew of vets stayed behind with a team of Marines to watch over the zoo. Moving all of the animals to another location just wasn't possible and animal rights activists along with the zoologists who worked there weren't about to let them all die off. Everything was fine until a week ago when some of the larger animals went missing. Hoffman locked it down and pulled out the staff.

Red's people, Hemosapiens, have been living under the surface of the planet for thousands of years. Supposedly, when Homo erectus started to evolve into Homo sapiens they split into two different tribes. Homo sapiens evolved normally and became what we know as humans. Hemosapiens were a cannibalistic group that would drain and drink the blood of their kill after each hunt. The massive intake of blood on a regular basis changed their physiology, allowing them to become stronger and faster due to an increased metabolism that burns through normal blood like fuel. They also evolved faster mentally and knew that they would have to keep humans alive and thriving in order to have a steady supply of blood and meat, so they took to caves.

Eventually they burrowed farther underneath the earth, waiting for a time when technology would allow them to reach to the stars and find other forms of life for sustenance. Unfortunately for us, the humans, they needed to do two things to make that happen. Take over Earth, and keep enough of us around as a viable food source in the meantime. Animals and kidnapped humans worked well for hiding under the surface, but they were looking to expand their roots. That meant a lot more mouths to feed and more room for the future generations. The timing was right, their technology was ahead of ours and rather than give us more time to catch up, they attacked.

Hoffman sent us in to the zoo to find out if the Hemos are responsible for the missing animals and, if so, to see if we can find an access point to their network below the city. It will be crucial to turning the tide and taking the fight to them.

I'm checking the straps on my day pack one last time when the light above our head turns green.

"All right boys, have fun!" Kelly turns around and smiles at Aden as we grab hold of the drop lines. I kick the rope out of the helicopter door and pat Aden on the shoulder. He turns to me and nods, then jumps out the opening. I follow just behind and touch down next to him on the pavement, then turn around and give Kelly a thumbs up. She disconnects the ropes, then takes off. The dark zoo gates loom ominously over us.

"This is...much scarier at night." Aden says cautiously looking around at every little shadow that moves due to the slightest breeze.

"I don't think it helps that we're hunting giant bloodthirsty cannibals that live in the darkness and want to turn our planet into a massive cattle farm." I walk toward the gates and look up at the untamed shrubbery that's starting to cover the entrance. Aden jogs up behind me.

"No, thank you for pointing that out. It doesn't help." Aden jumps at the shrill noise of a creature crying out in the zoo. Sounds like a bird of some kind, but I can't be sure.

"Look, let's just get in, find the hole, and get out." Aden chuckles and I shake my head ignoring his dirty mind. "Intel suggests that it may be located somewhere near the rear of the zoo as the first animals to go missing were the gorillas. Workers heard a commotion near the polar bear enclosure as they were being extracted, we should head there first."

Aden slowly turns his head to look at me and even in the darkness I can see how wide his eyes are. "They took out fucking polar bears? Do you know how big those things are?"

I turn to meet Aden gaze and grab him by both shoulders. "Look, we've been through this before and we've killed dozens of these guys. This is merely recon, in and out, avoid contact. Just keep one eye on the scope."

These assholes don't show up on thermal due to the fact that they're cold blooded. Red and his contact were able to re-engineer our holographic rifle scopes to register the material in their "suits". It was still hard to think of their Spartan like costumes as full combat suits. They show up as bright green on the dark gray output. Doesn't make seeing the surround area too easy, but we can pick them out no problem and the scope is small enough that we can use our free eye and peripheral to stay alert.

I grab his face with my left hand. "We're gonna be fine. Let's just get this done."

Aden nods and I smack his cheek before turning to the gates and cutting the chain that holds them shut. The growth is stopping us from opening the doors completely, but we're able to pull them back enough to slip in. I've been to the zoo dozens of times since moving to San Diego because the annual membership is cheap and with all the pathways it can be a really cool place to do a morning run. Right now though, I'm just terrified. Everything looks creepy with the excess plant growth and lack of light. It's like something out of a horror movie.

We stay to the side of the road all the way down to the polar bear exhibit and on the way we see animals huddled into the corners of their own enclosures. It's clear something's got them spooked. As we approach the polar bear pool on our right the water seems darker than it should, even without the lights. I climb up the fake rocks to get a better view of the enclosure and point my flashlight down at the pool.

"Holy shit," I mutter under my breath.

"What?" Aden asks climbing up behind me. "Holy shit."

The polar bears have been ripped to shreds; pieces of meat are scattered throughout the enclosure and floating in the water which is now red from all the blood.

I tap the comm in my ear, "Kelly, come in, over."

"Go ahead. Over."

"Hemos have definitely been here. Polar bear enclosure is a blood bath. No signs of entrance, we're going to continue on to...." We hear a scream pierce the night from behind us. It's coming from the elephant enclosure. Aden looks at me with those wide eyes again.

"What the hell was that, over?" Kelly asks.

"Sounds like they just attacked an elephant. Doubling back to the African exhibit, over."

"Be careful. You guys aren't prepared for a full-on battle, over."

"Will do. Contact when we have more info, over and out." My phone starts vibrating in my pocket and I pull it out to see 'RED' across the screen. I show it to Aden.

"It's about time," he says, "Answer it. I want back up."

I answer the phone. "Where are you?"

"Museum of man tower off El Prado. I can see you from here."

It still amazes me how heightened his vision is. Mix that with his increased hearing and strength and he can be a good distance away but still be accessible to help at a moment's notice. "Great. Can you meet us at the front gate? We just heard an animal being attacked, more than likely by a Hemo."

"Negative. The Hemos will pick up my scent. If you are trying to find an access point to the underground tunnels, you will need to find and track them without getting spotted." Unfortunately, he's right. He's more beneficial to us as a double agent than another soldier in the fray. He can't risk being seen with us unless absolutely necessary, just like he can't risk taking us to his access points. Luckily, we've found effective ways to cover our own scents, but the Hemos are much more attuned to their own, potent scent. "I can see the elephant enclosure from here but cannot currently see any Hemos. I will continue tracking you and if there is an emergency I will be there as quick as I can."

I hang up the phone and Aden is waiting for the good news. "He's in a tower in Balboa Park."

"So, we meet him out front, right?" he says with an uneasy eagerness.

I shake my head. "No. He can't be seen with us, you know that. Besides, he says they'll pick up his scent and it will attract them. We need to go in quietly and track 'em back to the tunnels." Aden's look drops back into disappointment and he pushes past me toward the elephant enclosure mumbling as he does. I don't like this any more than you do brother, but it needs to be done.

It only takes us a few minutes to get back up to where the elephant enclosure is and, to our surprise, it's much cleaner than we expected. The enclosure itself is huge, about the size of two football fields end to end and covered with dirt. There's a railing separating the walkway from the enclosure which drops down ten feet from where we are. We can also see several large metal tubes that look like trees throughout the enclosure that hold hay for the elephants to eat.

"Where are all the elephants?" Aden asks.

"I don't know, are you getting anything on thermal?"

"Nothing, not a goddamn thing." He's right. There are no readings at all, and no blood or sign that the elephants were here to begin with.

"Let's drop down into the enclosure and see if we can find anything." I move over to the rail and prepare to swing over the edge when Aden grabs my arm from behind.

"I *don't* like this. Something is wrong." No shit, remember the polar bear cage? "We literally just heard an elephant scream and there's nothing, not even blood. You saw what they did to the polar bears. Something's wrong."

"You don't ever get skittish." He doesn't. I can't remember the last time that I saw Aden this worried. He didn't even look like this when we attacked the group on the beach.

"Exactly. What does that tell you?" I look down at his hand on my arm, and grasp it, then pat his shoulder with my other hand.

"When have I ever steered you wrong?" I ask. "Just stay frosty." *Aliens* is one of Aden's favorite movies. That comment was enough to warrant a weak smirk and the releasing of my arm. We can't see the whole enclosure, maybe the elephants were attacked on the other side. Maybe the Hemos took them alive somehow. There must be a huge entrance to their tunnel system if that's the case.

Climbing down the side railing, we stick toward the edge and make our way around the entire enclosure. There's nothing to indicate that anyone was in the area recently. No heat signatures, no disturbances in the sand, no blood, nothing. I walk out to one of the metal feeding trees and Aden hesitantly follows. I know he's got this gut feeling and all, but there's nothing here, not a damn thing showing up on the thermal and if Red saw something he'd call.

I lean against the big metal tube 'tree' racking my brain with what's going on. There's something off, something in the air that I can't put my finger on and it's driving me insane. While kicking the dirt around beneath my feet, I focus on the small clouds of dust and try to think of what we're missing.

Battling these soldiers is getting harder by the day. They started to send greater numbers up after the beach. Increased strength and speed allows them to wear full body armor similar to Kevlar that's painted the color of flesh. They don't look like Greek soldiers underneath, it's just a scare tactic. Still, outside of blinding them, or blowing them apart, our only option is getting to the back of their neck to sever the spine, which isn't an easy task. We've made adjustments to our tactics, but we've also lost a lot people in the process. Red's been helpful, but the information he provides has its limits. He was sent up to complete recon and collect humans for food before the attacks started. Fortunately, he thinks we humans deserve to be left alone. Unfortunately, he's not privy to the battle plans. Whatever's going on here is out of his scope and way over our heads.

"I feel like we're being watched." Aden whispers behind me.

"There's no one here, stop with the…." My phone's buzzing in my pocket. I pull it out and see Red's name on the screen; I activate the call on speakerphone.

There's this whooshing noise of wind coming through the speaker and Red screams, "CONTACT!" so loudly that the speaker buzzes causing me to drop the phone. I look down at where it landed and Aden's arm falls to the sand beside it. It's no longer attached to his body and blood begins to pool underneath it. Rising my head I see Aden's wide eyes as horror takes over his face and he falls to his knees.

There's a Hemo behind him, blade drawn, and he's pulling it back for another swing. He's wearing a tight black suit, something that we've never seen before. As he drives the blade back toward my brother's head, I manage to get my shotgun up and unload a slug right into the Hemo's face. He stumbles backwards and I move forward firing again at his knee. It crumbles and he goes down. All I can feel is the white hot rage flowing through my body as I press the shotgun right into his face and fire one last time. His body slams down into the dirt and doesn't move.

I spin around and run back over to Aden, almost losing consciousness in the process. I'm not sure if it's because of how quickly I'm moving, the adrenaline, or the fact that what I'm seeing is actually sinking in. My knees slam into the dirt and I pull a tactical tourniquet out of one of my vest pockets and wrap it around the stump near Aden's shoulder.

"Something's wrong, something wrong," he's mumbling through hurried breaths. He looks up at me, "Daemon, something's," then he looks back down at his stump and screams. I smack my earpiece causing a sharp pain to shoot through my ear.

"Kelly! We need backup and exfil now! We're in the elephant enclosure, Aden's hurt bad, does Hoffman have men in the area?" I forgot to say *over*. The things you forget and then subsequently think of when your brain is running on adrenaline. Where's Red? Why didn't we see that Hemo? Are there more?

"I'm on my way. He's got a Marine platoon team heading toward the beach now, I'll patch you to their frequency." There's static on the radio and gruff voice comes through. "This is Lieutenant Mackelson, who..." I cut him off.

"Lieutenant this is Daemon Athano operating under Captain Hoffman in the San Diego zoo..."

Hoffman hears the transmission and interjects. "Athano! What the hell are you doing? This is a secure line. You can't compromise..."

Aden's starting to shake, I think he's going into shock. "Captain, shut the fuck up! ADEN'S DOWN!" There's a desperation in my voice that I've never heard before and it starts to crack as I plea for backup. "His arm...we have hard contact in the zoo, one hostile wearing stealth gear, possibly more. We need help." I just squeeze Aden tighter in my arms. "We need help," I say again.

Tears start streaming down my face. I've lost everything from my old life, I can't lose my brother, too. Even though I've butted heads with the captain since day one, he's well aware of how much Aden means to me. Hoffman delivered the intel of our parents' death and had front row seats to the emotional breakdown that followed. After that day we vowed to fight for the only thing that mattered anymore; each other. Hoffman knows he needs us, we're the only connection to Red, and if we fall who knows how quickly the Hemos will overwhelm the surface.

Hoffman's voice comes back through the radio. "Lieutenant, you are to reroute your choppers to Sergeant Athano's position at the zoo *immediately*. These are two of our most important assets in the field, drop in and eliminate any threats and ensure that they're given medical attention and extracted. This is your only priority, if they don't survive I'm holding you personally responsible."

"Yes sir!" Lieutenant Mackelson yells back.

Hoffman turns his attention to me. "Daemon, we're coming for you, hold on. The Hemo you came in contact with...is he dead? Do you see any more?" It hits me that I haven't looked at anything else since I got to Aden. I turn around to see the Hemo I shot standing over us with his blade in the air. His throat explodes and blood drenches us as a blade drives through from behind. He lingers for a second then the blade is ripped out the back of his neck and he's shoved to the ground next to us. Red is towering over us in a similar tight black suit. He looks at me and nods, then starts looking around the enclosure in every direction.

"We have company," he says rotating the blade in his hand and pulling a second one off his back. I can hear the sound of a chopper coming in from the east, and see a half a dozen Hemos approaching Red from the same direction.

"Coming in hot!" Kelly screams through the radio. "Take cover!" As I look up at her helicopter it hits me...she flies a transport. It doesn't have a weapons system. I drag Aden behind the large metal tube to our left and keep one eye on Kelly as she brings the helicopter within ten feet of the ground behind the Hemos. They turn around and she rotates the blades down into the dirt, moving forward and cutting them to pieces in the process. She's brought it too low though and the blades begin to break apart causing the body to smash into the ground and slide to a stop twenty feet in front of the metal tube we're hiding behind. I sit Aden up against the tube and move out to wave Kelly down. I can see Red fighting a few Hemos to my right.

Kelly's got a medical pack on her back and a shotgun in hand. "Down!" she shouts from five feet away. I hit the dirt and she shoots, hitting a Hemo behind me with a slug in the chest. He catches his footing, but she keeps moving forward and fires three more times knocking him to the dirt. She loads a dragon fire round and shoots, engulfing his body in flames. I scramble back over to Aden. Kelly is on her knees pulling supplies out of the bag trying to stop the bleeding with gauze.

"Lieutenant Mackelson is sixty seconds out, Aden's gonna be okay."

Okay? He doesn't have an arm. I'm supposed to protect my brother at all costs, make sure that he's always safe, but all I've managed to do is continually put him in harm's way. It didn't hit me until now just how dangerous our lives have become in the last few months. We've been lucky, so lucky, up until this point, but everything has changed in a heartbeat.

I'm at a loss of what to think or say, but before I have the chance to process anything, a Hemo approaches from behind. I turn and thrust my shotgun into the air with both hands, stopping a large blade before it lands in my skull. He slices my arms with a second blade and the shotgun drops. Red comes out of nowhere and takes his head off with a sword, but another Hemo attacks at the same time bringing his blade down on my right knee with all his might. It sits at the end of my kneecap separating me from my lower leg. I hear a *BANG* and then ringing as Kelly unloads a slug into the side of my assailant's head and Red's blade drives through his skull to finish the job.

This must be what it's like to be in shock. No, no, no, this can't be happening right now. I'm fine, it's a bad dream or something. I don't even feel any pain. The world is spinning; I try to stand and pain shoots through my leg as I put weight on the stump. It's not a dream. I'm going to die. I look back at Aden who's struggling to stay conscious as Kelly's continues to work on him. Red starts fighting another group of Hemos. I can hear a helicopter in the distance, but everything else is dulled.

"No, no, no…" I mumble. Kelly's done all she can on Aden and turns to me. "No, no, I can't…I can't die, I need…Aden needs me." Kelly wraps her arms around my chest from behind, and drags me next to my brother, propping me up against the metal pole. "I can't, it can't happen…" I grab Kelly's arm. "He needs me." I plead as tears roll down my face and my head falls forward.

"I've got you," she assures me. "You going to make it. Hey!" I look up at her deep green eyes. They're so vivid, even in the dark. "You're gonna make it," she's says clearly, taking her time with each word. I bring my left arm up and set it on her shoulder for just a second. There's a spray of red mist all over our faces and my arm falls to the dirt next to Aden. Kelly's in shock with wide eyes and Red tackles a Hemo to the left of us. She snaps out of it and frantically wipes my blood from her face. The helicopter. I can hear it so loudly now. Everything's starting to fade.

"I can't die...I can't die...I can't...."

The world goes black.

* * *

I'm snapped back into consciousness as pain jolts through my body. I scream and writhe, but it's no use. Two Marines are carrying me to the helicopter and my wounds are being sandblasted by the dirt that the blades are kicking up. It feels like my stumps are on fire and the pain is keeping me conscious. My head slumps back and I can see another two Marines helping Aden along. He's bleeding from the stomach now too, he must have been hit by something else. There are explosions going off all around and I can hear the *thump* noise of the Marine's grenade launchers. It's all starting to fade again.

I can't see, but I can hear Red arguing with Kelly about where to take me.

"You cannot help them, I can!"

"They won't make it that far! And why the fuck should we trust you?

Amidst all the chaos there's a pause. Kelly is questioning Red's decision and I know why. It's the same thought that popped into my head when he towered over me holding Aden.

There's a dull thud, presumably Kelly's fist making contact with Red. "You're wearing the same fuckin' suit, Red! The same fuckin' suit that allowed those bastards to sneak up on the boys!"

More black.

The world is in bits and pieces now. Some sound here and sight or blinding light there. We're in a helicopter for a while, there's more burning on my stumps. They start to pulse. I'm being carried somewhere. I'm awake, Red is holding me up against a wall and strapping me into something.

"You are going to make it," he says before closing a rounded glass door in front of me. There's a hiss and my vision fades as I look down and see tubes protruding from my skin.

I don't know if I'm dead, or if it's a dream, but I can still hear Red. I can hear him the way you hear your own voice when you're talking, as if I'm in his head.

"I do not know. It is only a theory. It has never been tried before. There have been theories..." His voice echoes and trails off. Poison is flowing through my veins. My entire body burns, and it's the last thing I feel.

Chapter 7: Down the Rabbit Hole

2.28 - 2468 - 56:754 Red Galaxy Standard

"Bloodpack Alpha member Delta-Alpha-Echo 6, your slip has been approved for docking. Docking procedures to commence in T-minus sixty seconds. Please ensure any and all loose equipment is secured prior to umbilical attachment."

"About freaking time," I say to myself without responding to the docking patrolman through the comms. Two damn months. Between waiting for the slow ass dropships to transport us to the recon facility on the outskirts of the Milky Way galaxy, the finicky instamatter machines to get us out of the galaxy, and then waiting for a small retrieval ship to bring us to the Patriarch, it took two damn months to get back. I slam the holographic button for the slip's open speaker system on the console in front of me. "Bill. Get your ass up here, we're docking with the Patriarch in less than a minute." He claims to have gone back into the small storage bay to try and grab some sleep, but I'll bet anything that he was looking for food.

I hear the door behind me slide open and Bill falls into the secondary seat to my right, rotates forward, and peers out the thin cockpit window. The small amount of blood running down his lower lip makes me shake my head as I turn my focus back to the holographic representation of our docking procedure on the console.

"You missed some," I hiss out of the side of my mouth. Bill wipes the area around his mouth a few times with the back of his left hand.

"Hey, it gave me more energy than sleeping would have."

I shake my head and mutter, "Maybe *I* wanted to get some sleep," under my breath.

"What?"

"Nothing." I just focus on the hologram in an attempt to not get frustrated by Bill's selfishness. There's really not much for me to do while we're docking. A large majority of space flight is automated these days. Outside of inputting coordinates and making sure the computer doesn't overheat or shut down, it's just a whole lot of sitting and waiting. Which is exactly why Bill slept for most of the trip in between rummaging through the storage bay for food while I manned the controls.

"Hey man, benefits of being the ranking officer. I would have brought you some, but I know you don't eat when you're tense."

He's right, I can't. I don't know why but I've never been able to eat when my mind is trying to figure shit out. Crazy me to worry over universe-shattering news like *Oh, someone you see as family has been lying to you for centuries*, what am I thinking? Hopefully Bill enjoyed the trip because the lack of food and sleep for the last month in this cramped up slip has me on edge. Not to mention the two weeks we spent in those small ass dropships that feel like coffins. Our longevity in life allows us to go months at a time without eating or sleeping if need be which is great for survival, but horrible when you need to kill time.

"So what's the plan?" Bill asks turning his seat to face me. "I mean outside of storming straight into Red's training bay and asking him what the fuck the deal is?" The entire slip jolts and I can hear metal snapping down onto the hull.

"Docking procedures complete. Scanning for airborne contaminates," the computer informs us. The vents start to hiss.

"No, that's pretty much it."

"You're really pissed off aren't you, LT?"

"Yes."

"You must be. You're always so straight and to the point when you're really angry," he teases.

"Fuck off."

"See?" I can't help but smirk a little. Luckily it's on the left side of my face and he can't see it. I'm not sure what I'd do if I didn't have Bill around, probably go mad and murder a bunch of people. What a fun game that would be. He grounds me, holds back the anger and rage with his half-witted comments and sarcastic attitude. Some people see it as annoying, but I find it comforting most of the time. He just always seems to enjoy life no matter what we're going through and that helps me push on through the tough times, which are plentiful. Most people see me as reserved and stoic, but that's only because Bill keeps my malice in check. I don't know why there's such hostility deep down inside, but I know I'll have to face it one day. It's the only thing in the universe I fear.

"Blood Pack Alpha, Captain Otto requests your presence on the bridge as soon as you've stowed your gear. Welcome back."

Bill slams his fist down on the holographic comms button. "Great to be back, patrolman!" he replies cheerily. "Come on, let's go debrief with the captain then talk to Red."

"I've got a better idea." I say jumping out of my chair.

"Oh come on LT, Captain wanted to see us. He's not stupid, he knows our slip already docked! How pissed is he gonna be when you go storming into Red's bay instead of going to see him?"

"He won't even know." I dart out of the slip's side door and jog down the ramp. Bill sighs behind me and then runs to catch up.

"Oh, man, what did you do?" He asks nervously as I power walk through the halls of the ship toward Red's training bay.

"Calm down. Vali cut the feed and looped an image of our ceiling. If he checks, it'll just look like I'm relaxing in my bunk for a few minutes." Vali is brilliant and has way more power then he should when it comes to stuff like that, but I trust him.

"Vali? Really?" Bill, on the other hand, does not trust him. Here comes the lecture. "How can you trust the guy? He has unlimited access to your brain and he's creepy beyond all belief." While Bill struggles to keep up, I spot Red's double doors and pick up the pace as the anger drives me forward.

"I'm not getting into this with you right now, Bill. Vali's done more than you know to keep us out of trouble, just drop it." He does, but only because the frustration in my voice is growing as we approach the bay. All these years, how could Red keep something like this from us?

I push through the double doors with so much force that they slam into the walls as we walk through, creating a ringing, metallic echo throughout the massive room. Red's training bay is the size of a large hangar and uses complex, realistic projections and holograms to help soldiers train for battle against virtual combatants. It's how we learned to fight Thyr without ever meeting one in the past. Red spends ninety percent of his time in this room. When he isn't training the constant stream of new recruits to fight the Plague War, he meditates for hours. Supposedly with deep meditation you can suppress the hunger. Personally, I've never had the patience to try and I'm not quite sure why you'd even want to. Might be good for Bill though, there'd definitely be less arguing on our missions.

Red is standing in the middle of the room, feet together, hands at his sides with his eyes closed. His chest is slowly moving up and down from the deep breathing exercises he's engaged in.

Bill rushes up next to me and whispers, "Do you really want to piss off Red too? I heard he used to have a pretty bad temper before he *centered* himself." I push Bill away and walk right up to Red, standing close enough to feel the breath from his nose on my neck. I'm a little taller than Red, but he's still pretty damn intimidating.

"Gentlemen," Red says without opening his eyes. "I heard you were on your way back. Have you already debriefed with Captain Otto?" He opens an eye and raises an eyebrow at me, curious as to why I'm invading his personal space.

"Vali's made the room dark, we need to talk," I say holding back a snarl.

"This room is always dark." Red says lowering the eyebrow while opening the other eye. He doesn't move otherwise. He has a point. Outside of the training holograms there was barely any light in the massive room.

"Not what I meant."

"You misunderstand my meaning." Red tilts his head slightly and squints. "This room is always dark. After all these years do you think I would let the High Order have eyes or ears in *my* space? Who was it that introduced you to Vali?"

He did. Red was always one to walk his own path, but I never figured he'd make it a point to stay hidden from the eyes and ears of the High Order. Then again, I never expected him to show up in a video helping humans, so I guess the lesson of the day is; you don't know shit. It makes sense that he wouldn't want people poking around in his business if he was previously involved in something of that nature.

I take a step back. "Look Red, we…"

"Found something on Earth. By your tone and flared nostrils I would assume…an underground facility." I glance at Bill then back to Red.

"How long have we known each other? Trusted each other? By the High Order, you're like a father to us!" I scold, blood boiling at the fact that he's been lying to us for centuries. My fists are shaking and my jaw is clenched; Bill sets his hand on my shoulder and I start to calm down. I take a deep breath and close my eyes. My muscles relax and the anger subsides making room for reason. Upon opening my eyes again, I look at Red. "I know what it looks like. I can understand wanting to keep it quiet from the High Order or anyone else, but us?"

It's not often that I let my emotions get the better of me, but there's no one in this world that we're closer to than Red. Bill and I were both alive and kicking during the Bloodwar. We fought side by side with Red for decades until our failure and subsequent capture stole everything from us. He says that our unit was caught in an ambush, and they dragged us away from the engagement before torturing us for information. Red risked everything to save us and he took a decade retraining us to be soldiers again. He even got us placed back into the Alpha program. No matter what's happened since that day, he's always been the one fixed point in our universe. Now two blurry videos on some ancient console under the surface of the Earth is making me question centuries of trust.

"I know you feel betrayed. But there is a reason for my insincerity. If anyone knew that that bunker existed, you would both be in danger and I could not let that happen."

I turned away from Red and start pacing around the room, I want answers and I want them now. "How can I believe anything you say, when you've kept something this big from us?"

Bill's curious too, I can see the wheels in his head turning, but he wouldn't dare interrupt my line of questioning. When it comes to playing the game in the field he can't wait to ask questions or dig deeper, until it gets personal. Then he clams up. Another reason we work so well I guess, because when things get personal I start making noise.

"I believe it is time for me to explain," Red says calmly walking up to me and setting his hands on my shoulders. "Please, sit." He motions to the ground. I sit on the floor and Red follows suit. He looks back at Bill who tentatively walks over to us, sits down, and pulls his legs up to his chest.

"Red, I have to know," I'm having a hard time formulating the question, but it's driving me crazy. "What you said about our amnesia, is that the truth?"

Red looks at Bill, then back to me, "The amnesia, yes," he breathes in deeply then out. The way it came to be," he slowly shakes his head. "No."

My heart is beating so hard and fast that I'm afraid it's going to break through my chest. "What happened?"

Red looks at me. "Do the names Daemon and Aden mean anything to you?"

Chapter 8: Rebirth

Feb 16th 2120 4:00am Earth Time

There's blackness all around. It's the only thing I can remember except for the occasional voice in the back of my head. The fact that I have no control over what it says indicates two possibilities; either I'm crazy and that voice is a separate portion of my subconscious, or I'm hearing someone else. The blackness makes me think that maybe I'm blind. This is the first time the thought has crossed my mind. I can feel my body, the rhythmic pumping of my heart, the rise and fall of my chest as I slowly breathe in and out. More recently I've been able to move my tongue from side to side, ever so slightly. There's something metallic, almost copperish that I'm able to detect.

I want to focus on my senses more, but the voice is getting louder. I can hear and feel a struggle. There's grunting and the noise of feet shuffling against the floor. There's a thud, then another, louder, reverberating through the back of my head near the voice and into my body.

BAM!

This time the sensation hits me like a wave. I have a body and limbs, but can I move them? I stretch my fingers and feel the muscles expand and contract as I form a fist. Maybe I'm not blind after all. Maybe it's all in my mind and comes down to understanding that movement is indeed possible. I breathe in deeply and command my eyes to open.

The world is blurry. Light exists, but not how I'd expect. It's dull, sedated, and weak. That doesn't stop it from causing pain. Pain to my unprivileged eyes, for they have not seen the world of the living for some time. I blink once and lighting radiates into my temples. Another blink, hoping my pupils will dilate and adjust to the brightness. They don't. My eyes open; my mind wants to close them, but I don't have control.

BAM! Again, and louder.

The light is temporarily obstructed as two men slam into a rounded glass door in front of me. I don't know who they are, but the one with his back to me feels familiar even though I can't see his face. They roll off to the left side of the room and continue fighting. Another man approaches the glass with dark red eyes and stares through the thick protective barrier before pressing a button to my right.

"Hello, Daemon," he says in a surly voice. Daemon? Is that my...

Searing pain shoots through my mind just under the surface of my skull and my eyelids clamp shut as I experience pieces of a past life. Killing on a massive scale, my brother, Aden, Red, Captain Hoffman, Kelly, the beach...the zoo. The pain remains but my muscles tense and rage forces the debilitating sensation to a dull ache as my arms quiver. Another flash of events crop up in my mind. Helicopters, blood, darkness, my brother is placed in a tube on the wall. Red lifts me up and straps me into the tube next to him. I open my eyes then reach down to the straps holding me in this glass cage and tear them out of the wall I'm held against. Red was the man pressed against the glass a few seconds ago, Aden is in the container next to me, and the bastard staring at me with those blood thirsty eyes is a Hemo.

A tingling sensation is building in my feet, it travels up my legs and into my chest. A fire beneath my skin manifests and it's escalating at an exponential rate. I'm not quite sure where this sensation is coming from, but if I have to guess I'd say it's the rage. I've just never felt an emotion affect my body like this before. There's barely enough room to raise my legs to my chest and press my feet against the glass. The Hemo's eyes go wide as I thrust them forward with all my strength. The glass shatters as I make contact with the Hemo causing him to fly fifteen feet and slam into the wall behind.

Before I have the chance to think about my next move I'm inches from the Hemo's face. I can taste the stench of feeble weakness exuding from his pores as I pin him in place against the wall and stare deep into his empty eyes. He has nothing but fear and hatred for my brother and me. A roar radiates throughout the room and just before I manage to pull myself away from the ever growing worry in his eyes to find the source, I realize that the sound originated deep within. What type of monster have I become? Surely not one who allows this pathetic excuse of a man in front of me to continue threatening the existence of my brother.

I'm not quite sure what's happening, it feels as if glass is slowly cutting its way through the fibers of my brain. My eyes are clenched tight; jaw straining which causes my ears to muffle the scuffle a few yards away.

Where am I?

Concentrating on the pain allows just enough relief in my muscles to slowly open my ears and let the sounds of the room invade my senses. A tall man in dark clothing trips the one he's fighting and pulls a thin, two foot square blade from his back, driving it into the fallen man's skull. He pulls the blade out and turns to glare at me as the deep black blood drips onto the metallic floor below. Natural instinct is overridden as I'm comforted by the sight before me and not frightened as I should by all rights be. I blink.

The blade leaves Red's hand and flies past my face at such a close proximity that I can smell the blood as it travels in front of my nose. I follow the weapon until it meets its target twenty feet to my left, through the heart of another Hemo coming to kill us. There are five more behind him who are undeterred by his sudden demise.

Why does my head hurt so much?

Daemon, I can hear Red say in the back of my mind. I turn and he tosses another blade at me handle first. On my knees I try to stand, but my entire body feels like it's shutting down, my muscles failing to communicate with one another, but somehow my fingers manage to grip the handle as it hits my palm. There's the faint sound of liquid dripping onto the floor and I notice that everything below my elbow is drenched in the onyx blood of a Hemo. What did I do?

My attention is drawn to the heavy sounds of boots against metal as a Hemo barrels toward me with a thin square sword drawn. Adrenaline releases into my system and enables my arms to react as our blades make contact and the ringing of metal reverberates off the walls. Another attacks and I slide to the left on my knees leaving just enough space to occupy the sword he would have brought down on my head. It slams into the floor next to me with an ear-piercing clang.

Muscle reactions increase, and my body begins to act on its own. I lift my right foot slightly and move it to pin the sword on my right to the ground with my boot. Turning my attention forward, I force the Hemo in front of me back with my blade, then bring it down on the neck of the Hemo to my right. It's a clean cut and after a fraction of a second, the head rolls to the ground behind me. I grab the corpse's sword and launch to my feet, bringing my blade and the sword together to form an X in front of my chest to block another blow from the first Hemo. One of them is standing guard at the door and Red is fighting the other two in the corner of my vision. Attention reverted forward, I force the assailant back once more, and when he attempts to swipe at my arm, I dodge out of the way and spin around him while ramming the sword into his abdomen. When he curls forward in pain, I release the handle allowing it to stick in his gut and hold his head in place while sliding the smaller blade through the side of his neck. A flick of the wrist sends blood and flesh to the floor as I slice his throat open and the lifeless body falls to the ground.

    The Hemo who was previously guarding the entryway is now at the control panel to the right and behind me. The door to Aden's container opens, the straps release and he falls face first at the Hemo's feet. Aden rolls over as the Hemo draws his blade. He opens his eyes to see my short blade fly over his head and pierce the Hemo's shoulder, pinning him to the wall next to the container. Aden scrambles backward slipping and sliding on the bloody floor before making it to his feet and bumping back into Red who has just finished dealing with his own kills.

    The Hemo reaches to remove the blade from his shoulder, but I rush over and drive the thin square sword into his other one so he can't move. Red walks over, looks at me, then draws back his blade before hacking off both of the Hemo's legs. As he hollers in pain, Red stands back up and looks at me calmly.

    "Limb for a limb, right?"

    "Speaking of which," I say looking down at my left arm and right leg. Both are intact, and I'm wearing some sort of tight black outfit and boots, not to mention I'm a good foot and a half taller then I remember being. I no longer look up to Red. In fact, if anything, he looks up to me. "What the hell happened?"

"We will get to that in a minute," he says turning his attention to the legless Hemo on the wall. Red drives the palm of his hand against the Hemo's forehead, slamming the back of his head into the wall. He leans close, digging his fingernails into the back of the Hemo's head. "How do you know about this facility?"

"You fucked up, Red. Your little pets are gonna burn." He looks at me and smirks. Aden walks up behind Red and stands next to me. "First, we're going to kill that annoying little shit in front of his brother's eyes," he nods at Aden. "Then we're going to tear you apart, limb by limb," he turns back to Red, "before we finally...."

Red's other hand snaps up and clutches the Hemo's throat, his nails dig deeply before he tears out a chunk of flesh leaving the windpipe exposed through a gaping bloody hole beneath his chin. What little blood is left in the Hemo's body trickles out of the massive wound and down his chest as he attempts to breathe.

"I *always* find a way to survive," Red whispers into the Hemo's ear before ripping the rest of his head off and letting it fall to the ground.

"Not the best interrogation I've ever seen," I say.

He turns his head to me and shrugs. "He gave me enough to..."

"What the fuck is going on?" Aden screams into my ear, finally managing to get back on his feet. My head is still in pain from whatever that containment unit did to me.

"Christ Aden, inside voice. Jeeeesus." I rub my ear that is now ringing due to his high-pitched squeal.

"Why are...Ah!" Aden screams, grabbing his head with both hands and collapsing to his knees. The expression on his face paints a picture of excruciating pain. Red and I both kneel next to him and I hold Aden up by his shoulder.

"What's happening to him? What did you do to us?" I ask Red frantically. Before he can answer, my own torment returns. My entire body is on fire, my muscles are contracting and I can feel the blood pumping furiously through my head. Blackness takes me once again. I'm seriously starting to get tired of this shit.

Chapter 9: Blood is Thicker Than...

2.28 - 2468 - 235:079 Red Galaxy Standard

    To say that Captain Otto is displeased with the fact that we didn't come straight to him after returning from our mission is an understatement. It's rare that the captain's emotions are visible, or even palpable, to the soldiers around him. Still, with the amount of stress he's under with the Plague War escalating the way it is, I don't blame him. Outside of getting annoyed with Bill's sarcastic side, and let's face it, who doesn't, the captain is usually pleased with our performance. In fact, he may not be one to sing praises on a regular basis, but he always treats soldiers in a fair and consistent manner. His current displeasure is more amplified than normal, sure, but not only did we disobey a direct order, there are several imminent threats, and right now all the shit is landing on his shoulders.

    What's worse is it turns out that our contact with the Thyr on Earth wasn't the only confirmed contact. In the two months that it took us to get back to the Patriarch, fifteen other recon squads confirmed contact with squad-to legion-sized combat groups spread across ten planets. We're one of two teams that made it back alive.

    The Plague has also continued to spread across the universe and two days before we returned, Plaguers started attacking the Red Galaxy which holds not only our High Command, but a large majority of our civilian population as well. Early strategists reading the Plaguers' attack patterns foretold this attack while we were operating on Earth, which is why the Patriarch was pulled back home.

"Simple orders gentlemen, that's what we're talking about here." Otto's tone is flat, his face red, and my primary goal right now is preventing him from raining a massive shit storm down on own heads, seeing as it all rolls downhill and he's currently the levy. I'm pretty sure he's still pissed at Bill for getting reamed out by Major Erislad about the lewd pick-up lines he used on a gorgeous blonde High Priestess. The huge smile on Bill's face isn't helping.

"Something funny, Sergeant?" Otto snaps at Bill. Just like the game, he finds joy in getting under people's skin, unfortunately for me it's usually with people who are above us.

"No, sir." He doesn't even have anything to be laughing about. I know Bill, normally I'd say like my brother, but as it turns out he actually is my brother. The whole situation with Red is going to take some time to sink in, for both me and Bill. Even though it doesn't show, I know he's having just as hard a time processing all the information that Red told us, especially the reason why he saved us, which in turn makes it pretty difficult to give Otto the attention he thinks he deserves right now.

Otto pushes himself out of the ostentatious, leather-wrapped chair behind his equally ostentatious wooden desk and walks around the side, circling behind us in the process. Real wood is extremely rare since we scorched Earth. Our most recent mission has validated that little forests have been thriving over the last few decades, but our people never go there. They certainly wouldn't go there to harvest something like wood. The captain is the only one I've ever met that is fascinated by it. I've always found it interesting that he's so adamant about keeping those pieces.

"Excellent. Then wipe that shit-eating grin from your face because I see nothing funny in the fact that the Plague War has spread to our home system. Do you?" he asks poking Bill...or Aden...shit that's weird. Regardless, he pokes my partner in the back of the head.

"No, sir," Aden says through clenched teeth. He hates when Otto pokes him in the head. I have a feeling that his rebellious nature is going to grow now that we're aware of our true origins. It might get harder to keep him in line.

"Thyr combat squads have been discovered on five planets in the time that you and your lieutenant spent in those damn pods," Otto stops poking Aden and switches his attention to me. He says it like it's our fault. Blame the damn High Scientists, they're the ones that have had to focus on weaponry instead of flight tech. Oh, and why's that? That's right, because *they* created a Plague that mutates our people into intelligent, bloody-thirsty monsters that want to kill or convert every last Hemo. Shit, now my inner monologue is starting to sound like Aden, or has it been that way the entire time? Maybe we're more like each other then I thought. At least I'm the filtered version of my brother.

"We've encountered two recon squads on as many planets," he continues, vilifying us for events we have no control over. "Didn't even know they had recon squads," pausing as if to contemplate the ramifications of that fact, he shakes his head before continuing. "And eight legions spread across three others. They've managed to kill all but you and another squad."

"Alphas?" I ask, knowing full well the answer.

Otto continues walking around us and glances at something on the wall as Aden shrugs at me and silently claps his fingers against his thumb in a chatting motion then points at Otto. I risk a quick glare at Aden before my attention is back on Otto as he rounds my left side and looks back down while addressing me.

"Yes, one other, India November Foxtrot. The rest were Beta teams." Captain Otto probably saw this as a chance for the Betas to get some field training, without realizing how large the Thyr threat actually was. It's probably part of the reason he's so frustrated and projected those emotions on us. I know he blames himself for their deaths. That explains why we lost so many men and why the other Alpha team survived. Aphrodite and Blaze are the two most ruthless, skilled Alphas in the universe. Well, besides us that is. Blaze and I are close, really close, but I feel like recent revelations may have fucked that all up.

We...or Hemos...are all about our own kind, we always have been. People make excuses for the way we spread across the galaxy, snuffing out other species. Oh we're just beating them to the punch, they'll say, or the best way to defend what we have is to stay on the offensive. I don't know that I ever believed any of that. We conquer because we can, and we're damn good at it. Point is, Hemos don't do well with non-Hemos, and especially not when it comes to the first species that we burned for taking a stand when we started to spread. How's Blaze going to react when she finds out Aden and I were human, or are human? Keeping this quiet is the only option right now and I can't do that if I spend more time around her.

"What were Betas doing scoping out the Thyr?" Aden asks.

Betas are Black Soldiers training to be Alphas, but there's a lot of weeding out before they reach our status. Even then, with the danger and frequency of the missions that we're given, seventy-five percent of newly appointed Alphas die within the first ten years of duty. If they get past ten, the likelihood of survival increases dramatically due to field experience and battle confidence, making teams like India November Foxtrot and us a rare breed. Any team that hits their centennial is very likely to make a second one, but that's not easy. Only twenty seasoned teams operate in the entire universe. That's a pretty small number considering there are approximately three trillion Hemos spread across the known universe, and roughly two trillion are active duty.

"We're stretched thin. The Plaguers' numbers have doubled in size since our last major encounter and even though our strategists were able to predict their ambitious actions, no one assumed their ranks would have swelled to the size they did." Otto finally reaches the other side of his desk but he doesn't walk around the final corner to sit back down. Instead, he pushes his clenched knuckles into the wooden desk and lets out a long sigh. After a moment he lowers his head and continues. "On top of the Plague War growing out of control and the Thyr poising for war on Earth, Mini K incidents across all worlds have grown to a dangerous level."

Aden leans over to me and whispers, "Looks like we're not the only jackasses to use that term," then chuckles under his breath but is abruptly silenced by Otto's fists slamming down on the desk.

"SERGEANT," Otto shouts, eyes now open and digging through Aden with a fiery intensity that I've never seen. Aden stays leaned over and merely rotates his eyes up to Otto. "What in this entire conversation is so humorous that you can sit here and make jokes while our people are on the brink of extinction?"

If I had to guess, I'd say it has something to do with the fact that we were engineered to be instruments vital to the Hemo's destruction. This was of course after they slaughtered the humans for being self-destructive and now they've pretty much signed their own death warrants in a similar manner while we, the instruments, didn't even know of our purpose until now. Oh the irony. We can't exactly say that to Otto though, or anyone else for that matter.

I look at Aden and mentally shake my head. "Well, I guess I find it humorous that you would send the two most lethal men in your military to a backwater, or lack thereof, planet like Earth and then bitch about the fact that we aren't around to help out when the shit hit the fan." Aden leans back into his chair, his eyes on Otto the whole time. "Sir." Aden's body loosens as he crosses his arms and legs out in front of him.

Otto snarls, then for what I would assume would be for the sake of his desk, bites his lower lip, clenches his fists, and sits back down in the ridiculously large chair. While leaning back and crossing his legs, he breathes in deeply, and interlocks his fingers over the top of his knee.

"If it wasn't for Major Erislad and the politics involved...I would have never sent you to earth. As much as I hate to admit it, I suppose you make a point, Sergeant. Then again, you have always been a pain in my ass so why should I expect any different?"

"Have I, sir? Wouldn't know. See my brother and I had a legit case of amnesia like two centuries ago in battle." Oh shit.

"Brother? If I remember correctly, you're an only child, Sergeant." Otto tilts his head and cocks an eye. I can feel my skin warm as I straighten my back ever so slightly waiting for Aden's quick wit to kick in.

"Brother-in-arms, sir. LT isn't just my superior officer. We're bonded by blood." In more ways than one. Little son of a bitch is going to be the death of me yet, whether it be by stress-induced heart failure or something else. Of course, Red would just probably revive me to go through it all over again. Is this what hell is like?

Otto eases back into his chair, unaware that Aden is referring to our newly realized deep, dark secret. "Yes well, aren't we all," Otto mutters almost under his breath.

"Sir," I posit, he nods. "How bad can the Mini K incidents be? They're mindless beasts."

"Bad enough for me to bring it up. Mindless or not they're popping up all over the universe and wreaking chaos wherever they go." He pauses. "Gentlemen, the battles are heating up, and I don't know why you didn't come straight to my office as instructed and, personally, I don't care. What I do care about is you following orders. You may not always agree with them, but if the most elite recon team in the known universe starts choosing which orders to obey or disobey, no matter how small, then word's going to get around. It'll spread like the Plague and all of a sudden we fall apart because two professionals couldn't report to an office on time. Understood?"

"Yes, sir," we repeat in unison. It's easy to understand his frustration given the circumstances and Aden's constant stream of bullshit. Can't have the military falling apart at a time like this. Hemos...well we...all of us will be lucky to survive a dual war with complications.

"Take a day, gentlemen, no more than a day. I want you here at this exact time tomorrow to go over your next mission parameters. Dismissed." He waves a hand at us and turns to the terminal in his desk.

Part of me wants to argue about the fact that we're ready now. With everything that's going on, it'll be hard to get some rest knowing that we've got plenty of energy to dive into our next assignment. Space travel does wear you down though and given the massive amount of information we received from Red about our past, maybe some time to process everything and center ourselves isn't a bad idea.

We get up from the uncomfortable wooden chairs, points for nostalgia but not comfort, and salute before heading out of his office. A few steps out into the hall and I grab Aden by the shoulder and spin him around.

"It's difficult enough trying to figure out what to do about our past, could you take it easy for a bit?"

"Hey, I'm helping the cause, bro. If I change my personality, then people would definitely get suspicious." He smiles that stupid toothy grin of his.

"Fine, just cut out the damn innuendos okay?" He doesn't answer right away so I squeeze his arm and jerk to let him know I'm serious.

The smile fades and is replaced with annoyed defeat, "Fine, fine, no more suggestive words or phrases. You're the brother. I mean, boss...boss. Simple slip of the tongue, won't happen again." He smirks playfully and yanks his arm away from my grip.

I shake my head and throw him a half smile, "Look, go get some blood. I'm going to make sure the captain knows we're on the level then head back to my room for some much needed alone time."

"Oddly enough, I'm not hungry," he says walking away. "Weird right?" he shouts over his shoulder. "Starving when an axe could split my head at any second, but put me on a ten-thousand-person command ship with infinitely enjoyable edible options and it leaves me." I watch Aden turn down a hall to his left and disappear before I start back to Captain Otto's office.

"Hey, boss?" Aden shouts from behind. I turn my head and see him out of the corner of my eye peeking around the corridor with his head and upper body, holding onto the corner near his abdomen with his left hand.

"That alone time...you'll be calling Blaze, won't you?" I shake my head. "Eh, eh?" My right hand falls to the sidearm strapped to my leg. "All right! All right, just kidding. I'm going, geez." I can hear him step back around the corner and walk away. "See ya tomorrow!" he shouts from down the hall.

Standing at the edge of Otto's door, I'm trying to figure out what to say to ease the tension a bit and reassure him that Aden, or Bill, and I are still committed professionals more than ready to pull our weight in the coming wars. No more bullshit assignments with everything going on. He can't afford to have us pulling shit detail with the battles that our people will soon have to face. As I run through scenarios in my head, I can hear Otto speaking in a hushed voice through the slightly cracked door. Red did say that our senses seemed more attuned than a normal Hemos for some reason. Probably one of the reasons that we're so good at our jobs. I quietly lean closer and slow my breathing to hear what's going on.

"You assured me this wouldn't be an issue," Otto says.

"It is not," I hear Red telling him. What's Red doing talking to Otto, and how did he get in there without us seeing him? Was he hiding in there the whole time?

"How much do they know?"

"You have trusted me all these years and I need the trust to continue if you want me to contain this. They are still our most valuable assets in the field. That has not changed."

"How. Much. Do they know?" Otto asks again, slower and more definitive.

"They discovered the facility. They know who they are and why they were changed."

Otto exhales in discontent. "What's it been, almost three hundred years?" He pauses, Red must have nodded in approval. "And we still aren't sure how to deal with this. We knew it would take a while to turn them, but the Bloodwar was just so incredibly ill-timed. Who knew Ellie would have pulled the trigger that early, well before the brothers could have been released. Humans turned Hemo, the perfect warriors." The captain sighs. "What do you do with two hybrids that were meant to topple a species but woke up too late?"

"The humans are gone along with their memories. Over the years as my blood slowly mixed with theirs, we became connected. Daemon showed signs of understanding my thoughts when they were first released, but that passed quickly. That much time in a comatose state allowed most of the memory tissue to decay causing..."

"*Most* of the memory tissue?" Otto asks cutting Red off.

"Or all. There is no way to tell. Even they would not know. Some memories could theoretically come back, but their mind decayed and was replaced with new tissue. Blank tissue. I cannot see any reason why they would have a desire to acquire vengeance."

Unlike Red, the old man is a patriot, through and through for the species. He always speaks of our genetic superiority over the humans, even though, now as it seems, they may have come first. I'm worried that he'll see us as abominations that need to be put out of our misery.

"What if we still wanted them to?" Otto asks Red.

Huh? Maybe not.

Chapter 10: Lightning Never Strikes Twice

Feb...uh...some year...noon maybe?

I can hear Aden's car sputter up the driveway and immediately reach for the remote to turn off the TV. After giving him so much crap about getting a big TV with his first paycheck, I'd never hear the end of it if he knew I'd been watching it more and more since he bought it. It's a stupid habit that's developed ever since that unreasonably large life-sucker started taking up space in my living room. I found my passion in the outdoors and don't want to get back into my old ways as a lazy couch potato.

Aden shoves open the front door and walks into the house just as I open a backpacker magazine that was sitting on the end table next to the couch. He looks at me, pauses, then chuckles as he turns to slam the door.

"What?"

"Come on, I know you use the TV when I'm not here. You can't start pretending to read something *every* time I come home."

I shake my head flipping a page in the magazine, "I don't know what you're talking about. There's plenty of other ways you could have spent your first check. You know, like getting a nicer car maybe? I'm always afraid that thing's gonna die on the highway."

Aden chuckles again as he walks in front of me and rounds the couch to the left to go into the kitchen. I can hear him open the fridge and pull a beer out then start to search for a bottle opener.

He continues to rustle through the drawers even though there's a magnetic one hanging on the front of the fridge.

"Or you know, maybe pay me back for all the craft beer you drink that *I* pay for?"

He stops and peeks his head around the wall near the end of the couch and smiles. "Hey come on, we don't want to be *those* kind of roommates. The ones that bicker over every little purchase." He ducks back into the kitchen. "You're more than welcome to drink my beer."

Of course his idea of beer is the cheapest box of cans that he can find in the local run down grocery store or mini mart. No beer is too cheap for my brother when he's the one paying.

"That's the thing. You don't buy beer." Aden's head shoots around the wall again this time with a cocked eyebrow. "Don't give me that look, I don't know what the hell you buy, but it's not beer."

He disappears back into the kitchen as my attention reverts to the magazine. Now, I love when he struggles over the simplest tasks, but the noise of him rummaging through the drawers is starting to get to me. I may have picked up the magazine as a diversion, but some of the articles in this month's issue look pretty interesting.

"Fridge door," I say flipping another page.

"Ah," he exclaims and I hear the clank and fizz of the bottle top before the opener and cap drop down on the counter.

Waiting until he steps in the living room, because it's just more fun that way, I declare, "Not where you found it," while slightly turning my head to shoot him a glance out of the corner of my eye. He sighs, walks back into the kitchen and I can hear the opener smack against the fridge door with excessive force.

He falls down on the couch to my left and sips the beer. "Better?"

"Well the cap is still on the counter, but I'll let it slide. Training takes time." I smirk. "Besides, you clearly have something you want to tell me." I flip another page.

Aden takes a long sip then sticks the bottle in between his thighs. "This is really good, kinda tastes like coffee."

"Well it's a coffee stout so I guess they're doing something right." Aden pulls the bottle out from his thighs and looks at it.

"Huh." He takes another sip and pushes it back between his legs.

"So, come on, spit it out, what happened today?"

"You know how you want me to get some direction in life? You know, annoying me like Mom and Dad used to annoy you?" he asks. Oh great, here we go.

"Sure."

"Well, I think I found something."

"Do tell," I say blandly admiring an advertisement for a portable backpacking stove. Aden would love this thing, it has a built in usb charger that gains battery life from the heat produced by cooking. There'd always be a way to charge my phone and I'd never have an excuse for turning it off. I quickly flip the page hoping he's too preoccupied with this newest of new life ventures to notice the ad.

"Well, I was down near SDSU looking at classes." Which I know means looking at girls. He's been 'looking at classes' for months now. Some days he takes a bag and pretends to be a student while hitting on said girls. "And I stopped into a recruiting office."

What? I drop the magazine on my lap and turn to look at my brother as the simplicity of the situation hits me. "Who's the girl?"

"What?" he stretches out the word in a high-pitched voice. "Pfsh, I...it's not...I do things for other reasons. I just think it would be good for me." I continue staring and raise my left eyebrow. "There's no girl," he presses. I tilt my head to the right. "It's...well, I didn't lie, she's a woman."

I pick the magazine back up and start scanning the page. "Uh huh. Exactly. What's her name?"

"I don't know, yet. At least I'm not quite sure, but I've seen her around campus a few times."

"Of course you have. Come on, details. What's she look like?"

Aden sips the beer again then sits up and leans forward resting his elbows on his knees. "Well she looks fit, I mean it's hard to tell under the baggy uniform..."

"ACUs," I correct.

"Yeah, right. ACUs. Anyways she's got green eyes, blonde hair, about five five..."

"California dreamin'." I say casually, looking back at the magazine.

"Yeah, man." Aden leans back into the couch and puts the beer between his legs then interlocks his fingers behind his head.

"What branch and MOS?" I can see Aden out of the corner of my eye turn his head in confusion. I close the magazine and toss

128

it on the coffee table then turn to him. "What's her *job,* numb nuts?"

"Oh, right. She's a Marine,"

"Combat Utility Uniform," I blurt out. Aden doesn't care, but he waits for me to explain the random outburst. I direct my eyes toward the ceiling while recalling the entire phrase. "M-C-C-U-U, Marine Corps Combat Utility Uniform. Yeah. Marines call it a Combat Utility Uniform."

"Uh huh," Aden could care less about the proper terminology, but not correcting the detail would have driven me insane. "I think I heard her say something about being a pilot." Now I'm the one chuckling. "What? What's so funny?"

"That's Kelly Tyler."

"You know her?" Aden shoots straight up from the back of the couch almost spilling his beer in the process as his eyes go wide.

"Yes, I know her. That station had me come in a few weeks back to talk to some kids about the National Guard. Brother, I say this with all the love in the world...you don't stand a chance."

Aden scoffs. "What, is she married or something?"

"No, but she's dedicated, driven, and focused on her career, not to mention wickedly intelligent. Worked as a Paralegal or something before going into the Marines. She's not going to jump in bed with some young little shit who joins up just to get into her pants." Aden's taken aback and feigns a look of pain.

"Combat uniform, not pants," Aden corrects. Well look at that, he does listen from time to time.

"Combat *Utility* Uniform, but yeah exactly. Not happening, bro." Aden sighs.

"Look, do you know why they bring her into the recruiting stations?" Aden shakes his head. "Okay, let me break it down for you. She's hot. You have two heads, one that you should follow and one that you shouldn't...get the picture?" Aden sighs and shrugs back into the couch. "Look, the military isn't filled with hot women, if you want to join up to get some direction or because you seriously want to serve, then by all means go ahead. I'll help you prepare every step of the way, but don't do it for a California dime."

There's a weird flutter in my chest and Aden catches my expression change as I squint for a brief second. "You okay, bro?"

What the hell was that? "Yeah, I'm fine. Must have eaten something weird."

Aden gets up and walks back into the kitchen. "I keep telling you to lay off the tacos in that little drive-up building. They got a 'D' rating from the health department last time I was there." He opens the fridge again.

My chest is starting to tighten up. "I didn't eat there today, besides they changed it to an 'A' last week."

"Good to know 'cause I'm starving. Wanna grab some tacos?" Aden shuts the fridge and walks back into the living room. "Hey, you sure you're okay?"

I lean forward, put my elbows on my knees and begin to rub my chest. "Yeah, my chest just feels a little tight."

"Indigestion is the leading cause of...." Before Aden can finish off spouting whatever fake fact he's concocted there's a loud crackle then a bang outside of our door.

"What the hell was that?" I yell jumping up from the couch. Ripping the door open, I run outside to see a large black circular burn mark in our driveway. "What the..."

Aden comes running out behind me. "What's wrong?" he asks, looking at me like I'm crazy.

"Look, something struck our driveway, I think it was lightning."

Aden looks down at the driveway then back up at me with the same weird face. "What are you talking about?"

"The burn mark right there and the loud noise, it sounded like lightning."

"There's nothing there, Daemon." I look at Aden incredulously. "And I didn't hear a noise."

This is unbelievable, he has to be fucking with me. Turning back to the ground, I look back to the burn mark, which is still in the driveway, then up to the sky and can see dark clouds gathering over our house fairly quickly.

"What are you talking about? Look, there are storm clouds right there. I think we should get inside it looks like it's going to hit again." I point up to the sky while watching them swirl and dance in an odd display of consuming darkness.

"I'm taking you to the doctor," Aden says with some fear in his voice. I look at him, shocked. "Dude, the sky is clear, besides lightning never..."

Aden's voice disappears; replaced by an ear-piercing reverberation and a searing pain. It's another lightning strike, but this time it hits me. The electrical surge jumps through my body and my head kicks back as my limbs quiver from the voltage. All my muscles are tense and it feels like my blood is on fire. Everything goes black.

I can hear a voice. A male voice but I don't know who it is. "Nothing. Hit him again!" The pain takes over once more, but this time I can feel it start near my chest. Why are they—whoever they are—doing this to me? Come to think of it, who am I?

"Come on, Daemon. Come on!" Same voice. Is that my name? He sounds worried, are they trying to help me somehow? Again the pain comes, sharp and fast through my chest before rushing through the rest of my body. I can hear a double thump, then another, then I can feel it. I think it's my heart. My body takes over and I gasp. Dry lips are greeted with stale air before my lungs pull it deeply into my chest. I draw in until it feels like they'll explode and then exhale all of the previously stagnant life within a second. My breathing continues and slows, but I can't open my eyes.

"Well, fuck," the male voice says. Two pieces of plastic clatter against the floor. "What's happening to us?"

I don't know who these men are, but they feel familiar to me. Odd, I don't know who I am, where I am, but these men for some reason...I'm connected to them somehow. In more ways than one it seems.

Another deeper voice answers. I can hear the second man's voice before he speaks, *you are a living miracle.*

"I'm not sure, but you were both in a coma for nearly a hundred years. Over time your body assimilated the blood, but there was brain damage. The new blood fixed the brain but some of your old memories are pushing through."

You may very well die from the stress, honestly I am surprised you are still alive, and equally surprised that the defibrillator worked. That explains the searing pain in my chest.

"Your new body is rejecting the old memories. Your new mind is treating them like viruses and trying to cleanse your system. Your brother should be okay for now."

Brother? The first man is my brother? No wonder I feel a connection, but why is it stronger with the other one? Why can I hear his thoughts?

"What comes...AH!" My brother howls in excruciating pain as he continues to forcefully expel the air from his lungs. When they're empty, he gasps for oxygen like having just been punched in the stomach then wails again. It's louder and more painful than anything I know and even though that's not much at this point, it frightens the hell out of me.

"Aden. Aden," the second man calls out. I hear him shuffling around as my brother falls to the floor. The clattering of plastic returns and a mechanical whine increases in pitch and volume until it's replaced by two thuds.

My brother's name is...wait...who am I? What's all that noise?

Chapter 11: Push Back

3.01 - 2467 - 002:845 Red Galaxy Standard

After overhearing the conversation between Otto and Red, there was no way I could have slept. I figure, what does it matter at this point? I've been awake for so long and have so much shit running through my head that one night isn't going to do much damage. Truth be told, even if I hadn't overheard the conversation, I wouldn't have slept because of the bomb that Red dropped on us. Hell, let's go a little further than that, even if we didn't talk to Red I would have been racking my brain about the human base. We don't stop and find the human base? Then I'm racking my brain about the next mission. Point is, I think too much, clearly. All this most recent shit aside, I probably would have stayed up anyway. No point in dwelling on it.

Still, there's not much else to do while I'm waiting for Bill...or Aden...outside of the Blood Labs. I'm still struggling with calling him Aden, but if I'm going to come to terms with this entirely different reality that's been kept from me all these years, then that's the first step. Otto contacted me an hour ago and canceled our debrief, then told me to contact *Aden* and meet up with a High Scientist named Alexander to get some new gear before going on our next mission. We've worked with him on a number of occasions, he's not too fond of Aden. Aden's sarcasm has been set on max ever since we talked to Red, which should make this meeting much more annoying than it has to be.

We don't normally get gear from scientists, so I'm assuming it's something experimental that they need to test before distributing to all of the soldiers. We've been test subjects for experimental equipment since the High Priests pushed the NSU Act through the High Order. The No Stone Unturned Act states that any active military personnel above a certain rank is subject to test equipment and weapons that the High Scientists say have reached their fullest potential in a lab setting but still aren't ready for mass production. This led to the creation of the Research Evolution and Accidental Personnel Emergency Repair division, or REAPER, which has been run by Alexander since its inception. I know what you're thinking, and yes, this was how the Plague was created. Luckily, after that horrible miscalculation, the use of genetic alterations was outlawed. Now we just get to test equipment that could very well blow up in our faces, or even worse, not work when we need it to.

As I'm waiting for Aden, I hear a clicking noise made by one particular tongue that I am all too accustomed with to my left. I turn to see Blaze leaning against the wall and shaking her head while looking at the ground.

"Bill's running late again? Seems like it's becoming a pattern."

"He's there when it counts," I say flatly while turning to look at her. She looks up at me and smiles, which would normally make me laugh or at the very least smile back. Blaze and I have been, oh how do I put this delicately...fucking around for decades on end. More recently things have started to go beyond just having fun. Aden thinks that she loves me. Scary thing is I know that I love her. Priorities though. All that needs to be dealt with at another time in the unforeseeable future. I can't even think of dealing with her until I've sorted the rising pile of shit that is my life out.

I know what she wants, so I'm going to try and keep things professional. "The captain said you ladies got into a little trouble on the last mission? Barely made it out of the clutches of the Thyr?"

"Oh, please," she quips pushing off the wall and walking toward me.

"Nothing you couldn't handle?"

"No, the bit about us being ladies. Ridiculous."

I smirk and look at the ground for a second as I think back to all the justification that Aden's given me over the years about why I should get together with her. Before I know it, Blaze is in front of me and I lift my head to meet her piercing gaze. Her bright red hair is shaved on either side and formed into a thick mohawk that's combed back to the rear of her head. The color of her hair is a stark contrast to her bright green eyes. Despite the rebellious hair style and the overly aggressive behavior, her face is delicate, beautiful, and altogether feminine. She leans on the door in front of me a cracks a seductive smile.

My mind is blank. I can't think of damn word to say, not while she's standing there like that looking fucking adorable.

After a minute of silence she says, "You promised me some time before your next mission."

"I did, that's right, but," before I have a chance to make up some bullshit excuse, she reaches around my waste and grabs my ass without looking away from my eyes.

"But?" she asks with a smirk. I cough. "Oh come on LT," I love when she calls me LT. It turns me into more of a bumbling fool then I currently am, but I still love it. "Impending war and all I know," the smirk fades. Blaze has always been tough as nails, except when it comes to me. We seem to have the same effect on each other and it's nothing that either of us ever expected.

"Somedays I just need a reminder," she says looking deep into my eyes. "It's," she sighs and shakes her hard. "It's all going to shit real soon and sometimes I need to be reminded why we fight. Today is one of those days."

Blaze just went from being sarcastic, sexy and confident, to exposed and vulnerable in a second, because she knows that she can when it comes to me. We've been there for each other through centuries of shit. Sure Aden and I experience it first hand, but Blaze and I, we help each other through the aftermath. She's seen a side of me that Aden never has and probably never will. I've never been more open with anyone and when she's in pain, it's all I can do not to fall apart, and now…I don't know. I don't know if I can be that anymore and I feel horrible not talking to her about why.

Thankfully, Aden walks around the corner as I snap back to reality. "Well, well, look what the Mini K dragged in," he taunts from behind me.

In a fraction of a second, the smirk is back. She looks past me and nods at Aden. "What's up, shithead," then looks back at me and smiles once more before saying, "LT," with a nod. I turn to watch her leave and she shoves Aden with her shoulder as he passes. Aden leans on the wall in front of me but turns his head to watch Blaze round the corner as she says, "I'm sure I'll see you later."

"Sleep well?" he asks before looking back at me.

"You know the answer to that."

"I guess not. You guys…" he draws out the words suggestively.

"No."

He shakes his head. "Damn shame. Body like that, I bet she's..."

Not in the mood for his antics, I cut him off again. "Trust me I know, just leave it."

Aden pushes of the wall and turns to face me. "Really?"

I wonder if all little brothers are this annoying. "What?"

"Figured you guys would have caused a few new bruises by now seeing as how long it's been."

"Yeah brilliant idea, bravo," I say slowly clapping. Then I lean in close and lower my voice, "we just found out we used to be human, changes things a bit don't you think? It's best that I distance myself, at least until I figure out what Red wants from us."

"I was up all night, too ya know. Can't get that damn High Priestess off my mind."

I smack him across the back of the head.

"Hey! That wasn't nice."

"You're so dense, are you fucking kidding me?"

"I was just being honest. Look there's no point in worrying about what will or won't happen right now. This is our life, may as well enjoy the perks," Aden looks back at the hall Blaze walked down and chuckles. "And trust me brother, there's plenty of perk there."

I slap him again with one hand and slam the other onto the holographic interface outside the lab door. "Stop calling me your brother." I look down at the interface which envelops my hand in a yellow haze of holographic lines and dust. The yellow blinks on and off for a minute before turning a consistent green. The door slides open and I motion for Aden to go through. "Shall we?"

He walks past me through the door. "Pfsh, you just want a shield in case any of this questionable tech explodes." I follow Aden in and the door slams shut behind me. It's only been about five months since we've been down in the REAPER labs, but it feels like a lifetime with everything going on.

"Nothing in our lab explodes," says Alexander, the highest of the High Scientists, who is standing behind a gurney with both his closed fists setting on the top, knuckles down. "Not unless we want it to." He cracks a smile.

Alexander looks up at us, his stark white, slim-fitting lab coat, reaching to the floor. His white hair is styled up in a short point above the center of his head sitting just above those albino eyes. They've always bothered me. No coloration, just flat white eyes.

"LT, you seem put off. Do the eyes still freak you out?" They do. I know they developed an ocular injection that allows increased vision by removing the iris and dyeing the inner retina white so that it receives and reflects the maximum amount of light possible. It just looks creepy, and in all honesty, I can't imagine the level of pain you'd have to go through before your mind adjusted.

"I just always think of how painful it would be. Some mornings my alarm beats me to the punch and turns on the lights in my room and I get the worst headaches from the lack of light overnight."

Alexander throws his hands up in the air and shrugs before letting them fall to his side. He walks around the gurney and starts gesturing with his hands as he speaks. "What's a little pain when it comes to progress? We're not so different, you and I. I seem to remember you being shot, more than once in fact?" He stops a few feet in front of us and looks Aden up and down before turning and staring at me with those dead eyes.

"Yes well, a laser discharge tends to cauterize most wounds the second it travels through the skin."

Alexander moves a step closer. "Ah, but the regeneration isn't pleasant."

"We have combat stims. Thanks to your teams."

Alexander raises his hand and extends his pointer and middle finger to the ceiling while keeping the rest curled, thumb holding them down. "Yes, I know. I developed them." He points the two extended fingers at my face and bounces his hand up and down. "But they certainly don't remove the pain entirely." He turns and walks back to the front of the gurney.

"All due respect, sir, how would you know?" Aden asks.

Alexander pauses. "We don't test everything on soldiers," he mutters under his breath. Another moment passes before he spins around with a huge grin on his face. "Still, my point is valid! We're both willing to endure pain to foster progress, are we not?"

There's really no point in arguing with Alexander when he's trying to make a point, he'll go at it all day and I'm pretty sure there's a war going on.

"Yes, I suppose we are," I agree, eyebrows raised, nodding my head.

He's leaning back against the gurney, tapping the edge with his untrimmed fingernails. It seems to be a growing fashion for some reason, I haven't the slightest clue why. Taking a few moments to read my body language, which is pretty much nonexistent because I hate having these conversations and don't want to feed his ego, he finally gives up.

"Well, we can philosophize at some other time, yes? I hear there's a war going on." He smacks the tables with his palms, then holds his left arm out to our right motioning to the next room. "Come, I have a new toy for you."

We follow him into a room we've been in many times before to test new equipment prior to taking it into the field. Outside of a few computers on a desk to the left of the entrance, it's essentially just a large, open rectangle. The room is two hundred yards long, fifty wide, with maybe seventy-five above us if I had to guess, and my guesses have gotten pretty damn accurate after all the launching we've done in our suits under tight circumstances. Alexander walks up to the desk where another scientist is sitting and points at something on one of the eight screens stacked in two rows.

"So come on Alexee, whatcha got for us?" Aden asks. Alexander hates when Aden calls him by that nickname. "It better be something that blows stuff up after that little tease when we walked in."

Alexander's back stiffens and he stops whispering to the scientist next to him. "Don't call me that."

Aden rolls his eyes and crosses his arms. "Okay big guy, whatever, but seriously boom boom, right?"

Alexander turns around with a straight face and then flashes us a half smirk before walking to the desk on the other scientist's left. I lean in to Aden's ear, "Is there a reason you have to push him like that?"

Aden raises his shoulders and eyebrows, "Um, hello, because it's fun?"

"Yeah well, ever hear of *faulty* equipment? May be best not to push him."

"Your partner's right," Alexander shoots over his shoulder before turning around with a thick mechanical looking black belt in each hand. "You really shouldn't antagonize the man who chooses how people live and die."

Aden takes a deep breath then tilts his head back and closes his eyes, before lowering it and looking back at Alexander. "Oh, come on *Alexander*, I'm just giving you a hard time, you should be happy, I only do that with friends." Alexander shakes his head.

"You must be friends with everyone," I mutter under my breath.

"Well, I can't help it that I have such a likeable personality," Aden replies with a wide grin.

Alexander walks up to us with the belts in hand. "Let's just say you're lucky Captain Otto holds you in such high regard. Even after you hit on his niece."

Aden shoots a look of shock at me and then mixes it with excitement before turning back to Alexander. "Oh shit," he chuckles. "That was his niece?"

I look at the ground and rub my forehead. "Geez, A...Bill" Shit, I almost said Aden out loud. I look back up at Alexander to see if there's a peculiar look on his face after my slip of the tongue.

"Were you gonna call me Ace?" Aden asks happily. "I'd totally be down with a nickname," he winks at me.

"No, I think he meant to say asshole," Alexander corrects.

"Different sounding vowels, big guy," Aden snaps back.

I point to the belts. "So, what are these?" Alexander turns his attention to the belts and I shoot a quick look at Aden, who widens his eyes to say *what the hell*? Shrugging briefly, I reach down and grab one of the belts from Alexander as he holds the other up in front of us.

"These, gentlemen, are your new combat suits. It's only right that you're the first to get them. Your little mishap with the Almathe a few years back allowed us to conquer their planet much faster than anticipated. The Muutahtion we mined was integral to the suits' construction."

"Ha!" Aden blurts out. "We should get captured more often," he jokes nudging me in the shoulder.

There's nothing to them. Our previous suits are light, like a second layer of skin, but they're still full suits that we have to get into. Once we put them on, they seal up from the back via nanotechnology and there's no seam to be found, then the helmet goes on and seals as well.

"Am I missing something here?"

Alexander smirks; he always gets excited when soldiers don't understand how to use his tech. "Put it on."

I do as he says and bring the belt around my waist from the back looking for a way to connect the two ends. "How does it..."

"Just press the ends together," Alexander instructs.

The second I do the ends fuse together and the belt shrinks to fit my waist. "Oh, that's interesting."

"The suit is calibrated to your bio signature," Alexander explains, pointing at me. "Which means if you're rendered unconscious or captured, your tech can't be stolen and used against you. In fact, once it's activated, the user is the only one who can remove it."

"Always good to know," I say, smiling back. Aden grabs the other belt from his hands and secures it around his waist.

"Whoa. It's snug, isn't it?"

"Your previous suits used nano-electro-stimulation to certain areas of the body in order to amplify your muscles. These are a little different, they use a form of radiation to increase your musculature output, but the sensors require a tighter grip on your skin in order to read the reactions properly. They've been calibrated a little tighter than necessary only because we'd rather overdo it than have the suits malfunction due to improper data. It may be a little uncomfortable at first, but it won't hinder your performance, which is greatly increased from the previous model as it is."

Interesting. "How increased?"

"Depending on the user and the conditions, anywhere from seventy-five to a hundred and fifty percent more than the old suit."

I raise an eyebrow at Alexander. "That's a pretty big predictive gap. You do realize our jobs, our lives, often depends on the limits of our gear, right? We need to know what we're capable of."

Alexander throws his hands in the air then lets them fall to his side. "Like I don't know that! There's only so much we can do in the lab, that's why you guys are here. The values will vary per user, the higher end percentages, we think, are only capable in extreme circumstances when the user's body is releasing a bunch of adrenaline. Count on a general increase of one hundred percent."

That's something we can work with.

"First things first," Alexander says grabbing something metallic off the table. He points the small metal tube at my head and I feel an intense pain in my temple before he points it at Aden.

"Fuck! What the shit was that?" Aden shouts.

"Neural links for your new suits," Alexander answers while setting the device back on the table. "The suits interface directly with your brain."

I nod and look down at the belt, trying to figure out how, or if, it needs to be activated beyond just being wrapped around my waist.

"Oh, you're gonna love this," Alexander says smiling. "Okay, just...act like the suit is taking over your body."

"What?"

"The previous iteration that you've been using is an actual suit. You step into it, then activate the nanoparticles which create a seal and let the unit conform to your body. When that happens, your muscles tense in anticipation of the event, it's instinct, an involuntary muscle reaction."

"Uh, okay. Sure."

"Well do that. The belt feeds off of your neural and physiological outputs. Think of the suit enveloping your body, and your muscles tensing in the same manner that you're used to when the nanoparticles constrict, then the belt will understand that and react." I just stare at Alexander questioningly, he has a penchant for practical jokes every now and then. "Seriously," he confirms, nodding.

I shake my head slightly and glance at Aden, who shrugs in disbelief. Okay, here goes nothing. The second that I tense my body and imagine the suit, the belt activates with a quiet whirring and clicking noise. I can feel pressure against my abdomen as the suit takes over, spreading from the belt like nanite dominoes which seem to appear from nowhere. A second later, it's up to my chest and down to my knees, another second and the pressure has reached my throat and covered my feet. It continues to construct over my clothing and boots, lifting me off the ground slightly as it creeps between me and the floor, then advances over my face. I close my eyes before it reaches them, not quite sure what to expect from my newly acquired radioactive cocoon.

"Holy shit," I can hear Aden say. He's muttering the words, but they're much louder than they should be, the suit is amplifying the sound.

My eyes are still closed when Alexander says gleefully, "Ha ha, see I told you." He sets a hand on my shoulder and there's a weird sensation that follows. "Open your eyes."

I hesitate, but then open my eyes and blink a few times, allowing them to adjust to the light around me. All of my senses, my vision, hearing, touch, even scent all feel heightened. I look at Alexander who's smiling, then turn toward Aden who closes his eyes and tenses his body. Seconds later the suit's complete and all I can do is copy his shocked expression, "Holy shit."

The suit itself looks like black pearlescent scales all over his body. It switches through a myriad of different colors, depending on what angle the light is hitting it, but remains dark with the base color staying black. The individual scales are small, about an eighth of an inch in diameter and flex to match the movements of his skin. The belt around his waist remains, but the rest of the suit below his head is clear of any external features beyond the scales. There's a menacing looking visor over Aden's eyes that's flat like glass but still retains the black coloration of the rest of the suit. Three scaled straps—for lack of a better word—occupy the top and sides of his head and attach to the top and sides of the visor. The outline of his mouth and ears are visible, but there's not any other external equipment covering them beyond the scales.

Even though it looks as if the suit is skin tight, I can speak and move freely. "Give me the rundown, Alexander."

"Very well. The suit interfaces with the neural link in your head and, as I said before, is calibrated to your bio signature. These are the only two suits we have and you're the only ones who can use them. You will notice an increase in all of your senses. A large majority of the scales have a microscopic needle that pierces your skin and attaches to your nerves and muscle tissue. The reaction time is as close to instantaneous as possible. You can move freely and the scales will adjust as need be, like a second skin."

Aden is hopping up and down and swinging his arms around but stops and looks at Alexander. "Wait, if our sense are increased, isn't that going to suck if we get hit?"

"Excellent question, Bill. No, it will not. The suit is able to determine which sensations are beneficial and which are harmful. You will still feel pain as to be aware of any injury, but the suit will release medication that increases your base regenerative cells and adrenaline to help you push through the pain and remain combat functional."

Aden starts hopping again, then gets low to the ground and is stretching in all different types of positions to test the flexibility of the suit. "Cool."

"Oh, you haven't even heard the best part yet," Alexander smiles. "The suit collects and stores kinetic energy from friction caused between the plates as you move about. That then becomes usable energy within the suit itself."

"Self-sustaining systems?" I ask, moving my arms around as I try to get used to the feeling of wearing this thing. I won't lie, it's pretty intoxicating. I feel...amazing. Soldiers are down the hall talking, and I can hear them. If I focus on their voices, the volume increases, but the second I direct my attention elsewhere they fall into the background. The Patriarch is currently moving through space, and I can actually sense the movement. I'm aware of every little sensation on my skin, and I even can focus my view down to the pores on Alexander's skin. These things are insane.

"That *and*," Alexander brings his hands up to his mouth in excitement, "you can use the stored energy as a barrier!"

We both stop and turn to Alexander; I squint my eyes in confusion but it ends up zooming in my ocular implants. I'm going to have to get used to a whole new bunch of body gestures. Widening my eyes reverts the view back to normal.

"What does that mean?" I ask. Alexander turns around and grabs a pistol off the end of one of the tables then points it at Aden.

"No!" I scream as he fires. Aden doesn't move an inch and the blast harmlessly bounces off his chest and burns a hole in the nearby wall.

"Damn it, Alexander!" the scientist sitting at the desk shouts.

"Oh shut it, Brent! The suit always redirects at an extreme angle," Alexander yells over his shoulder.

"Still...I'm right here."

"Nobody cares." He dismissively waves a hand to Brent and goes back to explaining the barrier. "The suit monitors surrounding activity and forms a barrier of energy on the outside of the scales in the event that anything faster than nominal speed makes contact.

Bill's jumping around created more than enough energy to redirect the pistol blast."

Aden's touching his chest where the laser hit. "I'm getting a display reading about remaining power."

"Yes, it will keep you abreast of how much is left. You're not totally invincible, just as close as we could make you."

"What's nominal speed?" I ask.

"If someone were to punch you, the barrier would activate and force the energy outward. That's why Aden didn't move when I shot him, the suit reflects the same amount of energy it receives."

Huh, that's interesting. What if... "Alexander, mind if I try something?"

"By all means, that's why you guys are here."

"What are you gonna do?" Aden asks.

I smile at him, which he can't see now that I think of it, then turn to the far wall two hundred yards away. Theoretically, this should be a pretty fun little experiment if the suit reflects energy back to any external force. I take off into the test chamber running as fast as I can, then halfway through the room leap forward, careful not to apply full force. It's still too much as I'm at the end wall faster than I should be and *Impact Imminent* is flashing red in the upper section of my visor. I smack into the wall and bounce backwards to the center of the room, where I land on my shoulders and bounce up, flipping back over my head. Somehow I manage to land on my feet the second time and the barrier doesn't kick in. I'll admit, that was kind of fun.

I jog back to Aden and Alexander and even though I can't see it, I know Aden's smiling under his suit. "Holy shit, that was awesome!" he hollers in excitement.

"Yeah, that was pretty fun," I say, smirking underneath my helmet.

"Now you're thinking with kinetics. Still, I would keep notice of your energy reserves before jumping off a cliff. The suit should calculate the force of any object approaching you and warn you if the reserves aren't enough to repel the object."

"When I landed on my feet, the barrier didn't activate."

"Yes, that's a default setule feature, same with your palms. At a microscopic level, the particles rearrange and fuse to any surface. It's meant to allow for climbing, or landings. Still, the suit reads the neural feedback of your link, all the control is done through there, so if you think of bouncing off the ground, the suit will deactivate the setule feature and let the barrier do its job. Eventually, all of it will become second nature and the suit will be a part of you."

"Our weapons and gear?" I ask.

"All tuned to the bio signature of the nanomachines in the suit. All of your equipment will lock on like it previously did."

We were a force to be reckoned with before, but as soon as we become fluid with these new suits, which honestly won't take long, we'll be damn near invincible. Just have to keep an eye on those energy levels.

"Well, this is like, one of the best upgrades we've ever received. What's next, LT?" Aden asks, hopping around Alexander, bouncing a little higher each time.

"Well, the Plague has been pushing into the Red Galaxy, I'd say it's time we push back."

Chapter 12: Starting from Scratch

3.02 - 2120 - 33:915 Red Galaxy Standard

I feel as though it's been a while since I've been conscious, but really I have no basis for that theory. My body is tired; limbs and head heavy. When I open my eyes with what little strength I have, light floods in and pierces the comfortable darkness.

"LT, can you hear me?" The voice is clear and soft while seemingly thunderous. It sounds familiar to me, but I can't place the name of its owner. Come to think of it, I can't even place my own name. There's nothing in the banks of my mind that should contain memories. What's going on?

"LT?" Once again the voice, calm and deep, waits for someone to respond. My eyes adjust to the surrounding area to reveal a stark white room. There's a tall man, dressed all in black staring down at me. His entire face is covered by some kind of cloth, with the exception of his red eyes and a small patch of horizontal skin around them. Next to him stands a scientist, or possibly a doctor, wearing a white robe with equally white, spiked hair. His strikingly, bright blue eyes stare with eager success. As if my awakening has somehow confirmed an overly difficult path taken to justify one's life's work. My mental musing fades and suddenly I realize, they're talking to me. I'm LT.

The words, "Where am I?" escape from my bone-dry vocal chords and travel over my lips.

Those vibrant blue eyes flicker with joy as I speak. After a quick, but meaningful smile, the man in the white coat answers.

"The Red Galaxy. More specifically the Grecillian solar system surrounding the Katkis star. This is Grecillian High Command Medical Center, on the planet Redantus, third closest to Katkis."

Doesn't ring a bell. "Who am I?" is next on the docket.

The dark and light men trade looks, then turn their attention back to me. "You don't remember?" the dark man asks in a tone which implies that he already knows the answer to his own question.

I look around the room, but don't see anything out of the ordinary. Tubes coming out of my arm that lead to liquids in clear medical bags, machines monitoring my progress, chairs, and a large curtain blocking half the room to my right. It all seems pretty standard outside of the two clearly opposite strangers looming over my bed.

"Why the fuck would I ask if I knew?" I pose with a rather aggressive tone.

The dark man smirks. I may not be able to see his mouth under the shemagh that covers his face, but I can tell from the creases underneath his eyes. Details. I don't know why but the concept of recognizing and categorizing the priority of sensory details is screaming out in my mind. My eyes flicker around the room, and I start hearing, smelling and tasting everything within range. Everything, everything provides some little clue, some small addition to the projection of the current experience. The understanding of how each entity will play out in my life is built, word by word as my mind receives the sensory information and builds a definition to help me proceed well informed.

"Judging from your tone, and your facial movements, there is still some of the warrior I once knew left inside." He nods to the white medical man, who leaves upon confirming his gesture. We're left alone to discuss whatever needs to be cleared up.

"Alphas are trained to trust their senses well beyond what normal people perceive. It is the difference between life and death in what we do. Each little detail allows us the chance to avoid death, which is forever on our heels. This skill also allows me to see and analyze the details in your own face, the micro expressions and the eye movements. Your mind is working at an accelerated rate, to processing everything around you to feed the fight or flight nature. Regardless of which path you choose, you will have all the information you need to proceed accordingly."

I take a moment to calm my senses, breathe in deep and stop the seemingly subconscious decision to access everything and anything around me.

"You really do not remember anything?" the dark man asks with confusion in his eyes.

Calm is replaced by frustration, "What the fuck are you talking about?"

"Well..."

"Look...whoever you are. I have a killer headache and just woke up in a hospital bed without the faintest clue as to who I am or how I got here. My mind is racing like a stampede of coked up race horses," *What's a race horse?* I shake off the random thought and return to my tirade, "and I'm being analyzed by a tall son of a bitch who looks like the grim reaper. So if we could skip the amnesia checklist, that'd be great. Okay?"

"I am sorry, I..." He struggles for words while looking down at the floor and shuffling his feet a bit. "We are friends. More than friends in fact, brothers-in-arms."

I'm a soldier? He said we're Alphas, it must be some kind of rank. That would explain the buddy/doc combo upon coming to, but what led to the amnesia? Outside of the headache, I'm not in pain and don't see any wounds on my body. I bring my left hand up and run it through my hair, searching for some kind of cut or bump on my head. There's nothing that I can feel. No injuries. So how did I lose my memory?

"It started as a way to create a more realistic training program," he says without me asking the question. "Then it turned into something else. The High Order wanted to know just how far they could push an Alpha and..." he pauses and seems to be struggling for words again.

"You lost two limbs. Your left arm and your right leg. There was also severe damage to your head and brain which mended over time, but caused memory loss. You have been unconscious for weeks. The bruise on your head is gone and your limbs have regenerated. The doctors knew you would survive due to the cellular regeneration of our kind, but the condition of your mind was left up for debate. It was very possible that you would wake up and never consciously return."

"You mean like, be braindead?"

"Yes."

"Yeah well," the doctor finally chimes in. "We're not always so lucky." The soldier, my brother-in-arms, shakes his head at the comment. This guy doesn't really act like a doctor. "I've got work to do," he says looking down at a display on his wrist. "I'll come back for vitals once they've gone down for the night. Red," he offers with a nod at the soldier.

"Alexander," Red offers back.

With the mention of Red's name, my eyes close shut and battle scenes flash through my mind. There's a man in danger, and it's hard to make out his features, but I can tell it's not the man I'm speaking to. A scream rings out, there's blood, the glint of a blade and the ring of it striking metal. My face must have reacted to the imagery because there's concern in the dark man's deep red eyes when I open my own.

"Flashbacks?" he asks.

"Let me see a mirror," I demand without answering his question. He stares at me for a second and then turns to the bedside table and picks up a mirror. I snatch the mirror from his hands and direct it toward my face. The image I see, the man staring back at me, is who I saw in the flashback. Blurry details or not, I was clearly the man in danger.

I close my eyes and again get flashes of another battle, chaotic scenes that I can't decipher, but I can see myself through another's eyes. I can see the me I'm watching scream, *Red*.

"Why am I seeing your memories?" I ask, tossing the mirror onto the bedside table and glaring up at Red. It's the only explanation I can come up with for these odd visions of past events that involve myself. Unless I had an out of body experience at some point that I'm recalling, but that seems slightly more ludicrous than the already ridiculous explanation I've devised.

He sighs, "You lost a lot of blood due to the extent of your injuries. When we finally got you stabilized, I donated blood to help with the regeneration. There is more contained in the code of our blood than just the simple genetic data. Memories may have transferred, almost like experienced echoes of my life." *High Scientists think that we may have a connection beyond that, but I do not want to worry him with too much right now.*

Okay, Red's mouth stopped moving after 'echoes' but I still heard his voice. That last sentence didn't come through my ears. I heard it in my mind, like I was thinking it. He's clearly not telling me everything, there's more to this story and my past and until I figure out what it is, I'm going to keep the whole 'hearing your thoughts' thing to myself.

A voice comes from beyond the curtain to my right. I didn't even realize there was someone else in the room, but Red did mention something about my partner. "Did you give me blood, too? Because I can kinda hear your thoughts." Red walks around my bed and pulls back the curtain to reveal another man who feels overly familiar to me for reasons unknown. In fact, his face has similar features to my own. Same chiseled chin, angular cheekbones, and a slightly smaller nose; I don't feel as kind as his blue eyes look, but they're very similar to mine. His dark hair is very short, unlike my own, and his lower face is covered in matching stubble.

"What did you hear?" Red asks the man while facing away from me.

"Uh...High Scientists think we have a connection, don't want to worry..." he leans over to look past Red, "him too much." He nods at me.

Red puts a hand on his own head, shakes it, then looks back at me. "You two may not have your old memories, but you have not changed." He looks back to the other man. "You still cannot keep quiet," then chuckles lightly and backs up to the foot of our beds so we can see each other and looks at me. "And *you* still want to hold the cards close to your chest. You heard me too, did you not?" he asks, raising his right eyebrow slightly.

I hesitantly nod in confirmation. "Okay, let us get the basics out of the way." He points to me, "Your name is Liam Tyrus, which is fitting since you are also a lieutenant. Everyone calls you LT." He points to the other man, "Your name is William Tate, everyone calls you Bill and you are a sergeant." Red glances back and forth between us as he continues to explain who we are. "You are a two-man Blood Pack Alpha Recon team in the Red Military and no, before you ask, it is not my military, the name is just a coincidence. It is the military of our people, Hemosapiens. Before the ambush, you were the most elite team that our military had to offer. You have run hundreds of successful campaigns across various galaxies over the last century. I trained you and we are...friends."

"What year is it?" I ask bluntly, unsure if I can accept what this Red is telling us, "and if we were a two-man team, what were you doing on a mission with us?"

"It's 2120. The mission you were on had shaky intel. Before I transferred into combat training for recon teams I was an operator. We worked together previously and you asked for an extra hand given the gravity of the mission. So we laid out the mission and requisitioned a Beta unit as well. A ten-soldier Black Ops team in training to become Alphas. The mission went south, the Beta team was taken out and we got separated. You were captured. Our closest forces were months out. I was able to find and rescue you within a few weeks. It is a good thing I was there."

"Shit yeah! LT, I know this is all new but give the man a break, he saved our lives," Bill says, pointing at Red.

Red's eyes soften, there's a slight crease underneath the right one and I can tell he's smiling. Not having any memories to reference is driving me crazy, but he seems genuine and outside of one bit of selective honesty, which we could 'hear' anyway, he hasn't given us a reason to doubt him. The jovial tone in Bill's voice warms my body...we must have been very close. He's right, I have no reason to be on the defensive with Red.

"Sorry Red, this is all...it's just very confusing and frustrating."

"No need to apologize. I cannot imagine what you are going through, but believe me when I say I am going to dedicate all my time to making sure you remember your training. Even if we have to start from scratch. You men have a passion, a desire to honor the battlefield and you will do whatever it takes to combat evil in any form. We need you."

What a weight. Nervously averting my eyes away from Red, I look down at my chest for the first time, and notice a round pendant of sorts around my neck. It's a little over two inches in diameter and the center section is hollow. The outside ring is made of dark, bronzed metal and a black wire is wrapped near the top of the ring before splitting and extending over the hollow section and wrapping about the left and right bottom area of the ring. There's a square section of the perimeter to the left that's cut out, and below that, 'alone' is engraved in the metal. Continuing around to the bottom of the right, there's another square section, cut out to the lower right and above that, 'apart' is engraved near the top.

Red must notice me eyeing it, because he says, "The talisman of an Alpha." I look up while he offers an open palm. "May I?"

As I lean forward and remove the pendant, Bill says, "Mine's looks different. It says 'always' and 'never' on it."

Red nods and offers his other open palm to Bill, who removes his as well. As Red presses the pendants together, I can see that the cut out sections of my ring match up with raised sections on Bill's. He holds them up for us to see. The rings fit together like puzzle pieces, with the wires forming an 'A' in the center hollow section and the words now showing a completed phrase.

"Always alone, never apart," Red explains. "The code of an Alpha, your soul. An Alpha team operates on their own, but you can always rely on each other. You are comprised of one creative," Red looks at Bill, "and one analytical," then turns to me before looking back at the talisman in his hands. "You both represent the best parts of each side. You train together, fight together, bleed together."

"Die together?" Bill asks.

"No," Red says shaking his head. "That constitutes failure and Alphas do not fail. Ever."

After a second of silence I say, "Interesting design."

Red pulls the talismans apart and hands them back to us. "Indeed, you both did a great job."

"We designed them?" Bill asks.

Red nods. "Each Alpha designs their own talisman as part of their training. You are one of two teams that had the idea to make them lock together. You do not just work together, your lives are intertwined. It is impressive that you felt the need to show this on your talisman as it is a representation of your commitment to the life."

I stare at the engraved writing on my talisman before slipping the chain back over my neck. For some reason, I find comfort in rubbing the engraved words on the ring. Alone and apart. Given the thought we supposedly put into the design, I can't help but fixate on those two words. Partner or not, was my life broken prior to the memory loss?

Bill's voice causes me the drop the talisman back onto my chest. "The other team you spoke of, who are they?"

"India-November-Foxtrot. Two Alphas who have been trying to surpass your superior battlefield skills for quite some time now. There is..." A short beep emanates from a device on Red's wrist causing him to stop talking and look down at it.

"We will talk more soon. For now, I am told you need some more rest."

Red nods at both of us and walks to the door, which slides open when he gets close. I haven't been able to hear anymore of Red's thoughts since Bill spoke up, which makes me think that he can control his thoughts now that he knows. He turns around before leaving and says, "It is good to have both of you back," then he walks out and the door slides shut.

I lean back against my pillow and sigh before turning to Bill, who's looking at me with eager eyes. Raising an eyebrow, I tilt my head.

"This is gonna be fun, right?" he asks cheerily. I shake my head and roll my eyes then look back at the ceiling.

After a few moments, I hear Red's voice in the back of my head again, maybe he can't control them. *Captain Otto, it's good to see you.* As I hastily turn back to Bill, I can see that his expression has changed. Sitting up with his eyebrows pressed together, it looks as though he's attempting to listen to something.

"Do you hear it, too?" I ask. He nods quickly without looking at me. We can't hear the captain's voice in our heads, only Red's. *Flashes, sir, nothing major from what I can tell. I know. It will take time, but we need them. I do not think so, sir. We are the only ones that know. Of course. I will, sir.*

"Sir, why do I get the feeling that we're being left in the dark?" Bill asks, turning to me with a straight face. Shaking my head, I turn away to think.

"I don't know..."

"We need to be careful," Bill says, cutting me off.

While turning my attention back to him, I offer a slight smirk. "Great minds...we're in this together. We trust no one but ourselves."

Bill nods. I lay back and close my eyes hoping for more flashes, but nothing comes. Staring into the red darkness created by my eyelids does nothing, despite my desire for something, anything to appear, but the medication they have us on kicks in. I pass out searching for memories that no longer exist.

Chapter 13: Employing Assets

3.01 - 2468- 1763:004 Red Galaxy Standard

"These new suits are great, right?" Aden shouts through the comms. I'm sitting across from him in the SWIFT (Special Weapons Insertion Fleet Transport) and drive my head back into the small metal headrest of my seat. He's right, these suits are great. I didn't feel anything just then, even though I moved with more force than intended and my suit's display registered a rear impact on the exterior. When will he get it through his thick skull that he doesn't have to...

"I'm just fucking with ya," he says in a normal voice. "Inside voices, right?"

Lowering my head, I stare at him through my visor as he lets his helmet recede just long enough to wink and click his tongue out of the side of his mouth. The suit re-engages and covers up his face while he's still smirking. I shake my head, chuckling to myself. I'm so used to his body language that I would have visualized him winking regardless.

"Hey, bet ya five blood coins these things don't take the easy way out," Aden says.

He's probably right. No way they'll just kneel on the ground and surrender when we show up, but keeping with tradition, I reply, "You're on. I can be pretty damn intimidating when I want."

Aden chuckles. "Yeah, sure big guy. Easy money."

Our pilot, Mike, hasn't updated us recently. We must be getting close by now. I've always liked Mike. He used to be an Operator like us, but never went for his Alpha tags. After spending a century or so as a field Lieutenant with the low-level grunts, he wanted to get away from all the bullshit. Can't blame him. He was an engineer for a while, and eventually settled on flight school after his appreciation for spacecraft grew. It was right around the time that we gained Alpha status. We actually met him in our off-world and deep-space survival class. All the pilots had to take it at the Alpha level in case their craft went down. We've been friends with him ever since and were able to pull a few strings so he could become our assigned pilot. Even though he's an officer, he always gets mad when we address him by title, so he's pretty much a perfect fit for Aden and me. I mean come on, we're not exactly the 'by the book' types.

I tap the right side of my helmet to activate the comms, but nothing happens. I tap it again. Brand new suits and they're already not working?

Aden must have been watching because he nods and says, "Hey. The display, remember?"

Oh, that's right. They had to go and change everything around on us. The new control interface is built into our visors. Our ocular implants interface with the neural link in our heads and the sensors built throughout the suit. There's a menu system built into the heads-up display on the inside of our visor and we can use a combination of physical gestures and mental-projective thinking to active and navigate. Look at 'menu', think of opening it, and the menu opens. Similar to how we activate our suits. Also, as long as we're not in combat mode, the suit will allow us to navigate through the menu by 'touching' the holographic display in front of us. There's nothing there, but the neural implant reads where the display is and how our eyes perceive the menu. If we reach out and 'touch' a button where it theoretically would be if it existed in physical space, then the suit registers that. Of course, I don't see a reason to wave my hands around looking like an idiot, so I go with option A. I'll leave the latter to Aden.

I open up a channel to the cockpit. "Hey Mike, what's our ETA?"

Mike replies without hesitation, "Just under two minutes, LT. Alexander wanted me to let you know that your mission's logistical information is available to access in your new suits. You're not only connected to command, but any vehicle that you may have the need to use that's been upgraded to support neural links." There's a slight pause. "Shit, that's pretty fucking cool. Wish that had that in my day."

I chuckle at Mike's remark then scroll through the menu on my visor. Sure enough, there's a tab on the right side of my display that says 'Mission Data'. After opening that, I can see a tab that says 'Logistics' then 'Vehicle Data' following that. An entire breakdown of information spreads across my visor, from time, to target, to payload, build date of the SWIFT, current pilot, previous pilot, statistical information about the abilities of the transport; everything and anything I could need.

"Pretty fucking cool is right." That's impressive. "Thanks, Mike."

"No problem, LT. Ninety seconds out."

I turn and look at Aden even though he can't see my face. "You ready for this?"

A little video from the inside of Aden's helmet pops up in the top left corner of my display and I can see that shit-eating grin of his. "As ready as I'm gonna be. Looking forward to finally kicking some Plaguer ass."

"How the hell did you do that?"

"Geez LT, didn't you read the instructions? There's a direct link video chat feature in the menu system. Come on, get it together," he snaps, making the video disappear.

"I was too busy going over the mission parameters and figuring out how to use the features that would benefit us in combat." I roll my eyes even though he can't see me anymore.

"Sixty seconds!" Mike calls from the cockpit.

A bright red circle illuminates on the floor to my right, in front of my seat and another illuminates in the same position on Aden's side. We both stand up and move to the circle. I hate doing straight drops. I don't know what it is, but there's always a buildup of anxiety in my chest just before we fall.

"Thirty seconds!"

There's really not much to be nervous about, especially with these new suits.   Life or death combat has been a majority of our waking existence, yet I never get nervous on the job, only before a drop. It always happens before the drop. Then it floats away like Aden's attention.

"It's been a while since we've done a straight drop. Want me to hold your hand?" Aden asks, rolling his shoulders backward a few times as he prepares for the fall.

"Hold this," I say, chucking him the finger.

"Five, four, three, see you boys in a few."

The red antigrav ring on the floor turns green as the floor inside of it disappears and we're launched out of the belly of the SWIFT. The antigrav ring is pretty important for a straight drop. As a safety precaution, Mike doesn't slow the SWIFT down to let us out. That ring calculates exterior conditions and propels us from the SWIFT with enough force to make sure that the atmosphere outside doesn't catch our bodies and yank us into the hull before we're clear. Obviously low level atmosphere drops, like this one, require more force.

I keep my arms and legs tucked together to create minimal drag on the way down. The anxiety is already gone and my mind is on the mission. I'm concerned. Grecillian High Command doesn't ever request support from an Alpha team, or any team for that matter. If they need help, which is rare due to the secrecy of its location, they demand massive support and get it. So why now, all of a sudden, is there a request for an elite Bloodpack Alpha Recon squad, to sweep the area for possible Plague incursions?

"You're thinking about the message, aren't you?" Aden asks through the comms. We're dropping through the sky and the audio is clear as day, no distortion or wind resistance making it difficult to hear. I can't get over how much I love these suits, but part of me is waiting for something to go wrong.

"GHC doesn't request BAR's to do scan sweeps if they think enemies have gotten through. They call in a battalion and sweep the entire area by force, so why request us?"

"Why request at all? GHC doesn't ask, they demand."

"Exactly what I was thinking." My proximity sensor is beginning to flash red as the ground approaches. "Prepare for landing."

We both slam into the black ground below, causing a dark cloud to shoot up into the air around us. As the dust settles, I look up to see Aden crouched down with both hands on the onyx ground, scanning the area with his visor. I turn to do the same behind us.

"Report?"

"My visor is picking up a trail of dirt in front of us that was recently disturbed, which explains why this is our insertion point, but I'm not getting any kind of readings. Whatever caused it, hasn't been here for a while. It leads up to GHC."

"Nothing behind. Proceed on the trail with caution, call out any disturbances or readings the second you see them." I turn around to see Aden stand up and follow the trail. Earth wasn't the only planet we torched when spreading across the galaxy. Grecil was one of the first planets that our people conquered after destroying Earth.

This is our first time on Grecil, so I keep Aden at a distance as I continue to scan the barren landscape. It's a wasteland, worse than Earth. There's black dirt, towering rock formations all around, and some small amount of light breaking through the dark gray clouds above. Katkis, the center star of the Gracillian solar system, doesn't have a chance to illuminate the surface of Grecil. The occasional stray ray of light is the only bit of star shine the planet gets due to the smoke clouds created when we torched the planet nearly two centuries ago. Our weapons weren't always as sophisticated as they are today.

I can't help but let my mind wander to the conversation with Red yesterday. Aden and I were once humans and Earth was our home. Earth was everyone's home. The Hemos evolved alongside the humans, developing under the planet's surface until they decided that the humans were no longer fit to rule Earth. They were convinced that the humans squandered the natural resources to the point of no return. Guess they never thought the war would end in the planet being decimated.

"LT, copy?" Aden presses through the comms.

"Negative, repeat last."

"Shit LT, stop drifting. There's no way in hell I'm going to start playing the responsible one." That's a hell of a thought. I've never daydreamed on a mission before. Our past, Red, Blaze, it's all fucking with my head, but that's no excuse. I need to focus, we can't underestimate the Plaguers and despite the new gear, we've never faced them in person. Combat intel isn't always dead on.

"GHC dead ahead by one mile," Aden continues without another jab, and he knows damn well that I appreciate that. "Still no readings. Recommend launch procedure to close ground."

"Copy. Confirm silent landscape." I stop and zoom my ocular implants in to get a better look at GHC. There's a valley between us and the massive building which is built into the side of a cliff. Most of the building is carved out of the cliff itself, and the rest was built out of metallic stone mined from the valley before us, which is known as the Black Valley of the Fall. Rumor has it that the building was made using Thyr slaves that were captured after the uprising of 2252, which is why it was built so fast. It was the last time, before our encounter, that a legion of Thyr was engaged by Hemo forces. Aden and I were on the other side of the known universe on a protection detail and battle was over so quickly that we didn't get a chance to participate. GHC is a dark building, meaning its existence wasn't even acknowledged until it was nearly completed. It now serves as a military headquarters for the Red Galaxy and is the command center for all Hemo dark operations in the universe. We get our orders from Captain Otto; he gets his orders from GHC. Only a handful of officers ever get to see the inside of that building, so it's not at all comforting that we're here to possibly confirm that Plaguers have broken through.

I cycle through the comms menu in my helmet. "Mike?"

"Copy LT, go ahead."

"GHC looks silent from here, is there a way that we can tap our suits into the security feeds?"

"From what I understand about the new gear, yes it should be possible, but if the building is dark you've got nothing to feed into. You're not getting any signals at all?"

I re-scan the building, hoping to get something, anything that lets me know that there's life inside. Nothing on thermal, electrical is nonexistent, and no nuclear or radioactive readings. Not only is there no life being picked up by the scanners, but the building itself seems totally dead. "Negative on signals. Building looks quiet, no signs of life or activity at all."

There's a pause before Mike responds. "That's odd."

That isn't exactly comforting considering the tone in his voice. "What's odd?"

"Well, I was an engineer before switching to Black Op piloting and our military buildings, GHC in specific, shouldn't go dark. There's backups to the backups which can't be overwritten and are genetically controlled by officers in the building. There's so much going on with the wars across the universe that it's imperative that the comms stay up. You could destroy two thirds of the building and most of the equipment would still work."

Well that's not good.

"I'm going to contact Alexander, see if there's something we can do to get the building powered up and you patched in, but I wouldn't get my hopes up."

"Another day in paradise, right?" Aden asks.

"Paradise or not, we need to get inside that building and figure out what the hell is going on." I look for a point of entry.

"Right hand side, halfway up the building we've got a landing pad, confirm?"

"Confirm," Aden agrees.

"Okay, that's our target. The suit has a built-in launch computer to calculate the distance and force needed for precision landings. Mark the pad, prepare to launch and let the suit do its job to ensure you hit the target."

"When did you learn about that?"

"When you were figuring out how to video chat." I reply snidely.

Aden turns around and looks back at me and his smiling face appears on my view screen. "Yeah, but this is a whole lot more fun." he says matter-of-factly.

"Precision landings could prevent death. Color me crazy for thinking that's more important." The video disappears and Aden turns back to the valley, dismissing me with a flick of his right hand off to the side.

"Distance 1.1260 miles, altitude .562 miles, adjusting for wind variables and gravity." Aden crouches down. "Sir?" he asks. He finds out we're brothers and still reverts to 'sir' when he's nervous. Old habits die hard I guess. I wait for the question. "This smell like an ambush?"

"Maybe." I activate my launch simulator and crouch down to the ground watching the numbers change as I tense my muscles with the right amount of pressure to jump the desired distance. Everything is in the green. "Launch."

It's good that these new suits have built in simulators, because we would have totally overshot the target if they didn't. I can tell the second we leave the ground that we're applying less force than I would have expected. Still, the speed is remarkable. I'm watching my visor count down the distance to the target and within three seconds we're at the halfway point.

"Gah!" Aden bellows. Before I have a chance to react, the right side of my visor is flashing red due to a proximity warning. I'm violently jarred to the left and off trajectory. My visor is blinking red again to the left as I slam into a large rock formation, breaking it into pieces before sliding to a stop in the black dirt.

Looking up, I can see Aden leaned over, sliding back with his left foot to the ground, right knee down while his left hand clawing at the dirt to slow down and the right in the air to help keep balance. He stops perpendicular to me, twenty feet away according to the informational green tag that's hovering over him through my visor.

"Mother fucker!" At first I think Aden's yelling at whatever went wrong with our suits, but then I see the Plaguer ten feet in front of him. Of course it doesn't hear him through the suit, just sees that ominous black metallic face staring back. I'm the only one who gets the privilege of hearing his anger now. Nonetheless, the soldier lowers into an aggressive position, letting out a raspy high-pitched, shrieking howl that cuts through the audio filters in my suit. I've never heard anything make a more terrifying noise. It sounds as if its throat is deteriorating as it shrieks. Other shrieks echo in the distance in reply, including one to my immediate right from the Plaguer that struck me. They knocked us out of the sky during an increased launch procedure? These things are much stronger and faster than we anticipated.

Aden's assailant leaps forward, but Aden doesn't hesitate and the suit doesn't disappoint, he dodges to the left and pulls the blade from his thigh, hacking at the Plaguer as it flies past. I regain my composure and look up at my own assailant as the visor tries to warn me of an incoming attack. Dropping to my back, I grab the Plaguer by his neck as he lands on top of my chest. He's wildly swatting at my body with long grown-out nails, but they do little to disturb the scales protecting my body. I grab the side arm from my right leg and shove it into the Plaguer's chomping mouth and rapidly fire three times. The first round explodes the back of his head in haze of red fire and chunks of charred brain matter and the second two fly through his skull and into the air, piercing the dark clouds above.

Aden kicks the body off my chest and offers his right hand, holding the soiled, gleaming blade in his left. "One shot wasn't enough?" he asks.

"Just making sure. Not like we're gonna run out of ammo." I look down at the body near my feet. "Well, you just met a Plague victim, what's the verdict?"

Aden steps past me and looks at the body. "Doesn't seem like much of a victim to me." He kicks the corpse twice. "Asshole, though? Check."

Before I can remind Aden that these shadows of our species didn't choose to be who they were, the visor alerts me of incoming signals. Aden snaps to my back as we both scan the area. "How many you got?"

"Uh...a lot."

That's an understatement. I can see at least twenty Plaguers leaping into our vicinity on my side and another fifty or so crawling at high speeds across the dirt. They move like animals on all fours, contorting their limbs to maximize speed.

Aden crouches down and swings his Ka, preparing to attack. "Hold on," I say, turning around and setting my hand on his shoulder. They're slowing down. The ones who leaped into the area are staying back by fifty feet and the ones scurrying across the ground are slowing as they get closer.

"What? You want to sit down and have a conversation with 'em? They just attacked us."

"Actually," a loud, deep raspy voice says to our right, "They were trying to contain you, but we didn't realize that the Alphas had gotten new suits." A Plaguer in an old frayed Hemo military uniform is walking toward us. He holds a hand out to the rest, who have now surrounded us in every direction, signaling them to stand their ground. I squeeze Aden's shoulder to signal the same and then walk in front of him a few feet to meet who I assume is their leader.

Looking him up and down without moving my head, I finally get a chance to see what the Plague does up close. The uniform is barely holding together, having been torn to shreds and his skin is peeling, exposed, and rotting all over his body. His teeth and eyes are black, but for some reason, despite the mass deterioration of outer skin, the muscle I can see looks to be maintaining its form, possibly swelling from normal size as there are visible stretch marks in the fibers. I use the menu to switch between the different optic modes in my visor, but these things don't stand out on any of them. They're not registering as life forms. Oh yeah, and they're walking around the surface of Grecil, a planet with poisonous atmospheric conditions, without sealed suits.

"Oh yes, we don't show up on optics. Real handy in a pinch," the Plaguer says drawing out the last syllable of the phrase.

"Can you hear me?" I ask.

"Yes. Our senses are well beyond what you would consider normal. Also very helpful in a pinch."

"Not mention the increased muscle mass due to the genetic changes," I say, pointing to the muscle fibers exposed on his right arm under a torn section of uniform and flesh.

He grips it with the opposite hand. "No points for aesthetics though. Tell me why you're here and we'll consider letting you live."

Aden roars with laughter behind me then lets out a little squeal as he regains his composure. The Plaguer leans, looks at Aden, then turns his attention back to me. "Simple version, we're here to deliver a message."

He walks forward casually and leans in close to my right ear. "Ah, and what would that be?"

I activate the video feed in my visor and wink at Aden, then sweep the Plaguer's legs out from underneath him and drive my foot through his skull. The body quivers for a few seconds before falling still. Switching on the external speaker in my helmet just to make sure they can all hear, I announce, "Get the fuck off our planet."

All of the surrounding Plaguers roar with anger and lower into attack positions.

"I don't think they liked the simple version," Aden says, pulling his side arm from his right leg and tightening his grip on the Ka in his left hand. I walk back over to him and draw my Ka out as well, then switch off the speaker system.

"Looks like we'll have to deliver the complex version. I owe you five blood coins."

"Told you they couldn't be reasoned with."

"Yes, you did." With a flick of the wrist, my Ka unlocks into dozens of razor sharp flexible tiles and grows in length coiling on the ground near my feet. "Yes, you did."

Chapter 14: Muscle Memory

3.17 - 2120 - 595:000 Red Galaxy Standard

    It's nice to be out of a hospital bed and off all of the mind-bending drugs they had us on in order to allow advanced regeneration to kick in. I still don't remember anything before the hospital and honestly that first day when we woke up next to Red is even a little hazy. I'm not sure what kind of a man I used to be, but instinct tells me that it's not someone who wanted to be laid up for two weeks listening to Alexander, the odd, white-haired doctor with vibrant blue eyes that we woke up to.

    As I walk down the hall and approach a set of double doors that are painted dark red, I hear Bill running up from behind.

    "Hey, LT!" Turning around just before reaching the doors, I let him to catch up. "What do you think they'll have us do?"

    I have no clue, but anything's better than laying in that damn bed. "Training, hopefully. The orders were vague, just report here at zero six hundred."

    Bill looks the heavy red doors up and down. "Well, these are a little ominous."

    I shove him to the side, push both doors open, and walk in. Hinges seem a little antiquated given the technology I've seen on the rest of the ship, but I'm still getting used to everything. Maybe there's a reason that these door exist. The room is massive, not only in length and width, but height too. The walls and ceiling are white with a circular pattern throughout and there's a flush black panel on the ceiling about fifty yards in. We both look around expecting to meet Red, but he's nowhere to be seen. I walk underneath the black panel on the ceiling, which is large enough to fit a small slip through it, and just stare. The double doors behind us slam shut and we both turn around expecting to see whoever closed them, but there's no one there.

"Okay," Bill lets out slowly. "What the hell is going on?"

"I don't know," I trail off looking back up at the black panel. Bill's head follows suit. Two loud thuds from behind us echo throughout the room and we spin around at the same time to see something that we never expected to find on our first day back on active duty.

A creature, for lack of a better term, nearly twice as tall as we are with similar physiology and dark olive skin is standing in front of the double doors fifty yards away. This massive creature's muscles are bulging out of its limbs and body like some kind of genetically altered super Hemo. It's bald and the only clothing that adorns its skin is a loin cloth covering its midsection and held in place by a thick leather belt. Around its neck is a gruesome necklace of Hemo heads that drips blood on its chest and the floor. It's holding a large, incredibly sharp axe in its left hand and an equally large pointed hammer with a long handle in its right. Luckily, it's looking down at the ground and doesn't appear to see us, yet.

"What. The fuck. Is that?" Bill asks under his breath trying to hold in a nervous chuckle.

I take a few, quiet steps forward, unsure of why I'm moving toward this very large, very dangerous looking brute. Awe and an odd sense of familiarity takes over as I stare, pushing away Bill's hand while he tries to grab my shoulder and pull me back. The creature lifts its head to reveal two solid silvery eyes, then curls back its lips, and let out a deep snarl before releasing a low, incredibly loud roar that resonates through my bones.

"Uh, I think you pissed him off," Bill says with fear in his voice. "Those are some really big, sharp teeth."

"I'm more concerned about the weapons," I say, lowering my shoulders and stance ever so slightly. The creature's finished its roar and tightens its grip on the weapons while continuing to bear its teeth.

I lean back. "What are you doing?" Bill asks. His voice fades as my body takes over and I spring forward. I can't answer Bill's question because I don't actually know what I'm doing. I'm reacting for some reason and I have no idea why.

The creature doesn't hesitate. It lowers its head, then shoots forward as well, swinging its massive arms and weapons up and down as it bounds forward, gaining speed. Just before we meet, the creature raises its right hand high into the air and prepares to bring the pointed hammer down on my head. Instinct takes over and I dodge, wait for the hammer to hit the ground, then use my forward momentum to leap up and grab ahold of the bulbous shoulder that orchestrated the attack. I swing my body around and straddle the back of its neck with my legs, lock my ankles around its throat, and choke as hard as I can.

It lets out another massive roar, which is somewhat stifled by the squeezing of my legs, then drops its weapons and drives its arms up into the air to yank me from its shoulders. My upper body goes limp and I roll backwards, away from its grasp, while my legs continue to squeeze in an attempt to suffocate the creature. I can feel the muscles in its neck tighten against the inside of my thighs as it fights to stay conscious. The back of my head bounces off its lower back, and like activating a switch, the creature drops its hands forward and tries to reach my head by rotating its hands up and under its back. I roll back up in just enough time to avoid another swipe of the paws and see Bill's muscles straining as he heaves the massive axe over his head in front of us. By the time the creature notices him, it's too late and the axe slams down into its knee, splitting the cap and nearly taking the whole leg off.

With a thunderous roar, the creature tumbles to the ground. I swiftly unlock my legs, hop up on its shoulders, then leap forward off of the creature and tuck into a roll the second I hit the ground. With my mind racing, I stand and turn around to face the creature while scrambling back a few feet as Bill runs to my side.

"What the hell was that? Are you okay?" he asks frantically.

"Yeah, I...I don't know, my instincts just kicked in." I turn to Bill as the creature breathes heavily through its teeth, then turns over on its back to look down at its leg. "What about you?"

"Really?" he cocks an eye and tilts his head. "Fucking someone up with an axe to the leg isn't instinct, genius, it's common sense. Axe, meet kneecap."

I shake my head and roll my eyes before looking back at the creature, then I grab Bill's shoulder. "Look," I point at the creature with my other hand.

It rips the axe out of its leg and blood shoots everywhere before slowing to a trickle. Lifting the axe into the air, it lets gravity take over and drops the nasty end on its open wound, separating the leg from body. It tosses the axe from one hand to the other, then reaches out and grabs the large hammer with its free hand. As the blood continues to pour out of the leg and onto the ground, the creature grunts, flips back over onto its stomach, pushes itself up on its remaining knee, then uses the support of the hammer against the ground to stand on its good leg.

"What the…" Bill can't finish his thought as it's interrupted by another deafening roar. Leaving a river of black blood in its wake, the creature starts hopping toward us with its hammer crutch.

"Take out the hammer," I say to Bill. Oddly enough he doesn't hesitate, but reacts much like I did when we first saw the creature. He runs forward and dodges a swing of the axe by sliding across the ground and grabbing the base of the hammer. He snaps to a stop, then yanks, causing the head of the hammer to slip and make the creature topple.

Somehow, it manages to retain both weapons in its hand as it hits the ground, but the hammer is pinned underneath its body. I run up and slam my foot down into its throat. It lets out a deep growl of pain, but tightens its grip on the axe and brings it back to swing at me. Bill grabs the creature's forearm with both hands and pulls back as hard as he can, momentarily preventing the swing. I bring my foot back down on the throat with enough force to hear a crack, and repeat the process one last time until my foot drives through the throat as it collapses.

Bill hangs on to the arm as the creature struggles to breath for a few more seconds before finally going limp. We both sigh, then drop to the ground as the adrenaline recedes.

I hear a clicking noise from the ceiling, followed by a whoosh, and the sound of boots slamming into the ground behind us.

"Interesting," Red says plainly. I look at the ceiling, then spin around on my ass to see Red with his arms crossed, leaning on his left leg, looking down at us. He's barely dressed. There's leather briefs just covering his midsection, a red cloak draped across his shoulders that reaches past the floor and a bronze helmet covering his head. "Not as interesting as that get up," Bill chuckles holding back a laugh. He hops over the massive corpse and jogs up behind me. "Please tell me we won't be fighting in that."

"It's ancient combat gear, numb nuts. Mostly worn as a badge of honor for those who have been around long enough to know what it actually is." I got that little nugget of information when I could still read Red's mind. I shake my head, jump to my feet, and walk over to him.

"And interesting? More like fucking annoying."

"The test or your inability to read my mind?" Red tilts his head toward me ever so slightly. He knew I was planning on keeping that little tidbit to myself, but more importantly, how the hell did he know?

I ignore his comment about the previously advantageous telepathy. "What the hell was that thing?"

"As I said, a test."

"A test?" I chuckle, turning around to look at Bill before turning back to Red. "Are you serious? It could have killed us."

With that, two soldiers dressed in full combat gear drop from the ceiling, landing on either side of Red.

"But it didn't, and we've brought you back from the dead once already," Red says without commenting on the soldiers.

Unsure of what's going on, and without thinking, I find myself quickly assessing the two soldiers. They're female for one. More muscular than I would expect, but still, there are irrefutable female qualities that can be seen through the tight fitting, pitch black highly dense grecene under weave, one of the hardest materials our people have ever created. It's odd, the darkness of the gear and the lack of sheen almost make it difficult to distinguish the separate pieces of the suit. There are flexible grecanium-plated boots, knee pads, elbow pads, and gloves protecting the areas that could take some impact in a fast moving battle. The helmets are built to be aerodynamic. They're attached to the suit around the neck with no visible seam, have a wide visor with a reddish orange tint on the front, and sweep back across their heads with a bit of the bulge near the rear. That bulge houses all the comm and locational gear, as well as the mission data. Hold on, why do I know all that?

"How underwhelming. Mediocre, in fact." A mechanical sounding voice says from the shorter soldier to Red's left. The taller one on the right doesn't say anything, and doesn't move, but I can feel her gaze jumping between myself and Bill. She's assessing us, just like I am them.

"They will be back to outranking you in no time," Red turns to the short soldier, who continues to stare at us. "It is amazing what they have retained."

"We'll see. Let them face off against Nox first." The short soldier offers a short grunt before they both leap over to the main doors we came through some thirty yards away.

"Whoa," Aden exclaims at the feat. "When do we get to do that?"

"All in due time," Red answers.

"They seemed peachy," I say dryly staring at the door as they leave.

"India-November-Foxtrot," Red says. "Your, competition, for lack of a better word."

"Who's Nox?" I ask, looking up at Red.

"It is short Nox-Ira," he says. "It is old tongue. Translates to night fury."

I look back down to the floor for a moment, trying to remember anything about the Nox-Ira or night fury, but nothing comes to mind. "She spoke like it's a person."

"It is," Red confirms confusing me further. I look at Aden and he shrugs, he's as lost as I am. "The Nox-Ira is a personality, a separate personality within our people. Some do not have the strength to summon their Nox-Ira, but it is a prerequisite to becoming an Alpha."

Red turns and walks toward the hulking corpse of the creature we took down. "Your Nox-Ira, mine, everyone's is a volatile creature. In times of extreme stress, pain, and mental anguish, your mind gets flooded with chemicals and emotions. It can be difficult to focus and make logical decisions geared toward your survival. At lot of men would break in those circumstances. Handing over control of the situation to the Nox-Ira allows you to avoid this. He will suppress emotions, he will ignore pain, and he will make the decisions that must be made."

"I don't like the idea of being a puppet," Bill mutters.

"Me neither," I reply quietly.

"You cannot be a puppet to yourself." Red says stopping in front of the corpse and turning to face us. "The Nox-Ira is you, and you it. You may not have total control, or even remember events that transpire while he is working, but make no mistake, it is indeed you. The animal that evolution buried deep within your soul."

The idea behind the Nox-Ira is appealing, but regardless of how Red describes it, or him, it still sounds like I'm taking a back seat. Maybe it's the memory loss, but that makes me really nervous.

"You will understand once you meet your Nox-Ira, but that is for the future. I have more to show you," he sets his pointer and middle fingers over the eyes and his thumb on the right cheek of the dead creature's head. There's a quiet hiss and the top of the skull folds open to reveal an array of bio mechanical parts in its head. "It is a training drone."

"So it's fake?" Bill asks.

"Yes and no. These creatures do exist, they are called…"

"The Thyr," I say, cutting him off. Bill looks back at me as I stare at the mess of machinery in the drone's head.

"Yes." Red puts his fingers in another odd configuration over the drone's face and the head snaps shut. He stands up and looks at me. "Do you remember anything?"

"No I…I don't know how I know the name. It just came to me."

"Like the fighting?" he asks. I nod. "It is muscle memory. Instinct if you want to call it that. Just because the memories in your head are gone, doesn't mean the ones in your muscles are."

"And the name? Thyr? How did I know that?"

"Latent information from my blood transfusion maybe, I am not sure. The good thing is that we are not really starting from scratch. So what have we learned from this?"

I look down at the ground as Bill and I stand there for a second letting all the information sink in and think back over the fight. Two weeks of feeling helpless and on day one we take out a massive creature without any weapons. Finally feeling confident and alive, I look back up at Red.

"We're badasses. Next question."

Red laughs, "Let us find out what else you remember."

A devious little smile creeps across my face, "Let's."

Chapter 15: The Dark Castle

3.01 - 2468 - 1822:234 Red Galaxy Standard

"Shit," I roar, crashing into the GHC's carved out cliff wall, as a few stones fall to the valley below.

"Activate!" Even though it won't make a difference, I clench every muscle in my body while bracing for impact. The visor flashes red at the same time that I shout the command and a fraction of a second later, there's five sequential *thuds* against my armor, followed by high-pitched shrieks that quickly fade away. I look below to see Plaguers falling into the deep valley, along with a few loose stones. The visor calculates that bottom is a little over a mile down.

Aden's clinging to the wall on my right and as I look up, his attention is still on the falling Plaguers. "Shit LT, it worked!" He continues to stare, but pauses for a second before saying, "Oh, that looked like it hurt. Love these new optics," at which point he laughs and turns his attention to me.

"We don't have much time. They're gonna keep coming. It won't take them long to scale the wall, assuming they aren't already in GHC."

The Plaguers didn't hesitate to attack after I smashed their leader's head in; they quickly overwhelmed us and made it nearly impossible to use our weapons. Our suits were able to deflect their attacks, but how long would it have been until their strength outwore our internal power units? Alexander had explained that the basic functions of the suit could operate on its own, regenerating power for over a century without having to replace the microscopic radioactive core, but the kinetic features, which provided the most protection, ran off of the built-up and stored power. The only thing we could do was forcefully stand up and launch to shake them off and get into a clear area, then launch again with more force to get out of there and formulate a plan. Luckily, the new comms made it really easy to communicate our ideas during a chaotic fight.

After attaching to GHC's cliff wall, we activated our kinetic barriers and any pursuing Plaguers bounced off of our armor and fell to the valley below. Hopefully, the climb will generate more power for the next attack, as we are now running on reserves.

"What's the plan?" Aden asks as we start climbing.

"Get into GHC and contain the fighting. It'll be much more difficult for them to overwhelm us in the corridors. We can create a funnel and take them out as they attack."

"Assuming GHC has corridors. We don't have any clue what the interior looks like. All that studying and you didn't even know about the video chat, and now your master plan includes some wild assumption?"

"Wild assumption? What building have you been in that doesn't have corridors?"

"Warehouses." he says proudly.

"You're shitting me right now, right? Why the fu...," I sigh, it's not even worth it. I flick my eyes from one side of the visor to the other, sending a floorplan file of GHC to Aden's video screen.

"Oh shit, how'd you get that?" he exclaims.

"Oh come on now, you should know that. Your bestest tech buddy in all the universe, Vali. He was able to gain access to our suits via the neural link."

"Oh, great. Now I've got that freak poking around in my new suit? I'm telling ya, there's no privacy these days."

Rather than start an argument with Aden about the merits of having Vali around with unrestricted access to our neural links, I decide to let it drop and just keep climbing.

As I reach the top of the cliff, also GHC's south wall, my visor alerts me to an incoming transmission. I activate the link as I'm climbing over the edge and onto the security walkway on top.

"Go ahead, Mike."

"Hey, you guys okay? I saw that little scuffle you got into."

"Yeah, we're good. Just trying to get a little home field advantage. Whatcha got for us?"

He sighs. "Not much unfortunately. Alexander confirmed that there's only one reason for the building to be dark. Nothing we can do from our end. Crew has to be dead."

"How the hell did the Plaguers manage to get inside and kill everyone?" I stand up, step to the edge and peer to the valley below as Aden hoists himself up to the walkway.

"Wait, how does this mean that everyone's dead? Did I miss something?" Aden asks, standing up and looking at me as I turn to him. "Couldn't an officer be threatened into shutting the building down?"

"Well honestly...it's above your pay grade *Sergeant* Bill, but all High Command locations implant neural chips, much like ours, into the officers who work there. The difference being," Mike explains, "that there's a built-in fail safe. In the event that the facility becomes overrun, the officers don't actually have the physical ability to do anything that would harm defensive operations or the facility itself."

Aden pointlessly scratches the side of his helmet. "Huh, so what you're saying is, gun to head, they just freeze?"

I nod. "Yes, but it goes beyond that. If the officer is in danger and doesn't take steps to remove the threat, the neural link will take over, forcing them to. Even if the actions result in self-destruction."

"Wow," Aden actually sounds surprised. He switches to an internal channel so Mike can't hear and says, "and I thought having Vali in here was bad," while tapping the side of his helmet.

"Yeah," I cock my head slightly and nod as he switches the internal channel off. "But if everyone is dead, the building shuts down as a fail-safe so invading forces can't attempt to mess with equipment. Right, Mike?"

"That's right. Hey, how'd you know all that? I just got done getting that information from Alexander and basically had to pry it out of him by telling him it's mission critical."

Vali sent me a bunch of files on GHC when we first landed, I've been reviewing them as time allowed. "I have my ways."

"Well let's hope it helps, you've got incoming."

Aden and I both look down the side of the cliff to see Plaguers near the bottom of the cliff leaping upward and grabbing hold, then leaping again. "Shit, they're moving pretty quickly," I say. "Let's get inside."

Aden and I run down the security walkway to a sliding door on the southeast corner tower, which is, of course, locked because of the building being dark.

"Any ideas?" Aden asks.

I hadn't even thought of the fact that the doors won't open since they're all computer controlled. "Shit. Mike, we've got a problem here."

"Yup, Alexander's working on it, patching him through."

A slight upward nod of the head to Aden and he dashes over to the edge of the walkway to keep an eye on the Plaguers scaling the wall.

"LT, it's Alexander. Is there a security panel on the left-hand side of the door? Over." I doubt Alexander spends much time giving out information to soldiers who are on mission, I can't remember the last time we ended a transmission with 'over'. You'd think Alexander would know that being a High Scientist, but most of his work centers on weaponry and armor so maybe it slipped his mind, or maybe he's just nervous. I look for the panel, but there's nothing that I can see, the entire frame around the door is smooth.

"Nothing that I can see, and there's no need to say 'over'. Modern comms detect frequencies in your voice and the visor displays when you've finished with the transmission. You should have a similar feature on your terminal next to the frequency graph."

"Uh, LT?" I ignore Aden, positive that he's just reminding me to hurry.

"Right, I knew that." I can hear Alexander typing and swiping through information at his research terminal. "Uh. Shit, they switched the doors out for GHCS E.X.T. Lockdown models a few years back."

"LT," Aden presses again.

"Well that's very fascinating, Alexander, but seeing as we have several dozen Plaguers scaling a wall to kill us, I'm more concerned with how to get in, than what model they used."

"I *know*. I know! I'm working on it," he responds, frustrated.

I slam my fist into the door then turn and look at Aden, who disconnects the blade grip from his leg, then with a flick of the wrist activates the extension process, and with one more flick locks the individual sections into place. The nanoparticles fuse the Ka together and he shoots a small glance my way before focusing on the cliff again.

"Work. Faster," he says to Alexander sternly.

"Mike, is your SWIFT equipped with..." before I can finish my question, a Plaguer shoots over the wall below Aden, who brings the Ka down on its head. The Plaguer was dead almost immediately as Aden's Ka was driven through its skull, but the momentum from its leap causes the body to continue upward. Aden's Ka continues to slice through the entire body, cutting it cleanly in half as both pieces fly up into the air ten more feet before falling back down into the valley below.

"Alexander!" I yell.

"I'm...I'm trying, I can't..."

All of a sudden, there's a thunderous mechanical pounding from inside the building which echoes throughout the valley. It happens five more times, getting progressively louder before the entire building lights up and the door slides open to the right.

"Aden!" I yell, as he takes the head off of another Plaguer trying to climb over the wall. I dart in the door, pull the rifle off my back, and turn to cover Aden as he runs inside. At least a dozen Plaguers pour over the top of the wall and I'm able to fire off three shots before it slams shut again. We can hear the Plaguers outside screaming and bashing their fists on the door.

I lean my back against the door and bump the back of my fist against Aden's. "Thanks Alexander, you're a life saver."

"Uh, guys, that wasn't me," he says, thoroughly confused. I stand up and look at Aden when a little message appears across the top of my visor.

'You're welcome. - V'

The message must have appeared in Aden's visor as well, because he chuckles and exhales, "Phew, I thought it was gonna be an ambush for a second. I'm kinda okay with Vali helping us out."

"Repeat last," Alexander says. "How did you guys get in, and who the hell is Aden?"

Vali must have garbled the transmission to prevent Alexander from hearing his name. It wasn't his real name, just a hacker alias, but I'm sure he didn't want Alexander poking around regardless. I'll make up a story later. I'd be nice if he was able to do it when I screwed up and shouted Aden instead of Bill. Sometimes the adrenaline clouds your judgment but combat or not, I need focus and watch what I say on open comms.

"Must be getting some interference, I said 'aiding'. I was covering Bill, we'll touch base later, Alexander, thanks for the help." I cut the transmission.

"One day you'll have to tell me what that was all about." Mike says.

"One day I will. Proceeding to command room." I break off the transmission then smack Aden on the back. "All right, let's get back to work. I'll take point." Pulling up the GHC schematics in my helmet, I expand them to cover my whole vision, then kick up the transparency so I can still see everything else.

"Copy that." Aden turns around to face the door which the Plaguers are still trying to open and touches his back to mine. The noise of them trying to break in is actually rather comforting, at least I know where they are for the time being. I think it'd be much more unnerving if the noise had stopped right away. Lockdown or not, we know there are other ways for them to get in. I'm more worried about the ones inside the building that I can't hear.

Making it through GHC is a pain in the ass, even with a map overlay showing me our current position. The whole place is set up like a maze with various halls leading all over the building like the branches of a tree. We finally make it to the central command room after twenty minutes of navigating through the corridors. The entire system is up and running since Vali rebooted it remotely, which still amazes me.

"Shit," I mutter under my breath as we reach massive central command room. The room is shaped like a giant sphere with stations positioned around the entire exterior wall, facing in. There are two more, increasingly smaller circular rows of command stations that recede into the floor closer to the interior of the room, then a circular platform in the middle surrounded by screens for the commanding officer. Oh, and there are Hemo bodies everywhere, blood splattered all over the consoles and walls.

Aden turns around, "Shit indeed."

'Center command console - V' appears on the top of my visor. I look over all the corpses once more then walk past the circular rows, down the steps, and into the center command console. "There's eight screens, what am I looking for?"

'Turn...turn...turn...Stop. File number 82113114 - V'

"It's locked with biological security code, the only person who can open this is the owner." The file unlocks and fills up the screen. "And, apparently, you."

Aden walks up behind me, continuing to scan the room with his rifle, probably wondering if there are any Plaguers masquerading as dead bodies, or if the corpses are infected and going to change.

"What is it?" he asks over his shoulder.

It takes me a second to realize what I'm looking at. At first it just looks like a bunch of numbers, dates, and initials, but it seems to be a security log. A few more moments and I understand why Vali brought this to our attention.

"This says that somebody shut down GHC from the outside so the Plaguers could get in."

Aden scans the room once more then runs up behind me. "What? What are you talking about?" Vali pulls up ten different security videos files that show the building's security features going down one by one and the Plaguers pouring in and slaughtering the personnel. He zooms into one particular video feed of the Plaguers emptying out the weapons and older combat suits from the armory.

"This is *not* good," Aden says.

Vali switches back to the security log and clicks on the details surrounding the day that the building was tampered with. "Oh fuck. This is worse," I say as my eye catches the name of the perpetrator.

The file disappears from the screen and a live feed of Captain Otto sitting in his office appears in its place.

"Gentlemen, I suppose you have questions."

Aden and I both turn to look at each other then back to the screen. So much information is running through my mind and I'm trying to figure out what the hell is going on that I can't focus enough to formulate words.

My lips quiver with a mixture of fear and rage as I barely manage to ask the first and most important question, "Why?"

Chapter 16: First Mission

7:12 - 2120 - 1100:003 Red Galaxy Standard

"Captain," Bill and I offer in unison with a salute.

I'm already a bit on the nervous side because we've been training for four months and this is our first time meeting Captain Otto since we've woken up. The old man appears to be carved from stone, with an angular, chiseled chin being the most prominent feature on his face. Thick, well-kept, short grey hair covers the top of his head and his dark brown eyes make him seem kinder than I expect. This is exemplified by the slight smile he offers before motioning to the old wooden chairs in front of his desk.

"Gentlemen, please sit."

We hold our salute for another second, as customary, then round the chairs and have a seat. I shift in an attempt to become more comfortable, but fear it's impossible with such an antiquated material. Word around the ship is that he's stern but fair, and won't tolerate failure. That last part worries me as I'm sure being ambushed and robbed of our memories would be considered failure.

"They're shit for comfort," he says, pointing at the chairs.

"Not at all, sir," I respond, lying through my teeth. Sitting in this chair is probably the most uncomfortable I've been in the last four months of training, and at one point, a Thyr drone nearly ripped my arms off.

"You can cut the crap, Lieutenant. I've sat in them myself."

"Why keep them?" Bill blurts out. Both the captain and I turn to look at him. "I mean, is it some kind of superiority technique...sir?" Bill glances to me out of the corner of his eye, catches the deadly glare I'm firing his way, then turns his attention back to the captain with a practiced look of dumbfounded curiosity. The tension in the room is palpable as Captain Otto's ice-cold stare bores through Bill and the uncomfortable chair that he occupies.

To my surprise, Captain Otto rolls with laughter. "No, Sergeant, it's not." Loosening up his shoulders, he lays both arms on the wooden desk before us. "Red was right, you may have lost your memory, but you haven't changed." He turns to me, "and judging from that glare you're giving your partner, neither have you." I ease up as the captain looks back at Bill and continues, "I don't keep them to make you uncomfortable in my presence, as your superior, which you may want to remember when speaking, Sergeant. I keep them as a reminder."

"A reminder of what?" Bill asks.

"Humans." We both look at each other. "All of the furniture in this room was from Earth."

"I was under the impression that we scorched Earth, sir?" I ask. "Furthermore that any items associated with the humans was subsequently banned by the High Order."

"We did, and it sounds like you've been reading up on our history."

"No memories, sir."

"Yes, that's right." He nods looking at the desk for a brief moment. "Well, some of those who played integral parts in its burning were able to confiscate and remove certain items before the final blow was dealt. The High Order looks the other way given our sacrifices in the final days of the war. The chairs you're sitting on, this desk, my chair," he leans toward us so we can see the back, "which is slightly more comfortable with leather padding over the wood." He eases back into the chair and points to one side of the room, then the other. "The picture frames, the small table against this wall, and the armoire against that wall, all made of wood. It amazes me how well it lasts given proper care, and yet, a simple flame could destroy it forever." The old man pauses for a moment, staring past us at nothing in particular. It seems as though he's reminiscing about something before the war. "Still, fascination aside, I keep all of this to remind myself of the human's plight, to keep my priorities straight." Captain Otto pushes the chair back, stands up, and walks around the desk.

"You see, the humans believed they were the only intelligent life in the entire universe. A rather egotistical stance to take considering how large the universe really is. They stopped working for the benefit of their own kind and began fighting against one another for money and power." He stops behind us, setting a hand on each of our shoulders.

Awkward. That's how this whole situation should feel. I want to shove his hand away and scream I'm a fucking soldier not some pup straight out of the black who needs to be coddled and nursed. I want to do this, but don't. Outside of the fact that he's my superior and I don't want him to be pissed at us right off the bat, my mind feels surprisingly accepting of the situation. I want to be angry, but the truth is I'm comforted by the slight gesture and I don't know why. The relaxation, the warmth created from a simple gesture, that is what I am angry at. If Bill feels the same he doesn't have a problem acting otherwise. He shrugs the captain's hand off, who just smirks and continues.

"It's very difficult to progress as a species when you're constantly sabotaging your fellow man to get ahead." He continues walking again. "But what's the point? If you're not progressing, then what spoils do you truly get from stifling your own people? By the time we came along it wasn't too hard to take over a world that was already drowning in disarray and confusion. They had no idea how to work together, and were so afraid to that they couldn't mount a significant defensive."

Making it to the other side of his desk, Captain Otto sits back down in the high-back, leather-coated chair. "These relics remind me of what unity can accomplish, and what we need to do in order to further ourselves. If we don't stay focused, it wouldn't take much for a single flame to come along and render us all to ash." He gestures to all the furniture. "Much like this wood."

"I feel like some kind of reference to 'trial by *fire*' is coming next," Bill teases.

Squinting at Bill, Captain Otto grunts in confirmation before swiping through files occupying the built-in screen on top of his desk. Bill looks at me for the usual head tilt and grimace that screams 'shut the hell up' before offering a smirk and turning back to Captain Otto.

"Gentlemen, Red tells me you're progressing well, faster than he expected in fact, and that you're ready for the field."

"Yes, sir," I fire out...man, now I'm doing it...I mean, I *say* before Bill has a chance to open his damn mouth again.

"Excellent to hear. I won't lie, I've come to like you boys over the years and want to make sure you've fully recuperated, but at the same time I need you in the field. Before the ambush you were the best two operatives I had. I hope that still holds true."

"We've been trained by the best, sir. We won't let you down."

"That you have, and I have all the faith in the universe when it comes to Red's skill and judgment."

"What's the op, sir?" Bill finally asks an appropriate question.

Captain Otto flicks his finger across the desk toward us, then does it again. "The files have been forwarded to your VOK." What the hell is a VOK? We're both unintentionally staring at Captain Otto like two numb nuts fresh out of boot. "Variable Operations Knowledge? The biokits that pair to your suits?" The blank stares continue. "I'm guessing Red didn't get the time to go over field equipment. Head down to Alexander in the research division, he'll get you suited up."

The same Alexander that helped us recoup? Why was a scientist from the research division hanging around in the medical facility?

"He works both fields." The captain answers as if I asked the question. "I've seen that look before when explaining all that Alexander's involved in. The division heads up is officially named Research Evolution and Accidental Personnel Emergency Repair." The surprise on my face must be as easy to read as the confusion from a moment ago. I'm making a mental note to work on hiding my reactions more efficiently. "He creates things that take away life and give it back. In very specific circumstances of course."

Placing his left palm flat on the desk, Captain Otto pulls a hologram into the air, creating a mirror image of his screen for us to see. "Now, back to the mission at hand, scorched or not, the Earth is ours. It has been for almost fifteen years now, since the Bloodwar of 2106." A holographic model of Earth appears and zooms in to a highlighted, rectangular land mass, as a red locational light starts blinking on the map. "Even though the humans are gone, it turns out they made contact with an alien species almost a hundred and seventy-five years ago in 1947, in what used to be the southwest United States and then possibly some sixty years later in a northwest region of that same area." Another red dot appears to the left and above the original. "The species, known as...huh, this is a weird one...Kuh-lin...was in its infancy back then, but their exploratory envoy apparently made a deal and vowed to return in peace to help the humans once their technology had advanced." He swipes the desk causing the map to disappear; a profile of the Kuhlin species with a picture of one of them takes its place. It looks humanoid but the skin is refracting light and seems to almost...glitter. "Well, they're back, and not really happy to find that we've turned the human species into ash."

"Where do we come in, sir?" Bill asks. Wow, two for two. He really must be getting tired of battling training drones.

"You're going to head down to the Earth's surface and deliver a message."

"What's the message, sir?" I ask.

"Get the fuck off our planet." Captain Otto swipes the mission data hologram to the left of his desk, causing it to disappear, and then leans forward. "We didn't come halfway across the universe and spend two years embroiled in a short but bloody war that eventually led to us scorching a perfectly good planet just to listen to some pansy-ass species of glittery freaks that warped into the area complain about losing their first contact." Captain Otto leans back into his chair. "Scorched or not, long term, the Earth has value to us. I want them gone, *now*. I don't care how you do it, but make sure they get the message loud and clear *and* that there's at least one of them left to take that message back to the rest of their people. Questions?"

"When you pulled up their profile, they appeared to reflect the light, is that their armor or skin, sir?" Hopefully it's the latter.

"We think it's their skin. An initial scan of the area hasn't indicated weapons of any kind, even their ship seems to be unarmed, a diplomatic transport of some kind." I trade looks with Bill, unintentionally showing my dismay over the simplicity of the mission.

"Look, I know this probably isn't your choice assignment for getting back into action, but we need to make sure you're fit for field work. That includes making sure that you follow protocol, don't get flashbacks, and that you survive the drop procedures, considering how extensive your injuries were."

"Sir, we haven't had any flashbacks since waking up." As long as he doesn't consider reincarnated information and muscle memory to be flashbacks. "And all of our vitals have been top notch since we started training."

"I understand, let's just look at this mission as a formality, okay? Get 'em gone, get back, and we'll talk about the future of our species and your role in expanding it when you're done. Copy?"

"Copy, sir," we both reply at the same time.

"All right, dismissed." Captain Otto salutes.

We both stand, salute back, hold it for a moment, then round the chairs and walk out of the captain's office.

Just as we're out of earshot from the captain's office, Bill starts complaining. "Well, this sucks."

"It does, but the captain has good reasons."

"How would you know? We're in the same boat, dipstick. We don't remember anything from before the ambush, we don't know him, we don't know military protocol other than what Red's crammed into our heads for a hundred hours straight only to be rewarded with a few hours of sleep. We don't know what his reasons are or what missions we used to go on prior to the ambush, but from the way they treat us, I'm guessing it's not a crap messenger mission like this."

I stop walking and grab Bill's shoulder, spinning him around to face me. "One, we're soldiers, regardless of what our situation is or how familiar I feel to you, remember the chain of command, shithead. And two, if there's the chance of something weird happening with some kind of post-traumatic stress when we jump back into the shit, I'd rather find out on an op where the targets don't have weapons."

Bill shakes his head, "Psfh, it's still bullshit."

"Lover's quarrel?" A female voice interrupts behind Bill. I look past him as he turns around and see Blaze leaning against the wall at a cross junction in the hall. Blaze was the shorter of the two soldiers who dropped in on our first training session. The one who made the snide comment. Aphrodite is her partner and Lieutenant. We've seen them around the ship since that day in the training room, traded jabs here and there, but haven't really spent a lot of time with either of them. To be fair we haven't had time to spare and I don't even know if I would that I could. Something about her makes me uneasy.

"Like the ice queen can even understand love," Bill mumbles. He's not exactly fond of Blaze. Probably because they're so alike it's ridiculous. She's witty, sarcastic and at most times a total ass. That's on the surface though and while it seems my partner is quite skilled in combat and strategic planning, he's not the best when it comes to reading people. I'm confident that there's another side to Blaze that we haven't seen yet.

"Anyways," Bill says louder looking back at me. "That's my cue." He nods, "Sir," then walks down the corridor and turns left away from Blaze.

"I don't think your partner likes me very much," she says loud enough for him to hear while turning to watch him leave. He mumbles something as he continues down the hall.

"He doesn't like competition."

Her head snaps back to me. "None of us do. That's why we're so good at our jobs." Good point. "So, they've got you taking baby steps on your first mission?"

She must have overheard us. "Didn't anyone ever tell you that it's not polite to eavesdrop?"

She takes a few meticulous steps closer. "I make it a point to figure out what's polite and then do the exact opposite," she says with a devious smile.

I chuckle, then start to walk toward her with the intent of sliding right on past and heading back to my bunk. I think she's trying to flirt with me and I don't need this shit right now. "Huh, why am I not surprised," I say under my breath.

She grabs me by the arm, hard, but not forcefully and I stop out of sheer surprise, somehow without letting it show on my face. "Red says that it's unlikely your conscious memories will return." I cock my head slightly forward waiting for her to continue. She moves in, her lips twisted in a smirk until her face is only a few inches away from mine. All of a sudden she blinks and there's a look of confusion on her face, as if she forgot what she was doing or had planned to say.

"You okay?" I ask.

"Yeah I just," the confusion remains as she searches for the words to describe what just happened. Then without saying anything, she releases my arm and starts walking in the opposite direction. She yells back, "Don't get yourself killed on a practice mission," without breaking stride. I can tell from the tone of her voice that's she trying to be sarcastic and snide, but there's lingering bits of fear and confusion.

"Man," I say to myself, "and I thought we were fucking weird."

Chapter 17: Wake Up Call

3.01 - 2468 - 1915:839 Red Galaxy Standard

It's only been five seconds since I asked Captain Otto why he overrode the security in GHC and let the Plaguers take down our most secure military compound. My breathing increases with every second he doesn't answer and the pounding of my heart is so loud that I almost don't hear him speak. Problem is, he's not talking to me.

"Are we secure?" he asks while turning away from our feed and glancing down to what I can only assume is a separate feed on his desk's built-in screen. One of the screens in front of us to the left of Captain Otto flickers to life, and a man with a blank black mask similar to our own tilts his head as if he's reading the expression on my face.

"Yes," he answers in a mechanically-garbled voice, without separating his gaze from mine.

"How secure?"

"I wouldn't be able to hack it," the man replies, still staring at me.

I retract my helmet so the Captain can see the look of frustration on my face. "Who the *fuck* is this?" I demand as Aden looms over my shoulder and moves a little closer to get a better view retracting his helmet as well.

Captain Otto ignores me and continues his conversation with the man on the other screen. "Excellent. Clear the Lieutenant."

Aden and I glance at each out of the corner of our eyes. "Clear me for what?"

"He's talking about me." A voice answers from behind us in the main doorway to the command center. I know that voice, but it sounds different, confident. Aden and I turn around to see Mike casually walking down the steps.

"Mike, what the hell are you doing here? How did you find a secure location to land the SWIFT?"

He walks up onto the command platform and smirks. "Don't worry about the SWIFT, big guy. It's all under control." His tone is different and this new swagger filled with attitude that he's giving off is altogether foreign. I've known Mike for a long time, but the man standing before me is a total stranger. He salutes Captain Otto on the screen. "Captain," then turns to the man in black, "Vee."

Aden and I both turn to look at the man in black. "Vali?" we ask almost at the same time. He answers with a quick nod. Neither of us have ever met Vali in person or for that matter, via video feed. We've never seen pictures of him and always communicated through our suits via text. He was referred to us through Red which, given the situation about our past, makes sense now, but how do Mike and the captain know him? Speaking of which...

"Aren't we missing someone?" Mike asks vocalizing my next thought. Well, that was creepy.

Captain Otto adjusts his camera to show Red standing behind him. Vali taps the side of his helmet and the visor collapses from left to right into a little square, then flips up near his ear as the top of the helmet collapses back and disappears into the neck just like the bottom portion does in the front. Staring back at us is an absolutely stunning, blonde-haired young woman with bright green eyes.

"Holy shit!" Aden screams pointing at the screen. "Vali is that hot High Priestess I hit on?" His eyes are wide with excitement and Mike chuckles behind us.

I look at Captain Otto. "Vali is your niece? Somebody tell me what the fuck is going on." This is all way too confusing and it still doesn't explain why Captain Otto sentenced this entire facility to death. All my energy is focused on not exploding before I get some answers, instead I just growl, *"Now."*

"Gentlemen, you were once human."

Aden and I both freeze like statues. The smirk fades from Aden's face and we're breathing shallowly, staring at Captain Otto with wide eyes. Given what I've seen over the years, I wouldn't put it past him to orchestrate this whole mission as some sort of trap to catch us off guard. He's planning on putting an end to the humans once and for all, and like fools we walked right into it. My right hand slowly creeps toward my side arm as the tension silently builds in the stuffy dark room.

A faint metallic whirring from behind me cuts the silence. It's Mike's laser pistol powering up, the sound of which increases slightly as he raises the weapon and presses its barrel against the back of my head.

"Easy, Hoss," he orders. "Let him finish."

Captain Otto waves a hand at the screen. "That isn't necessary, Lieutenant Mackelson." Lieutenant Mackelson? Mike lowers the side arm and the noise subsides as he re-attaches it to his combat pants. "These two want to know the truth. They need to know the truth. It eats at them like a parasite from the inside, always forcing them to stick their heads where they don't belong. Well, now they finally get to hear it."

Captain Otto eases back into his leather chair. "Gentlemen, with the exception of Red here," he points his thumb back at Red, "say hello to the last remaining vestiges of the human race." Extending both hands out, he points one at Mike and the other at Vali.

It's hard to tell if I'm more nervous now than I was a few seconds ago. My heart is still racing and my mind is trying to catch up with reality, but I can't seem to formulate words to ask even the most simplistic question.

Luckily, Aden is seemingly less affected by the news at hand. He turns to Vali and smirks, offering a quick nod before saying, "What's up baby, wanna repopulate our race?"

She chuckles and shakes her head while Mike scoffs behind us. "You were a little bit smoother when you were human," she says.

Mike playfully shoves Aden's shoulder from behind. "It's this new body, memories or not, all the strength has made him cockier."

"Besides, I thought you didn't like me," Vali adds with a playfully innocent smile.

"Uh yeah, when I thought you were some pathetic, nerdy, hacker *guy* poking around in my head. Come on you're in my neural link, are you telling me you can't take a little peak at my memories? Just another piece of hardware to hack right? Look at one of the times I thought back on that banquet and you'll see what I really think," he says, winking and making a clicking noise out of the side of his cheek.

Vali shakes her head, "Luckily, It doesn't work that way dipshit. I don't want to know what's going on up there."

Aden laughs and the sound helps my mind finally pull itself back together, allowing my lips to comply with the situation. "Hold on...we all knew each other? Are we the only ones who lost our memories?"

"Yes," Captain Otto answers, ignoring the playful rhetoric of Aden, followed by Vali's half-disgusted, and surprisingly half-interested responses. "Red filled you in on how you came to be, during the emergence of the Hemos in 2014, but he didn't tell you what happened after you went under."

Aden and Vali turn their attention to Captain Otto as he leans forward in his chair, setting both elbows on his desk and interlocking his fingers together as is common when he explains something.

"My name was Captain Hoffman when I was human. I was the Marine Corp Officer assigned to the San Diego emergence incident. You and your brother had already assembled a group of civilians in the area to fight back, thanks to the information that Red was providing. During the recon mission at the zoo that led to your injury," he points to Mike, "Mike, then known as Lieutenant Mackelson, rerouted his team to the zoo to offer extraction." He then points to Vali's screen, "Vali isn't my niece. Her name was Kelly back then. She was a pilot who routinely transported you two to and from mission sites. She was also working with Red prior to the emergence and anyone else's involvement. She was, and still is, the most experienced person when it comes to information surrounding the Hemos, their history, and their emergence. Now she's a hacker and an information broker working undercover in the High Science division under the guise of my niece."

This is insane. "How come we were the only ones to lose our memory?"

Red moves from behind Captain Hoffman and points the camera in his direction. "Because my research surrounding the technology to convert you was not ready. You were the first and only because, if I did not put you in those tanks, you were going to die right there. It was a shot in the dark at best that worked out in the end, more or less. The amount of blood you lost, plus the depth of the medical coma you were put in had side effects. I did not have time to properly prepare your bodies, and when my blood started to convert you, it caused your old white cells to attack the new, foreign tissue most notably in your brain. Once the conversion was complete, your bodies rebuilt themselves, but your memories were gone."

"Not all of them, though," Kelly chimes in. "I mean some part, something lingered. We thought you guys were going to be blank slates, but you continually display traits of your former personalities." She points to me, "You were always a natural leader and strategist, you still are. And you," she points to Aden, "are still a little shit."

Aden cocks his head and smirks at her, "We had something, didn't we? In the old life?"

"Maybe if you'd grown a pair and talked to me," she shoots back without missing a beat. I wonder how long she's been waiting to say that.

Throwing my hands in the air I demand, "Okay, it's been over two centuries, can we put a cork in the whole sexually repressed energy thing for just a few more minutes?" Aden raises a finger, getting ready to say something sarcastic, but I swat it out of the way and slap my hand over his mouth. "Priorities, you little shit," then look back to Red, "continue."

"Your situation immediately revealed a great deal of information which allowed me to make the conversion safer for other humans. It was still questionable when Kelly went under, but she insisted." Kelly's smile fades as she stares at Aden with a longing that clearly shows that she had given up hope on ever having this conversation, and is relieved that it's finally out in the open. Quickly realizing the emotion emitting from her face, she averts her gaze, pretending to cough and rub her welled-up eyes. It's clear that she cares for Aden a great deal, even if it was never said.

"It was a little rocky at first, but with her body prepped and the changes made to the conversion process, she stabilized and advanced much quicker than expected. After doing multiple scans of her brain activity and seeing that the cortex remained unaffected by the process, meaning she would retain her memories, Captain Hoffman suggested putting Lieutenant Mackelson under to use as an undercover operator given his combat experience. It had become clear that the Earth would be lost in the war. Years later, when the last of the humans were on the brink of extinction, I convinced Captain Hoffman to go under as well."

Everyone remains silent as Aden and I process the information at hand. It seems as though he's finally taking this seriously and trying to understand what this means for us, which is exactly what I'm thinking about. There's one question beating in the back of my head though, and it's the same one that I asked the Captain when his face showed up on the screen in front of us a few minutes ago. "Why?"

"Excuse me?" Captain Hoffman asks gently, pushing Red behind him and turning the camera back to his face.

"Why? What's the point?" I look at Captain Hoffman, then Red, Kelly, and glance back at Lieutenant Mackelson before turning back to Captain Hoffman. "There's four of us, and one turncoat. All this secrecy, all the lies and deceit to keep us alive, what's the point?"

Lieutenant Mackelson shoves me from behind which causes me to stumble, and almost fall into the monitors. "What's the point? What's the fucking point? Oh that's right, you don't remember when they slaughtered us by the millions, strung people up like cattle after skinning them alive; you were at a fucking slumber party." I turn around as he rushes forward, stopping an inch from my face. "You want to keep playing little Hemo bitch and you've got the stones to call Red a turncoat?"

"Get out of my face," I snarl coldly.

"Lieutenant," Red says calmly but firmly through the screen. Lieutenant Mackelson bobs his head and chuckles before turning and walking a few steps away, pacing in place near the edge of the command platform.

I back up and turn to the screen. "Seriously, what's the plan here? Just take down a whole race out of revenge? Huh?"

"We took down the most secure military facility in the known universe in minutes," Captain Hoffman proudly states.

"Yeah, bravo," Aden interjects, clapping mockingly. "Stringing us along like puppets the entire time, and working with those animals in the process." He points to the dead bodies throughout the command center. Lieutenant Mackelson scoffs and mutters something under his breath, but I can't hear what it is.

"This is just…" Captain Hoffman tries to explain, but the pent up anger inside is building up.

"This is ludicrous, that's what this is!" I holler, cutting him off. "You people are living in a psychotic dream. You want to dismantle an entire species with five people and a savage pack of genetically altered misfits who were tortured in a lab somewhere? Talk about false hope...and did I miss the part of humanity that believed in genocide?"

Lieutenant Mackelson growls and lurches toward me, drawing his sidearm in one quick motion and grabs me by the neck, shoving the barrel into my temple. "Genocide? Genocide is killing our whole fucking race and eating or experimenting on the poor souls who didn't get the chance to die in battle! Women, children!"

With my back stiffening slightly, the rage in his eyes continues to burn through my skull as Aden maneuvers his head around from behind Lieutenant Mackelson in order to speak into his ear.

"Put it down, now." Aden's got his Ka pressed into the Lieutenant's spine, but he doesn't yield.

"Aden!" Kelly cries from the screen.

"Put it down or I'll cripple you with a single thrust and spend the next century torturing your shadow of a body until you beg for death...then I'll take the time to get creative."

"Lieutenant!" Captain Hoffman scolds.

The Lieutenant bares his teeth and yells in frustration. He tosses the pistol to the floor, pushes Aden aside and walks down off of the command platform, kicking one of the dead bodies a few times before pacing up and down the steps.

I pat Aden on the shoulder and turn back to the captain, speaking loudly enough for the lieutenant to hear. "I don't remember any of that. All I know is this life. You can't ask me to throw that away."

"This life is already on its way out," Captain Hoffman says, looking down and typing something on his desk.

"What do you mean?"

He continues to type, but quickly gets frustrated. "Stupid piece of...Kelly can you?" The video of him shrinks to encompass half the screen and the other half is filling with classified documents from the High Science division.

Kelly chimes in to explain what it all means. "Hemos were experimenting with genetic conversions way before they took over Earth. I've found black documents tracing back to the late eighteen-hundreds referencing some queen who was trying to mix our two species. Before taking over Earth, they decided that the Homo Sapiens were too weak of a race and that only certain people actually took to the conversion and embraced the stronger, foreign genes of the Hemos. It was out of sheer luck that it worked for you, and Red's brilliance to decrypt the data your bodies provided, that pulled it off for us."

She navigates to a specific document. "After the scorching of the Earth, they began looking for other species, and they found one."

"The Thyr," Captain Hoffman says. "The uprising of 2252 wasn't because they saw us as a threat, it's because we started abducting and experimenting on them. The High Council wants to genetically splice us with the Thyr in order to make some kind of super species."

"Designed for one reason," Red says, leaning down into view.

"Genocide," Kelly finishes. "They want to enslave any species that is of use and slaughter any that isn't. This is who the Hemos are. After wiping out the humans they got a taste for blood and now everything revolves around cleansing the universe. It's Hitler on an unbelievable scale." I offer a look of confusion and she shakes her head. "Never mind, it's just really horrible."

As I take a deep breath and look at Aden to get his read on things he lowers his eyes to the floor while thinking about everything. Fighting an entire race bred for death wasn't exactly in the cards when Red brought us up to speed a few days ago. It's a lot to take in.

"That calculating that you're doing right now," Kelly says, pointing at my head. "That's your human side. It's still in there. You're still great men and you know that what they're doing is wrong. You know you can't walk away from this; even if you can't remember why you're fighting, you know you have to."

After taking another deep breath, I point to Lieutenant Mackelson. "He's an asshole."

"No argument," Kelly says, nodding.

I look back at Aden who's nodding to me with absolution in his eyes. I've seen that look before on missions. It shows up when we have to go way off course in order to do what needs to be done, even though it'll land us in a world of hurt. This is going be a shitstorm.

Without taking my eyes off him I ask, "Where do we start?"

Chapter 18: A Glittery Mission

July 19th 2120 - Earth Standard

"What's it called again?" Bill asks Mike through the comms. I know what he's doing. Mike hasn't caught on yet, but after four months of training with Bill for twenty hours a day and I can pretty much pick out every little tic. His voice goes higher when he's trying to be an ass and trick someone into making a fool of themselves.

Mike explains it one more time, stressing the frustration in his voice as he pronounces each word. "Savage. Lance. Of. Woe."

Bill couldn't be any worse at trying to contain his laughter; breathing heavily, snorting through his hand, and trying not to move around too much. He finally gives, screaming through both hands. "SLOW!" He chuckles. "It's called SLOW." He exhales as if a weight has been lifted off his chest. "Your vehicle of woe is called SLOW, haha. Oh man, it felt good to finally say that."

Mike thinks for a second before agonizing over Bill's realization, "Damn it! You've gotta be kidding me. How did I never see that?" he sighs. "Talk about an oversight."

The SLOW banks to the left as Mike focuses on the mission for a second. "Okay, we're through the atmosphere. Landing in sixty seconds in the northwest section of what used to be called US."

Bill turns and looks at me with a tilted head and cocked eyebrow in disbelief. "Who the hell would name a place US?"

He's right, that's weird, but then again, from what I hear the humans weren't exactly normal or logical in most of their activities. "As the captain stated it's short for the United States, but I guess it was frequently reference to as US. Seems rather lazy, although from what I hear the humans were weird. I wouldn't put it past them to be so self-involved that they did it on purpose to call a large location like that 'US'."

"You have no idea," Mike whispers through the comms. That's also weird. Before I have a chance to question Mike's odd behavior, he calls out the specifics of the drop point. "Okay, we're touching down on the edge of some scorched little town. Thirty seconds, get the door ready."

Mike isn't actually going to land the SLOW, just in case the aliens we're here to chat with decide to go hostile. It's protocol. Even though we've scanned for weapons, there could be something down there we don't know about. I look over at Bill, point my finger in the air, then spin it around in a circle signaling him to get ready. I stand up and position myself just behind the square drop doors on the floor. Bill does the same on the other side. That's when it hits me.

My knees go weak, there's an odd quiver in both hands and a wave of heat washes over my skin even though the Grecene suits are designed to control body temperature. I think back to the first time I saw these suits, in Red's training room, on Blaze and Aphrodite. My head starts spinning, and the nausea makes it difficult to stay focused on the mission, let alone the drop procedure that we're about to engage in for the first time since we came to. I take a deep breath and exhale, hoping that the action will eject the odd sensations from my body.

"Fifteen, open drop doors," Mike bellows from the cockpit, snapping me back to reality, and like that it's gone.

"Hey. You all right?" Bill asks.

"Uh, yeah," I shake my head and input a code on the wall to my right, then tap the green release button on the touchscreen. The square doors in the floor below us separate into the bottom hull of the SLOW and I can see the scorched black pines rushing by underneath, followed by an old road that Mike maneuvers us over.

Before Bill has a chance to follow up on my weird behavior a couple of massive four legged creatures with dull gray and green skin jet across the pavement below. Neither of us get a good look at what they are because of the speed.

"Mike, I just saw some pretty big creatures run across the road beneath us. Any idea what they are?"

"Huh, no. I didn't seen anything in the intel about local wildlife. I heard most of it was killed off years ago, but it is likely that other species could have left something behind. That or our new friends brought some pets. Either way, keep your heads on a swivel down there."

The blurred black pavement slows and Mike turns around to look at us as we hover twenty feet above the ground. "All right, gimme a call when you need exfil. I'll stay within emergency range, thirty second touchdown time. Be safe." He salutes us then turns back to the cockpit.

"You ready?" I ask Bill. He smirks and jumps through the open drop doors. I follow, landing on the black pavement below a second later and we immediately start scanning the area as Mike takes off.

The place must have been a lush forest at one time, but now it's just a sea of burnt tree stubs to either side of the road. They look like eerie black pillared statues leading us into town. Light is scarce as the excessive cloud cover above makes the entire area look like an ominous, colorless ghost town. "Report?" I order.

"Getting a few different signals a mile in, but that's it. Those creatures we saw must be out of range already." Bill's crouched down on the road, looking straight at the ruined town in front of us. "Which is fucking insane."

That *is* insane. Our scanners reach out to roughly ten miles. No way those creatures could have gotten out of range in time, unless they're fast as shit or can teleport. Hell, maybe they don't show up on scanners, which is an equally discomforting thought. Nothing we can do about it now. Besides, Bill will never admit it, but we're both a little on edge. Easy mission or not, we're in unfamiliar territory and it's our first time back in the field. Adrenaline is raging through my system, forcing my senses into overdrive, and I know it's the same for Bill. Readings or not, we'll be able to hear or see those creatures well in advance if they decided to come back and check us out. Okay, I need to focus, which reminds me…"Maybe we could stay on point, Sergeant."

"Sorry. The signals I'm getting have to be the Kuh-lins."

I turn around, tap his shoulder and continue watching our rear. "No signals behind, proceed forward, slowly. Call out any movement."

"Roger," Bill confirms. He stands up and moves forward while staying low, but keeping a fairly quick pace.

"Hold," he says as we reach the edge of the town. I pause and wait for him to explain, but instead hear him walk off the road. While turning around, I see him walk up to a metal sign and wipe away the black soot that's concealed its text. The surface underneath is mostly rusted away, but the sign is green with white lettering and reads 'City of Forks, Population 3,175.'

"Why would they name a city after an eating utensil?" Bill asks, turning around with a confused grin on his face and shaking his head. I'm still getting used to having a small, constant video feed to his helmet camera in the upper right side of my visor. "What the hell was with these humans? Where's your house again, Johnny?" he mocks in goofy high-pitched voice. "Oh it's in Forks," he changes to a different, lower-toned voice, "Forks?" then back to the other one, "Yeah, Forks, US."

"I don't give a shit. Stop messing around and get back on mission."

"Okay, okay. Just curious, that's all." It seems like he's always curious. That's going to get us in trouble one day.

"Freaking humans," he mutters while hopping back down to the road. All of a sudden there's a beeping in my earpiece and my VOK bracer starts vibrating on my right arm.

"Hold," I command. Bill turns around with a curious look on his face and I turn down to the flexible screen wrapped around my wrist to see that it has gone black, before a message appears in white lettering.

"What is it?"

"Remember how Red said he was going to put us in touch with that intelligence expert that works under the radar?"

"What, he's touching base now?" Bill twitches his head, gasps, then jerks his arm off to the side before looking at his own VOK screen.

"Little beep through the earpiece, followed by a vibration on your VOK unit?" I ask.

"Yeah it...what the hell?"

"What?" I literally just told him that the hacker touched base. His message to me was just a basic greeting, what could he have sent Bill that would make it act so weird?

"It says, 'Good luck, be safe - V' and has a little smiley face next to it." Bill's face is painted with a mixture of disgust and concern. "Who the hell did Red say this guy was?"

"Huh, that's odd. Mine just says 'Good luck -V'. Red didn't say much, just that he would be useful in a pinch and was able to do stuff that regular intelligence couldn't." Bill looks at me with a cocked eyebrow and then looks back at the message. "Maybe he likes you," I offer innocently.

He looks back up, the concern melts away leaving only disgust, "Ew. This dude's creepy, let's just get back to the mission." He starts walking back up the road.

I'm barely able to contain my laughter, but doing a much better job than Bill was earlier. "Maybe you guys could get dinner when we get back and..."

"Shut up," he snaps. "Can we please just," his left arm shoots to the ground at his side, with straight, stiff fingers driving toward the ground. "Mission at hand. This is serious shit. Life forms five hundred yards ahead, seven of them." Even though Bill's right about staying on mission, I'm making a mental note to torture him later about his new found admirer. What are friends for?

Some of the clouds move away, allowing the sun to break through as we round a couple of ruined houses. Most of the structures in the area only have foundations and some old plumbing remaining. Perpendicular to our position is what used to be a very large, old brick building. It's all rubble now, burnt to a crisp like everything else in this town, and most of the planet for that matter, but parts of it are still cropping out of the ground in certain areas. It must have been a facility of some kind, maybe educational or a social gathering place for the humans.

"Are you seeing this?" Bill asks with a high-pitched voice. I am, and it's freaking weird. In front of what remains of the large building, are seven glittering...things...standing just off of the road. They're bipedal creatures, a little smaller than us, yet vary in height and are shaped in a similar manner. I'd almost mistake them for humans if it wasn't for their twinkling skin. Honestly, I'm having a hard time figuring out whether this an actual mission or the captain and Red are just screwing with us on our first day back to active duty.

"I am. Are you seeing or reading any weapons?"

"Negative." One of the shorter males moves forward by a few feet and waves to us. "But uh, one just waved."

"Thank you, Sergeant." I say sarcastically. "Let's just...let's go deliver our message, I guess." As I walk past Bill and approach the seven creatures, the cloud cover moves in front of the sun again blocking its light. The sunlight dims over the creatures, and they transform from the diamond-like exterior to normal clothing draped over pale skin. They now look like, from what I've heard at least, what humans would look like. Only with really bad fashion sense.

The male who walked in front of the group and waved now has pale white skin and puffy brown hair pushed back over his head. There's three males and three females behind him. They all seem...fairly attractive as far as humans are concerned but too...pretty. Almost in a dark, fake way.

While approaching the pale male with puffy hair, I can sense a weird air of smugness radiating from his eyes and oddly shaped mouth. I stop ten feet in front of him. "My name is..." before he can finish the introduction, a shot sounds out and the back of his head explodes, spraying blood all over the rest of his people. They stand in shock as the body falls backwards to the ground.

Bill jogs up next to me and is staring at the body with an odd look of hatred in his wide eyes.

"What the fuck was that?" I press.

"I don't know man, I just…" he's shaking his head. "There was something about that smug little son of a bitch. I just couldn't look at him anymore." A few more shakes of the head and he turns to look at me with a wide grin on his face. "But hey! Message delivered, right?"

Shaking my own head, I look back at the body on the ground. The others have snapped out of shock and are kneeling by the newly appointed corpse. The women are weeping as the larger and shorter men step in front of them in what I can only presume is a protective stance. Like it's going to do any good. A taller, older man with short blonde hair approaches us with a stern look on his face.

"Which one?" Bill asks.

"The stern one," I assert, pointing to the male walking toward us.

It takes all of two seconds for Bill and I to raise our side arms and fire off five more shots. The tall blonde male who was walking toward us, raises his arms to block his face and cowers in fear as the others fall to the ground. He slowly lets his arms down and turns to look at the six dead bodies.

"You've been chosen to deliver a message." I say coldly.

"What message?" he growls over his shoulder while beginning to whimper.

"Tell the rest of your people to stay the fuck away from Earth. It's under control of the Hemosapiens."

He spins around with puffy red eyes and tears streaming down his face. "What other people?" he barks. "We were the only ones!" Turning back to the bodies, he falls to his knees and continues to cry.

Bill leans over to whisper in my right ear, "Uh...I guess we don't have anything to worry about." He nudges me with his elbow. "Hey, hey, ask me what I think of their clothes." I slowly turn my head to look at him and perk up my eyebrows. "Come on, come on, ask me."

I sigh, knowing full well that I'm going to regret asking, but finally give in, "Hey Bill, what do you think of their clothes?"

"Wouldn't be caught dead in something like that. Ha!" The man on the ground throws back his head and wails to the sky, probably overhearing Bill's sad excuse for a joke. Bill shakes his head and chuckles, "Ah, wouldn't be caught dead. Whooo." After a few seconds of congratulating himself for such a classy comedic retort, he turns and gawks at the weeping man in the dirt and scratches the side of his neck. "Hey, we should uh, put him out of his misery or something? Seriously, he's like...really taking this whole thing to heart."

Poor taste in comedy aside, Bill's right. It'll be more merciful if we just put the sobbing sap out of his misery. I raise my arm and fire a single round through the back of his head then watch the body slump into the mud.

"Well, that's that. Pretty easy first mission if you ask me," Bill says, putting his pistol back into its holster on his leg. The clouds part as the last bit of sun is shining down on us and Bill looks up at the beautiful colors radiating through the gray sky.

"Hey look, it's twilight. That's really something with all the colors in the sky. I was reading up on Earth a few days ago and did you know they had all these different names for the solar and lunar cycles?"

I wonder if this is going to be any indication of our lives from here on out. There's a level of indifference washing over my body that I'm not entirely sure I'm comfortable with. Seven kills in a matter of minutes. These poor, defenseless creatures that ended up being the last of their kind. We just caused a species to go extinct and you know what? Looking at the bodies, I really don't give a shit. I just tilt my head to the side and think of how the blonde one fell at an odd angle compared to the others. Is that sick? I think that's sick. Is this what I have to look forward to?

"Like it wasn't just night *and* day." Holy shit he's still talking. "There's the twilight, then there could be a new moon, that's when it doesn't even show in the sky. Or an eclipse, that's when the sun gets blocked by another planet in the system."

By the High Order I hope I become more oblivious to his rambling over time, "Shut up."

"And sometimes when the sun comes up they called it breaking dawn. How funny is that? Like the sun or the sky is broken or something."

"Just...shut up, Bill." I tap my comms earpiece. "Mike, we're ready for exfil. All alien life eliminated. Over."

Chapter 19: A Blind Bet

3.01 - 2468 - 1940.186 Red Galaxy Standard

A deafening thud echoes through the facility from the entranceway to our rear, and Captain Hoffman's eyes grow wide on the monitor. Lieutenant Mackelson runs up from behind and nearly knocks me over in the process.

"I thought you took care of it," the captain questions over my shoulder.

"I did," Lieutenant Mackelson insists, "but it won't hold forever. We need to move. *Now*." He jumps over to Kelly's monitor. "Make sure everything's clean."

"Of course."

"What's going on?" I demand.

Captain Hoffman tries to explain while Kelly and Lieutenant Mackelson are rushing through the screens in front of them, "Well, this involved a lot of moving parts and the most important part of all was making sure we got you and your brother informed as quickly as possible." Another thud echoes through the halls. "We had to make sure..." then another.

"Short version!" Aden scolds, rushing over behind me.

Captain Hoffman's gaze turns apologetic. It's the first time I've seen the old man look sorry and it's unnerving given the ominous noise thundering through the halls.

"The Plaguers don't know that we let them in."

"Come again?" I ask. Another thud, louder this time.

Lieutenant Mackelson answers over his shoulder while pulling up security feeds on the screen to the left of Kelly's. "The Plaguers don't know we're helping them. They think we came to take 'em out, so now they're trying to prevent that from happening." Aden glances at me as I turn back to Captain Hoffman. Another thud; it sounds like the massive front door to the facility is beginning to crack which would take an enormous amount of strength seeing as it's comprised of metal and stone.

I fume at the screen, clenching my fingers into fists while I speak, "Your plan is to arm the Plaguers in order to help us take down the Hemos, but you haven't secured their support by explaining what you're doing?"

"Lieutenant Mackelson is taking a proactive approach in setting up communication with the Plaguers, but we couldn't ignore their threat to the Red Galaxy and raise eyebrows. We didn't have time...." Other thuds echo and the cracking noise almost drowns out the low boom of whatever's hitting the door.

Lieutenant Mackelson stops what he's doing and turns around to face us, cutting off Captain Hoffman in the process. "Look, we made a blind bet and if it doesn't work out, that's really going to suck, but right now, we need to get the fuck out of here." He points back to the security feeds, "You can track their movements from that terminal. You need to hold them off while I get back to the SWIFT."

As I follow the lieutenant's arm to the video feeds, I realize that his left bicep looks slightly bigger than the right one. Before I have a chance to ask about it, I hear the door to the facility crash open as echoing sounds of stone and metal bounce down the walls.

"I'll be on comms!" he exclaims, dashing out the door where Aden and I came in. He may be an asshole, but he's all business when it's necessary. It's funny how similar his use of rage is to Aden's comedy when there's no need to focus. Turn up the heat though and they both become calm, collected professionals, ready to do whatever needs to be done. If nothing else, he'll have my respect for that alone.

I can hear the Plaguers' horrific, shrieking growls as they rush through the halls trying to locate us. Aden jumps over to the security screens, "Shit!"

"What do we got?" I ask, whipping out my Ka and locking it into place.

"We have *a lot* of company."

"Give me a number, Sergeant."

"Hundreds. The fuckers are gushing through the doors like water, running over each other and..." he pauses and leans in to squint at the feed, "they're climbing on the fucking walls and ceiling."

"That's new," Captain Hoffman says. "Kelly, make sure to record the feeds."

"On it," she replies, "but we need to get off this transmission, the virus I installed can only veil so much from any possible prying eyes."

Captain Hoffman nods at Kelly's video on his desk, then looks up at me. "We'll be watching. Get out of there and make it back in one piece. We need you." His screen goes black.

"Aden," Kelly beckons. He turns from the security monitor to look at her. "Be safe." She beams a beautifully radiant smile at him with a small hint of concern, then switches off.

Aden offers an optimistic smile at the blank screen then looks at the floor for a second before looking up at me. "Her smile's not as creepy now that I know she's a really hot chick." He turns back to the security screen. "A strong, intelligent, patient..." Aden's voice trails off and there's a look of longing on his face that I've never seen before. "Amazing..." his voice trails again. I give him a minute to see if anything surfaces from the past. Aden notices me watching and his eyes go wide before he recovers, "Amazingly hot chick. Shit man."

There's something else there, but Aden has to figure that out on his own. Besides, I've got my own shit to deal with and this isn't exactly the best time to stop and have a brotherly conversation on lost memories and love. "I'm happy for you. Let's just make it out of here so you can cash in on that smile." I activate the comm channel with Lieutenant Mackelson. "How much time do you need?"

"Five minutes," he hollers. I can hear the wind rushing past his mic in the background and almost jump back at the noise. The first damn mission and I'm already spoiled by our suits.

"Make it three," I counter.

"We're gonna have a hard time lasting one," Aden says, drawing his Ka and locking it into place. I pull out my pistol and he does the same. "We've got thirty seconds till they swarm through that door." He's referring to the one that Lieutenant Mackelson originally entered through, the one that leads to the front of the complex. "What's the plan?"

"Same as before. Funnel them into a tight spot and take them down. We'll go out the way we came in." I point to the door on our left. "Toss me your Ka." He does and at the same time I toss my pistol to his newly freed hand. "You go first. I'll stay low and hold them off with the Kas. You provide cover fire from behind as

234

we progress back up to the security walkway." I almost contemplate having Aden use our rifles, but the pistols will be much easier for him to maneuver given the situation.

Aden takes a moment to digest the plan and looks like he's going to complain about the fact that I'll be in front of him holding back the Plaguers, but he doesn't have a chance. Several of them streak past the doorway. Without saying a word, I motion to our left with my head and Aden runs toward the exit as quietly as possible. Unfortunately, it doesn't do much good. The second I reach the door I hear one of the Plaguers let out a scream at the entrance behind me. I turn in the doorway to see him glaring at me without lips as saliva gleams off his sharpened teeth. The commotion of his cohorts savagely barreling through the halls abruptly stops, only to be followed by their noisy change in direction. He lets out another scream and almost instantly a barrage of other Plaguers tear through the door, knocking him over and spreading across the floor and walls.

"LT!" Aden screams from behind me up the steps.

"MOVE!" I flick my wrists to unlock the Kas, allowing them to break apart into sections and flow like whips onto the ground. The nanoparticles that comprise them extend the newly flexible Kas out to a length of ten feet and I immediately flick them forward to take out the closest Plaguers. Eight of them go down between the two swings. I rotate, side step an attack, and launch several more of my own. As the Plaguers start to overwhelm the room, I turn and bound up the steps. We run through the maze of tight, raising corridors, making our way back to the security walkway on the top of the building.

At the last set of stairs, Aden takes a position forty feet above me and begins to rain lasers down the steps, missing my head and shoulders by inches. I can hear the Plaguers crash through the tunnel below and howl as the lasers explode upon impact. Pulling up a live feed of the area behind me on my visor, I abruptly stop, spin, and flick the Kas down the steps then watch as they sever a few heads and continue to split others Plaguers in half. Heads and torsos topple to the floor as fresh Plaguers rush over their fallen comrades. Aden keeps them at bay with the pistols long enough for me to assess the situation below. I can see limbs trying to continue the fight even though they're no longer attached to their owners. Interesting.

More Plaguers push through the mass of dead bodies and I snap back to life, turning and leaping up the steps as Aden rushes up to the door above us. Stopping ten feet in front of him, I turn and convert the Kas back down to four feet as they lock back into place beyond the grips. Aden starts to volley rounds down the stairs and I prepare my stance for the oncoming wave of bodies. I connect the base of the handles and the nanoparticles fuse together, providing me with a single weapon. A thin double-bladed sword with a single, two-handed handle in the center. The stairway is wide enough for me to use a variety of techniques to carve up the wave of Plaguers who haven't figured out that they're already dead. They can join the amassing pile of meat and bone beginning to clog the stairway below.

The first volunteer for my newly formed death stick to make it past Aden's fire gets four feet of nanosteel shoved through his abdomen. I bring my foot up to his chest and force him back down the steps, knocking aside dozens of Plaguers as he flies into the wall at the bottom. The second and third are taken out at the same time as I sweep the back end of the Ka across the front of me to the left and take their heads clean off. I continue to dodge and move, trading the front Ka with the rear in one continuous fluid motion as bodies start to build below. Aden ends twenty more in a matter of seconds and now they're having a hard time getting past the pile of dead.

"I'm on my way, boys. Where are you?" Lieutenant Mackelson triumphantly assures through our comm with the loud noise of the SWIFT engines tearing through the background.

"Went out the same way we came in. Which way are you coming from?"

"South."

"Great." I slice open another couple of Plaguers and cast a few others down the stairs. "Come at GHC. When you're a half a mile out fly vertically and then hit the thrusters on my mark."

"Roger."

Need that door open? - K illuminates across the top of my visor and I nod. The door behind Aden slides open.

"Cover fire!" I turn and run toward Aden, who continues to fire until I'm five feet away. Then he turns himself and leaps out the door. With Plaguers on my heels, I vault through behind him to hear the door slam shut and a howl of pain pierce the air as I hit the ground. Aden's laying on the walkway to my left and nods to the door. I turn back to see the upper half of a Plaguer laying on the ground flailing its arms about, with a stream of blood leading back to the side of the doorway.

"Ew," Aden groans.

Pointing past Aden to the SWIFT in the distance I shout, "There's our ride, let's go!" The SWIFT banks up exposing its underside.

Aden's face pops up on my visor. "Are you thinking what I think you're thinking?" I smirk. "Oh, shit." Plaguer screams echo through the valley and my visor lights up red to the sides and bottom warning me of incoming signals.

"Launch!" We leave the walkway as a slew of Plaguers land behind us. Several seconds later, we slam into the bottom of the SWIFT, and the setule feature allows our suits to lock onto the outer hull. Just like at the cliff, we activate the kinetic barriers before a few Plaguers hit our backs and they bounce off, falling to the valley below.

"Hit it!" I scream to Lieutenant Mackelson.

The thrusters kick in and our bodies jerk down momentarily as we shoot into the sky, still attached to the SWIFT. I look down to see a dozen other Plaguers fly by beneath us, then turn to look at Aden who's doing the same.

He looks up at me and laughs, "Holy shit."

"Lieutenant, pull just below the outer atmosphere and let us in."

I inhale deeply. For a moment I don't breathe. I hold it all in and just when it feels like my chest is going to burst, I let the recycled air escape my lungs get sucked back into my helmet's filter. My chest moves up and down at an increased pace to make up for the momentary lack of oxygen. It feels like I'm starting life over, like I'm seeing the universe for the first time.

Looking to the stars above, the shimmering light reminds me of the reflective gleams that could be seen on the outside of Aden's suit the first time he activated it yesterday. It's only been a day and so much has changed...everything has changed. I used to be a soldier following orders, now I'm one of five individuals who are the last remaining members of a previously extinct species. The life I knew, hundreds of years, was a lie all along, and the people I swore to protect are looking to wipe out every other lifeform in the universe. We're outmanned, outgunned, and overwhelmed in every possible way.

There's only one thing that hasn't changed. Aden's my brother and like these new suits, he's a part of me. Whatever comes next, we'll tackle it together. That's all that matters to me now.

Chapter 20: Hurry Up and Wait.

07.15 - 2139 - 564.029 Red Galaxy Standard

"This is hands down *thee* most boring op we've ever been on!" Bill groans loud enough for any creature within a mile radius to hear.

"Shut the hell up!" I hiss through my teeth. "We're on a recon mission and you're going to..."

"Blow our cover?" he asks stalely. "We've been posted in this spot for ten...days. TEN DAYS!" Okay, Bill tends to get a little cranky when he doesn't eat for a while, even though we can survive for months at a time without a fresh intake of blood. It's too bad we don't have anything convenient to take on mission with us. I want to be angry at him, I want to reprimand him for speaking so loudly on a recon mission, but part of me agrees. This is ridiculous.

"Look, just calm down, okay? We've had a nice bit of action for the last nine years or so, but getting a mission like this isn't necessarily a bad thing." I sit up and lean against the rock to my left, Bills squints at me for a second, tapping the side of his rifle and trying to figure out whether or not I'm tricking him into disobeying an order. "Sit up, I don't care what the pre-op protocol said. I'm tired of lying here, too." He re-adjusts his pack, sits up, leans against the rock across from me, pulls his knees up and lays the rifle in his lap.

Our first mission after the rehab nineteen years ago was pretty easy and, even though the following years weren't too crazy, the High Order kept us busy. Everything was pretty routine, a lot of recon ops with the occasional assassination, or prevention of assassination. While it was all fairly straight forward, those first ten years were by the numbers. We got into a routine and became more connected than any other recon team out there. It didn't take long before Captain Otto upgraded us back to Alpha status. Then the Feeleye war flared up.

High scientists had been experimenting with the last remaining humans from the Bloodwar of 2106. They essentially bred a small society of humans on a distant planet in the Cruciatus solar system at the far end of the Red galaxy specifically for genetic testing, trying to figure out a way to synthesize their blood, making it easier for us to feed. Of course, they hadn't figured anything out yet, and we're technically not supposed to know any of it, but it's good to have an inside track into these types of things. Problem is, the planet they chose to breed the humans on was already inhabited by the species known as the Feeleye.

They had similar physiology, but were thin and muscular with the ability to switch between running on all fours and standing whenever they felt the need. It provided them with more agility overall; quicker on land and more nimble on the trees and mountains, especially since their fingers and toes had hooked nails that allowed them to climb most natural surfaces with ease. Their increased ocular structure allowed for greater vision during the day and night. The war should've lasted a few years, but given the fact that they had grown accustomed to the planet and the terrain, it took nearly a decade. It was more of a nuisance than anything.

"Have you heard any more from *Vali*?" Bill asks snidely.

"I really don't understand what your problem is. He's saved our asses on a number of occasions." Time and time again, Vali has come through for us on missions. I was a little skeptical at first when Red told us to make contact, but he's already saved our lives more times than I can count. In the beginning of the Feeleye war the intelligence was spotty at best. Communication was horrible and the new tech that they sent us into battle with was constantly failing. We lost a lot of great men the first year, and Vali's constant stream of information is the only reason we survived.

The High Scientists finally got their shit together and developed an experimental research division to close the gap between lab and combat. Because of our survival rate, Bill and I were selected to test the new gear in battle, the first of which was armor. It's the same suit we're wearing today. They figured out a way to make the grecene under weave denser, then used it to sew together small grecanium alloy plates that cover our entire body. The whole suit is specifically designed to shrink to a predetermined size—five percent smaller than the user's body—when a small current is fed into the straps, which then tighten. The constriction of the muscles offers greater performance and strength at a considerable increase to the grecene under weave and grecanium pads we had previously been wearing. The design of the weave also allows for increased distribution of force upon impact, so instead of a bullet feeling like a full on smack from a crowbar, it feels like normal punch. At the same time, the material is much more durable and holds up under repeated battles after being hit multiple times. These new suits can take over a hundred hits before having to be replaced, whereas the old ones could only take fifteen at most. After the first year of testing and computing data, the High Scientists determined that they increased our survival rate by two hundred and fifty percent in battle. I don't know if the numbers are true, but I'll take it.

"It's the smiley thing again, isn't it? I don't know why you make such a big deal out of it," I scoff while waving a hand in his direction.

Bill purses his eyebrows and twists his lips in disgust. "Well...he doesn't do it to you, of course you don't." Shaking his head, he sets the pointer finger from his left hand on his forehead and runs his thumb and middle finger down the inside of his eyes a few times. "It's just creepy, man." He gives up, letting the left hand fall to his knee.

"That aside, he did pass along a rumor," I offer. Bill straightens his back and perks up his eyebrows. "Apparently, Alexander is working on a new suit." That makes him smile.

"It's about damn time! These things are so uncomfortable, especially around the creases. They definitely didn't think of..." he adjusts his hips and pulls at the portion of the suit in front of his crotch. "Well you know." Straightening out each leg, he takes the time to stretch and contract the muscles, then pulls them back up into the same position.

"Yeah well, there are rumors circulating the ship that Alexander's a eunuch. So maybe he just didn't think of it." I look out to the west, left of my location, at the vast, lush valley of blue ferns, then down to my scanner. Still quiet.

"Oh, man." Bill squints and sucks in his lips, looking like he just bit down on a Klydarian sour horn fruit. "That would suck. But you know," he glances up to the sky, mulling the topic over as he speaks, "it kind of makes sense with how much time they spend in the lab, remove temptation and all that." Looking back down at his rifle, Bill starts checking the firing mechanism to make sure everything's in working order, even though he's already done it three times since we've been here.

"How's uh," Bill keeps cleaning rifle, "How's *your* situation...fairing?" I inquire. He stops and looks up as I nod down at his gun...the one below his rifle.

244

With a shrug, he goes back to cleaning the actual rifle. "Eh, I don't know what it is." He stops to flick a little eight-legged bug off the end of the barrel, then drops his arms to the ground letting the rifle balance on his knees before looking up. "It's weird, you know? Have you ever had something with a female, something...special?"

Bill and I had some R-and-R before the Feeleye war and kind of made it an unspoken rule not to spend time together off mission. Our rec time was so precious and we spent so much time together that we would just split and do our own thing whenever possible. We don't pry into each other's business. If it wasn't mentioned previously then we don't ask and we don't dig if the other one doesn't want to talk about it. That being said, it doesn't really matter, we pretty much tell each other everything anyway.

"A few little trysts here and there over the years." I start chuckling, "That one chick, remember? The uh, the singer who was into feet."

He starts laughing, "Really, you?"

"Yeah well, it was short-lived. No matter how hot she was, the feet thing became weird quick. Obviously, I don't remember from before...you know." Of course there's Blaze as well, but he doesn't need to know about that. Blaze and I both agreed when we started fooling around that it would be kept between us. Seeing as how much time we spend apart and the odds that we may never come back from a mission, we didn't see the need to get too serious about it. We also didn't see the need to hear everyone else's opinions on the subject. The life of an Alpha isn't exactly built to allow for normal relationships. We enjoy being around each other, and that's hard enough to find in this universe.

He laughs and then exhales, "Yeah. Well, I don't know, whenever I try I just, I get this anxiety in my chest, I start to feel guilty. I don't remember ever having something committed, but when I go to...I just feel like I'm doing something wrong for some reason, and I can't. Makes me wonder if I had someone before the whole amnesia thing. Maybe a female that no one else knew about." He slowly shakes his head, then starts to clean the weapon again.

Unsure of what to say, seeing as I don't really have any experience in relationships that I can recall, or advice to offer on faulty male equipment, I check the scanner again, then the horizon. "Huh, that's weird."

"What?"

"I'm not getting any readings."

"Okay, why is that weird? We've been here for ten days with no readings."

"Which is fine," I point to the horizon on my left, "but what's that?" Bill raises his head and follows my arm, looking past the never-ending field of blue ferns, out to where air meets earth. Where the deep red sky and the blue plants meld into some sort of purple haze, there's a thick fuzzy black line in the distance that encompasses the whole horizon.

"That *is* weird." He squints, then pulls the rifle off his knees and holds his right arm out like a platform to steady the gun as he stares through the scope. "It looks like it's moving. Hmmm. I don't know why it would be dark, but, some kind of incalescence from the midday sun reflecting off the surface?"

I look up at the bright blue and white sun, then back down to the horizon. "Can't be. We've been here for ten days and haven't seen it the whole time. It was definitely hotter yesterday."

He continues to stare through the scope with his right eye, keeping the left closed. "Maybe the heat from the sun is interacting with some expulsion from the local plant life and it only happens every so often, or what about some kind of natural phenomenon?"

"Possible, I guess. Keep an eye on it for a sec, I'll ping Vali." Looking down at the VOK unit on my wrist, I tap out Vali's secure cloud address. He answers immediately.

What's up?

Black haze on the horizon, haven't seen it before. Are there any recorded natural phenomenon or meteorological activity that might cause it?

Hold... The three periods blink out in succession, then back on as I wait. *Nothing recorded. What about your objective?*

Still not spotted.

You misunderstand. There's a slight pause between transmissions. *What if that's your objective?*

There's a sudden realization of our insignificance in the universe as Vali's suggestion causes me to stop breathing. Sounds fade, but I can tell that Bill's trying to speak to me, only his voice is drowned out by the stark understanding that we're in a lot of trouble.

"LT? LT?" Ambient sound and air begin to flow again, slow at first, then fast as my heart starts pumping way past its normal operating rate. I look up and Bill's eyes which are fixed on me. "What's wrong? What'd Vee say?"

Scrambling to a knee, I grab my rifle and point it at the horizon, staring at the black mass through my scope; it's gotten considerably larger. "Oh, shit."

"What?"

"Look closer."

Bill pulls the rifle back up and shoves his eye to the edge of the scope. The darkness is slowly increasing in size, and I'm assuming he sees what I see, because he murmurs, "Oh, shit," as well.

The darkness we see is a mixture of shadow and black dirt being kicked into the air. The mass moving toward us is the very thing that we've been sent to find, record, and bring back, given the chance. A large nomadic species that travels in herds. Only it's not one, it's tens of thousands, possibly more, running at us full speed in some kind of a stampede.

"They're gaining ground quick."

"Yep," I acknowledge, standing up.

"What are we doing?" he asks nervously.

I look around for some cover or escape plan, but the field of blue ferns stretch out for miles and the only thing within sight, outside of the herd heading toward us, is the two Hemo-sized rocks we were sitting against. Judging by the size of these beasts and how small the rocks are, we won't last long huddled behind them. "Working on it." Transport's too far away, we're fast but can't outrun them for long given the speed at which they're gaining ground. Going east or west is out of the question since they encompass the whole horizon, spreading farther out as they get closer. Looking down at the rock to my left, I get an idea.

"Get on the other side of the rock." I point to the one behind me that Bill was leaning up against.

"Not gonna do much good on this side," he barks over his shoulder, following the order regardless.

"I know." Pulling a grenade off my chest, I spin the center ring around until the red dot lines up with the ones on the top and bottom portion, then quickly place the grenade just behind the rock and face the three red dots toward the ground. As I jump toward Bill, the grenade goes off, shooting a cloud of black dirt into the air. Our grenades can double as directional proximity mines and are designed to penetrate thick walls and doors.

I leap up to see a deep hole in the ground four feet wide by ten foot long and rush over to the edge. "Let's go!" I wave to Bill, looking out at the creatures who are now gaining ground at an incredible speed. The 'cloud' of creatures appears to be at least twenty feet tall and I can start to make out heads and limbs. They'll be here any second. Bill hops over the rock, rips off his pack, tosses it in the hole, then presses his hands to his sides and jumps in. He disappears into the darkness and I follow immediately after.

I land sooner than expected and would have preferred a little more space between us and the stampede. The soil must be pretty dense as the directional grenade only created a hole about ten feet deep. As I land at the bottom, the light from above is obscured by hulking massive bodies, and limbs that are kicking dirt down onto our heads. The creatures grunt and squeal as they fly past above, with one in five or so tripping on the edge of the boulders above.

After an hour of being squeezed into the small hole, with no signs of the stampede letting up anytime soon, Bill leans over to me and yells, "At least we're not laying down anymore!" then smirks. I guess it's all about the outlook.

Chapter 21: The Never-Ending Day

3.04 - 2468 - 203.115 Red Galaxy Standard

My bunk on the Patriarch isn't a rock, it's not hard packed soil, or even a muddy clay river bed. For most people that would be a good thing, but with the amount of time we spend in the field, it's way too soft for me get any quality sleep. I stare at the cold gray ceiling above with my legs crossed and bounce my foot out of a mixture of boredom and contemplative curiosity. We made it back to the ship a little over twelve hours ago and Captain Otto aka Hoffman suggested that we all take some time to let the gravity of the situation set in. Luckily, our little stunt at GHC put the Plaguers on guard and when Major Erislad sent an entire company down to re-secure the building, they fled back to the edges of the galaxy with all the gear they had stolen. For once, we've been blessed with the gift of time; time to figure out what our next move is and time to figure out how we plan on securing the allegiance of the Plaguers.

At least that's what Captain Hoffman said. I think he's more concerned about letting me and Aden really truly accept our new situation. We're all on the same side and this is the right course of action, given what the Hemos have done and who they've become; a ruthless virus spreading throughout the galaxy, attempting to wipe out any species that stands in their way.

The more I think about what we're trying to do, the more it makes sense. It's been hard for me to look at the Hemo culture objectively all of these years. I woke up in a hospital bed and was trained to be a killer from day one. I was told about our so-called race and never had a reason to question it because it was all I knew. Granted, it was all part of Red and Captain Hoffman's master plan to give us a flawless undercover identity, which is great, but at the same time it makes the current acceptance very difficult for me, regardless of how it instinctively makes sense.

Then there's Blaze. We promised each other that we'd never let things get serious, because even though we're the best in the universe, any day could be our last. We were just having fun and blowing off steam and even though we've never openly talked about it, things have become so much more complicated than that. I feel as though I've almost thought of her the last few days more than the Hemo situation. I love her, that's set in stone. It'll never change, even though it was never meant to happen.

I finally stop bouncing my foot and activate the helmet and visor on my suit. I need to get my mind off Blaze. Kelly sent us a bunch of detailed intelligence files that she had recorded and kept safe over the years. It's not a complete history of who we were as humans, but gives us an idea based off of her time with us in the field. I've been reading through them little by little over the past twelve hours. Pulling up the file on myself, I start to read one of her assessments.

Daemon and his brother are invaluable to our team and, for that matter, the survival of the human race as a whole. Upon learning of these two civilian soldiers and the recon operations they had started on their own accord, I immediately suggested to Captain Hoffman that we pull them into the fold. At the time, the captain was unaware of my involvement with the informant Red. Red had been trying to find a way to teach us how to fight back without involving the military, as it would likely end badly for not only himself, but for us as well. We, as humans, have a habit of fearing what we don't know, and Red and I were both concerned that they would attempt to capture and interrogate him upon his immediate discovery. Even though it was unlikely that they would succeed, it was very likely that the Hemos would have found out about his treachery in the process, and we couldn't allow that to happen.

Daemon and Aden's parents had rushed out to meet them when the emergency situation was declared in San Diego, but their flight was taken down by a Hemo operative before it was able to land. The event crippled both Daemon and Aden. The only saving grace was the trust they put in each other and what started out as intelligence-gathering turned into a vendetta to kill as many Hemos as they could. Upon realizing that they were outnumbered and overwhelmed by the Hemo presence, they decided to put their trust in Red, who approached them after I made him aware of their situation and drive. They were hesitant at first, but he offered information that no one else could at the time...a way to kill their enemies.

Captain Hoffman had a difficult time accepting the fact that a band of civilians led by two sarcastic brothers was the only shot we had at fighting back and that for all his power and command, the military hadn't been able to learn anything of worth. It took some time, weeks in fact, but the Captain came around to how valuable they truly were. Their experience in the field, due to Red's information, allowed them to train our soldiers and begin to push the threat back, although it came at great costs.

I kept the information on my visor, but receded into my head and contemplated what she wrote. We fought for our parents and what the Hemos took from us. I don't know if I'm more annoyed by the fact that I can't remember what it feels like to lose them, or that I'm glad I can't. Even before I found out who Aden really was to me, I couldn't see living my life without that sarcastic little shit by my side. We've been to hell and back together and I honestly don't know what I would do if he was killed, and that scares me. I can only imagine what it would feel like if the people who bore and raised me were unexpectedly cut from my life.

I'm fed up with sitting in my room with all this shit going through my head alone. Aden and I have a boundaries thing when we're off mission, but I need to talk to someone about this. While swinging my legs over the bunk, I disengage my helmet and hop down to the ground. As I walk through the halls of the living quarters, I wonder how Aden's dealing with the whole situation. He's never been one to dwell on his feelings, at least as long as I've known him, but a lot has changed in the last few days.

A couple minutes later, I'm in front of his room and press the white holographic call button to the right of his dark gray door. The holographic outline turns blue as I press it. All of the rooms are soundproof to help the soldiers sleep through the loud noises of the ship and its crew. If the button is red, the room is unoccupied, white occupied, and blue confirms the transmission of the alarm. There's also green, which allows the person to speak through the intercom system, but people rarely use it.

The door slides partially open and Aden thrusts his sweaty head through the opening, staring at me with wide, frustrated eyes blocking the entrance with his body. I look down to see that he's naked, with the exception of the combat suit's belt that's securely wrapped around his waist. "Hey buddy, what's up?" he asks, grinning at me.

Closing my eyes for a second, I shake my head and try to rid my mind of the image that I just saw. "What the hell are you doing?" I open my eyes to see a flash of pale flesh from over his shoulder and part of what looks like a nipple.

"I uhh…" he gawps, trying to come up with a reasonable lie.

"Hello, Vee," I offer over Aden's stumbling of words. He stops and purses his lips together then glances to the left, then right, waiting for a break in the awkward silence of Kelly trying to figure out whether or not she's going to respond.

"Hello, LT," she finally replies meekly, out of view behind Aden.

I look back at Aden, who smirks and confirms the obvious with a slight nod of his head. "We uh, had a lot of catching up to do," he explains.

As I wave a hand to stop him from speaking, he chuckles while I start walking away. I stop ten feet from his door and shout over my shoulder, "Never answer the door like that again!" The door slides shut behind me and the corridor is dead silent once again. I can't express how glad I am that the rooms are soundproof.

Good for him. While I'm trying to figure out all that I can about our past lives and who we were, he's living a piece of it with someone who meant something to him. I could tell by the look on his face that he was happy, and it wasn't just because of the sex. He's always had a problem connecting with women, even though having the time to try was sparse for us. They were either too focused on their career and viewed him as a childish soldier or used him only to throw him out when they were done. None of them had the chance to see past his playful sarcastic demeanor for who he really was. Now he has somebody who knows more about him than I do, or than he does himself for that matter. A smile creeps across my face as I walk down the hall, thinking about his companionship. It's nice to see a little bit of light in our new found darkness.

There's no way I'm going back to my room, I can't just sit there and read intel files on our history for another twelve hours. I can pore over hours of intel for a mission, but for some reason it's different when I'm looking at my own past life. I'm craving the truth, but at the same time finding it difficult to read through someone else's words. Maybe Red can offer me some more insight.

I turn the corner and look up to see Blaze walking toward me with a smirk on her face. "Hey." She stops a few feet in front of me and leans against the wall. "We just got back, I heard the captain gave you boys some time."

Shit. All I want to do is go back to bunk with her and get lost. I want to get out of my head and let her intoxicating scent envelope my body until nothing else matters, but I can't. I don't know where she stands. She's a Hemo. She's part of it all and I need to distance myself from that if I'm to stay focused and move forward.

I nervously chuckle. "Yeah, but Plaguers, still work." *That's not even a complete sentence. What the hell was that you idiot? Pull your head out of your ass.*

Blaze brushes the idiotic comment aside with a shake of her head. "All the more reason to take advantage of the time we have." She moves forward, seductively rotating her hips with each step. I'm a hip man, she knows this. "It's been way too long."

Fuck, now I'm starting to think about the last time we were together and I can't...damn it. I chuckle again, "Yeah, ha."

She doesn't even acknowledge how stupid I'm acting right now, so she must really want to fuck. She gets that way. "So your room?" She shrugs her shoulders and glances at the ceiling, "Or mine for that matter," before staring back into my eyes with unbridled lust. She's practically on top of me, her hand reaching for my belt.

"Yeah," I cough. "No, I mean." I set a hand on her wrist pushing it away from me. "I really need to talk to Red." That didn't help, she pushes her hand back and clamps down on my buckle. "I have to meet with Red and go over some intel, seriously." I clench my teeth behind pressed lips and push her hand back before walking around her and down the hall.

"Liam," she shouts from behind me. It's rare that she calls me by my first name. I stop at the corner and spin around hiding half of my body down the next hall. Her demeanor has changed. She's trying to hide it, but I can read the signs written all over her body. Confidence and persistence has turned to confusion and pain in rejection. "Are we..."

"Yeah, we're good. I just...we'll talk soon."

I disappear down the hall. After I'm out of earshot, I stop and take a good few minutes to slam my head against a wall while calling myself an idiot over and over. *We're good?* What the fuck was I thinking? Oh probably that I didn't know what else to say and I didn't want to hurt her just yet, you know, before we dismantle the entire race. Fuck me I'm stupid.

I arrive at Red's training bay, my mind still on the encounter with Blaze and push through the double doors with just enough force to cause them to swing open and touch the walls without an obnoxiously loud sound. To my dismay, Red is nowhere in sight and to make matters worse, Mike or as Captain Hoffman called him, Lieutenant Mackelson, is standing fifty yards inside the hangar engaged in holographic drone training. He blows the head off of a Thyr and its body falls to the ground, joining the twenty some other lifeless bodies that currently litter the area around him. With his back to me, Lieutenant Mackelson turns and looks over his left shoulder to see who entered.

"End session," he says coldly and with that, the bodies, blood, and weapons disappear. "What the fuck do you want, *LT?*" He's been bent out of shape ever since I questioned their…our…whole crusade at GHC.

I walk forward, weighing my options of just leaving and returning to my room, bored out of my mind, or trying to mend the burnt bridge between myself and the lieutenant without knowing why he hates me so much. "I was uh, looking for Red."

He reaches over his shoulder with his right hand and lets the Ka snap to the back of his suit, then takes the pistol in his left hand and sets it on his thigh where it stays. "He's with Captain Otto. Trying to figure out what our next move is, given that the Plaguers have pulled back." I continue walking forward and try to get a good look at his arms to see if they're still different sizes. They appear to be even again, but I can swear they're bigger than they used to be. He turns around to face me, "Anything else?"

Inhaling deeply, I try to figure out what to say before stopping a few feet in front of him. "Look, I, uh," I look down at the ground in an attempt to swallow my pride, "I shouldn't have said what I did back at GHC about it being pointless and all." I raise my head back up and apologetically stare into his dark eyes.

There's a palpable bitterness as he stares back with that cold, dead, blackness from the dark places that soldiers never talk about. "Fuck you," he finally states, raising his eyebrows and slightly bouncing his head in acknowledgment.

I don't know if it has to do with the fact that I'm still coming to grips with the entire situation or that I don't have Aden around to help control my anger, or that I'm just sexually frustrated and worry that things will never be the same with Blaze again, but as soon as he says those two words, my blood begins to boil. My skin, which is supposed to be regulated by my suit, feels hot and there's this burning pit of hatred that's churning in my stomach. No matter how hard I try to quell the anger brewing inside, I can't, and it's not long before it explodes in the form of a well-placed jab to the lieutenant's jaw, knocking him back ten feet before he falls on his ass. Luckily, he's wearing the combat suit that Aden and I used to use and the helmet's on or I would have shattered his jaw from the raw power of my new scaled suit.

As I stand there with the muscles of my arms clenched and my fists out to either side of my body, he shakes his head quickly, then glares up at me. Doing a kip-up to get back on his feet, he bolts forward as I activate my helmet and lower into a defensive stance. Here's hoping I don't kill him.

Chapter 22: Mini My Ass

08.20 - 2139 - 599.029 Red Galaxy Standard

It's been a while since Bill and I have been down to Alexander's lab. Supposedly they've been working on a bunch of new tech for us to take into the field, including new suits, though it's been over five years since they've finalized anything. Not really a significant amount of time, but for a while there they were churning out tech left and right. It seemed like every time we came back from a mission they were giving us something new to try in the field. Hell one point, they were flying it into the mission on drops ships. I know you're busy, but put this new, ridiculous, untested piece of tech through the paces would you? Give me a break.

Honestly, I don't really care that we haven't been to his lab in a while. Alexander's okay, he just creeps me out a little. He has this weird way of dealing with people, as if nobody can ever fully understand what he's trying to say. So he'll stare at you like you're too stupid for any of it to sink in. It's a little annoying.

I round the last corner before the lab with my eyes to the ground, thinking about the creature that we just spent the last few days hauling up to the ship. To my surprise, Bill's leaning against the doorway that leads into the lab. "Look at you. All on time and shit." I'm surprised that he's here at all.

"Look at *you*," he fires back. "Basically have a fucking hop in your step. Something light a fire under your ass?"

"I don't know what you're talking about." I do. We had a little time after the mission and Blaze just so happened to have a free hour before heading out to her next assignment. It was cutting it close, but we managed to give each other a few new bruises.

"What is it called when something lights on fire, and it's burning really fiercely," Bill closes his eyes and looks at the ceiling as if the word is just on the tip of his tongue. "I feel like it as starts with a B as well, just like burning, but more, like a wildfire...like if a regular fire had *hormones* and was raging!" With 'hormones' Bill eyes shot open and he stared at me with that dumb little smirk of his, that, I know your secret smirk that I just can't stand.

"Drop it. Besides annoying me, what the fuck are you doing here?" I say quickly in an attempt to get him to change the subject. Luckily he does.

Bill cocks his head, "Oh, come on. The amount of trouble it took to haul that annoying piece of shit up here after laying around for ten straight days, you don't think I'm gonna want to hear what Alexander found out?"

Leaning against the door frame across from Bill, I offer a look of shock. "It's just that you've never really been one to care about education before."

"Education? Shit, I just want to learn how to kill the sonuvabitch in case we find ourselves in another stampede." Bill slams his palm into the touchscreen to his right. The door, which slides open, disappears into the wall next to me. He essentially leaps into the room with enthusiasm.

"Yup, there it is," I say under my breath, following close behind.

As we enter Alexander's lab something feels off, but I can't pinpoint what it is. All I can do is stare at the hulking monster secured by massive chains that penetrate the floor, fifty yards in front of us. It seems so much larger in a confined space. The creature is kneeling and still looks to be about twenty-five feet tall. Head hung low between its massive shoulders, I follow the arms down to the overly large hands which are formed into fists with the knuckles pressed into the ground. The skin is a leathery dark gray and appears to have patches of toughened scales that slide between each other over the joints and creased sections of skin. It reminds me of a holo report I read about some creatures on Earth called reptiles. They had toughened scales all over their body to protect their organs and they would overlap to allow for movement. Only with these creatures, the scales didn't cover the entire body, just certain points. While the limbs are overly large in a muscular way, the stomach is bulbous to the point of being out of place with the rest of the body. It's breathing at an increased rate and as we get a few steps into the door, it inhales deeply and looks up at us.

The eyes are small, black, and set just above a wide mouth that stretches to either side of its face. There's a bone-like structure that spans the top of its bald head and extends out several feet on either side. The creature either has enough mental capacity to remember that we were the ones who captured it, or is just threatened by the fact that we entered the room. It roars, baring large, sharp, onyx teeth and spitting phlegm all over the lab in the process. The sound is deafening and continues for ten seconds as its muscles tense and it lurches forward. Bill and I stop in our tracks and lower into a defense flight stance out of instinct before seeing the chains tighten around the wrists and neck. Electricity surges through the restraints and the beast's pitch increases with pain as it falls back, lowers to its knees, then finally quiets, dropping its head back to the floor.

"Don't worry," Alexander says, fifteen feet in front of us, standing over a desk to our left. "Those chains are made from a synthesized Osmium alloy and held together with a magno-electric current tied to the ship's core. The harder it pulls, the more electricity, the stronger the chains become." He turns around to face us. "It's unbreakable." Alexander's eyes are stark white and I must have made a weird face upon seeing them. "Oh come now, they're just eyes."

We walk up to Alexander. "Okay, first things first," I assert, raising a finger. "What the hell is the deal with your eyes?"

"Ocular injection for increased vision. Irises are removed and the inner retina is dyed in order to allow for maximum absorption of surrounding light."

Bill inhales sharply and I squint at the flat white spheres staring back at me. He looks like a shadow of his former self, almost dead. "That sounds like it hurts."

"Immensely," he replies without hesitation, "but that's not why you're here." Sticking his left arm out toward the creature he says, "Your quarry," then begins to walk toward it.

"I'm good, uh..." I look at Bill who's nodding in agreement.

"Come now, don't be afraid you two, it's perfectly safe." Alexander waves a hand for us to follow. I sigh, Bill shrugs, and we both jog to catch up.

With the initial shock of seeing the creature subsiding, I realize what seems off about the lab. "Did your lab get bigger?" I ask, slowing down to Alexander's pace as we come up behind him.

"Yes. We knocked down several other labs to extend them into one large open lab and test facility. We now have two hundred yards of open space in front of us instead of seventy-five."

"What the hell do you need that much space for?" Bill asks.

Alexander glances back, "Oh, we've got a few things in the pipeline." He turns back to the creature. "But enough about that, onto the catch of the day! Behold the Diakaiju, or as I like to call it, the Mini-K."

"There's nothing mini about that thing," Bill scoffs.

"It is compared to some rumored prophecies of man." Bill and I look at each other in disbelief. I wouldn't want to stumble across whatever makes this thing look small. "Anyways, we've learned a lot in the few days that we've had this little guy strapped up. The skin is excessively tough, making it difficult to breach with traditional weapons. Their olfactory cavities are internally larger, much like ours. That's why it roared when you entered, it could smell a new presence in the room. This seems to make up for how small their eyes are and in turn how weak their vision is. They're carnivorous, judging from the shape of their teeth and the contents in its stomach that we forced out."

"Forced out?" I ask.

"Yes. A well placed, sharpened electrified Osmium-E rod to the stomach."

"You forced it to hurl, then rummaged through the aftermath?" Bill asked, clearly disgusted by the thought.

"Anyways," Alexander continues. "We also learned from scans that the creature is harboring offspring."

"Why didn't you just scan the stomach contents instead of making it throw up?" Bill presses.

Alexander and I both ignore him. "It's a she and she's pregnant?" I ask.

"Well, technically, no. It's asexual. This particular creature is carrying three separate litters which are all at a different stage of development, for a total of twelve unborn."

"How bad did it smell? I can only imagine what it would be like to sift through all that upchuck."

Alexander and I stop walking and turn to stare at Bill.

"Fine! Fine, I'm done." We continue staring. "Seriously! I'm done, just...go back to your boring nature segment."

Alexander shakes his head and turns to me, "Bottom line is," he motions to the creature on his left, which is now only about thirty feet away from us, "they're extremely resilient and reproduce quickly. That, coupled with their size makes them a pretty big nuisance in the grand scheme of things. Your report says that the stampede lasted for hours?"

"Yes, it did. Which reminds me, that many creatures? Why didn't they show up on our scans, or to our equipment on the ground?"

"Well, they're warm blooded, but we think that the thickness of their skin blocks them from our scanners. We're looking into it. We still have a lot of testing to do."

With a nod, I turn to my right, face the creature, and walk a couple steps closer to get a good look.

"How do we kill it?" Bill asks.

"Well, that's one of the things we're trying to find out, but we think it has a fairly similar brain and nervous system to our own. Cripple one or several major organs and it should go down."

"Doesn't look like our rounds will penetrate this skin." I muse while pointing at the hardened sections.

"They won't," Alexander affirms. "That's the other reason I asked you down." He taps me on the shoulder and I turn to see him motioning us back toward the door. "Come with me."

At the command desk near the door, Alexander's assistant has laid out four new firearms for us to test. Two rifles and two pistols.

"Now you're talking!" Bill beams, running over to the desk. "What are these?" he asks, picking up a small metallic disk sitting next to one of the rifles. At a quarter the size of a thumbnail, he pulls it close to his eyes and squints to get a better view.

Alexander snatches it from his fingers while walking past. "That is your new ammunition. Osmium-E."

"Just like the chains?" Bill points back to the creature.

Alexander stops at the end of the desk and turns to look at Bill with surprise. "Have you actually been paying attention for once?"

"Been paying attention to how boring you are," Bill mutters as he picks up the rifle.

Alexander sighs. "Yes, like the chains. Osmium is the densest naturally occurring element on Earth and upon taking control of the planet, we were able to strip mine enough of it to figure out a way to synthesize and improve it. Hence the E, for enhanced." He picks up the other rifle on the table. "These weapons superheat the rounds, which takes a great deal of energy, then fires them out of the barrel at an astonishing twenty-thousand feet per second. As the round flies through the air, it heats further and, upon hitting its mark, spatters into hundreds, at times thousands, of molten drops that tear through the target."

Alexander looks like he has more to say, but is abruptly cut off by Bill's rifle fire. Following the barrel of the rifle, I just barely catch a small outer section of the Mini K's left shoulder explode into a red mist which causes the creature to throw its head back and roar at the ceiling.

Bill spins around with a smile on his face. "Well good news, it works!"

Chapter 23: Realization

3.04 - 2468 - 299.205 Red Galaxy Standard

    There's no reason this should be happening. Not like this, at least. Lieutenant Mackelson didn't hesitate to charge after the cold cock to his jaw caused him to fly back on his ass. He had it coming. Hell, even before this whole realization of who he actually was and putting a gun to my head at GHC, he always had a little attitude in everything that he did. I used to think that it was just friendly bullshit between soldiers, but now I can see that it wasn't.

    I'm on the ground as Lieutenant Mackelson reaches back for his third punch. The first two hits made the display in my visor twitch and readjust the output. That's something that didn't even happen after I ran into the rock face outside of GHC and I slammed into that thing with a shit ton of force. The blows that he's landing are too powerful, way more powerful than his older model combat suit should be putting out.

    I jerk my head to the right, dodging the third blow and let his fist slam into the floor below. A video feed pops up on the right side of my visor and shows his fist make cracks in the floor. He pulls it back and the nanoparticles in the floor repair the damaged section, making it appear as if nothing had happened. Repositioning my head catches him off guard and allows me to swing my left fist up and make contact with his temple. I don't hold back. A loud, deep crack echoes throughout the room when I make contact, causing his helmet to hiss out an electric fizzle as he tumbles off to my right.

Lieutenant Mackelson rolls twice before stopping on his stomach. Meanwhile, I roll backward, hop up to my feet, and raise my head in just enough time to see him doing the same. Damn, he's fast, faster than a mere pilot should be.

The entire right side of his helmet is cracked. He glares at me with furious anger, then glances to the crack in frustration and rips the helmet off, tossing it over his shoulder. A faint hiss rolls over his back as Lieutenant Mackelson disengages the combat suit from behind and begins to peel it from his shoulders. The suit conforms to the wearer, but for some reason his muscles seem to swell as he pulls it off and kicks it to the right. Standing there in a white, sleeveless muscle tee and a pair of black, tight fitting undershorts, his gaze lowers. "Come on, *Lieutenant*. Let's fight like real men," he growls, "if you can remember what that even means."

Rotating my jaw and flexing my facial muscles from the pain of his jabs, I imagine the suit dissipating back into the belt and it does just that. Then I undo the front and toss it off to the left, near Lieutenant Mackelson's suit on the floor. With the exception of my sleeveless tee being black, we're now equals. Though his whole body, the tone looks larger than it did at GHC which is odd. Regardless, it won't do him any good.

He rushes out of rage, crossing his right arm over and making contact with my left cheekbone. I stumble backward to my right knee as the blow reverberates through my entire body and pain shoots across my face. He strikes again in the same place, grabbing a section of the shirt over my chest with his other hand, and then again, raising the fist's contact point slightly to strike my eye socket.

Lieutenant Mackelson is looking to cash in on his fourth hit, but before he does, I catch it in flight with my left hand. He keeps pushing and the strength it's taking to push back and keep the fist where it is causes a bead of sweat to run down the side of my face. I bring my right arm up inside of his left, cave the elbow with my right forearm, and grab the back of his neck. Before he has a chance to catch on, I yank his head forward and bash my forehead into the crest of his nose. He jerks back howling, "Fuck!" and sprays blood all over my face in the process.

My head is spinning at the combined effect of his hits and mine and the strength in my legs is all but nonexistent as the adrenaline temporarily subsides. I fall backward, just barely catching myself by forcing my right palm back down onto the floor under my ass, followed by my left one, then finally sit down with a thud. Lieutenant Mackelson is also feeling the effect of my hits as he shakes his head and nearly loses his balance after taking a few small balancing steps in an attempt to stay vertical. Blood soaks the front of his once clean white shirt and is spattered all over the ground at his feet.

I have just enough time to regain my bearings and stand before he's able to do the same. His head is still down as he brings a hand up to clench his nose and blow the snot and blood to the floor. "Well, we know who wears the pants in your family," he mutters through his hand. "Doubt that little pissant you call a brother could've delivered a blow like that."

"AHH!" I scream, as the heat radiates from my body, rage pushing me forward before I have a chance to think. Lieutenant Mackelson raises his head and the knuckles on my right fist barely miss his cheekbone and smash directly into the bridge of his broken nose. He stumbles to the left as I press forward, uppercutting his jaw with my left fist and causing him to fall backward to my right.

I should have him, but somehow in the blinding confusion of blood pouring into his eyes, he has enough sense to drive a foot into the air and makes contact with my genitals as I close in for another hit. The pain is excruciating and the numbness spreads from my midsection to the rest of my body. My thighs tighten, forcing my knees together and I fall to the ground, grasping myself without any hope of reaching out for support. I groan and hit the floor on my side which forces the air from my chest. The thud feels like a shockwave of tenderness that rolls through the numbing sensation across my skin as I try to breathe.

 Lieutenant Mackelson rolls away from me to his right and tries to regain his footing, only to stumble and fall on his stomach. I can only hope that the uppercut rattled him enough to keep his world tumbling for a few more seconds until I can regain my breath and get back to my feet. He manages to make it to his knees as the numbness subsides in my limbs; it still burns in my midsection, but at least I can stand.

 He's still on his knees with both hands on his thighs for support as I steady myself and stomp toward him from behind. It takes a lifetime to reach him five whole feet away, only to have my goal of catching him off guard shattered by an elbow to the stomach. The numbness returns, trading places with the air that's expelled from my lungs. I gasp in an attempt to replace it, but can't and fall forward onto his shoulders. Lieutenant Mackelson spins to his left and shoves me to the ground near the last location of his right knee. Before I have a chance to react, he moves again, sliding onto my chest and pinning my shoulders to the ground with both knees.

 Closing my eyes I clench the lids shut with what little strength is left in an attempt to drive the numbness from my extremities that's been caused by lack of oxygen. I gasp again, trying to get much needed air into my lungs, but the action is interrupted by Lieutenant Mackelson's fist making contact with my nose. My eyes snap open and the light temporarily blinds my vision before it's blocked by another fist that slams into my eye. He continues to swing at my face with alternating fists, each punch delivering more pain than the last, but also loosening my respiration and driving out the numbness. My face must be boring him, as the seventh hit drives into my left clavicle and snaps it in half as his knuckles sink into my shoulder. I wail in pain and wince as he pauses to look over his nasty handiwork. The perfect time to strike.

    Through squinted vision, I can see him raise both fists above his head for one massive strike. As he does, I drive my feet into the air, roll the lower part of my spine off the floor and wrap my ankles around his chest from behind, locking them into place and preventing his arms from going past his midsection. He shockingly claws at my feet as I reach down deep, summon all of my strength and shout, pulling him back and causing him to flip over my lower half and land on his stomach a few feet away.

    I kick up from my back and plant my feet firmly into the ground. There's a second wind of strength surging through my body after tossing him to the ground like a rag doll. The pain caused by my broken clavicle and swollen face is dulled by the insurgence of adrenaline into my bloodstream. Face down, he pounds a fist into the ground, then lifts his chest off the floor. He drives his other fist into the ground for support and pulls his knees underneath his waist, holding his body up on all fours.

    There's a mad fury burning in the dark pit of my stomach and it forces itself out past my curled lips and gleaming teeth in the form of a monstrous roar. Nox-Ira is awake and he wants blood. My body is low with arms out to the side, muscles tensed and fists clenched as I force the raw emotion from my core. Memories shoot through my head reminding me of the last time Nox howled in a similar manner. I had just been released from Red's transfusion container and realized that some Hemo thugs were trying to kill my brother and me while we slept. The memory which previously escaped my mind seems so vivid now.

After what feels like hours, the growl subsides and I take a deep breath of fresh air to regain my strength for the coming battle. Lieutenant Mackelson's head is still hanging low while his back bounces up and down from the hurried frantic breathing. He's seething at the floor, exhaling spit and blood below until a response comes from the dark side of his own Nox-Ira, but his has changed. It is not a roar, and it does not sound like any creature that I've ever heard, save one. It's a high-pitched scream, a shriek of deep-seated torment and pain. A terrifying wail that enters my ears and rolls down my spine, vibrating my ribs and rattling my insides as it does.

It's the sound of a Plaguer.

Chapter 24: Stressed

02.04 - 2251 - 001.674 Red Galaxy Standard

"I still can't believe they found Thyr," Bill throws his hands up into the air as we're walking down the corridor that leads away from the docking bay. "Like actual Thyr, man!" he turns and shouts in my ear.

I rub the inside of my eyes with my left hand, then use the right to push his face away from me. "Yes, I heard you," I grumble. "And they claim," I correct him. We've just gotten back from a sixth month mission, with lots of killing, barely any sleep, and even less food. I'm not in the mood for Bill's unusual perkiness. All I want to do right now is take a shower, hit the mess hall, then get some rack time in before they figure out where to send us next.

"Do you think we'll get to fight 'em?" he beams, hopping up and down as we continue to walk. I close my eyes for a second and visualize my bunk. "LT!"

I shake my head, "I don't know, man. Look, I have no clue how you can have this much energy after I had to wake your ass up *again* halfway through the Scorlitic mission."

"It's exciting, this type of shit, it's the reason we exist! Not the sweep and clean bullshit they've been having us do for the last few decades." I glance over at Bill and he's rubbing his hands together. "We've been training and kicking ass since our accident what, a hundred and thirty-one years ago, to fight these bastards and now we might finally have a chance. All these other missions, they've just been appetizers leading up to the main course! It'll be full on war!"

I can't take this anymore, six months of Bill is pretty much my limit. Luckily, we've reached the corridor that splits off to my room, which is right across from the showers, and the mess hall is straight ahead. I turn the corner and head to my room.

Bill slides to a stop. "You're not gonna grab some grub? I heard the chefs were experimenting with something called pork blood. Supposedly the fat makes it really good."

"Gonna grab a shower first and change, feels like I'm covered in shit," I bark over my shoulder without stopping.

"Suit yourself."

There are days when I don't know how Bill keeps it all together. Maybe it's because he doesn't take anything to heart and just lets it all slide off of his back. I used to be able to do that, but more recently I've been having a hell of a time. Maybe it's just all the fighting. We find a new species that has something we want and we drive them from their homes and take it. Hell, it doesn't even seem like the reasons are all that justified anymore. Some days I feel like our people have become the bullies of the universe.

I shake my head, then smack the side of it with my open palm. I'm just tired, there's no point in philosophizing and trying to figure out what it all means. I'm a soldier and there's a job to do, that's it.

Some random soldier that I don't even notice bumps into my shoulder as I'm walking through the hall getting lost in my own head. He bounces off the wall before spinning around and shouting, "What the fuck, man?" I turn to face the new found frustration that's keeping me from the sweet clarity of a hot shower and bare my upper teeth. My brow tightens and I glare through the little shit of a private as if he's responsible for every last thing that's gone wrong with my life. A low hiss rolls off the air as it escapes my lips.

"I uh...sorry, sir," the private fumbles out of his mouth before tossing me a quick salute and bolting down the hall away from me. The salute was pointless. Unless you're on the command deck or in the field, rank doesn't mean anything. "Rank is fit for decisions and battle!" Captain Otto explained to us before our first mission years back. "It holds no place in soldier's leisure time and therefore is not acknowledged." I guess the military has a point to some degree, but I can't see it making a difference if we did implement it. Respect among the ranks is a big deal to our people, and even if it wasn't, leisure time only lasts so long. No point in digging a hole of shit to return to when your shift is up.

I take my time in the shower. After finishing, I lay in my bunk, staring at the ceiling, almost too tired to make my way to the mess hall. My body is drained, my muscles are sore, and my mind can barely function, but I know if I don't eat, I'll just wake up with stomach pains and there's been enough of that over the last six months. I reluctantly swing my legs over the side of the bunk and slam my palm into the holographic button to the left of my door. Holographic controls, I shake my head at the notion. Never thought we'd see this kind of tech a hundred years ago. Now it's all standard issue junk that nobody gives a second thought. I've been oddly nostalgic recently.

As I walk toward the double doors leading into the mess hall, I can hear the commotion from a crowd of soldiers shouting over each other. I try to avoid the mess hall during busier hours because of the cock diesel, piss and vinegar younger guys that tend to get rowdy in their off times. Last thing I need is to get caught off guard or in a bad mood and accidentally break someone's arm, or worse, kill them. Nothing would happen of course, because even though rank doesn't count when it comes to interacting with your peers, if you bite off more than you can chew, you deal with the consequences. I'm not talking about the ones dealt by the military either. Personal matters are personal matters, you better be able to handle your shit. That being said, I deal with enough violence in the field, I don't need it in my free time too, even if it's justified.

I walk through the double doors leading into the mess hall and it's swelling with soldiers who are drinking synthetic blood and carrying on about the Thyr presence that High Command supposedly found near Earth. Bill is sitting at a table near the end of the room by himself and I nod to him before pushing through the throng of soldiers and make my way to the distribution machines. I glance over at Bill once more, who's oblivious to the noise around him and staring down at a mug of blood. The exhaustion must have finally caught up with him. Even if it didn't, Blood Packs don't really mix with the normal soldiers, especially Alphas. We're trained at a tactical and intellectual level that's way beyond what normal soldiers are used to and therefore get frustrated quickly when having to deal with them. Still, some of them never learn.

I pour myself a mug of the pork blood that Bill was ranting about earlier, turn, offer a slight nod to Aphrodite and Blaze sitting at the opposite end of the room, then proceed to the right end where Bill is. Blaze barely acknowledged me which is rare given the amount of time I was away and how long it's been since we've fucked. Even though the exchange was brief, I can tell they're on edge and slightly frustrated with the amount of commotion in the room. I had Vali pull their most recent field report while we were on assignment, and the mission they just finished was almost as frustratingly long as ours. Like me, they wouldn't be here unless they were really hungry.

Bill looks up as I approach, but a few feet before I reach the table, a particularly large and ignorant looking soldier steps in front of me and blocks my path. I stop, slowly lift my head, and gaze up at the soldier's eyes above me. He's a good foot taller at least. After taking note of the look in his eyes, I glance to my right at the soldier behind him, to see the little shit I bumped into in the hallway.

My eyes return to the sack of meat in front of me. "Is this the guy?" he asks over his shoulder.

"Yeah," the little one sheepishly replies.

I continue to focus on the lumbering beast in front of me with an ice cold gaze that tears through the back of his skull. It doesn't make him uneasy, which is odd and, quite frankly, unfortunate for him. This one must be especially stupid.

"Who the fuck you think you are, plowing through guys in the hall and acting like you own the place? Growling like an animal and shit."

I release my gaze and lean my upper body to the left so I can see Bill. "They move?" I ask.

He looks up from his mug, lets his eyes dart around ever so slightly, then lowers his head back to the mug. "Na," he scoffs lightly. "She smirked a bit though."

The massive soldier in front of me smacks the side of my left face in an attempt to get my attention. "Hey! I'm talking to you." I straighten back up and return my gaze to his eyes and ease the tension in my shoulders. "Did who move? What the fuck you talking about?" he asks curiously, clearly annoyed by the fact that I haven't backed down or shown any kind of fear. At this point, I notice six of his buddies move in from behind out of support, three on either side. There's eight in total now, counting this lumbering idiot and the little mouse behind him. I wanted to avoid confrontation, but I guess it just isn't in the cards today. It's sad as

I'm sure the on-board medics have more to focus on than trying to save eight knuckleheads from the indifferent grasp of death.

"Did you see the smack, Bill?"

"I heard it." I can hear him sip the blood again, loud and clear to instigate the three soldiers in front of him.

"Hey!" the big one in front of me yells.

"They still watching?" I ask Bill, keeping my eyes fixed on the soldier in front of me this time.

There's a pause before Bill answers, "She's shaking her head."

"What the hell are you talking about?" the soldier demands.

"Look over my shoulder." The soldier cocks an eyebrow, unsure of whether or not I'm trying to trick him in order to gain the upper hand. "I'm serious, look straight over my shoulder, you should see two women sitting alone at the far end of the room."

He glances up, "Yeah, so?"

"They're Alphas," I explain. "Two of the best in the universe. In fact, there's only two other Alphas who are superior." The soldiers continues to stare, but there's a sudden sense of panic in his eyes as his tiny brain starts to piece everything together. One of the soldiers to the left moves and I hear Bill's cup tip over onto the table.

The entire mess hall has fallen silent as everyone has their attention turned to us. Some of the soldiers know not to mess with us, some of them can spot Alphas a mile away by the way we carry ourselves, and some of them are just clever enough to pick up on a fight when it develops. The silence is broken by the sound of Bill's metal chair swiftly skidding back against the floor as he shoots up to his legs. Then I hear a head being slammed against the table in three quick successions. I can only assume it's the ass who spilled Bill's mug.

All of the soldiers turn to Bill, including the big one in front of me and I can now see past them as Bill pulls the soldier's head back into the air by his hair. Blood sprays out of his mouth as Bill pulls up, causing the body and legs to stiffen. He lifts a foot into the air and slams it down onto the soldier's knee, causing it to collapse backwards with a spine chilling crack that resonates throughout the mess hall. Bill releases his grip and the soldier crumbles to the ground, wailing in pain.

"Blood for blood," Bill mutters under his breath before spitting in the soldier's face. Bill's Nox-Ira is awake and a ready to shatter bone. Though more serious then Bill's normal demeanor, he's always gotten a kick out of breaking bones. My Nox prefers to pummel more than anything.

The other seven soldiers are in shock as the mess hall falls quiet again with everyone eagerly waiting for them to make another mistake. A low growl escapes my throat, filling the air with tension as the big soldier in front of me slowly turns back around. I don't want to fight, but all the rage and frustration from the last several decades is boiling over and I can't control it. My Nox is angry and it's been too long since I've let him out to play. I don't have a choice anymore. The only other sound in the room is Aphrodite and Blaze at the other end of the room, laughing hysterically at the entertainment that we're about to provide. These soldiers are about to learn a very painful lesson.

You don't fuck with an Alpha, but more importantly, don't ever wake their Nox-Ira.

Chapter 25: Sacrifice

3.04 - 2468 - 306.596 Red Galaxy Standard

Controlling my emotions when Nox's bloodlust is in full throttle is damn near impossible. I don't even know if bloodlust is the right term to describe what happens to me, but given our predilection for blood as sustenance, and also a silent reminder of an impending victory, I can't think of any better phrase. It starts with the awakening of Nox, a process that Red helped us perfect in training. Rage tenses my muscles, causing adrenaline to be released in heaping quantities throughout my body. Then my blood begins to warm and the heat increases until it feels like liquid fire coursing through my veins and scorching my organs along the way. This causes muscles to throb and my stomach to seize until the anger deep within takes over. It all converges in my throat and erupts out of my mouth like a thunderous storm of destruction and madness, a frightening audible representation of the transformation that has taken place. There's anger and pain and strife and contempt in the noise that is not my own and, afterward, the body I inhabit is no longer mine. It's something altogether animal. Nox-Ira has taken over and has full control.

If memory serves, which at this exact moment is questionable, this is only the second time that Nox has engaged in full bloodlust in the last three hundred and forty-seven years of my knowledgeable existence. Though I've let him take over on multiple occasions, he doesn't always manifest in this hyper-aggressive manner. Most times, he simply helps me focus and quell pain. Red previously explained how it happened when I broke out of the transfusion chamber, right after awakening on Earth. He claims that side of Nox was something he had never seen in another Hemo. I don't remember it—well, not all of it—but I remember the same sensation I'm feeling now. Fire, followed by darkness, followed by a lightheadedness and lots of blood. Red thinks that it has something to do with the Hemo blood unlocking an animalistic need in my genetic code. I don't know if that's true or not, I'm just hoping to keep a little more control this time, as I'd really love to watch the light in Lieutenant Mackelson's eyes dim as I beat him into the floor.

    Of course, that whole plan may have gone better had he not transformed into a Plaguer before my eyes. After rushing toward him in a fit of rage, the Lieutenant's newly acquired speed allowed him to move out of the way and proceed to launch me into the wall behind him. For some reason, maybe it's the bloodlust, I find myself having an ample amount of time to reflect on the situation while I'm soaring through the...nope.

    I slam into the sidewall from the sheer force of Lieutenant Mackelson's throw and stick into the newly formed crater my back has created. It only takes a second for the nanoparticles to begin repairing the damage behind me as I slowly get pushed from the wall and slump onto the floor in a crumbled mess. Before I have a chance to assess the situation, my back is up against the wall again with the Lieutenant's grip tightening around my throat. At first, the fact that he's so fast seems out of place with the other Plaguers that we've interacted with, but then I remember the benefits of my suit. Heightened senses, reaction time, endurance to pain; it becomes agonizingly clear how much my suit does to keep me alive.

    There's something humbling about being outmatched by a new predator on the evolutionary galactic food chain, even if it is the byproduct of experimentation.

Another shrill scream pierces the air as it escapes Lieutenant Mackelson's lips. The grip around my neck loosens, only to tighten again a second later as his head drops. It sounds like he's sobbing.

"What did you lose, Daemon?" he shouts into his chest. "Your parents? Is that what the war took from you?" Lieutenant Mackelson raises his head and glares into my eyes with his own, which are now bloodshot from the Plague raging through his body. His breathing has accelerated to near hyperventilation and his shoulder and chest muscles ripple as the crunching sound of bone can be heard under his skin. His biology is changing before my eyes. The virus is turning him into a more prolific hunter, a more prolific killer. He winces and wails in pain, but to my surprise it sounds normal like the old lieutenant that I knew.

"Did you...lose...a family?" I raspily squeeze out as his grip continues to fluctuate around my throat. All I can try to do is appeal to the Hemo in him, or possibly the dormant human in him. The normal scream indicates that the virus hasn't fully taken over yet.

He wails humanlike again in frustration and then begins to punch my face with his free hand. The hits come hard and fast at first, landing just above my cheekbone, but begin to scatter around my face as he loses control. The fist breaks form as he claws and swats, slicing my skin open and causing blood to roll down and drip from my chin. Though his grip around my neck continually fluctuates, it never loosens to a point where I can escape. The scraping stops as the Lieutenant snaps the free hand to his side, grasping his abdomen in pain and wincing once more. A Plaguer shriek causes my ears to ring as it escapes his throat. His head raises and he glares into my eyes.

"I lost myself...GAH!" Both his hand griping my neck and his own side tighten as he shrieks and his eyes clamp shut. "My men, my only family." One hand tightens around my neck as the other forms a fist that he drives into the wall next to my head. The fist opens and clamps back down on my neck as he pulls me forward and slams me back into the wall. He does it again; each hit rattling my bones more and more as I wait for one of them to give in to the sheer force of the impacts. I can feel my shoulder snap out of place on the fifth hit.

He pulls my face close to his and opens his eyes. "Fifty men. That's what it cost to save you and your little brother." Another brief wince before the eyes shoot open. The cornea of his eyes have almost entirely lost their white coloring to the concentration of swelling red veins. The virus has almost completely taken over. "The fighting flared up after Kelly and Red evacuated you two." Spit flies out of the lieutenant's mouth as he tries to speak through the pain and clenched teeth. "I lost an entire platoon. The only ones who meant anything in my life."

He lets out a Plaguer shriek, then rips me off the wall and throws me back into the middle of the training room like a rag doll. I land on my knee, which shatters from the force of the ground, then roll to an excruciating stop on my back. My head falls to the right and my combat suit, in its belt form is laying on the floor ten feet away. I roll onto my stomach and begin to claw my way toward it. My arms reach out and dig into the ground as my muscles contract in an attempt to pull me closer to the last bit of salvation I may have in the world of the living. Six feet; all I have to do is reach the suit. If I can get it strapped on and activated, the suit will release medication directly into my bloodstream. It won't heal me completely, but it can speed up the regeneration, numb the pain, and hold my broken bones in place while giving me the increased strength to fight back. Three feet and I hear a whooshing sound.

Lieutenant Mackelson's left foot lands on the back of my wrist, pinning it to the ground and his other foot slams into the center of my back. He slides the foot on my wrist down toward my elbow, reaches down, grabs my hand, and snaps my arm backwards, shattering the radius and ulna. I wail in pain as tears stream down my face and drip onto the floor with a mixture of blood from my open face wounds. The lieutenant hops off my back and flips me around. He pins down my shoulders with his knees and leans in close.

"I sacrificed my life, my family, my species and now, the only humanity I had left with the hopes of raining death on those who made me suffer so horribly and you merely see it as your last choice? IT'S THE ONLY CHOICE!" He raises a fist again to continue the beating and I wonder whether or not the pain will keep me conscious as my vision begins to fade and my body numbs.

On the verge of passing out, the room darkens and there's a soft, warm breeze that sweeps across my cheek. I turn to look at the source and Blaze is lying next to me on the floor smiling. She's a hallucination, the real Blaze wouldn't smile at my pain unless it was also for pleasure. This is disturbing for two reasons. I've been in a lot of hairy situations in the field, combat stress mixed with physical pain and exhaustion. This isn't the first time that I've been on the verge of death, but it is the first time I've hallucinated due to it. The second reason is understanding that I love Blaze is no longer enough. It's clearly something that I can't run away from, which means that I have to live and figure out a way to make things work. I have to make her understand what we hope to accomplish. Problem is, impending black out and all.

My eyes turn back up to Lieutenant Mackelson as he's violently knocked from his perch on my chest by an unseen force. I look up, then turn to my right to see Red in full combat gear let out a deep roar, the likes of which I've never heard from him. It sounds like my inner demon, Nox will try to reach up and warn Red of what the lieutenant has become, but my arm falls to the ground before I get the chance. The frustration from passing out only quickens the darkness. Shit.

Chapter 26: Ramifications

02.04 - 2251 - 020:932 Red Galaxy Standard

"Yes, sir," Captain Otto says for the twentieth time into the video call coming through on his desk. "No, I totally understand, sir." Bill and I can't hear who he's talking to for some reason.

Bill leans into my left ear and whispers, "He must have one of the new nanoimplants they plan on putting in us," and nods to Captain Otto. Something tells me they wouldn't test combat equipment on the captain before perfecting it through other means.

"I'm sure ours are a little different. We've been out for over six months, and I don't see them testing combat gear on the captain," I respond in an equally hushed voice.

"I'll take care of it, sir," Captain Otto says sitting down at his desk with sincere reverence. He salutes, then taps the screen to end the call. His facial expression and demeanor immediately change from sympathetic to infuriated. Maybe I can quell the oncoming storm a bit before it hits.

"Captain Otto, I'd just like to apologize for what happened in the mess hall…"

He slams his fists into the wooden table, "Shut your *fucking* mouth, Lieutenant!"

We're definitely in the shit now. I don't think I've ever seen the captain lose his composure like this before. He's gotten frustrated with Bill's bullshit, but has never yelled at us before. We haven't been in a scuffle on the ship for years, but then again, none of the previous ones were this bad.

Right after Bill shattered the drink-knocking-over-soldier's knee, the rest of his buddies snapped out of the oh-shit-shock they had fallen into. Brains took a backseat to instinct, or they would have picked up their fallen buddy and scurried out of the room. But, unfortunately for them, and now it seems for us, they decided to attack.

Stupidly, the two to the left of me, who were standing with the knee-shattered soldier, rushed Bill first. He blocked a punch to his left with the same arm then used his opposite fist to crush the throat of the secondary soldier. That poor sap immediately gasped, but was unable to breathe and fell next to his wailing buddy on the floor. There was no chance of him getting up again. Bill proceeded to grab the throat of the punch-thrower and keep him at a distance as he swung his right arm around to backhand one of the other three approaching from behind. The bitch-slapped-soldier stumbled to one knee as Bill kicked another in the stomach with his right leg, pushing him back into yet another one who was rushing in. The soldier that I bumped into in the halls, now on my right, watched in fear as the big guy in front of me did the same. And who could blame them? In a matter of seconds there was one guy who was probably going to die, one awaiting judgement at the end of Bill's grasp, and three on the floor.

Bill was stressed from how long we'd been in the field, that's not even a question, so I totally understand why he reacted the way he did, but now it was my turn. The big soldier finally snapped out of his shock-induced paralysis and made a move to attack Bill. That's when my protective nature took over.

He attempted to lunge toward Bill, but I stuck my left foot in front of his, then rotated to his side, grabbing the back of his neck. I switched my weight and placed my right foot behind his legs and pulled with all my might. The towering giant went crashing back to the floor as I let go and watched the back of his head smack the ground with a spine-tingling crack. He wasn't moving too much, just sliding his limbs around a bit, but I hadn't survived this long as a soldier by assuming situations were as they appeared. I gave him a swift kick in the face, followed by another to the gut, then the groin for good measure. When he rolled over there was no question that he was going to stay down for a while. Meanwhile, some other little shit built up the courage to attack me from behind. Can't see how given the show that Bill was putting on. Whatever this guy did, wasn't that impressive or smart and before I knew it, I had flipped him over my back and driven a palm into his chest. I'm confident I cracked his sternum.

As I looked up to make sure Bill was okay, I could see four guys on the ground, one of which was moving. Bill had the remaining soldier in his grasp, back pressed to his chest, with the soldier's arm locked out to the side. Bill's free hand snaked around his shoulder as they struggled. Well, the soldier struggled. Bill wasn't putting forth a lot of effort. A second later his hand grasped the soldier's chin and snapped his neck. The soldier went limp and Bill didn't waste any time pushing his corpse to the floor.

Physical altercations are monitored via the security cameras throughout the ship, and the mess hall is a hotbed for such activity, so medical personnel are dispatched fairly quickly. As the last soldier hit the ground, four EMTs rushed through the door to administer treatment. "Lieutenant," one of them saluted as he rushed by. It was more than clear by the way he carried himself and the smirk painted across his face, that he was once an Alpha.

And that was that. Shithead know-it-all soldiers who are still green to the military shouldn't go puffing their chests out at spec ops. Two of the soldiers died, four were in critical condition, and the big ass leader had a bruised ego. The little pissant that hit me in the hall, inadvertently starting the whole thing never did join the fight. He just cowered off to the side.

Only that wasn't that. Normally speaking, the whole incident would be chalked up as a scuffle in which junior soldiers bit off way more than they could chew. Today though, that wasn't the case.

Turns out, one of the soldiers who died in the scuffle was directly related to Major Erislad, a one major prick who thinks more of his position in the military than what common sense might otherwise dictate. Even though this was just some barbaric meeting of the minds for our people, the major didn't see it that way. Not everyone abided by the soldier code of honor.

Now, judging from the captain's reaction to the video call and my attempt at easing his tension, Bill and I are looking at months, if not years of shit duty. The captain takes a second to compose himself, then loosens his clenched fists. He raises his head to look me directly in the eye. "You boys listen to me and you listen well." He switches to Bill's eyes. "Don't you ever, EVER," his eyes shoot back to mine, "apologize for something like this again. To ANYONE!"

Come again for LT? The captain continues before I have a chance to transform the confusion on my face into words. "The only reason that our people has survived all this time is because of soldiers like you. You spend more time in the field on a single op than most soldier do for a half a year." No shit. "You're the soldiers who follow orders without questions, soldiers who do what others won't, soldiers who do what needs to be done. Part of that is weeding out the societal rejects who think they're fit to be in our military. They think they're fit to honor themselves with our uniforms when, at times, they're clearly not."

He glances down at the monitor on his desk and spits. "The *major*," he says with disdain, "seems to have forgotten that duty comes before blood. Duty comes before personal bullshit, religious beliefs, and any kind of vengeance that we see fit. Duty is EVERYTHING! Otherwise we run the risk of ending up like the humans did—*dead*...with a scorched planet seized by those who are worthy."

The captain breathes in deeply and relaxes back into his leather-bound wooden chair as Bill and I process the situation and try to understand how we're not actually in trouble. Sure, rank doesn't mean anything when you're off duty, but shit rolls downhill. That's just a fact of life. The captain has always been there for us as a guiding light and even though we don't remember what he was like before the accident, I feel like he's been more supportive since it happened. I have no facts to support that theory, other than a little voice in the back of my head that says he's been taking it easy on us.

After a few deep breaths, the captain leans forward once more, setting his forearms on the desk and interlocking his fingers. "Promise me here, this isn't an order. This is a request from someone who's known and guided you throughout most of your adult lives. You boys promise me….that you'll never apologize to anyone who doesn't deserve it. *NEVER* compromise what you've become. You boys are the saviors of our race, even if you don't know or accept it."

Bill and I stare at the captain for a second, then glance at each other really quickly and confirm in silence that he's being honest. We turn back to him and say in unison, "I promise."

He looks both of us in the eye for five seconds exactly, then relaxes back into his chair. "Good. Now listen, I fought as hard as I could. We were going at it for a good twenty minutes before you boys got here, but in the end, his brass is shinier." Well, this can't be good, here comes the shit detail. "You boys are being reassigned. The major seems to think that you two need a break, given the amount of time that you've spent in the field recently.

"But sir," Bill speaks up, "not to toot our own horn, but aren't we the best operatives you have?"

The captain closes his eyes and shakes his head, "Yes!" He takes a second to compose himself, then opens his eyes and glances at his desk before turning his attention back to us. "Trust me, nothing infuriates me more than knowing my best two operatives are going to be stationed in the Outer Rim somewhere, when we've got actual work to do." Well, that explains his anger after ending the call with the major. There's a small sense of relief that washes over me knowing that his frustration has nothing to do with us.

"Unfortunately, there's nothing I can do about it. He's our superior, and while *some* soldiers don't take duty as seriously as others, I intend to see it through. I expect you will too."

"Yes, sir," we affirm.

Well, all things considered, the situation could have been a lot worse. I know Bill will go stir crazy and well, I probably will too after a while, but I'll deal with that when the time comes. Besides, given my musings over whether or not our actions are morally right in the context of the universe, maybe I do need some time to unwind.

"You boys are going to be stationed in security detail on Lanans in The Outer Shores. It's essentially a bunch of high ranking officials and rich proprietors that want to stay as far away from the action as possible." Huh, the whole 'fight our war, but keep it away from us' attitude. Seems oddly human for our race based off of what I've heard. "I don't agree with it, but I'm just a captain. Listen, you boys get out there and keep your heads low," he zeroes in on Bill when saying the second part, "and *get back here*. I can't afford for you to be stuck in The Outer Shores with all this Thyr business going on."

"Ah ha!" Bill screams, as the captain and I jump in our seats a bit. "So we *did* find 'em."

"Yes, we did," the captain says solemnly. "So behave and get your asses back here so we can crush the threat. Understood?"

"Yes, sir."

The captain salutes us, signaling the end of our conversation. We salute back, stand, and exit his office.

"What's the plan?" Bill asks as we walk down the hallway.

"Like the captain said, keep our heads down and get our asses back here," I reply.

"Maaaaaannnn. This is gonna be so boring," Bill whines.

I don't respond because he has a point. It is going to be really boring.

* * *

The darkness descended like a hurricane, ferocious and bloodthirsty. There was a moment, oh the briefest of moments when I had hoped to escape its wrath, but that moment was torn away by the violent winds, hope replaced by pain and death. It was gone, all of it and I was helpless in the grasp of the storm. Trees burned with the fury of a star drive as the forest rendered to ash. There was no fuel left to feed the inferno, but still it raged on. My soul, my life, the force that kept me moving was ripped from my chest over and over. Each time I tried to call for help, the darkness reached in the open cavity of my pain's portrayal and yanked the vocal chords from my throat. It was useless. All of it so useless.

"GAHH!" a furious, throaty war cry escapes my lips long and hard as I drive my first toward the enemy. My punch is stopped by a rock-hard surface as frozen terror clenches my face. My blood is racing, liquid fire that burns as the darkness that consumed my soul. My mind dashing from one offensive thought to the next, eyes searching for the unstoppable force that prevents me from vanquishing the unseen enemy. The rage swells within and blinds my conscious self from the world as is.

"Liam," a timid voice said over the winds, the carnage, the fiery battle of my nightmare. The icy grasp on my face is a palm, and the immovable force now wrapped around my enraged fist its opposite. The fist that hugs my own loosens as the ghosts of my past melted away. The cold palm on my cheek directs my eyes up from the bed, to meet her gaze.

"You're with me," Blaze says, soft and kind. "Look," she presses, timidly tensing her hold on my face, and I did.

As my chest heaves up and down, I stare at those beautiful emerald eyes until the nightmare fades further away, to the point of being a distance memory. No, better yet, just a dream. A faint recollection pushed deep into my subconscious, never to return again. It didn't matter much, there are others to take its place.

So many others.

The weight of it all hits, pulling me down into her chest as the tears come ravaging through my system. Blaze doesn't judge, she doesn't question, she just pulls me closer and rocks back and forth ever so slightly, singing something unintelligible but soothing in my ear. The sweet, lucid tones keep the demons at bay while reality takes hold. The stock of my life, my deeds, and all that I was unable to do to help others in need.

Alpha's leave their ghosts unspoken, albeit understood by the blood of a fellow warrior, for just the night prior our positions had been switched.

Chapter 27: Déjà Vu

3.07 - 2468 - 992:010 Red Galaxy Standard

I feel as though it's been a while since I've been conscious...and I have this strange, overwhelming sense of déjà vu. I'm exhausted, my limbs are heavy, and when I open my eyes with what little strength I have, light floods in and pierces the comfortable darkness. Great, I'm in a recovery room of the medical ward.

"LT, can you hear me?" Aden's voice echoes through my ears as I'm still coming to terms with the lighting situation. Closing my eyes, I attempt to lift my head off the hard pillow, but the entire room begins to spin and I immediately drop it back down to the bed. "LT?" Aden tries again. "LT!" he almost shouts.

"Aden...just shut the hell up," I mutter, barely loud enough for myself to even hear. Turning to my right, I slowly open my eyes to see Aden laying on his back on the bed next to my own with his arms behind his head, smiling at me. "What's so funny?"

"You mean beyond the simple joy of pissing you off just by talking too loud, annnnnnnnd that you just fucked up and used my human name without knowing who else was in the room?"

Shit. Well, if there had been anyone else, he wouldn't have called himself human. Turning my head back to the ceiling, I exhale, "Yes. Besides that."

"Well, thanks to the mother-of-all ass-kicking you took, and trust me it was, I had three extra days with Kelly. I'm sure you could imagine what we did with that time." Aden makes a clicking noise out of the side of his mouth.

"I could venture a guess."

"Well, you know how…"

"Don't," I cut him off. I'm happy that Aden's finally found someone, but the last thing I'm in the mood for is an overly long and detailed story of his conquest. As I breathe in and out a few times, the palpable awkwardness continues to grow. I can feel the smile fade from Aden's face as I keep my eyes closed and ask, "What?"

With almost a whisper he replies, "I'm glad you're still here, bro."

The door to the room slides open as I sit up and open my eyes to see Red walking through the door. Everything's still spinning, but I deal with it. "Doing much better I see," he offers from under his shemagh. His left cheekbone and eyebrow lift slightly as he half-smiles. I'm becoming a pro at understanding his facial expressions by reading the small visible patch of skin around his eyes.

"Thanks to you," I nod. "So, you killed Lieutenant Mackelson?"

"Well duh, right?" Aden asks before Red has a chance to answer. "Which I've been meaning to ask, Red," Aden turns to him. "We have Plague scanners all over the ship, how was it not picked up before he turned?"

Red lowers his head and walks to the left hand side of my bed so he can see both myself and Aden as he speaks. He raises his head to look at me, "That situation is a little more complicated than it appears." I turn to look at Aden, whose eyebrow is cocked in confusion, then turn back to Red. "Captain Hoffman tasked the lieutenant with finding a way to connect with the Plaguers. Their command structure is still a mystery to us, and any attempt to communicate with their supposed officers was met with extreme hostility. We needed a way into their ranks."

Holy shit. "Mackelson exposed himself on purpose?" I ask in horror as my jaw drops to my chest.

"What the…" Aden mutters under his breath behind me.

"Yes," Red confirms. "We were running out of options and more importantly, time. The High Scientists have been working on a way to mix our genetic code with the Thyr for almost a year now and they are near completion. We needed to take action."

That's what the lieutenant meant when he talked about sacrificing whatever humanity he had left. "How could you let him do that?" I demand. "How could Hoffman?" I push myself up into a seated position on the bed, ignoring the near debilitating vertigo that sends my head into a tail spin. Is there no end to Hoffman's need for vengeance, or the lieutenant's blind faith in his quest for justice?

"It is unfortunate, but necessary," Red answers stoically.

Swinging my legs over the side of the bed, I hop down onto my feet and stagger for a second, waiting for my bearings to calibrate. Red is directly to my left and I push him away with my pointer finger. "What do *you* know? You sold out your own race."

Before I have a chance to turn and walk away, Red's left hand snaps up to my neck and spins me around, pinning me to the wall behind him. There's a slight quiver in his grip as his brow tenses for just a moment before relaxing. "Hey!" Aden shouts and moves to intervene, but Red's right hand flies up to silence him. Aden freezes in his tracks as Red turns his attention to me. This is the first time that Red's ever show any hint of aggression toward us. In fact, come to think of it, I can't ever remember him showing aggression toward any Hemo, outside of training. This simple act has caused both Aden and me to freeze in place.

"Please do not confuse my collective nature for a lack of emotions. For centuries, *my* people had such great potential, but they threw it all away in a mad dash to claim the Earth." Red leans in close to my left ear. "Desperation will make people do crazy things, it does not matter whether they are human or Hemo. My people threw away their chance at a peaceful life when they started committing unnecessary acts of genocide to further their own goals." Red's grip loosens around my neck as he steps backward and I drop back down onto the floor. "There were precious few of us who saw the path we were headed down for what it was and decided to take action. I would rather kill every last one of my own than watch another species disappear from the universe. It is also unfortunate, but *necessary*."

Still fuming, I push past Red. Ripping my hospital robe off, I grab my casual clothes from the bed that Aden was sitting on to get dressed.

"Wait a minute," Aden directs toward Red. "You didn't answer my question; the ship has atmospheric sensors to detect the Plague, how was we he not caught upon boarding the ship? Also, why did it take so long for him to change?"

"Kelly made sure that the sensors were turned off upon our arrival and kept them off, even though the systems continued to read normal in the control room. As far as the change, we think the dormant human blood in his system, or the fact that his genetic code was originally different, confused and slowed down the process," Red answers. I look up and Aden's shaking his head, no doubt annoyed by the fact that Kelly didn't say anything to him and that subsequently lead to my life being in danger. "We actually assumed that the lieutenant was immune and thus no threat to the ship. We were wrong. Luckily, he was able to control his actions long enough for us to get him off the ship and back on mission."

"What?" Aden asks his face going white.

"The lieutenant is off the ship and back on mission."

"So the asshole of all assholes maims and nearly kills my brother and you didn't put him down?" Aden yells. Red almost looks offended by the idea that Aden wants him dead. Yelling at Red is pointless, he's just another soldier doing what he's told. I know exactly who to direct my anger at.

I push past Aden and barrel toward the door. "Where are you going?" he asks.

"To have a little chat with *the captain*," I snarl out of the side of my mouth. As I'm storming down the hallways with anger burning in my gut, I realize that I've been following commands my entire life. Now, with the knowledge of our past and what we're about to do, I finally feel like the shackles have been released. There's nothing holding me to a sense of honor or duty anymore, other than the need to kill those responsible for ruining so many lives. If Aden and I survive this, there won't be much for us to do other than roam the galaxy for a quiet place to live out the rest of our centuries alone.

I slam the holographic button on the side of the captain's doorframe and rush through the door with renewed purpose and fire. Captain Hoffman looks up from his desk with a smile. "Ah Daemon, it's good to see you up and around again." I walk around his desk as he spins to face me. Without thinking, I grab the collar on his uniform and yank him from his chair. There's no time to for him to react before I start punching him repeatedly in the face.

Aden rushes through the door, with Red following casually behind. "Daemon!" Aden shouts from the other side of the desk.

I hit the Captain a fifth and final time, enough to get his nose bleeding and produce a nice cut on his lip, then shove him back down into his chair. He spits blood onto the floor, then looks back up at me, "Feeling better, I assume?"

"I'm done with being left in the dark. I'm done being manipulated." I thrust my pointer finger toward his face. "You want our help, then you better tell me everything right fucking now. That or I just slit your throat with the knife secured to the bottom of your desk," he glances down at it then back up to me, "and call it a day. I'll be tried and executed, but I really don't give a shit anymore."

Captain Hoffman rotates his jaw, rubs his thumb across his lip, and looks at the blood. He reaches over to the top center drawer of his desk. I can see Aden out of the corner of my eye. At this angle, there's no way for me to tell whether he's more shocked or afraid of my outburst, but my eyes don't leave the captain. He removes a handkerchief from the drawer below.

Captain Hoffman dabs the cut and says, "I take it Red informed you of the lieutenant's valiant sacrifice?" I nod once and the captain looks back up at me. "Well then, you have it all. No more tricks up my sleeve. Lieutenant Mackelson will use his newly acquired status to infiltrate the Plaguer ranks and make them aware of our situation. The enemy of my enemy is my friend. With any luck, the armament that we gave them at GHC will act as an olive branch of sorts in order to join forces. If that doesn't work, we do have something else they want."

"What's that?"

He glances at Red briefly, then back to me. "Kelly was able to gain unrequited access to GHC's servers after shutting them down. She has full control over all of their communications."

That will definitely come in handy when the fighting starts. "What's next?"

Captain Hoffman smirks, "Grab some grub, take a nap, train in Red's bay, I don't really give a shit as it seems like you're beyond accepting some of the more trivial orders. The lieutenant will make contact with us as soon as he has something to report. Latest intel shows the Plaguers falling back out of the system after our little confrontation at GHC. I've filed you both under medical leave to keep you on the ship and ready."

That won't last forever; Major Erislad is going to see our leave before long and demand that we're put back on active duty. Hopefully, Lieutenant Mackelson will report in sooner than later and we can get moving. I turn and storm out of the captain's office without so much as a salute or another word.

Aden jogs up behind me in the hallway. "Hey, do you mind if I go talk to uh,"

"That's fine," I say, waving my hand. I need some time to think and Kelly's probably the only person that will keep Aden out of trouble.

Aden grabs my shoulder, pulling me to a stop and walks in front of me. "Are you sure you're okay? You've been a little on edge since all this shit started coming out."

I bring my right hand up to Aden's face and cup the side of his cheek, wrapping my fingers around the back of his neck. "I'm fine." I pull my hand away, then lightly smack his cheek and walk by. "Tell her I said hi." Aden starts walking in the opposite direction. "Oh, and Bill," I say, turning around; he stops and turns to look at me and smirks at the fact that I used his Hemo name again. "Don't give her a hard time about not telling you." He offers a slight smile in the corner of his mouth, nods quickly, then leaves.

Still feeling a little rattled from the fight and not wanting to go back into a bed at the moment, I head down to the mess hall for grub. It's off-hours and the room is pretty much empty accept for one soldier I catch in the corner of my eye with their head down. I'm not feeling chatty at the moment, so I head over to the blood dispensers without checking to see who it is.

"LT," says a gentle female voice behind me. I turn around to see Blaze standing there holding an empty mug. There's something about her that seems off, I've never seen her like this before. "Well, you," she searches for a word. "You look like shit," she offers with a soft chuckle and a head bob.

I smile and look at the floor, unintentionally shuffling my feet, "Uh, yeah. It's been a rough couple of days," then look back up to see concern in her eyes.

"Yeah, I heard you were in the infirmary. Everything okay?"

"Yeah it's," I scoff, "nothing to write home about. I'm fine, thank you for asking."

"I didn't know you had family."

"I," I shake my head and laugh, "No, I was just turning a phrase." She nods, seemingly embarrassed by the misunderstanding. She has to know that I've been avoiding her, it's written all over her face.

Aden's busy, my body is in no mood to train, and I don't want to go back to my room, so maybe the universe is finally pushing me to talk to her. "Do you want to just chat for a bit?" I ask offering a hand out to the chair next to me.

She smiles, staring into my eyes for a moment before nodding, "Sure, that'd be nice." I sit and look at the table, then scan the empty room. Avoiding eye contact probably isn't the best way to make her feel better.

"Hey remember..."

"Were you..."

We both start at the same time cutting each other off. There's a nervous exchange of laughter before we both smile and she says, "You go."

"I was just, I was thinking about that time we uh," I yawn and rub my eyes. "Remember when we talked about what we'd do if we could actually retire some day?" She smiles and bites her lower lip. It feels good to see her smile. Things may be complicated but I'll take any little offering of joy where I can get it. "What about Oderia?"

She closes her eyes and shakes her head as if the motion will reverse the question I just asked. "Oderia?" she repeats questionably. "Like the Feeleye's home planet?"

I grab her empty mug and walk over to one of the distribution machines and pour her a fresh cup of synthetic blood before doing the same for myself. "Yeah it wasn't all bad, I mean look past the skirmishes, the missions, the war." I walk back over to the table and sit down, handing her cup back. She mouths 'thank you' and holds on to my hand as it's wrapped around the cup. I nod and continue. "There were lush yellow forests, gorgeous clear red waters on the cost, fruits, indigenous life that's not the Feeleye that we could hunt for food."

Blaze pulls the cup out of my hand and takes a sip. Then she shakes her head while setting it back on the table. "No, no, no.

When I leave this all behind, I want to leave it all behind. That means new planet, new life."

I blink a few times, then purse my eyebrows at the thought. I must be visibly nervous because she asks, "What?"

"You said when," She looks at me and shakes her head slightly as if to say 'so?'. "When, like instead of 'if', you said when."

Now she's the one who's nervous. "Yeah, I...don't you want that some day?"

Boy do I. "I...of course," I yawn again uncontrollably. "But the circumstances of our life, the reality of what we are..."

Blaze takes another sip from her mug then stands up. She walks behind me, sets one hand on either shoulder and leans in close to my ear. "You need to get some rest." Then she walks toward the door, and it slides open. She stops, and I'm still looking at the mugs on the table, thinking about how serious she is over leaving this life behind.

"Hope isn't a bad thing Liam. Just because they're dreams now, doesn't mean they can't come true." I cock my head slightly, but don't turn to face her. Another second and I hear her walk out of the room and the door slide shut.

Chapter 28: The Outer Shores

05.15 - 2251 - 304:293 Red Galaxy Standard

Everyone reacts to deep space travel differently, especially when travelling a great distance. Star drives help the process and greatly reduce the time it takes to reach intergalactic and even universal locations, but there's still a toll. Physical and mental.

Bill has a tendency to sleep and eat his way through most of our trips. I can't really do either. Sure there's systems in place to knock us out for the duration of the flight, but I prefer conscious contemplation. Something about being out of it for extended periods of time just bothers me.

It's always interesting to see what pops up in my mind during extended travel. Just a few moments ago it was a dissemination of tears. There's not much too them. Lacrimal grands secret protein-based hormonal fluids with a natural painkiller. That's pretty much it. A chemical reaction, produce by your body based off of external stimuli that leads to an emotional response. So why then does it seem to have such a lasting impact on us? How can the very person that stops my tears, then be the only cause when she's not around? At times it all feels unknown, yet oddly familiar.

I almost don't notice, but Bill stumbles into the cockpit as we approach The Outer Shores.

"Bloodpack Alpha member delta-alpha-echo-six, your slip, one-six-three, has been approved for landing in hanger Delta.

Proceed to bay door number two and reduce overall speed to comply with Red Military standard one-one-five-six."

The female operator directing us to the hanger sounds quite attractive, which isn't really a surprise considering The Outer Shores is a haven for the rich and famous. This whole assignment is a load of shit. Bill and I are going to stick out like sore thumbs. Trying to prevent him from getting into trouble over a twelve month detail here is going to be really difficult.

"She sounded hot," Bill beams in the co-pilot seat next to me. Right on time. I'm actually surprised he's sitting up here to begin with. Usually, when it comes to extended travel, he goes into hibernation mode in the cargo bay, just sleeping and feeding.

"What's the deal?" I ask while adjusting the slip down to trafficking speed and inputting the coordinates for our landing hangar. I look up at Bill to see him staring at me with a cocked eyebrow and a questioning look on his face. "Oh, come on. You never concern yourself with logistics. Usually I have to pull you out of an isolation chamber when we reach our destination."

Bill smirks, then idly waves a hand in my direction. "Pfsh, what are you talking about? The logistics of long distance space travel..." He breaks and starts laughing hysterically for a few seconds, then exhales with a 'whooo' at the console. "I couldn't even get halfway through that." He looks back at me. "You know exactly what it is. You're just off because you're focusing on how much this next year is going to suck." That I am. "Or possibly because of how much you'll miss Blaze," he mutters.

As right as he may be, I ignore the comment. Things with Blaze are getting....interesting for lack of a better term. We both entered into the whole idea of continued physical congress because there's really not much else to do in your downtime. Sure you can train, and we both do extensively, but you've gotta be able to blow off steam and get away from the life, even if it's just for a few hours. Lately though it's just been, I don't know. There's something else between us and I don't know that either of us understand what it is yet, so we're unwilling to address it.

Turning my attention back to Bill I ask, "The women?"

"The women!" he swoons. "By the High Council, the women. We're going to be surrounded by some of the richest and hottest women in the galaxy. It's a numbers game, LT. Thousands of them, two of us, it's gonna play out in our favor sooner or later."

Yeah, there it is. Bill can have his fill, or at the very least try. I can only imagine all the cheesy pickup lines that are running through his head right now. As I initiate the landing sequence for our slip, it hovers above the opening hangar bay doors below. "Look, just remember why we're here, okay? We're pulling security detail because some of the brass, i.e. the major, wasn't happy with our actions. Let's not make it any worse than it already is."

"Worse than it is," Bill mutters, shaking his head. "Listen to you! We've essentially been given twelve months of R and R around hot women and you're worried about getting *in trouble*." He brings his hands up and mockingly forms a quotation symbol with two fingers on each hand. Our slip lands on the metal floor in the hanger and bounces to a stop as the hydraulic legs stiffen in place.

"Bloodpack Alpha member delta-alpha-echo-six, please proceed to the hangar officer with your partner for debriefing. Welcome to The Outer Shores." While the first part of that message was all professional, it's clear that the female operator smiled during the welcome part and it isn't lost on Bill, who's smiling back at the speaker.

"I'm telling you man, she's a ten. I can hear it in her voice." I smack Bill across the back of the head as I get out of the pilot's chair. "Was that necessary?" he moans.

"Apparently," I confirm, punching the unlock code into the blue holographic interface next to the Slip's hull door. It slides to the right and disappears into the hull as a thin metal ramp extends down to the hangar floor from underneath the ship. I look back to Bill, then motion a hand out the door, "Let's go. I don't want to be late for the debrief."

Bill shakes his head, gets up, and walks past me down the ramp mockingly mumbling, "I don't want to be late for the debrief." We get to the bottom of the ramp and there's a double-wide door on the wall in front of us, then a small clear walled office to the left of the door with a friendly-looking female hangar operator that waves us over. "What did I tell you?" Bill whispers as we approach. He's got a point, she's wickedly attractive, almost too attractive to be believable. You'd never see a woman like this on the Patriarch, but personally speaking, I'm more attracted to strong-willed women who can handle themselves in a fight.

We walk up to the clear wall and a glowing blue map appears to the right of the operator. "Gentlemen, welcome to The Outer Shores. Major Erislad has requested your presence in his office, which is highlighted in red on the layout to my left." She points to the map and, sure enough, there's a room that's highlighted in red with a glowing white dot labeled 'Major Erislad' in the center. Two holes appear in the clear wall in front of us and the operator motions to them. "Gentlemen, your right wrists please."

We both place our wrists through the holes, which firmly close around them. "This whole 'gentlemen' crap has gotta stop, sweetie, OW!" Bill screams as a sharp pain shoots into my vein, then immediately dissipates. My entire right forearm feels warm under the skin.

"What was that?" I ask as the hole opens back up and releases our arms.

"I apologize for the momentary pain. Here in The Outer Shores, we like to make sure that everyone has access to any information that they may need in order to make their stay more pleasant. Nanomachines have been injected into your skin and if you look at your forearms, you'll see a small, glowing blue dot near the inside center of your wrist." I rotate my arm around to look at the inside of my wrist and can clearly see a pulsing blue dot where she described. "Tapping this dot will activate the Information Control Enzymes in your skin, also referred to as ICE. Activating ICE will allow you access to a wide variety of information, including various maps of our facilities and messages from other members."

I tap the blue dot with my left pointer finger and the dot stops pulsing at its brightest point, then expands an interface across my forearm in the same luminous color and offers several different options. It's essentially an advanced VOK unit that's built into our arms. Pretty impressive tech, but I guess when your compound has a limitless budget, this is the type of stuff you can afford. The thought has never crossed my mind until now, but it makes me sick that more money isn't put into keeping us alive. I know Alexander's department faces budget issues from time to time.

"Your directional maps have been updated with the locations of your living quarters and will direct you to Major Erislad's office. Have a pleasant day," the operator says, before turning around and typing away at the clear screen to her right. The map on the wall disappears and the large door to our right slides open. I take one last look at the operator, then proceed to walk through the doors and down the hall.

"Uh, *bye*, I guess." Bill says to the operator behind me expecting some kind of response. Lifting my right forearm, I can see a map of the floor we're on, with a red dot representing my position and a white line leading to Major Erislad's office. There's a readout of our *distance to destination* at the bottom of the map that decreases as we walk.

"Well, that was a little odd," Bill says jogging up from behind. I look over and he's scratching his arm where the map is to see if anything happens to it. Nothing does.

"What's odd?" I ask, fairly confident that it has something to do with how creepily robotic the operator sounded as she spoke to us.

"She didn't even respond to the raw sexual vibe that I was throwing off." I stop walking and stare at Bill. He keeps walking for a few steps, then turns around and looks at me. "What?"

"That's your take away from our interaction with her? Really?"

"Well, duh," he insists. "You've experienced my vibes before, you know how powerful they can be on the lady folk." I shake my head and walk past him toward the major's office. "Seriously though, like, look at me!" he yells from behind.

"Just shut up, Bill."

The corridors on the base are fairly similar to other military bases that we've been to, with one stark contrast. They're total overkill. The materials used in this base are made to look opulently extravagant. There's no question that it's operated on the basis of money and not that of military protocol, which is odd, because it is still a military base. Its primary functions are mainly centered around political needs and not combat, but it's still odd to see, given the internal operations of our government. Clearly, the materialistic wants of the political wing of our species has grown in the decades that we've spent embroiled in their wars. I already hate this place.

As we approach the major's office, I stop and turn to Bill. "Look, do me a favor...promise me you'll keep your mouth shut when we're in there." He stares at me with confusion and feigned pain. "I *don't* want to be here. We don't belong here, we belong in the field, and even though you see this as a fun little vacation, I know you'll come to hate it soon, too. Let's just do our stint, keep our heads low, and get the hell out of here, okay?" Bill purses his lips and nods. "Good." I press the holographic 'call' button to the side of the major's door and it slides open almost immediately.

The major, who we've never met prior, is sitting behind his desk, staring at us as we enter. I can already tell that we're not going to get along by the snide look of entitlement painted across his face. "So," he growls, "you two are the soldiers who killed my nephew and put his friends in critical condition. What do you have to say for yourselves?"

Before I have a chance to think of something that won't get us in trouble, Bill offers his version: "The green, arrogant little shits needed to learn their place. I'm confident they're well aware of it now, especially your nephew. Sir."

I catch the major fuming behind his desk before turning to gawk at Bill. He glances at me momentarily and offers a slight shrug as if to say, 'Hey, I didn't actually promise I wouldn't say anything', then turns back to meet the major's glare with his head held high.

Here we go.

Chapter 29: The Unexpected Visit

3.20 - 2467 - 001:103 Red Galaxy Standard

I'm startled by the clapping sound near the twin doors behind me as the last holographic Thyr falls to the ground in a bloody digital mess. I didn't hear anyone come in, but that's not really uncommon given the size of Red's training area and the amount of holographic Thyr that I just took down. I've also been training without my suit since the ass-beating I received from Lieutenant Mackelson a few weeks ago, and thus don't have the heavily amplified senses that I've grown used to.

Part of me hopes that Blaze is back from her most recent recon. I still haven't explained my distant nature and why I've been pulling away. We had a nice talk that night in the mess, about where our lives were heading—or where my fake Hemo life was heading. It just felt so good to be around her again, intoxicating to the point where I couldn't think straight. Everything has been so fucked up since I found out the truth that I couldn't bring myself to talk about the new reality of my life. I just wanted to be with her. I wanted something in my life to feel familiar. To feel like home. Fuck, how do I explain it? How will she react?

Disappointment washes over me as I turn around to see Alexander walking toward me with those dead white eyes still clapping in a very deliberate and robotic fashion. It's odd to see him in the white pants and shirt that he's wearing, even though it's the same get up that he dons under the lab coat. For some reason, the absence of the lab coat changes his entire persona.

"It really is amazing to see you fight. I'm a little hurt that you're not wearing the new suit we made for you," he feigns sadness with a smirk and shrug, "but you're still quite incredible on your own."

"End session," I demand coldly, releasing the holographic blade and sidearm, which both disappear into blue pixelated dust before hitting the ground. A quiet mechanical hiss emanates from the floor as the Thyr bodies disappear. "You've seen me fight before."

"Video feeds are so much different than real, live, unadulterated action." He stops ten feet from where I'm standing and folds his arms behind his back. "It's pretty amazing."

Since the fight two weeks ago, I've been splitting my time between obsessively training, figuring out how to talk to Blaze, and training even more. Occasionally some time with Aden crops up when he's not with Kelly, and we all wait for word from Lieutenant Mackelson. Suit or not, I don't want to get caught in a situation like that again. I've never felt so helpless in my entire life and given what we'll be facing in the coming battles, it can't even be the faintest hint of an option. I'm a little frustrated that Alexander is here; I don't have time for pleasantries.

"What do you want, Alexander?"

"Why do I have to want something?" he jests.

I scoff. "Because in the, what," I look up at the ceiling to do the math in my head, "almost three hundred and fifty years that I've known you, we've never interacted outside of your lab." He glances to the left and bobs his head in acknowledgment before looking at me again. "We're the same race but a different breed." I point at him, "You make the toys," then myself, "I make the sacrifices."

Well that seems to have riled him up, as he's the one scoffing now. "You Alphas. You're so narrow-minded." He juts his head forward, widening his empty white eyes. "Do you know what it's like to live in physical pain every second of your life? To feel as though your head is being crushed at all times and to find a way to push past that pain for the betterment of your species?"

Not in the mood for this attitude, I rush forward and grab him by the throat, picking him up off the ground. Judging by the look on his face, if he was still standing on his own two feet, he'd have stumbled backward on his ass. "Cut the shit. Do you want to go tit for tat on all the different hardships that we've had to endure over the years? Huh? Because I've gotta tell ya, we'd be here for a while and I'd come out ahead by a long shot." Releasing him from my grip, he drops a few inches back onto his feet, as I turn and walk a few paces away. "Tell me what you want." I stop, turning around to face him. "Because as far as I can tell, you're either here to hit on me, or ask for my help." I shrug my shoulders and shake my head. "Regardless, I feel like you're going to be disappointed."

Alexander rubs his throat for a second, clears it, then glances at the ground with a scowl on his face before looking up at me. "I've been told this room is dark. Is that true?"

"Who told you that?"

"Is it dark?" he presses.

"Yes, it is. Now who told you that?" I demand.

Alexanders turns his back to me and starts pacing around as if he's trying to figure out how to tell or ask me whatever's running through his head. "A hacker named Vee. I don't know his real name." Clearly not. Alexander assumes Kelly is male just like we did. "I started poking around in order to find more information about some disturbing rumors that I've been hearing. I wanted to know if they were true before figuring out any course of action."

This doesn't sound good. It sounds like Alexander may know about the fact that we were once human, or for that matter, just that someone in general was once human. "What about Vee?" I ask.

He stops pacing and turns to face me. "He approached me over our system when I was digging for information under what I thought was a dark ID, but this, this hacker is so much more advanced than I could ever be. He blew through my defensive matrix like it was nothing and already knew everything about me. Even hacked into my security feed to describe what I was doing while he was sending messages." Alexander shakes his head and stares off to the end of the room. "I've never seen anyone out-tech me."

"What a pity. Stay on point, why are you bringing this to me?"

He snaps back to reality and walks right up to me. I don't move or break my gaze. "He told me that you were one of a few well-placed individuals in contact with him. He said that you knew all about what the High Order had become and told me who you really were." Oh great, here we go. Why in the hell would Kelly trust Alexander with our past? Granted, it would be great to have an inside guy in the research department, but Alexander would never betray his own race. He believes in purity and loyalty above all else. It's one of the main reasons that he was promoted to the position that he's in. He'll do anything to advance our stance in the universe.

He leans in close to my ear, even though I told him the room is dark. "I know about the genetic splicing that they're doing with the Thyr. I know that you're trying to prevent it and I want to help."

Well, that is...unexpected. Kelly is playing Alexander. She's been able to secure his support, support that we'll dearly need, without actually revealing our true nature. I've got to say, I'm impressed and honestly a little intimidated. I bring my hands up to Alexander's shoulders and move him back away from my ear. "I told you, the room is dark."

He frowns and looks at the ground. "Sorry. I just, I'm not quite sure who to trust."

Okay, time to throw him a bone. If Alexander plays his part in the destruction of the species, I don't see any reason why he can't just walk away from everything in the end. I set a hand on his shoulder. "This goes up to the highest level of our government. Are you sure you want to be a part of it? It could mean dismantling our species as we know it, or dying in the process."

Alexander takes a second to consider the weight of what I've just told him, then lifts his head and stares at me with an emotional depth that I've never seen from him. "If the High Order is splicing us into Thyr hybrids," he pauses, making sure that he wants to commit to the words that are about to cross his lips, "they need to be stopped, and if they can't," he shakes his head, "then I don't want to see what they become."

I nod and squeeze his shoulder in a show of support before releasing him from my grip. "I want you to sleep on this. It's a big decision to make."

Alexander nods in confirmation and bites his lower lip while closing his eyes, before opening them. "I've made up my mind."

"All the same." I allow a slight smile in the left corner of my mouth to let him know that our relationship to each other has changed and for all that he knows, it's for the better. Well, technically it is for the better, regardless. At least now there's a chance that he won't get caught in the fray when the killing starts. "Take the time anyway. I need to speak with Vee, as well as the others involved, and find out what our next move is."

His gaze wanders off to the side of the room as he continues to process how quickly everything has changed, then he turns and walks toward the doors of the training room. I find it interesting that there's something in the universe that can still surprise me after all these centuries. Even though Alexander's always been upfront about his loyal nature to the purity of our race, I would have never expected him to act on anything that placed it in question. I guess it just goes to show the lengths that people will go in order to support their beliefs. If Alexander can see how wrong the High Order is in fucking with the natural order of the universe, then maybe our actions aren't as questionable as I first thought. I'm still not comfortable with genocide, but I'm confident that Aden and I won't let it come to that. Not fully.

I walk over to the doors and tap the blue holographic interface for my ICE unit, pulling up Kelly's dark feed, and patch the video into the door's security terminal. Her smiling face promptly appears in a holographic box above the interface.

"Lieutenant. What can I do for you?"

"I thought this was a quiet channel?" I ask.

"It is," her eyes go wide as her smile spreads, "unbreakable."

"Then please, just Daemon."

The smile fades "I don't uh…"

"Do you call Aden Sergeant?"

"Well," she pauses, "No. But to be fair, you're not fucking me."

I can't help but burst out laughing, it feels good amidst all the life changing shit that's been going on. Prior to her coming out about being Vali, I only knew her as the prim and proper High Priestess that Aden disgusted with his vulgar pick-up line. It's humorous to see this side of her. This down-to-earth, sarcastic female that seems a little too perfect for my brother. I've had enough of this military for the time being, so I'd love some sense of normalcy before we blow everything to hell or die trying. "Still, let's drop the formalities when it comes to our...more open conversations. Do it for me. Please."

Her smile returns after my unintended laugh and she nods in approval, "Very well, Daemon. What can I do for you?"

"I just had an interesting conversation with Alexander."

"Did you now?" she asks through a snide smirk on her face.

"I did indeed. Who else is aware of this little side project of yours?"

She tilts her head and looks to the ceiling, biting her lower lip. "Actually, you're the first to know."

"Hoffman doesn't know?" I ask surprisingly.

She looks back at me through the monitor, her face beaming with joy, "Nope. Consider it a little present for everything he's done to keep you in the dark. I leave the information at your disposal."

A slightly sadistic smile slowly spreads across my face as I think of all the ways I can frustrate the captain by keeping this information close to the chest. All the things we're about to take on and I'm getting into a pissing match with one of the, well now five, other people that I can count on to try and make it out of this alive. It seems petty, but then again, I can't remember the last time I've had a chance to be petty.

"I see those wheels turning again," Kelly says shaking me out of my little mental wonderland. "Why don't you let the mischievous human side come out and play for a bit?"

"I'll think about it." I lick my lips and glance at the ceiling as my head bobs in thought before looking back at Kelly and raising my eyebrows. "Thanks again."

"Anytime." She smiles once more, big and bright before switching off the feed.

Chapter 30: Delayed Vengeance

01.30 - 2252 - 504:102 - Outer Shores Common

"Thinking back, I'm kinda surprised it wasn't worse," Bill says, leaning against the doorway of the banquet hall. Security detail, isn't exactly enjoyable, and Bill's working on my last nerve. I don't know how many times I have to tell him, it's almost become involuntary at this point.

I keep scanning the crowd, "Stand up straight." Bill rolls his eyes, then pushes off of the wall and straightens out. He folds his arms behind his back and a half smile creeps across the left side of my face so he can't see it. Today's crowd seems pretty docile. A bunch of rich, young, privileged yuppies throwing some kind of black tie social event to slap each other on the back and celebrate something pointless. None of these kids look to be more than a hundred years old and I'd bet my life that none of them have ever seen combat, through a vid stream or otherwise.

"I'm just saying."

"You're always *just saying*, Bill."

"I know." He pauses trying to figure out a different way to say it, but gives up. "I'm just saying, we're over the six month mark and nothing happened past that initial blow out. We're in the clear. It's unspoken protocol."

I can't tell what's worse, this mind-numbingly, boring security detail, watching all these rich little shits, or Bill's boredom-induced rambling. With nothing better to do, I play along while continuing to scan the room for threats. "What the hell are you talking about?"

"It's an unspoken rule in the ranks, man. If you piss off your superior, and he doesn't punish you within six months, you're in the clear. Come on, everyone knows that." Bill keeps his hands folded behind his waist, then leans back against the wall again.

I turn to look at Bill. "Wait, what if you're on mission for more than six months and don't have any kind of comms?" It's not out of the realm of possibility. Comms went down all the time during the Feeleye war.

Bill looks at the ceiling in thought as one of the rich little shit's father walks over and says, "Gentlemen, could we keep up the professionalism please?" Bill snarls at the well-dressed man, then straightens back up and starts to scan the room as I return to my previous stance. "Thank. You," he says slowly and deliberately, pronouncing each word as if it's hard for us to understand him. He turns and walks away muttering, "untrained animals" under his breath.

"Maybe you should focus more on actual protocol and less on unspoken rules," I tease Bill.

He scoffs, "Oh, give me a break. This shit isn't protocol. There's no reason for us to be here." He throws his left hand lazily out at the crowd. "Look at these people. They don't even know what's going on in the rest of the universe. They don't know what the true cost of all this is. The safety of their little slice of heaven."

I hate to admit it, especially since agreeing with Bill at times can make me feel, well, dirty for lack of a better word, but he's right. None of these kids, and more than likely their parents as well, understand what it takes to secure their protection. They look at us with disdain, see us as antiquated, blunt tools of force left over from an age long forgotten that went extinct with the humans. They think the Thyr are a bedtime story told to children who won't listen to their parents and the Feeleye war was drawn out as a political stunt or some form of population control. We lost a lot of great men and women in the Feeleye war. Men and women a hundred times better than these cowardly, rich snobs.

"Well, looks like we got our punishment after all. Another six months of this shit." I glance at Bill, then quickly direct my attention back to the crowd.

Now that the ostentatiously boring dinner party is finally over, after continuing well into the night, Bill and I head to our respective rooms to pass out. It's amazing how exhausting standing around doing nothing can be. I offer a weak wave to Bill as he continues past my door to his own and mutters something about it being bullshit that his room is farther. I don't have the energy to listen or the inclination to respond in any way other than opening my door and collapsing on my bed. I will give The Outer Shores this, the beds here are incredibly comfortable and spacious. Some of the staff laughed at the accommodations that we were given, but compared to our rooms on the Patriarch, this is a five star hotel. It's always interesting how perspective comes into play with inanimate objects. It's not like people, where you could possibly misconstrue their intent or meaning. An object is an object, so its level of functionality or satisfaction is solely based off of the user's use for it and their previous experiences. I had problems falling asleep on something so comfortable for the first few months, but I'm finally getting used to it. Not that that's a good thing. Once this was all over, I'll be going back to stiff bunks and sleeping on rocks.

Before having a chance to pass out completely, on the verge of darkness and bodily exhaustion the likes of which I'm not used to, the communicator on my desk begins to beep. I roll over and grab it, surprised to see the name 'Captain Otto' across the small screen in bright blue letters, and tap 'receive'. The captain's face fills up the screen. "I was just about to grab some rack time, Captain. What can I do for you, sir?"

His eyes are wide with an odd combination of excitement and fear. Looking down at the bottom of the communicator, I can see that Bill is patched into the call as well. "Get your asses up right this second. I sent a request five minutes ago to the major. There's been no response yet, but he has to reinstate you into active duty."

I launch out of the bunk and set the communicator on the desk, as I throw my boots on and change into my casuals. "What's the situation, sir?" I ask, pulling a clean shirt over my head.

"Lieutenant Nyla and Sergeant Utha," it always sounds weird when the captain calls Blaze and Aphrodite by their real names. There's a small pang in my chest as my mind makes the connection between Blaze's actual last name, Utha, and her call sign. I'm not sure whether this makes me happy, or worried, but I don't have time to dwell on it right now. "They confirmed a Thyr presence on Earth and two other locations in the Milky Way galaxy. We need to get you boys back into action now to spearhead the continuing reconnaissance and disruption of their mobilization." I jam my feet into the combat boots near the foot of my bed and they let out a few faint clicks as the material shrinks tightly around my feet and ankles. Picking up the communicator and rushing out the door, the captain continues. "This petty little squabble that he has with you needs to end. Initial reports put their numbers in the millions and if we're going to ensure that they don't have a chance to spread and colonize, we need every available Alpha active and in the field."

Bill flies out from a corridor on my left, slamming into the wall on my right as he pulls his second boot on and it secures around his foot. He drives it to the ground and pockets his communicator now that he can see the captain on mine as we continue toward the major's office. "You boys need to convince the major to reinstate you and get back here ASAP. I hope you've stayed under the radar and on his good side the last six months. Over and out." The captain taps his screen and the video feed goes black.

I shove the communicator in my pocket and turn to Bill as we rush down the hall. "Well, this should be interesting," I say. "Let's hope your whole six month theory is correct."

"Dude, there's no way the major will hold us here when there's an imminent threat to High Command out there. He can't possibly be that much of a selfish ass." Bill may be confident, but I'm crossing my fingers. From what we've seen in our time here, there's plenty of powerful people who are no longer making decisions that are based on the best interests of our race.

As we round another corner, the major's office is just ahead on our right. The door slides open before either of us have a chance to tap the holographic call button on the frame. The major is sitting behind his desk, staring at us in the hallway. "Gentlemen, please come in," he says kindly and offers a hand to the chairs in front of his desk.

Bill and I hesitate for a second, glancing at each other before entering and cautiously sitting down. His voice is never this pleasant when he's addressing us. "I just received a request from Captain Otto. I'm sure he's taken the liberty of informing you directly?"

"Yes, sir," I respond with a nod. "If I may, sir?" The major approves with an extended hand over his desk that says 'continue'. "I know you're not quite fond of my partner and I, and to be honest you have good reason. I would like to once again apologize for our actions on the Patriarch that resulted in the unfortunate passing of your nephew and for the bluntness of my partner on several occasions since arriving at this installation." I look at Bill and so does the major before we meet eyes again. The apology is hollow. I just hope my acting is better than the major's ability to disseminate fact from fiction. I know the captain told us to never apologize, but it's clear the major gets off on having control. I don't mind doing some boot licking if it can get us away from this shithole. "But, now there's a common enemy in space, poised to attack the High Order in an attempt to wipe out our species for good. We may occasionally be inappropriate, but we *are* the best at what we do. Please sir, reinstate us into active duty so we can do our part to quell this threat to the High Order before it has a chance to gain ground."

The major purses his lips and looks down at his desk, reflecting on everything I just said. Bill and I afford a quick glance at each other as he offers a raised eyebrow in approval. The major lifts a tablet from his desk with the captain's request displayed on the screen. "I have here the captain's request for you to be reinstated into active Alpha duty immediately." He lowers the tablet and swipes his finger across the screen before showing us another communication. "And here I have a report from Brigadier General Fanderia. Would you like me to read it for you?" Oh shit. The major clears his throat and turns the tablet around to read the message.

"Major, I concur with your conclusion. The information that we have thus far about the Thyr presence in the Milky Way and subsequent galaxies holds no threat beyond what the forces stationed there are currently capable. As you stated, I see no point in reinstating Lieutenant Tyrus and Sergeant Tate as they would be better fit serving as security in The Outer Shores on the rare chance that another species would see this as an opportune time to strike at some of our people's most influential members located at your facility. Please convey this information to Captain Otto." The major sets the tablet back onto his desk, folding his arms over it and looking back up at us.

"This is bullshit," Bill mutters.

"What's that, Sergeant? I couldn't hear you," the major quips, staring at Bill.

"This is bullshit. Sir," he barks back, much louder.

"Turns out that I *am* that much of a selfish ass, Sergeant. You two little shits are going to be stuck in this facility for a while, long after the Thyr threat has been eliminated." He looks back and forth between us as he speaks, raising his voice with each word. "You're going to continue playing babysitter while your fellow Alphas get the chance to fight the one enemy that you've trained your whole lives to fight, but have never had the honor to meet in battle. You're going to stay here and prove that this antiquated society of barbarism that we've cultivated is no longer useful. You're going to prove that whether or not there's a protocol for it, that self-involved, egotistical assholes such as yourselves won't be allowed to run around and do WHATEVER THE FUCK *THEY* WANT!" The major takes a second to compose himself, "And that there will be consequences for it."

The major takes a deep breath and closes his eyes before tilting his head to the side and opening them back up. "Now get the fuck out of my office," he says, emotionless. Bill and I shove our chairs backward as we stand, snap off a salute with contempt and storm out.

Chapter 31: Welcome to the Party

3.23 - 2468 - 645:982 Red Galaxy Standard

Aden bolts out of the corridor to my left and I'm struck with an odd sense of nostalgia as he clips the combat belt around his waist and runs into the wall on my right with his shoulder. The scaled suit consumes everything except his face as he turns to acknowledge me. "What's the deal?" he asks with a grin as I dart by.

I can hear him following close behind, "Not quite sure, Hoffman just said suit up." There was an unusual nervousness in the captain's voice when he called my room.

"It didn't sound good." Simple math really. There's only two things that could have the captain so worried. Either he found out that Lieutenant Mackelson is dead, or the Plaguers are attacking again, but in greater force. Whatever it happens to be, it's bad because we were told to head straight to the command center instead of getting debriefed in the captain's office.

Red lights are flashing across every console in the command center as we come rushing through the door. The officers and tech operators are screaming at each other from across the room and various bits of field info and videos are riddling the dozens of holo screens. Aden and I slide to a stop just after passing the threshold of the door, shocked by a chaotic mess that we have yet to see is this room. As we're looking around trying to get a read on the situation, I see an officer out of the corner of my eye tap Captain Hoffman on the shoulder and point to us.

"SHUT UP!" the captain roars over the noise. "All irrelevant personnel get the fuck out. Now," he demands, pointing at the door. Ten men and women gather their things and quickly rush past us and out the door. We're left with the captain, five officers, Aphrodite, Blaze, and a single comms tech. "Gentlemen," Hoffman offers pointing at the large transparent command screen behind him, "the Thyr have entered the war."

With the exception of the emergency alarms radiating from various consoles, the room is eerily silent. A variety of emotions wash over me as I try to actually process what the captain just said. "Fuck me," Aden exhales. That's an understatement. We're all well aware that the Thyr were rebuilding their ranks, Earth and the thirteen dead recon teams were proof enough of that, but this is something else entirely. I look at a console and see five large ships on the edge of the Galician galaxy.

"Those are," I start.

"Not what we expected," the captain says. "Each recon team reported squad- to legion-sized Thyr collectives at each of the ten planets reconned. These are warships, corp sized. We estimate their crew size to include one hundred, possibly more, legions."

"Did you say legions?" Aden asks in near disbelief.

The captain nods. "So about the same size as the Patriarch," I affirm. Close to a half million troops per ship. That's a lot of soldiers.

"Yes, if scaled up to accommodate their size that is," Captain Hoffman turns to us. "Gentlemen," then Blaze and Aphrodite. "Ladies," Blaze shakes her head at the notion as the captain turns to the screens displaying the five Thyr warships on the edge of the Galician Solar System. "Intel shows the ships docked near Morrina, the furthest planet from Grecil, so at least that's something. With all five ships, we're looking at a force of somewhere near the tune of two point five million, and we have no idea how many more are on the way."

Blaze steps forward, "Two point five million, when none of our recon teams found..."

"Reported." I correct. Everyone looks at me. "Thirteen teams didn't come back. We escaped a legion ourselves."

"Two point five when none of our teams *reported*," she repeats as everyone's attention turns back to the screen. I can see that she's annoyed with not only the fact that I cut her off, but also that I've been pulling away more drastically in the last few weeks. "None reported any substantial forces. It's not unlikely to assume that this is a bulk of their force. If that's the case, we shouldn't have a problem."

I scoff out of uncontrolled response to the observation. Everyone looks at me again and I immediately regret having not held the reaction in.

"What?" she asks snidely.

I shake my head. "I think the Thyr have already proved that it's a mistake for us to assume anything."

The captain nods, but Blaze presses the point. "Really, Lieutenant? Is that from your extensive battle experience against them? Where were you during their discovery and subsequent uprising two centuries ago?"

We all know the answer to that, so there's no point in me saying anything. I get that she's angry with me, but it's clouding her judgment and unfortunately making her look foolish in the process. I may have reconciled with the fact that I love her, but it doesn't mean that I'll allow her to make such ignorant insinuations.

Besides, I was always led to believe that relationships were about bettering your companion.

"Where were you?" I ask.

That riles her up. Her face gets red and she all but leaps forward to lay one across my jaw. "Fighting the Thyr, you condescending asshole."

"Sergeant," Aphrodite says firmly.

I raise a hand, signaling to Aphrodite to let it be. "Captain," Blaze continues turning away from me. "There are over fifty million soldiers in the Red Military along with over five million Betas and a thousand Alpha teams, why are these ships even considered a threat?"

"How many were there?" I ask.

"What?" Blazes asks frustrated.

"How many Thyr did you fight in 2252?"

Blaze holds her gaze for a moment, before diverting her eyes to the ground while attempting to recall a specific number. "Like five thous…"

I don't let her finish. "Four thousand, three hundred and thirty-eight. Against ten Alpha teams and a force of ten thousand Betas just to *really* drive the point home. You know how I know this?" I don't pause for an answer. "Because I've spent the last two centuries and longer, studying everything about our enemies. Every encounter, every battle recording, every fact and known facet of their species. Battle experience is a small part of what it takes to make tactical decisions." I walk past everyone, to just below the screens and point to the enemy ships.

"*That*, is not four thousand, three hundred and thirty-eight soldiers. It's well over two million and we have no fucking clue whether it's the last of their species or a fucking welcoming party sent to knock on our front door." I drop my arm and walk over to Blaze.

"They're considered a threat because we have no idea what we're walking into. We thought they didn't have recon teams, they do. We thought they didn't have or wouldn't be willing to use cloaking tech, they do. Hell, we thought they were fucking extinct." I pause briefly to point back at the screen before stopping in front of her. "Two point five million, and a few months ago we thought they didn't exist." I move to within an inch of her and stare into her eyes. "Those fifty-five million soldiers are spread throughout the known universe, most fighting off growing numbers of Plaguers. There are one million reserve soldiers left on Grecil, five thousand Betas and at this current time, two Alpha teams within the vicinity. By the time it takes us to pull back a significant enough force to make the Thyr run and hide, they'll have easily overwhelmed our forces, that is of course, assuming that the Plaguers don't notice this once in a lifetime opportunity to jump in and join the fight *AND* that the Thyr forces engaged in this attack are limited to what we see, which I can guarantee you isn't true. Not enough? Recent reports from intel drones in the galaxy suggest that Mini K have been popping up and breeding at an unseen rate. Have you ever tried to face off against a rampaging force of Mini K? Because we have, and I can tell you right now, that would fuck up any battle, no matter what size."

Blaze's face is red again, her eyes burning through mine as we stare at each other. Her, out of willful stubbornness born through anger, and me out of frustration. I know she's smarter than this. I know I have an impossibly difficult mission before us and we're different species and everything is fucked up beyond belief but if I'm going to find a way to save her, she needs to be smarter than this.

"Ever wonder when these two are finally going to get it over with and fuck?" Aden says behind me. I turn to seem him leaning toward Aphrodite's ear.

"Okay, enough with the pissing contest," Captain Hoffman says, ignoring Aden's comment. "LT's right, there are too many variables in the air, too many things to go wrong, we can't afford to assume anything."

Blaze pushes me aside with her shoulder and steps over next to Aphrodite, then stares at the caption without looking at me. I turn back to the captain as well.

"What about that extra recon unit?" I ask referencing Mackelson.

The captain answers before Blaze or Aprodite have a chance to ask what I'm talking about. "No word. We have to move forward without the intel, however precious it may be. So here's the deal, current intel shows that the Thyr have started launching short range, but fairly large vehicles down to the surface of three planets within our system." The captain turns to the screens, then highlights and expands the view to show us a large view of the ships and the surrounding planets.

"Morrina, Saudade, and Sodadi." The names appear beneath each appropriate planet in white.

"Colonials?" Aden asks squinting at the screen. He can see perfectly fine, it's a just a physical tick that manifests when he's thinking.

The captain nods while glancing around to each of us as he speaks. "That's what we're thinking, yes. Forward operating bases within our galaxy for them to coordinate the coming war. As they push forward, they'll become more secure locations for their incoming forces to check in at before joining the battle. This is just the beginning."

"Look I love Galicia as much as the next Hemo, but why not just evacuate and wax the planets?" Blaze asks matter-of-factly. She seems to have calmed down a bit. It's not a bad idea, but I already know the answer.

The captain shakes he head. "Each of these planets have a substantial Hemo colonial presence due to the amount of raw minerals and beneficial wildlife. Evacuating them could be possible, but they took centuries to cultivate on and under the surface. We can't risk destroying that much work. They Thyr were smart if only for picking these planets." The captain turns around to face us. "I'm not going to lie; this is the start of a long and bloody war, even if the Plaguers don't come back. We need to strike fast and hard in order to avoid any unnecessary collateral damage that we can."

I shake my head. "These fuckers are deviating from what we know, hundreds of years of accounts. That makes them unpredictable and extremely dangerous."

"Trust me," the captain says, "I know. This is one of the many decisions that is out of my hands. You all have the best tech, training, and skills in the universe. Put them to use."

"What's the plan?" Aphrodite asks.

"India-November-Foxtrot, you will drop down onto Saudade and covertly assess the situation of the first Thyr dropship. Once any and all intel is called in from a distance, I will give the green light for an assault on said ship." The captain turns to look Aphrodite in the eye. "Intel gathering doesn't stop there. Assault the force in a manner that allows for the retrieval of their ship and any possible equipment. Alexander is dying to get his hands on whatever will help us gain an edge and we have yet to see small colonial ships from the Thyr."

"Understood," Aphrodite and Blaze say at the same time.

The captain looks at Blaze, "No deviations. Understood? The Plaguers could be back at any moment, so we need to do as much damage and gain as much intel as possible. We need a more solid idea of what we're dealing with so we can formulate a plan for the re-enforcements that are en route."

"Any details on that?" Aphrodite asks. It's the first time she's spoken up outside of trying to reel in Blaze. Her mind is trying to account for every possibility, just like mine.

"The million soldiers stationed in Galicia will be active and ready within twenty hours. Initial forces being pulled back will consist of five hundred thousand soldiers within three days. Five alpha teams will be in the Galaxy within the week. Beyond that we just don't know. All other local forces, Betas included, are engaged with the Plaguers and other species. High Command won't deem the situation in need of an emergency recall until they have more info.

"Yes, sir."

"What about us?" Aden asks. The captain turns around to address us. "Given your new suits, you two are going to try something a little bit more," the captain hesitates as if to search for the correct word, "aggressive." Aden and I look at each other with anticipation and smallest bit of concern that's only visible to us due to our centuries of working together. "You're going to sneak onto one of those battleships unnoticed and figure out how to take it down from the inside."

Aphrodite and Blaze shake their heads and trade looks out of a mixture of jealousy and disbelief as I take one long blink, hoping the captain isn't serious. He is.

"Understood," We say together

The captain saw our hesitation. "You're battle-hardened reconnaissance professionals who have excelled at everything we've thrown your way."

I can hear Blaze whisper to Aphrodite, "Except that mess at The Outer Shores."

Though it was never confirmed in official military records, rumors spread about my involvement of an escaped captive during our last stint at The Outer Shores. Seeing as the captive was supposedly so top secret that there's no record of its existence, I always reply to the rumors the same way; I have no idea what you're talking about.

The captain glances back at Blaze, "You have NO equals in this military," then sets his gaze on Aden. "I'm more than confident you'll pull it off." Aden nods. "The High Scientists have built a small slip that is just big enough to carry you two over to the ship and should be invisible to Thyr sensors."

"Should?" Aden asks.

"As your lieutenant stated, the Thyr are deviating from normal battle procedures, but that shiny new cloaking tech they have, we developed decades ago. If our sensors can't pick up this slip, it's unlikely theirs will."

"Well that's reassuring," Aden mutters.

I catch Blaze staring at me. There's pain in her eyes, behind the anger she uses to push it aside. "If that's all, Captain, we'll grab our gear and proceed to docking." I'm eager to get this mission underway. It's not going to be easy, but standing in the same room as Blaze, knowing how much I've hurt her is worse than whatever awaits us on that ship.

Captain Hoffman nods. "Dismissed." I look away from Blaze as we turn and head to the door. "Gentlemen," the captain calls out. "There's more work to be done, so get your asses back here ASAP." We both offer a thumbs up over our heads without turning back and head out the door. "Good men," I hear the captain say as the door slides shut behind us.

"You gonna talk to her?" Aden asks as we jog down the hall toward the docking bay.

"I think that would make it worse."

"Not to sound morbid, but it may be your only chance."

"She doesn't want to talk to me. Besides, the last thing I need is to fuck up my head before a mission like this."

We round the corner. "Brother," Aden says glancing at me for a moment. "I hate to break it to you, but our heads are well past fucked up."

Isn't that the truth.

Chapter 32: Blink

08.15 - 2253 - 124:123 - Outer Shores Common

You'd think that, given all their money, these people would have more to do than throw parties and banquets for themselves, but that's pretty much it. I can't even begin to understand why people would want to do the same thing over and over again for months, hell years, or in some cases decades, on end. Never leaving the planet, never leaving the galaxy, just sinking in to the same old routine for the rest of their long lives. Then again, as one of them so eloquently reminded me the other day, we are not 'cut from the same cloth', so I can't see them understanding my life either.

I haven't heard Bill say anything for a few minutes, which is odd for him, but then again I'm not usually daydreaming during security detail. This particular brand of extended torture is starting to get the better of both of us. A part of me feels like shit for letting my mind wander; it's not the way I approach any job, but this could hardly be called a job anymore. We're essentially living statues at this point, we barely move unless no one's watching. I turn to see what's got Bill so silent and he's intently staring across the room at something.

"Bill?" I ask slowly. I can only assume he's spotted an attractive female, but he's giving off a creepy vibe. "Whatcha lookin' at?" He doesn't respond, but his eyes dart to another section of the room. "Bill, it's impolite to stare, besides you look like a creeper." His eyes dart back to what he was originally looking at. Great, there are two women he's interested in. "Bill look, I'm sure they're both attractive but..." his left hand clamps down on my right wrist.

"Something's wrong," he says sternly.

I shake my head, "Look if they've got boyfriends then just don't go after them."

He turns to look me in the eye. "Something. Is. Wrong." I can tell from the seriousness in his eyes that this has nothing to do with women. He lets go of my arm and turns back to the crowd, letting his eyes dart around the room in every direction.

"Talk to me, Bill." The playfulness in my voice drops away as I split my attention between him and the crowded ballroom.

"Something's wrong. I'm trying to place my finger on it, but it's hard to see..." his voice trails off as his eyes squint at the crowd and he leans forward a bit before relaxing and straightening out. "There's something off about a few of the guests."

Well thanks for narrowing it down. It's not often that I get worried, but when Bill stops joking around, especially before I do, I know things are serious. "I need more to go off of, give me something here," I press, trying to get some information on what we're looking for and how dangerous it is.

He waits for a moment to respond, eyes still darting around the room as his lip slightly curls. "Some of the patrons are off." He squints again before continuing, "There's something off about them, I don't know what yet, but I don't think they're Hemo. It's just, it seems crazy."

"Bill seriously, anything here to go on, I'm not gonna think it's crazy."

He inhales deeply, holding it for a second, then lets it out. "Some of the patrons have been disappearing and reappearing in different spots."

Yeah, he's crazy. "What do you mean?"

"So far I've noticed three different people be in one spot, on one side of the room and then a second later they vanish and I catch them in a different location. A location that's way too far for them to have run to unnoticed."

"You actually saw them disappear and reappear?"

Bill turns his head toward me for the briefest of seconds, glancing at the ground as if to judge the validity of my question. "Well, no...I..." He looks up and locks eyes with me. "Look, I know this sounds crazy but one second they're there and then someone walks in front of them and they're gone. Then I search the room and find them in a different location. Like on the other side of the room."

Not only does this sound totally implausible, but damn near impossible. We don't have any kind of teleportation device anywhere near capable of performing a feat like what he's describing, and we're the most advanced species in the known universe. Bill tries to turn back to the crowd, but I bring my right hand up to his forehead and direct his head back to me. "Bill, there's no kind of tech out there that's capable of what you're talking about."

His upper lip quivers and he's clearly offended by the insinuation that it's either not happening, or he's lying. "Just look," he demands. I sigh, then turn back to the ballroom. "The young bald guy in the all-white suit, shirt and vest with the black tie to the left of the bar." It takes a second, but I'm able to zero in on who he's talking about. At least I think I do, I don't see any other guys in the area wearing all white with a black tie.

"Okay. What now?"

"Just watch. He seems to be on a pattern of every thirty seconds or so." I still have my doubts as to what Bill claims is going on, but there's only been a few times that I can remember him being this serious. If what he says is true, we're going to have a real problem on our hands. Still, it's going on twenty seconds now and the guy hasn't moved. He simply walks over to the bar and orders a drink. Hardly the actions of a grave security threat. More than thirty seconds.

"Bill, I don't..." A stunningly beautiful woman in a tight blue dress walks in front of our dark mystery man and he's gone. "What the..."

"I've got him over here," Bills says before I have a chance to choose an expletive to express my shock. I slowly turn to my right to see the same man standing near the entrance of the ballroom and leaning against the wall with a drink in his hand. It's damn near fifty yards away from his previous position.

"Fuck." That was the expletive I was searching for.

"He's not the only one. Redhead, ten o'clock, tight white dress." I blink a few times and pinch the back of my hand to make sure that I'm actually awake, then get eyes on the redhead. "Her...rotation, if you will, seems to be a little longer. She's around forty-five seconds." Bill must have been watching her the entire time I had eyes on the bald guy, because sure enough, it took just under forty-five seconds for her to disappear as well. It happened in the same exact fashion, someone walked in front of her and she was gone.

"The bar." Bill nods at the bar where the redhead is apologizing to an older guy that she bumped into. He smiles and offers to buy her a drink, flagging down the bartender.

"I spotted another three while you were watching the bald guy," Bill elaborates. "I think that's it. Five in total, at least from what I can tell. They're all wearing white and they all seem to have some sort of black accent on their outfits." The redhead did have a black sash across her waist. Without responding to Bill, I quickly scan the room looking for any other patrons who are dressed in mostly white. It doesn't take long for me to spot the other three, now that I know what I'm looking for. Actually, they're the only ones in the party who are dressed in white. These upscale rich people sure do like their colors, odd that it would be something to work out in our favor.

"I've got all five now, too," I confirm. We both keep our eyes on the ballroom, watching the mysterious, alabaster strangers jump around the room without ever actually seeing them disappear. "Have they done anything else out of the ordinary?"

I can feel Bill's eyes on me. "What, disappearing into thin air isn't fucking enough?" he quips.

Good point.

"I'm just trying to figure out what the hell is going on here."

"Yeah well, now you know why I was so quiet. I thought I was seeing things at first, but then thought there's no way a couple of drinks would do that."

I turn and glare at Bill. "You drink on duty?"

"Oh come on, like you're shocked," he says without turning to meet my eyes. "Most of the whiskey here is older than these kids, I'm not missing out on that. Besides, this isn't duty, this is standing still for eight hours at a time."

I turn back to the ballroom mumbling, "Not tonight it isn't."

Chapter 33: Damn Arrow

3.23 - 2468 - 680:231 Red Galaxy Standard

"It's quite astonishing, really," Alexander says with a huge smile on his face as Aden comes running into the docking bay. He wanted to say goodbye to Kelly quick before we got underway. I don't blame him. I'm still going back and forth about talking to Blaze before we leave.

Alexander turns around and points to the mini slip that will be taking us to the other side of the Galician Solar System undetected. "The physics behind it are amazing. Remember those creatures you came in contact with at The Outer Shores?"

"The Apparitions?" I confirm.

"Yes, precisely. We reverse engineered their..."

Knowing full well that this is heading toward a drawn-out explanation of the tech that we're about to use, Aden stops Alexander before he has a chance to drag us down the science wormhole. "Hey! Alexee," that of course earned him a scowl. "Look, I'm glad you're excited about your new toy here, but we're on the brink of a second war and time is kind of a factor. Less dissertation, more book with pictures."

Alexander pouts for a moment, annoyed by the fact that his detailed explanation of how the craft works will have to wait for a later date. "Okay, well," he brings his pointer finger up to his lips and taps them out of frustration, "Essentially, though this is really dumbing it down, even for you, there's a beacon on all three planets. When we activate the beacon on Saudade, it acts like a magnet to your slip and pulls you through space at an accelerated speed."

"How accelerated?" I ask, hoping to make up for Aden's dampening of his spirit.

"Well, you see," he says with a smile.

"Remember, book with pictures," I remind him.

He shakes his head. "Really fast," he blurts out. "That simple enough?"

"How long will it take us to get to Saudade?" Aden asks.

Alexander walks over to the slip, leans over and takes one last look at it, while referencing the computer on his wrist, which is probably completing the final preflight diagnostics. "You'll be there in under an hour."

I look at Aden with wide eyes and he returns the gesture. "Alexander, that's incredible." Across the system in under an hour, without using a wormhole or negma—also known as negative mass drive—is insane. Hell, even with a negma it would take weeks, maybe even months to get there. "What about navigation? At those speeds, we won't be able to react quickly enough if, say, a meteor or something crosses our path."

Alexander scoffs without turning away from the computer on his wrist. "Please, it's taken care of. The bio-computer in the ship monitors and resolves all that for you. I'd explain more, but apparently you don't have the time."

I throw my head back in frustration, then look over at Aden and jut my head toward Alexander. He purses his brow, silently asking *what?* I jut my head again. Aden sighs, "All right look Alexander, just as soon as we get back you can explain it all to LT, he'd love to listen." Thanks Aden. "But seriously, we have to get going, impending doom and all that. Is it ready to go?"

Alexander taps the screen on his forearm a few times then stands back up and faces me without acknowledging Aden. "It's all set. Controls are fairly standard; the bio intellect inside will help you along. If you need anything else you can reach me on my normal channel."

I walk over to the small slip, which essentially looks like a large, deep black tube with a pointed front no wider than five feet and barely long enough for two seats, one in front of the other. The side of the slip is just open, without any kind of defining door that can be seen. Both of the seats look like a pretty tight fit, but I manage to slide into the front as the chair and cockpit form to my body. The interior must be made up of the nanomaterial that our suits are constructed from. Aden gets into the back seat and Alexander backs up a few steps.

"The slip will connect and interface with the nanomaterial in your suit and the seats will change to match a more optimal comfort level if needed. It'll also monitor your biometrics and most of the navigational options will be routed to your visor and be selectable in the same manner that you activate your suit's functions." Alexander glances back at Aden briefly, then looks me dead in the eyes. "Good luck, gentlemen." He offers a slight nod before tapping the interface on his forearm, at which point the slip's opening begins to close with little blocks of nanomatter like our suits.

It's barely sealed and Aden's already on my case. "What was that?"

"What was what?" There's a small jolt to my back as the slip connects to and begins to interface with my suit. I activate my helmet and the visor appears across my face with a slightly different interface than I'm used to. *Apparition 1.1* is displayed in the upper right hand corner and *Ghost Drive* flashes across my display then fades away as I'm left with a variety of options. "Whoa."

A video of Aden appears in the upper right corner just beneath the *Apparition 1.1* title. "Don't change the subject. What was that little nod he gave you? He's never done that before, and there was this...look on his face." The slip begins to slide forward, even though I haven't heard the engines start up.

I activate Alexander's comm channel. "Hey Alexander, we're moving but I don't hear anything."

His chuckle echoes through my helmet. "Wouldn't be much of a stealth slip if it made a lot of noise, would it? Primary objective after you interface with the slip is to jettison from the Patriarch and hold position aside her until you select a destination or manually fly it. If you scroll to destinations on the right of your visor menu, you should see a list of all the planets in the system. We've already installed gravitational beacons on all of the planets. Just scroll to Saudade and select it. The slip will take over and offer suggestions along the way. If at any time you need to drop out of the gravitational slide, just switch to manual flight and your normal holographic controls will appear in front of you after it slows down to a manageable speed."

"Thanks," I say before closing the channel. Aden is still staring at me through the small video screen in my visor. "Oh yeah. Hold on." I open our secure channel to Kelly. "Hey Kelly, are we dark?" A video of her pops up underneath Aden and I select Saudade under the destination menu while waiting for her to reply.

"As always," she says with a smile.

"Thank you. Aden, your girlfriend..."

Aden turns flush red and cuts me off, "Whoa whoa, are we? I mean, labels are like, I don't know that she wants to be referred to as..."

Before he can finish, Kelly cuts in, "As what, shithead? What the hell else would we be?" she screams through the mic. "Please, please finish that sentence," she says sourly, before stopping abruptly and glaring into her camera.

"What, uh," Aden swallows, "what did my *girlfriend* do?" he asks in a high-pitched voice.

"Wise choice, jackass," Kelly growls.

I can't help but chuckle. "So anyway, as I was saying, your girlfriend pulled Alexander into the fold without telling him that we were humans."

Aden's eyes go wide and he pushes his lips out. "Wow, that's...how the hell did you do that, hun?"

"Oh, he's okay with the *hun*, but the girlfriend thing is an issue," Kelly exhales.

"Alexander is a purist, plain simple. I contacted him as Vee and gave him the details on the plan to splice Hemo and Thyr genetics and he thought it was appalling. Then I directed him to Daemon."

Past the initial little slide of us moving out of the docking bay, I can't feel the slip moving or hear any engines, so I direct my attention back to the flight display for a moment. We're already moving and we're moving fast. There's a small map of the system and our slip is zooming across it. I can't believe that I don't feeling anything, this tech is remarkable. Maybe I will sit down with Alexander when we get back and have him explain it a bit.

"Yeah, she could have warned me first, but I played it cool and got him on our side."

Aden looks up at the top of his helmet and takes a second to absorb the information, then looks back at the screen, "Hey, while we're on the topic of people acting weird, what was with Blaze?" He glances off to the side, presumably at Kelly, then back at me with a puzzled look.

"Huh?" I feign ignorance.

"She looked..." Kelly starts.

"Fucking pissed," Aden finishes.

"I was going to say frustrated."

"Well sure but,"

Their conversation fades from my perception as they ramble on and for a second I'm wrapped up in recalling more than a few nights with Blaze. Nights where we actually had the chance to enjoy each other's company. To just lay there and soak each other's energy and love. I almost don't notice Aden and Kelly having a silent conversation with their eyes. "Wait, hold on a second."

Aden's eyes shoot back to the screen. "What?"

"What going on between you two?"

"Whaaaat are you talking about bro?"

"What's with the eye conversation that you and Kelly were just having? Once you both get into your weird little ramble sessions I either have to walk away or tell you to shut up fifteen times, so what's up?"

Aden laughs, "I think you're seeing things." I keep staring and all of a sudden he stops laughing and gets serious. "Okay look, bro. We're worried about you, that's all. You started pushing her away."

"What did you do?"

"It wasn't right, I know I may have stepped over the line, but..."

"What. Did. You. Do?" I demand, enunciating each word.

Kelly looks around the room she's in, avoiding eye contact with her camera and Aden finally caves. "Okay, I said goodbye to Kelly, but I also stopped by to tell Blaze that you love her."

"WHAT!"

Aden chuckles nervously. "Yeah and we're patched her in so you could talk."

"ADEN!" Just after I scream his name in frustration, Kelly and his feeds drop and Blaze's beautiful, yet hurt face is plastered across the inside of my visor. Her jaw tenses and tears begin to well up under her vibrant green eyes. I try to switch the feed off, change it, do something, but Kelly's locked our feeds onto each other. There's no use. For a moment I just stare, I can't think of anything else to do and her eyes have always had this power over me. I don't want to deal with this right now and I'm furious for Aden thrusting it on me.

Blaze finally breaks the silence. "You fucking asshole!"

I nod. "That seems to be a pretty fair assessment, yes."

She takes a breath, "You avoided me."

"I did."

"You pushed me away."

"That's true."

"You were going into your most dangerous mission ever without even talking to me."

"Correct."

"You love me."

"I uh," I breath in deep and take a moment. Why can't I just say it? I know it's true, she knows it's true, hell Aden knows it true, but I still can't bring myself to say the words. Is it because of who I've become? Or what I'm going to do next? She doesn't know who I really am and what we plan on doing. Could she accept it? Could she get on board and fight back against the tyranny of the High Order?

"You don't have to say the words," she says snapping me back to the conversation. "But if it isn't true then say so."

I stay quiet.

She thinks for a moment, then looks over my face and slightly raises her eyebrow. It happens when she's come to a conclusion on something. "There's something else isn't there?"

I look away from the screen and swallow, "There is. Something from my past."

"Hey," she says waiting for me to look back. "Hey." I take another second then look at her face. It's more beautiful in that moment then it even has been. She doesn't need to say the words, it's written all over her face, in her eyes.

Blaze shakes her head, "I don't care what it is."

"But..."

"No. Shut up you stubborn bastard and listen for once in your life. I don't care. It doesn't matter to me. Tell me or not, whatever it is it doesn't matter. We've spent centuries with each other. There is nothing that can scare me away now, you hear me? Nothing."

Don't be so sure.

Her back stiffens. "Now I'm going to give the orders for once, you hear me, Lieutenant?"

"You always have," I mutter with a half-smile. This causes her to smile as well.

"You're going to get on that ship, you're going to take it out, and then you're going to come back to me. You're going to hold me in your arms and regardless of what you do or don't say, I'll know that love me and you'll know that I'm not going anywhere, I promise."

I nod silently.

"Then you're going to fuck me into an orgasmic coma and we're going to kick some more ass."

This causes me to burst out laughing. That's the woman I fell in love with. Feminine, crude and all together deadly.

"I can get behind that," I say with a smile.

"Fuck yeah you will," she says with a wink.

Chapter 34: Catch

08.15 - 2253 - 435.398 - Outer Shores Common

"Gentlemen, I want you to explain what happened," Major Erislad pleads with a kind voice. It's the nicest he's sounded since we were shipped to The Outer Shores two years ago. Hell, he even sounds nicer than when he led us to believe that we might get restored to active duty. For the first time since we've met him, I'm not wondering whether or not he's serious. He is. I can tell by the tone of his voice and the somber look in his eyes.

"Why? You have the damn security footage," Bill snaps. He, on the other hand, still thinks that the major is just setting us up for failure. I can't blame him. Two years of boredom torture with the occasional tongue lashing for something trivial that we did or didn't do would make anyone believe that he was just screwing with us again.

"Because we have an alien life form in custody and footage that caught nothing but fractions of what happened," the major explains to Bill. "The electronics seem to have reacted to their…jumps." He looks at me for a second and cracks a warm smile before turning back to Bill. "Because my wife and daughter are alive, thanks to you gentlemen. Please."

Bill sighs and after another moment of silence I bump his arm with my shoulder. "All right! Fine, but cut that 'gentlemen' shit out." The major nods in approval and offers a hand out over his desk, signaling Bill to continue. It's better if Bill tells it, seeing as he was the first one to spot and observe the Apparitions, as we're calling them, at some length before I noticed them. Besides, he deserves the appreciation after all. "We were on statue duty in the master ballroom and I only had a chance to sneak in two drinks beforehand, so it wasn't enough to totally zone me out. More like make the boredom more palatable than usual."

I let a nervous chuckle escape by accident. "Bill, I don't think the major needs to hear some of the more uh, pointless details of the night. Try to stay on track, maybe just stick to the facts." The major raises an eyebrow in judgement, in an attempt to tell if Bill is being sarcastic or not.

"You didn't want to tell the damn story and he wants to hear what happened. Are you going to let me tell it my way, or are you going to interrupt every time I say something uncouth?" he yells at me. I can tell he's enjoying this a little too much. I take it back, it's not that he thinks the major is setting us up. Bill knows that we finally have the upper hand and he's going to use it to say what's been on his mind for the last two years without the fear of repercussions. It's kind of smart, in a Bill sort of way.

"Uncouth? What? Have you been reading the *word of the day* entries on the your box of blood crisps again?" Okay, maybe I'll play along a bit. With the exception of a few hours ago, it's been a long and uneventful two years.

Bill raises his voice and throws his hands into the air for theatrics, "Oh, here we go again! *Bill's stupid!*" he mocks. "He couldn't possibly have more than a ten-word vocabulary."

"I never said that."

"How the hell am I going to tell the damn story if I'm only familiar with the most basic words in our language, huh?"

Now I raise my voice. "I didn't say that! Why do you always have to put words in my mouth?"

"Why don't *you* tell the damn story? I. Can't. Talk. Good. No. More."

"Gentlemen, please!" the major yells.

"Stop calling us 'gentlemen'!" we both yell back at the same time.

The major closes his eyes and sighs, then sets both hands on the desk in front of him. Bill and I have a brief moment to smile and wink at each other before he raises his head to look at us. "Sergeant, please continue with the story. You won't be penalized for whatever you say. You have my word."

Well, that was a mistake.

Bill squints at the major, then seemingly satisfied, sinks back into the uncomfortable chair. "Okay. Well, like I said, I didn't get a chance to drink enough to dull the abysmal atmosphere of pompous boredom before the massive, *look how small our dicks are* banquet."

"Sergeant," Major Erislad says, in hopes that he'll just continue.

"Oh right, there were women too, I don't want to sound sexist...wait I had something for this." Bill taps his lower lip with his pointer finger as the major shakes his head, already regretting his decision to let Bill off the hook for saying whatever comes to mind. "Gold digger's convention of old hags?" I'm doing my best to hold in the laughter tickling the back of my lips.

"My wife and daughter were there," the major says flatly.

"Oh, right. Speaking of which, nice work! Your wife was the only non-hag there." Bill leans forward and talks out of his lower lip in a hushed tone. "Must have cost a fortune to make her look like that, bet she shows her appreciation in your chambers, eh?" He leans back into the chair again. "And that daughter of yours," his voice gets higher, "not much to look at in the face, but turn off the lights and..."

"Bill, on point," I interject.

"Right," he confirms, pointing at me. The major inhales deeply, holds it, then releases it back out. "Anywho."

The banquet went downhill pretty quickly once the Apparitions realized that we had a bead on them, but they didn't know that we were Alphas. After Bill pointed out what was going on, we did our best to seem disinterested and keep them in our sights at the same time, which is easy to do with one or two targets, but five is a different story.

Just after the redheaded female jumped to the bar and flashed her pretty eyes to get a drink from the well-to-do businessman she bumped into, one of the males jumped over to the entrance and closed the doors. The other two males covered the two remaining exits to the room and the second female, who had short, black hair, jumped straight up on the end of the bar behind the redhead. All of the attendees wowed and clapped in amazement, assuming it was some kind of after dinner spectacle that had been prepared.

"Ladies and gentlemen!" she roared, getting their attention. The ballroom fell quiet. "A terrible crime has been committed by your species on the universe. The extermination of the Feeleye has not gone unnoticed and it has been decided that you shall pay for those crimes."

Hushed conversations erupted throughout the hall as people were trying to figure out if this was some kind of political stunt or a sick joke, but we knew better. "We need to..." I turned to address Bill, but he was already gone. "What the hell?"

"Tonight *you* shall pay for a brutal crime, with a brutal de..." I assumed she meant to say death, but the declaration was cut short by the closed end of a fist that Bill let loose on her jaw. She fell off the bar, smacked her forehead on the edge and rolled onto the ground next to the redhead below, as various men around the room gasped and woman shrieked in shock.

"Women, right?" Bill pointed to the black-haired Apparition on the floor with his thumb. "They sure can yammer on." He threw his hands up and shrugged. Before anyone had a chance to figure out what was going on, the redhead swiped Bills legs out from under him and he slammed on to the bar on his back. I rushed over, pushing through the crowd in order to get to him as quickly as possible, but by the time I could see what was going on Bill was swinging his body around, alcohol bottle in hand, ready to smack the redhead, but both her and the brunette had disappeared.

"LT?" Bill said questioningly as he slid off the bar, looking frantically around the ballroom.

"I'm working on it," I replied, also looking around to where they disappeared. There was no sound, no visible indication as to when they would jump so it was difficult to track them down once they did. The high society types still had no clue what was going on, but started to give us some space upon seeing the two women disappear.

"Hey, can I ask you a question, LT?"

"Uh...now, really?" The remainder of the Apparitions had disappeared, or at the very least I couldn't tell where they had jumped. The crowd seemed to be harder to scan since the patrons were huddling together and discussing what just happened.

"Ever think I could hook up with one of these chicks?"

"That's your question right now?" I went to my knees as something blunt hit me in the back of the head. Bill turned around, but the Apparition responsible was gone by the time he did. I let out a grunt and my knees slammed into the floor,

"Son of a bitch," I said, getting back on my feet with the help of Bill. I saw the bald-headed man appear on the other side of the room near the door. Hmmm, maybe... "Bill, we need to move." Before he had a chance to respond, I pushed through the crowd and darted over to where we had previously been standing post.

After a few minutes of scanning the room, Bill leaned into my ear and whispered, "What are we doing?" The Apparitions were nowhere to be seen, but they hadn't attacked us either. They came here to attack, to kill, but now they weren't doing anything. What were they up to? Waiting for us to make a move?

"When you saw them jumping, where did they go?" I asked quietly. Bill pointed out the different locations of all five Apparitions and where he saw them jump to. "Okay, I think I have a plan." I stepped down from our perch and started walking amongst the crowd, appeasing people as we walked across the ballroom. "No, they're still here, but don't worry, we'll catch them," I said with confidence. Bill followed suit, assuring the patrons of similar claims. We walked around the ballroom for ten minutes, avoiding all of the spots where Bill had previously seen the Apparitions, but there was no sign of them.

Then I walked over and leaned against the bar where I had last seen the two women. I could feel eyes on the back of my neck and turned to catch the wrist of the redhead trying to bring a knife down into my skull. She disappeared and I shouted "Catch!" to Bill before spinning around and sinking my fist into the black haired's stomach behind me. Bill had been standing at one of the two locations where he had seen the redhead in the last half hour, the other being my location. She reappeared in front of him and he grabbed her wrist, rotated the blade out of her hand, spun her around and dug it deep into her spine.

When the female in front of me curled over her knees and fell to the ground, I activated the stun points in the tips of my fingers and touched her head, allowing two hundred thousand volts to surge through her temple. Her muscles tensed and quivered as she fell to the ground. I didn't think I'd ever get a chance to use the embedded stun feature that they implanted into our hands during security orientation. I have to admit, it was kind of cool.

Bill's quarry was dead and the floor around his feet slowly filled up with blue blood that poured from her wound as my target remained still on the ground. The three remaining males made their whereabouts known right after the stunned chick hit the floor. The bald guy was now standing near one of the exits in front of me and screamed out in agony. Another male reacted in a similar fashion near the front door next to Bill's kill and the remaining male seemed to let out a war cry of some kind to rally the other two.

"So these creatures, they could only jump to specific locations?" the major asks Bill, breaking his recollection of what happened. He leans forward on the desk, seemingly interested in the story.

"From what we experienced, yes, it would seem that way," Bill answers.

"What about the other three?"

Well, two of the three males seemed to be consumed by rage and one attacked each of us separately after their emotional cries of distress. It was pretty clear that they were involved with the women that we just dispatched. Now rage is a funny thing, it can give you an unknown amount of power to fight off your enemies, but it can also blind you from the simple fact of what's happening in the immediate area.

That's essentially what happened. Every time that Bill and I would get the upper hand in the fight, these guys would jump back to their predetermined locations and use the chaos of the panicking crowd to attempt a sneak attack. I have to give them this, they were fantastic hand-to-hand fighters. At first, I was curious as to how they planned on killing everyone in the ballroom without weapons, but it became pretty clear that this was a personal vendetta. They wanted to be up close and personal, orchestrating one death after another with their bare hands. They had the skill, but unfortunately for them, they weren't counting on two Alphas as a security detail.

Now, as they were trying to use the teleportation to their advantage, Bill and I were sneaking closer to each other, one step at a time with every bout. It didn't take long before we were only a few feet apart and Bill and I are no strangers to using more than sight to react quickly in a fight.

I dodged a punch to the face which sailed past my shoulder and into Bill's hands as he reached backward over his own shoulder. Ducking down, I connected with a jab to the ribs and the assailant was caught off guard as Bill tightened his grip around the Apparition's wrist and heaved him over his back. He flew forward and tumbled into his brother-in-arms as they both fell to the floor. The third male saw this as a good time to intervene, but was focused on his friends on the floor and Bill as he approached and not my fist flying into his temple. They weren't the only ones who could use the chaos of the crowd to their advantage.

"What about the forks?" Major Erislad asks.

"Well," Bill pauses, thinking back, "we didn't have any weapons beyond the integrated tasers and LT had already stunned one. Given the trouble they already provided, I thought it was best to end them." Bill shrugs, "The first thing I saw walking toward them that I could use was two forks on the table to the right. So I snagged 'em, and buried one into each of their throats." He chuckles to himself. "Ah, who says you can't have your cake and eat it too?"

In any other outpost, this might seem odd. Not Bill using forks to kill aliens who look like us and can teleport...well yes maybe that too, but I was actually referencing just the forks. Most members of the military are confined to synthetic blood rations, which is really all we need to survive. Some posh settlements however, have started more solidified, supposedly more indulgent dishes that require actual utensils to eat.

The major ignores Bill's poor excuse for a joke and turns to me. "And yours?"

"They must have a similar physiology to us, because my punch to the temple stunned him pretty good. I had enough time to get a proper grip and snap his neck without any trouble."

"Hmm," the major muses while looking down at his desk. An uncomfortable amount of time passes and our previous position of dominance over the office seems to fade away with every passing second. Finally, he taps the desk with his knuckles and raises his head to look at us with a wide grin. "Well, gentl...er...soldiers. I believe thanks are in order. Maybe I misjudged you." He offers his hand out to me and I hesitantly shake it. "A dumb, blunt instrument wouldn't have had the wherewithal to dispatch those creatures so quickly." He offers his hand to Bill, who just stares at it. "My mistake." Bill purses his eyebrows and tilts his head, trying to read the major. He finally shakes his hand. "What can I do to repay you boys for saving my family and a large majority of our patrons?"

"With respect, sir," Bill says, "we'd like to get back to fucking work, like in the real universe."

"Ah, indeed." The major smiles again. "I think that's in order. I'll contact Captain Hoffman immediately and prepare your transfers. Lieutenant?" I'm still thinking back on the fight with the Apparitions as the major turns his attention to me. My head jolts and I look up at him. "Anything else you can think of?"

"Yeah." My lip curls at the thought of the danger that those Apparitions could present. The female I stunned had a lot to answer for. "I wanna talk to her."

Chapter 35: Infiltration

3.23 - 2468 - 755:328 Red Galaxy Standard

"You forgot didn't you?" I ask Aden.

"I...well no," I squint at him through the video on my visor. "Yeah fine, maybe I did for like a second."

"How do you just forget that we're humans planted into a different race's military for centuries as sleeper agents with the intent of eventually killing every last Hemosapien that roams the universe as revenge for the slaughter of our people and burning of our home planet some four hundred years ago?"

Aden pauses before answering, "I mean, when you put it like that." I shake my head. "Are you mad?"

I exhale. "I was at first, but I do love her. She needed to know, even if I can't say it for whatever reason."

Aden nods and stays quiet for a second. "We can't kill them all."

"I mean, it's a long shot."

"No," Aden says firmly. "We can't kill them all."

I bob my head in response. Aden figured it out before I did. I don't think I ever really believed that Captain Hoffman's whole plan for genocidal revenge was really an option. Hell, I don't even think that the captain believes that it's really an option, but with everything we've learned over the last few weeks, I just wanted some direction. I wanted some orders, because it felt comfortable. It felt like the life I've known for so long, but Aden's right.

"No we can't. Genocide is not an option, it never was. I think the captain knows this, we just need to make him understand."

"Blaze and Aphrodite are just the start." As Aden's talking a message pops up on my visor from the slip. We're approaching the Thyr war ship. "There are good soldiers out there, great ones who don't believe in what the High Order stands for."

I deactivate the shielding over the top of our small slip and the entire upper section turns clear, allowing us to see the space around us. "Geez," Aden says. "That's a big ass ship."

"It's not much bigger than the Patriarch, for the Thyr that is." I remind him. Still, seeing a Thyr ship this size is quite impressive. It all but blocks out the stars in front of us making the area seem like a void with its flat black hull.

"Yeah but everyone on the Patriarch isn't trying to kill us," he teases.

"Yet," I say.

He ignores the comment, "And the Patriarch isn't filled with Thyr AND might I add, we know where everything is on the Patriarch." That's a good point. I hope Kelly can help us figure out how to take these beasts down, otherwise we could be on one for months and not even know what we were looking for. "So, how are we docking?" Aden asks.

"Well, I went through the files that Alexander prepared for us and it looks like there's some kind of docking bay."

"Yeah, on the side closest to us."

"You read his mission prep notes?" I ask, shockingly.

"Well, you weren't talking to me for most of the trip, and there's nowhere to go. What the hell else was I supposed to do?"

"I don't know, I figured you'd be talking to Kelly about me and Blaze. Or planning your next sexual adventure with her."

"Please. I'm a professional." When you want to be. "Besides, I already knew you and Blaze would patch things up, but right now I just want to go blow some shit up." There's the Aden I know. I guess there's no fighting with my brother's true nature.

Holding back a chuckle I say, "Okay, well according to Alexander, we just need to lock our slip to their hull, pop the top, float outside, activate a breach stabilizer, and then cut through the bay door with the plasma torches built into our suit's pointer fingers. Oh, and on a side note, our suits have plasma torches." I really have to go back and read through the detailed instruction manual that Alexander put together for us. Add it to the ever growing list of shit to do.

I maneuver our slip into position next to the docking bay door then use a gravity field to lock onto the hull. "Hey Alexander, I've got a question."

"Reading you, go ahead LT."

"Given the ship's size and complexity, is it fair to assume that they'll be able to read a hull breach in the docking bay from the command center or operations room and that there will be a crew on staff in the docking bay when we break in?"

There's a slight pause. "I think it's safe to assume that, yes." Fantastic, before I have a chance to ask my second question, he answers it for me. "But if it's anything like the Patriarch, they'll send a team to investigate since the breach stabilizer will prevent the vacuum of space from collapsing the hull once you've broken through. Or they may just assume it's a malfunction since they're not dead and leave it be. May I remind you, this is precisely why we invented the Mini SWIFT." Mini SWIFTs are tiny recon drones that we can deploy in situations like this to get some layout and troop information, so we're not going in totally blind.

"Okay, thank you," I say flatly, closing the channel.

"That's a pretty wide girth of shit that could happen. Nothing will happen, or they'll send a team to kill you the second you start cutting," Aden says.

"You know High Scientists, always leaving plenty of room for interpretation."

I release the top section of our slip and float out of the top. Our suits have small gravitational retraction fields, similar to the tech that allows our slip to stay attached to the hull without actually touching it. I point my palm at the hull and activate the field at a low level. The field slowly pulls me over and locks my palm against it. Aden does the same, locking on an arm's length to my right.

"Place the breach stabilizer nodes," I command.

We both detach small metallic cylindrical devices from the side of our legs that are two inches in diameter and separate them into two equal pieces. Then I proceed to place the flat end of one against the hull above me and another to the left. Aden does the same below and to his right. "Activating breach stabilizer." A bright blue laser shoots out of all four nodes and reads our body signatures, then proceeds to scan the hull and weave a holographic-looking, rounded shield between us and the void of space. The whole process takes five seconds and once it's complete, an artificial gravity field activates, allowing us to walk on the bottom interior of the bubble.

"Activating plasma torch. I'm going to send in a mini SWIFT before we get started and figure out what we're getting ourselves into." Aden nods and leans against his side of the bubble with his arms crossed. I scroll through the menu system in my visor and activate the torch on the end of my finger, then place my finger on the hull and trace a small circle no larger than a half inch in diameter. I insert the small pill-shaped drone in the hole, then flick it through to the other side. With the video feed linked to my visor, the drone activates and flies to the top of the room where it affixes to the ceiling. It starts to rotate in place at extremely high speeds, collecting data from the interior of the room and building a real-time 3D model. Luckily the little guy is quiet enough that the Thyr won't see it unless they look for it, and scans won't pick it up.

A little red light starts blinking on the upper left of my visor and I look at it to open the digital schematics. The docking bay is huge, the MS measured the interior of the room at two hundred by five hundred yards with a small operations room off to our right.

"Well, there's a shit ton of little transport ships and a few bigger colonial transports for moving gear down to planets, but it looks like we only have to deal with two guards in the operations room."

Aden's video feed pops up on the right of my screen. "Dealing with two guards won't be an issue, dealing with them before they sound an alarm is a different story. Considering we're not already dealing with an alarm, I think it's safe to assume that their system is based off of atmospheric conditions and not hull integrity."

Well done, brother. "Possibly, but we've made the mistake of underestimating the Thyr before, let's not do it again. For all we know, they're acting normal while their men gear up to deal with a silent alarm that's been tripped." I open a secure channel to Kelly.

"Hey Kelly, the mini SWIFT we sent in has a connection to the Patriarch, correct?"

"That's correct, it streams real-time information to the Patriarch so the captain can monitor your progress."

"Excellent, so if it can send, it can receive, right?"

"Yes, but I'm not quite sure what you're getting at."

It's unusual for me to out-tech Kelly, or anyone for that matter, so if this works, I'll take a small moment to gloat silently. "Okay, so the MS is made out of nanomachines similar to ones that comprise our suits. Can you hack the MS to breakup and redirect the nanomachines into the Thyr's operations terminal and gain control of their network? Or at the very least, get a peek at their system so we know what to expect?"

There's a pause on Kelly's end and Aden looks at me through his camera with a mixture of bewilderment and surprise. "I uh, wow. I don't know, I've never tried something like that before, but logically speaking, yes I should be able to." I can hear her typing away on her terminal. "Give me a few minutes."

"Where the hell did that stroke of genius come from?" Aden asks.

I'm actually not quite sure. "I don't know. I've just been thinking about the tech we use more and more as we go out on missions and it just seemed like something that might work."

It only takes Kelly another thirty seconds to break apart the MS and infect the Thyr docking bay operations console. "Okay, I don't have full access, I can't change anything...yet. But I'm rerouting the interface to your visors." She hums to herself while typing away, "Annnnnnd you should be seeing it now, give me one more second." There's more humming, which has a bit more of a triumphant sound as she completes a technical feat that no one has done or even thought of yet. "Okay, so now you have access to the interface and the information contained within the ship in your visor. You can cycle through their database without being detected."

"Well that was surprisingly quick, Kelly. Thank you." I don't even know if my plan is going to work, but the fact that she was able to pull it off in under a minute is very impressive. I was a little worried about her skills possibly suffering from the amount of time that she's been spending with Aden, but it's clear that's not the case.

"Don't mention it." I can tell she's smiling by the tone in her voice. "The interface and base code is actually oddly similar to our own."

"That's weird," Aden points out.

"It is, but let's put a pin in it for the time being, we've got work to do. Kelly, keep at it, see if you can gain control over their systems, it could be invaluable to taking the ship down. I'm closing the channel, but feel free to open whenever you've got something."

"Will do, already working on it."

"Okay, so according to their system here…"

"Hold on," Aden interrupts.

"What's wrong?"

"Why is the language system in English?"

I just assumed that Kelly or our suits converted the language and didn't even stop to think that maybe that wasn't the case. "Hey, Kelly?"

"Yeah, Aden's right, it shouldn't be in English."

Okay, that's a little unnerving. "The Thyr don't speak English, so why the hell would their system be in English? Is there anything you can see on the back end that explain why?"

Kelly groans. "Hold on…well, the system is set to display several different languages depending on the user. It probably defaulted to English due to programing language I used to hack the system, but still, it has no reason to be in the system at all."

"I don't like this," Aden says with a worried look on his face.

"Okay well, there's nothing we can do about it now. Kelly, keep us updated, let us know if you find anything."

"Will do."

"As I was saying, aside from the unnerving shit we can't change, we don't have anything to worry about at this time." I scroll through the interface. "And you were right, the monitoring system is atmospheric, not hull-based. There's also a large maintenance ventilation system that runs throughout the ship, just like the Patriarch, so we should be able to use that to move around."

"We've got an access point near the floor to the right of our position," Aden adds.

"Let's get in there." We both activate our plasma torches and create a cylindrical hole in the wall that's just wide enough for us to crawl through, roughly four feet wide by three feet high. I use the gravitational field on my hand to pull the heavy chunk of metal into our atmospheric bubble and then push it out behind us. The bubble creates a new pocket around the piece of hull and keeps it from floating out to space. Aden climbs through and drops silently down to the floor. I follow, feet first, and use the field in my glove to pull the piece of hull back into place. Holding it steady with the field, I partially seal it with the plasma torch on my free arm, then drop down to Aden.

Even though we've got access to the system, a 3D layout of the bay and locational information on the only two guards here, Aden's scanning the area for threats. Ever the professional when need be, good man. I tap his shoulder and motion for the maintenance access duct to our right. Luckily, we make it into the duct system and seal the entrance without any trouble. After getting a safe distance in, I stop Aden in order to look over the schematics of the ship.

"Okay, hopefully Kelly will be able to gain unfettered access to the ship's systems, but we can't bank the mission on that. We need to find the ship's drive and see if we can overload it and, at the very least, leave it stranded without power for life support or defensive systems."

I'm scrolling through the database and something seems too convenient about these schematics. "Are you seeing what I'm seeing?" Aden asks. Then it hits me like a hulking Thyr running full speed.

"This entire ship is all too similar to the Patriarch," I confirm.

"What the hell is that all about? The Thyr created their own technology way before we came across them and while some of the theories are similar, their technical approach and aesthetics are wholly different than ours. Not to mention, might I add again, they don't speak English!"

Something's going on here, there's no way in hell this is just coincidence. High Command wants to splice Thyr genetics with our own and then five corp-sized battleships show up in our solar system packed with soldiers and the ships have strikingly similar tech? No, this has to be connected.

I reopen the channel to Kelly. "Kelly, have you noticed anything else in the..."

She cuts me off before I have a chance to finish. "Yeah guys, you aren't going to believe this. These ships were built by High Command."

"Fuck me," I mutter.

Aden and I sit in silence, letting the reality of the situation sink in as Kelly gives us a moment to process everything.

"Sir? Can we go back to being bored now?" Aden asks nervously.

Chapter 36: Just Keep Moving

01.12 - 2465 - 965.651 - The Void

"MOVE!" I scream to Bill behind me, praying, hoping that he's ahead of the game. Luckily he is, and I hear his laser rifle fire off a few rounds, followed by the quick thud of his boots close behind while I continue forward at full speed.

It's funny, our laser rifles don't actually make any sound when they fire, but we modified the weapons to have the option for our shots to sound like old physical caliber rifles. The sound can help your situational awareness on the field, and it can be used to weaken the enemy's resolve. Continuous rifle fire, followed by the painful death howls of your brethren will eventually crack even the most hardened soldier.

Usually I'd take the rear and make sure that Bill was safely in front of me, but circumstances dictate otherwise. I wouldn't be surprised if they've already surrounded us. Ironically in this situation, heading out first is more dangerous than staying behind, even with the throng of soldiers on our tail.

"Reload," he states loudly but calmly. I slow my pace to a stop and rotate, firing at the oncoming storm as Bill passes me, reloading the coolant chamber of his rifle. Lasers are a force to be reckoned with in the field, but it doesn't take long for a radioactive emitter to overheat when it's on rapid fire.

"Where the fuck did they come from?" I yell over my shoulder as I start shuffling backward while continuing to fire. One of them bellows a deep shout of contempt as I blast a laser through the head of his neighbor and shear off half of his skull. The Almathe are a glorious species of two legged creatures who are as brutal as they are beautiful. This was meant to be a simple recon mission on their home world of Peagle in the Bodley universe, but everything went south when they discovered our mini SWIFT taking scans of their city. The Hemo reputation is getting out into the universe and the general consensus is; kill on site.

"What does it matter?" Bill fires back. He's right, it doesn't. "Good to go, lead the way!" I rotate back around and start running forward down the tight canyon once again as Bill slows and provides cover fire to our rear. We've been in more than our fair share of hairy situations in the past, but this is probably the least confident that I've ever felt about getting off of a planet alive.

The Almathe stand at a height roughly between eight and twelve feet and due to the excessive gravity on Peagle, and tend to be about two hundred percent stronger than your average Hemo. Our new high-density compression suits put us in a similar strength range, but they've still got the advantage when it comes to height and body mass. They live off the land, strangers to technology as we know it, and have short white hairs that cover their bodies. When engaged in physical altercations, the microscopic sensory receptors on the ends of their hair cause the strands to tense, creating a biological high density grecene-like effect. The strands expand and harden, covering the open space between each other and create positional armor wherever the body requires it. Lucky for us, their faces are free of hair, but they have hardened, sharpened, thin bones that protrude from their foreheads that can be used for slicing, stabbing or just any kind of general evisceration. Needless to say, the key to staying alive involves accuracy and keeping your distance.

"How we doing up there?" Bill asks.

"Uh, well," Not too good. I don't really have an answer for him, we're in a narrow canyon with stone walls that are over a thousand feet tall to either side with no end in sight. Judging from the screams and laser blasts behind me, the Almathe have no intention of letting up and I'm starting to catch glimpses of them on the ridges above. I'm beginning to think this is an ambush.

"That good, huh?"

"Just keep running and give me a few seconds!" I shout, picking up the pace.

"I'm not sure that I can fulfill that request, sir."

He said 'sir'. Shit, he's as worried as I am. There has to be a way we can get out of this. Behind is not an option, clearly. Forward will work for now, but I'm pretty sure that...yup, the Almathe have started climbing down the walls. "Contact up high, descending fast!" I rotate up while continuing forward and begin to take down Almathe that are climbing down. Sniping head shots at fast moving creatures, six hundred feet in the air while sprinting isn't exactly easy, but I make do. You have to love muscle memory. Shooting is essentially an autonomic function at this point.

"Okay, I'm done with this shit," Bill growls. "Fire in the hole, find cover!"

"Cover? What fucking cover?" I yell back. There's a rush of burning cold that sweeps over my body from behind, followed by an explosion that knocks me to the ground. My hearing is replaced by a high-pitched ringing; I lift my head and open my eyes to a stark, dusty coldness that burns my retinas even through my suit. I can see the blurry shape of a dead Almathe in front of me and dig my fingers into its hairy hide, pulling the body on top of me. Before I have a chance to ask Bill what the hell he did, there's another explosion from above. I glance up in just enough time to see a pile of stone block out what little light shines through the canyon opening and fall on top of us.

Against the odds, I'm not dead. Well this is...pretty amazing and a little unexpected, to be honest. I was able to curl beneath the Almathe's body above me, so it absorbed a large portion of the falling debris, but I'm still sore from the impact. There's enough room for me to rotate around and face the area where Bill was behind me. I open my mouth and try to speak and even though the cold is gone, my throat is met with a raspy, dry sensation. After a few silent failures, I manage to squeeze out, "Bill."

There's no response. I'm just about to try and call out again when a small boulder in front of me shifts. With a groan, it rolls toward me to reveal Bill's smiling face. "Hey boss, what's up?" Well at least he's not calling me 'sir' anymore. Scared or not, I can't stand that shit.

"What the hell just happened?"

His wide smile fades as he smirks and looks at the rocks above us. "Well, I still had the overheated coolant cartridges on hand from the last time I reloaded. So I took it, tossed it at the fuckers behind us and blasted it with a laser, which in turn caused the unit to explode and force blast a frozen wave out toward us and the Almathe behind us. Then, I took the second one and did the same thing at the canyon walls in front of you, causing them to collapse as we continued to run."

That was, "Ingenious." I didn't actually mean to say that to Bill; by the High Order, he'll drag that out for months, hell, years if he can.

"Well, I mean," he looks off to the right with a wide smirk, "brilliant would have done it, but I guess, yeah it was ingenious."

"Okay, just slow the hell down. We still have a pretty big problem to deal with." I wrestle my arm from the rubble for the sole purpose of tapping him on the forehead with my pointer finger. "One *you* created."

He thinks for a second, "How are we going to get out of here?"

"How are we going to get out of here," I confirm, just after he finishes.

"Well, let's look at the positive."

"Please Bill, tell me the positive is in this situation."

He looks at me with that oh-so-Bill, *come on,* look, "We've been awarded the greatest asset that any warrior can ask for." I wait for him to finish. "Time."

Well then. He is one hundred percent right. Short of an exfil or barrage of ordinance to blast the Almathe from the surface of the planet, that is exactly what we needed. I'm reminded of what Red told us during training, *Visualize the escape, just breathe, there is an escape, there always is*. Okay, we have time on our side. I look up as a low growl radiates through the boulders above me. Correction, we have *some* time on our hands, but regardless, we have time and we need to use it. *There is an escape.* "So what's next?" I ask.

"Oh no," Bill starts shaking his head. "That's all on you. I'm the blunt instrument, I provide cover and time, you provide the damn plan."

I can hear the Almathe above us throwing the rocks aside and digging their way down to our position. "How many shots do you have left?" Bill's lips expand, revealing that wide smile of his.

After a few moments of continuous digging, the Almathe break through the rocks above us. They keep at it even though Bill's firing as fast as he can. I guess they assume that he'll run out of coolant, or shots or whatever seeing as they don't know much about our technology. Which is really just a testament to how badly they want us seeing as the dead are starting to pile up. That does offer a few more minutes as they have to stop to move the dead. Something tells me it only enrages them further though. Maybe it's the decreased intervals between growls. Luckily, they don't know our weapons. Unless they were able to observe our reloads and relay the information to their teams, which is unlikely given their technology.

After freeing ourselves from the surrounding rubble, we break through the barrier of corpses and Bill takes out three soldiers before his coolant chamber beeps once through the comm in our helmets, signifying that he has five shots left before the firing sequence shuts down to prevent overheating. Five more shots ring out and five more Almathe go down in a heartbeat. Two more drawn out beeps come through our comms, signifying that the coolant chamber needs to be ejected. He rips the small cartridge out and yells, "Pull!"

The Almathe may have a directive to apprehend or kill us at any cost, but that doesn't mean that they're ready to die. Regardless of how much we prepare, no soldier is ever ready to die. The look of shock painted across the faces of our pursuers merely solidifies my point. As the soldiers take a second to process their options, they turn to run in what seems like slow motion while I pull my side arm and zero in on the cartridge that's no bigger than my thumb. Meanwhile, Bill grabs a corpse in each hand and yanks them over us in protection as I fire, closing my eyes immediately.

The dead bodies are enough to block out a majority of the blast, but the wave of frozen pain that precedes still manages to lick our faces with a burning sensation, not to mention thrust a large stone into my face, breaking my helmet and, subsequently, my nose. The blast dies out and I push the debris away, bringing a hand up to my nose and cheek, wiping the blood away and flicking it to the ground. "Son of a bitch," I lament, climbing out from under the stone coffin.

I can hear Bill rustling behind me. "Hey," he coughs, "I didn't say anything about it being painless," he mutters underneath the chilly soot and smoke. We're able to climb out from under the mess that he made with his initial blast of the double empty cartridges and get a view of what we're up against in the canyon. It's not much.

The aftermath of Bill's makeshift bombs pretty much leveled any opposition in the area. With the exception of a few shots that he's firing into the remaining Almathe that didn't feel like dying in the explosion, we're alone.

"All right, well let's get the hell out of here," Bill says triumphantly.

"I don't like it," I grumble.

"You don't have to like it. There's nothing to like about this situation, let's just get the hell out of here while we can."

Unfortunately the canyon walls are a little too high for us to jump over, so forward we go. "All right, let's get to the edge of the canyon and call for exfil as soon as we can get some solid coordinates."

Despite the fact that we can't see the end of the canyon, it only takes us twenty minutes to make it out to the open fields of Peagle. There's a very low shrubbery that resembles Earth's grass and it covers the landscape as far as I can see. Even though we made it out of the canyon without any further trouble, I can't shake the feeling that we're being watched. "Call for exfil," I command Bill, while staring out at the endless fields.

"That's a negative, sir," he says from behind me.

I turn around slowly to see Bill staring at the top of the canyon walls that we just escaped from. There are Almathe covering not only the top of the walls, but the canyon itself. We don't have any chance of outrunning them in the open fields of Peagle and the dropship would never make it in time to save us. Not that it matters, I can see now that our comms were damaged in one of the blasts. There's a chance that we could take them on in hand-to-hand combat, but these creatures aren't the Thyr drones we've been trained to fight or the Feeleye. Their armored fur and sharpened horns make them a pretty deadly force up close. It's a gamble, but there's only one other option left.

I walk past Bill and pat him on the shoulder as I take a few steps in front of him. "Go on then. Why hesitate?" I ask with my language filter on, the one thing on my helmet that wasn't damage by the blast debris. I don't speak Almathe, but this handy little device will do the pleasure of translating it for me. It will also translate their voices to English through our comm unit

A particularly small Almathe leaps from the top of the right canyon wall and lands in front of me with a thud, tossing moss and dirt up into the air as he does. He stands and looks down at me. "You shall all be killed on sight."

I walk up to him so there's only a few inches between our chests and look up at his cold, dark eyes. "Do it then," I whisper. He doesn't move, but the slight change of emotions in his eyes suggests that he doesn't agree with the command that he's been given. "Go on. I'm not one for waiting."

There's a slight pause. "You do not fear the pain, the lasting darkness that we bring?" he asks, nervous about the fact that I'm unfazed by his threat.

"No."

"Why?" he demands.

"My life is comprised of waiting for death. If you're willing and able, then I'd not only be impressed, but honored to die by your hands."

The Almathe studies my face; he studies my body language searching for any kind of weakness or dishonesty in what I've just said. Satisfied that he's found none, he replies with, "You are unworthy of death." I stare back, slightly offended by the statement, but he clarifies. "You do not fear death and therefore it does not welcome you. The laws of Almathe are dictated by the Bull, but his laws are dictated by code."

"And what does the code state?"

"The code states that any enemy of the Almathe who shows courage in the face of death shall be spared." It seems too good to be true, but hell, I'll take it. I glance back at Bill and smile. This doesn't seem like our normal run-of-the-mill luck, but who am I to judge providence? "It also states that you are to be brought before the Bull and he shall decide your fate."

Of course. There's the catch.

"Splendid," I reply through gritted teeth. I sigh. "Lead the way."

Chapter 37: Dropping In

3.23 - 2468 - 836:022 Red Galaxy Standard

"So, what the hell are we going to do now?" Aden asks as we sit in the dingy, dark maintenance shaft of the traitorous High-Command-built Thyr ship.

"Our jobs, Sergeant. All this does is make our other mission easier to fulfill. Kelly?"

There's a pause. "Yeah, sorry. I'm still here," she says nervously.

"I need you to find out everything you can about who commissioned these ships to be built. I want you to get me a direct line to Alexander that's secure from any curious ears and I want you to do the same for the captain and Red, understood?"

"Yeah. I've already got the channels set up for Red and the captain. I'll patch them through to your visors and I'll contact you when Alexander is set up."

"Thank you."

"Daemon, Aden," she says quietly. She called me by my first name, that's just as bad as Aden's 'sir'.

"Yes?" we reply in unison.

"Be careful. If the High Order is involved, there's no telling what you'll be walking into. This could be a trap. We've been under the radar for a long time, we've been careful, but who knows if it was enough. Also..." she pauses again and the tone in her voice tells me that she doesn't have much confidence in the question that she's about to ask, "Do you really think we can trust Red?"

"Do you not?" I snap quicker than I should have.

"No, I, it's just, he's Hemo. He's always been an enigma and we don't really know much about him prior to the scorching of Earth. We only know what he told us."

I look up at Aden, who cocks his head to the side with a 'she's got a point' look on his face. "I trust him."

Kelly stays silent, presumably waiting for Aden to say something, but he stays quiet as well. "Okay," she finally answers. "That's good enough for me. I'll get to work and contact you when Alexander is available."

"Thanks." Closing the feed to Kelly, I turn my attention to Aden. "Go on." He plays around with the hilt attached to his leg, then looks up to me and shrugs. "Lying to us for hundreds of years when he could have just killed us and been done with it to begin with? Come on, you really think that's a possibility? Why would he do that?"

He inhales deeply, holds it, then forces it out quickly. "I don't know. I mean, why would the High Order commission warships for the Thyr? Maybe they're fucking with us. Maybe this was all an experiment to see what Human/Hemo hybrids would be capable of. Hell, they're ready to splice us, or well, themselves with the Thyr. You really trust Red that much?"

I think back to the day after Lieutenant Mackelson beat the crap out of me and I woke up in the medical bay. I think about Red and the look in his eyes when he put me against the wall and spoke of why he turned on his own people. "Yes, I do," I say with a slight nod before patting him on the shoulder. "Regardless, we've got work to do. We'll use the access that Kelly's secured to get us to the core of the ship and we can figure out how to take this thing down." I nod forward, "Lead the way, I'll follow. I'm going to open up a channel with the captain and Red to fill them in as we move."

Aden starts moving forward through the cramped shaft and we don't get more than a few feet before I have a video feed open to the captain's office. Red is standing directly behind him, arms folded, face covered by the shemagh as usual. "Daemon, Kelly said you needed to talk on the secure channel, what's going on?"

"We're on one of the Thyr ships over Saudade and Kelly's gained access to their system using the nanomachines that make up one of our mini SWIFTs. Sir, the ship was commissioned by the High Order." Captain Hoffman turns and glances up at Red, who nods before the captain directs his attention back to the screen with a somber look on his face. "Did you know about this?"

The captain's face curls. "No, Lieutenant. You demanded that we be forthcoming with information and we have been. We had a few theories, but we never imagined anything like this."

Fair enough. "Kelly's trying to find information on who commissioned these ships, do you have any idea who it could be?"

"Our best guess lies with General Vietus. He's been at the forefront of the Red Military's genetic splicing experiments for over a century now and believes wholeheartedly in its ability to advance us as the one true superior species. While he's more than a few ranks above Major Erislad, they're close friends from before the Bloodwar and hold very similar viewpoints."

"Oh yay, our old buddy," Aden chimes in as he rounds a corner.

"Yeah, your old buddy," the captain confirms. "After that incident at The Outer Shores last year, he's convinced the Thyr program is our only option and while his influence isn't as great as the general's, they're closing the gap between the fanatics and the non-believers."

A message shoots across my visor that the connection with Alexander is set up and he's waiting for our call. "Captain, we need you to coordinate with Kelly and try to find out as much as you can about what's going on and who's involved. We have to know how deep this runs and how close they are to being successful."

"Pretty damn close I'd assume, considering the five war ships in the galaxy," Aden quips.

"Are those orders, *Lieutenant*?" the captain demands with a firm tone. "Remember your place."

"Remember you race, *Captain*," I fire back. "I didn't always have a commanding officer." The captain looks back at Red again, who meets his gaze but doesn't move or say a word. "What?" I ask. It seems like they're having a silent conversation and the topic is me and not about what I just said, but something deeper.

"Nothing, Lieutenant," the captain says, returning to the screen. "Is there anything else for now?" he asks flatly.

I chuckle. "Yeah, hold on. I'm patching Alexander into our feed, he knows we're fighting against the High Council, but doesn't know we're hybrids, hold on."

"WHAT?" the captain fumes at his camera, slamming his hands on the desk.

I mute the feed for a second and Aden laughs. "Well, that was fun."

"I know, right? It's the little things." I unmute the captain, "Just one more second, sir."

"I can hear you!" he screams. I mute him again.

"Oh, just like old times." I can see the captain out of the corner of my eye stop screaming and he turns ghost white. I patch Alexander through to our feed and unmute the captain.

"LT, Bill good to see you." He notices the captain and Red. "Oh, sir," he salutes quickly. "I, uh, I didn't realize you and Red would be on as well."

"Relax Alexander, we're here to help. We know all about the High Order's plans," he says as the color returns to his face.

"Sir, I'd just like to say that it's an honor to work with you on this and I'm glad that your views match up with my own. We can't allow the High Order to taint the universe with a bastardized species meant to accomplish their own self-serving goals." The captain nods. "What can I do to help?" he posits to anyone willing to answer.

I take the lead. "The Thyr ship that we're on now is of Hemo origin."

Alexander's stark white eyes go wide. "By the High Order."

"Unfortunately, yes. We need you to find out who on the High Order approved this. We need to find out who's involved. You'll be working directly with Vali, who will make sure that your actions go unnoticed. Understood?"

He contemplates the task at hand before answering. "Yes I, of course, sir. I'll do my best. If there's nothing else, I'll get to it."

I nod in approval and Alexander's screen shuts off.

"A heads up would have been nice," the captain starts to argue.

"Well, that's calling the kettle black," Aden replies, cutting him off as he stops above a vent.

"Yeah, in the middle of a hostile ship right now, Captain. Gotta go." I cut the feed. "I think he's a little annoyed with the way I informed him."

"Eh, fuck 'em."

"Why did you stop?"

"What the hell was with the captain?"

"The way he reacted to what I said about not having a commander?"

"Yeah, that and…" With that the vent gives way and Aden falls into the room below. I can hear a lot of heavy movement as I scurry over to the edge of the vent. Aden's laying on his back in what looks like a mess hall with his hands up, surrounded by a dozen Thyr who rushed over with their blades drawn. He looks up at me. "Heh heh, sorry for dropping in boys." The Thyr follows Aden's gaze up to me.

"Shit." In the short time that it takes the Thyr to realize that they're in trouble, Aden draws the hilt on his leg, flicks his wrist to extend the flexible Ka blade and swings it in a full circle, slicing half a dozen Thyr legs off in the process. I dive through the opening head first and rotate my legs around, landing on my feet just as Aden rolls to the right, jumps up and locks the Ka into place, blocking a strike to his head. I stand and press my back to his, extending my own Ka and blocking a blow directed at the side of my neck.

"Well, there goes the element of surprise," Aden chuckles as he advances on the three Thyr in front of him. I duck and rotate around, kicking the blade I blocked into the knee of the Thyr to my right.

"Not yet!" I spring into the air and swing my own Ka around, bringing it down on the back of the Thyr's neck who tried to slice through my own. "I don't hear any alarms!" The body of the now headless Thyr falls to my right as I land in front of the one who took its blade to his knee. He's falling to the floor, so I take my side arm and press it to the back of its head and fire while thrusting my Ka into the air and over my shoulder to block an attack from the rear. The back of our suits have several different nanocameras built in to gives us an extra edge in battle.

Before I have a chance to turn and take out the Thyr behind me, Aden fires a round over my right shoulder, taking care of it. "Well that was fun, right?" I can tell he's smiling under that helmet of his.

"Just finish off the rest." The six initial Thyr that he trimmed the legs off of in the beginning are rolling around on the ground, trying to make their way toward some of the nearby consoles to set off an alarm. I can hear Aden dispatch them one by one as I run to the nearest console. The interface is so similar to that of ours that I have no problem hacking into the security feeds for the ship. I reverse the feeds from this room and loop a small clip from before we hit the ground. "There," I say to Aden, who's putting away his weapons as I turn. "Hopefully that..." Alarms begin to blare and the room goes dark for a second, before flashing red lights paint the interior. "Right, so maybe not."

"Uh huh, back into the vent?" Aden asks with a shrug.

A large door to the entrance of the room forty feet behind Aden slides open and a bunch of Thyr rush in wearing heavy metallic armor and carrying rifles. "Yup, into the vent. Now!"

Chapter 38: The Challenge

01.22 - 2465 - 102.520 - The Void

The Apparition's confinement is overly nice for a prison, but given that The Outer Shores is more of a political getaway than your normal military installation, it doesn't surprise me. I walk through the outer doorway of the isolation chamber and the biometric scanner that reads my body emits a low, soft tone. The machine continues to repeat the sound for a few seconds before sending my credentials to both of the guard's ICE displays. I stop in front of them as they look over the information. Once everything checks out, they simultaneously tap a control on the inside of their wrists activating the door.

The cell itself looks more like a small, two room apartment than an actual isolation chamber. The main room has a state-of-the-art nano couch and chair, both of which mold to the user's form, depending how they sit, and there are a variety of entertainment options on the far wall from the door. The left room is a bedroom with a digital fireplace and large bed in the center, built for comfort. There's also a walk-in bathroom and shower on the far left. The wall to the right has a dispensary built into it that takes trash and dirty clothing then delivers clean clothing and allows the user to pick a variety of food and drink from across the universe to suit their needs.

The black-haired, female Apparition that I stunned in the ballroom last night is nowhere to be seen. Walking into the bedroom, I turn to my left first, but catch her out of the corner of my right eye hiding next to the doorway. I stop without turning around.

"I wouldn't try it." She's absolutely silent. In a room this quiet with sound dampeners in the wall, I should be able to hear something, but there's nothing. Not even the slightest bit of sound from her breathing, or her heart beating.

"It'd be pointless. I was stripped of all weapons coming in, even if I wasn't, they'd seal and gas the room to knock you out in the event of an issue." I slowly turn around to face her. "That aside, I'd just kick your ass again."

The Apparition stands barely over five feet and her black hair is now auburn but still cut short, landing just below her ears. Maybe it was dyed. She's wearing the plain white short-sleeved shirt and leisure pants that are given to all inmates in the event of an arrest and has her hands at her side, fists clenched. Her supple, upper lip quivers at the thought of me putting her in her place and even though her makeup has been washed away, revealing her stark white skin, she is still a very attractive young woman. We stare at each other for a moment before the tension in her forearms begins to ease and her fists loosen. Her strikingly bright blue eyes dart all over my body and face while her brows dance upon her forehead in an attempt to read my intentions.

After a few moments she asks, "You are a warrior?"

"I am."

"Free me."

I chuckle, "I don't really see that happening." She seems hurt by the comment.

"These people here are not worthy of life. They no longer represent what your people once were."

"Yeah, no argument here."

"And yet you protect them?" she asks, cocking an eyebrow, visibly confused.

"Who are you? I've been all over the universe and I've never met anyone or even heard of any species like your own with your teleportation tech..."

She scoffs before I have a chance to finish, turning her back and walking toward the corner of the room. "I had almost forgotten of your people's ignorance. Believing whatever they're told, jumping to conclusions based off of what they see and not what's truly possible." She turns to face me again. "Is that why a warrior such as yourself would choose to protect these cowards? Someone told you a story and you listened?"

"If I'm so ignorant, then why don't you enlighten me?"

She rushes forward and even though her head only comes up to just above my stomach, the glare in her eyes and scowl on her face presents quite an imposing presence. "You so blindly follow the instructions of your leaders, regardless of how clearly inept they are. You'd never believe the truth; my words would be falling on deaf ears."

I return her gaze without moving or blinking until she finally turns and walks into the main room. "Consider this," I offer, following behind. She stops in the middle of the room but keeps her back to me, staring at the wall with the clothing dispenser. "I've been stuck in this hell hole of a base for over two years due to the ineptitude of my leaders. I'm a warrior, I don't belong here. By capturing you, I've finally been granted leave. Soon the High Order will send a team to retrieve you and the High Scientists will torture you and tear you apart in an attempt to figure out how your teleportation works. They won't care who you are. They won't care where you're from or what your plans were. They'll take what they need and kill you in the process." She lowers her head, then turns around and looks me in the eye. "The last two years I've spent at this facility have felt like two hundred, so you can understand how much I want to get back to my real life, yet I'm here with you and I'm willing to listen."

We stand there for what seems like hours, staring at each other with ice in our veins, neither one willing to blink for fear that the other may mistake the situation for a ruse. Finally, she looks down at the couch and I sit down.

"We're now known as Revenants, but were once called..."

Bill punches me in the shoulder. "Shit, Bill, what are you..." I take a look around and realize that I'm sitting on the cold stone floor of the Almathe holding cell.

"I can't remember the last time you dozed off on a mission," he teases.

I look at him, dazed, then glance around the small cell that's barely large enough to hold us to find that nothing has changed. Looking up, I see an Almathe standing guard on a metal grate, some forty feet above us. "Me neither."

"Bad dream?" he asks.

"I was thinking about the Revenant and the last conversation we had," I explain quietly, still staring at the grate above. Lowering my head to look at Bill, he shakes his head in reply.

"Forget I asked."

"Yeah."

But of course, with Bill it's never that simple. He looks down at the ground and starts shifting his body around. "You think it's true?"

I honestly don't know, but not a day goes by that I don't think of it, or her. Before I have a chance to answer, there's a metallic screeching from the entrance above. I look up to see the Almathe that decided we weren't worthy of death moving the unlocked metal grating away from the top of our deep cell.

"The Bull will see you," he says loudly without shouting. The only reason we can understand him is because they carry around our helmets to translate their speech. They don't understand the tech or the idea of our nano-implanted comm units, but they know it works. He turns to his left and grabs a rope from another soldier, lowering it down in the pit so we can climb out.

I turn to Bill and say, "Be ready," under my breath. He nods in approval. When you've fought together for several centuries, there's little if any explanation needed for intent. Bill is an extension of my body, and I his.

The Almathe soldier leads us into a large chamber of sorts with six guards following behind us. They stripped us of all our weapons and even managed, painfully, to get our combat suits off leaving us more vulnerable than ever. The chamber is open at the top and has stadium seating all around the edge carved out of stone and extending over a hundred feet in the air. The Almathe soldiers have filled the seating to the brim and begin shouting and hollering at us as we enter. The center of the chamber holds a small platform that is raised slightly off the ground on top of which stands who I can only assume is The Bull. The Bull looks like an Almathe, but instead of having white skin and fur like the rest, he has bright red skin and fur and is missing the typical Almathe bone protrusion from the forehead. In place, there's an indentation in the top of his skull forming two ridge-like outcroppings on the left and right side of his head.

"SILENCE!" he shouts in a deep, loud voice to his fellow white brethren that are jeering at us. They respond immediately with silence as his command echoes around the stone, before exiting through the round opening above. As we reach the center, the Almathe soldier behind pushes us toward The Bull, who's now only fifteen feet away. "You are the ones who killed so many of my soldiers ten cycles ago." He must mean cycles of the sun; we were captured ten days ago. "Speak!" he orders. Hold on, he speaks English, this isn't coming through our comms. We haven't encountered any Almathe who speak English yet. At least we have something for the intelligence file on the very rare chance that we survive.

Bill attempts to talk, but I quickly slap a hand over his mouth. "We are," I confirm.

The Bull looks at Bill with his deep red eyes, then back to me. "Cacully tells me that you do not fear death." He jumps down from the little platform and walks up to us, pressing his chest against mine and staring deep into my soul. "What if I were to slit your throat right here?" he asks.

"I would die."

"And this does not frighten you?" he fires back without hesitation.

"It would be more of a relief than anything else."

The Bull tilts his head from side to side, reading my eyes, looking for the smallest amount of weakness or dishonesty. Seemingly satisfied, he lets out a long and hard high-pitched laugh and looks back at the man who captured us, the one named Cacully. "It seems as though you've finally found one who is worthy!" he looks at Bill, "or two for that matter!" The entire chamber cheers at the notion.

"I'm sorry, worthy for what?" Bill asks over the exorbitant laughter of The Bull.

The Bull calms himself and turns his attention back to me. "You warriors wish to go home, yes?"

"That would be preferable."

"Excellent!" He turns and hops back onto the platform and throws his hands up in the air. "Then we shall have a trial by combat."

"Us?" Bill asks.

"Yes."

"Versus you?"

"Yes!"

"I'm sorry, I don't mean to question the validity of this trial, but your hair or natural armor alone gives you an unfair advantage, even though there are two of us. I request the use of our armor to even out the challenge." Very smart, Bill.

"That will not happen," the Bull laughs, "But you are right. Therefore, I shall have Cacully sheer the hair from my body. Thus shedding my own biological armor and leveling the challenge." Damn. The armor would have been more beneficial to us, he's still stronger, even without his hardened exterior. The Bull shoots a hand out to Cacully behind us, "It has been decreed, so it shall be done! Cacully, bring the shearing blade quickly. There's no need to keep these fearless creatures waiting. If they welcome death, then I shall bring it to them!"

Chapter 39: The Pain of Irony

3.23 - 2468 - 850.932 Red Galaxy Standard

"Why the *fuck* were those Thyr carrying rifles?" Aden yells as he rushes through the shaft ahead of me. "Thyr don't use rifles!"

"These ships were built by the High Order, I think it's safe to say that whatever we know about the Thyr is either a lie, or no longer applies." We can still hear the sirens in the ventilation shaft as I'm looking at the security plans and there's only so many places we can go hide. "It's not going to take them long to pin down our location. We need to get out of here and take our chances moving through the corridors and fight our way to the core of the ship."

"That's all well and good, but there are at least five hundred thousand soldiers on this ship, who now have rifles that look like they match our own." Aden stops at a T intersection. "We need to split up."

"What?"

"We stand less of a chance fighting our way through the corridors than we do in the vents. If we split up, we'll be harder to find. I'll head to the right and try to get to the control room and see if Kelly can help me access their systems and cause some havoc. You head to the left, get to the core, and find a way to overload it."

I pull up a video feed to Aden. "I don't like this."

"Neither do I, but it's the best chance we've got."

"He's right," Kelly chimes in as a little video of her pops up under Aden on the right side of my visor. "The ladies are still silent and making progress on Saudade, but the ground force is much larger than expected and I've just found dropship schedules to ferry thousands of soldiers down to the surface of the planet. You two need to find a way to take down that ship or Blaze and Aphrodite are going to have a hell of a lot to deal with. Maybe more than they can handle."

"Did you inform them of the incoming soldiers? We may need to pull them out and reconvene with Hoffman. They need to be aware of the fact that the High Order is involved." I know it'd be hard for them to accept as Alphas, but if worst comes to worst we can just pull them out before the soldiers get there. It's a recon mission first and we've gained tons of intel from getting access to this ship's computer. Not to mention that everything's changed since finding out the High Order is involved, even our previous plans as part-humans. Priority number one is to stop the High Order and dismantle their plans to control the universe. There are too many good Hemos who are just following orders and if they knew the truth, just like Alexander, they wouldn't want to be a part of all this deceit and betrayal. It's time for us to convince everyone else how ridiculous the captain's genocide plan is.

"Do you think that's the best idea?" Kelly asks. "Pulling more people into the fold?"

"Look, I know we had plans to take down the Hemo race as a whole, but it's clear that their society, our society, is the way it is because of the High Order."

Kelly stays quiet waiting for me to continue and Aden nods slightly to show his support. "We've spent our entire lives killing and that's the same reason that we want to destroy the Hemos. Don't you see? It makes us just as bad. We need to dismantle the

406

High Order and stop the Thyr from working with them, there are some good Hemos out there that can be saved. We fix the Hemo society instead of wiping it out." Kelly and Aden are silent, both staring at me while she processes the idea of letting the Hemo race off the hook for all of their past crimes. "Soldiers aren't to blame for war. We know better than anyone that they're just following orders."

A giant smile spreads across Aden's face. "You love her so hard!"

"Really? Now?"

"You love Blaze, you want to marry her, and have like eighty kids. She's totally changed your mind!"

"Awww," Kelly swoons.

"Not you, too," I moan.

"It's just really cute," she smiles while biting her lower lip and gives me a starry eyed look.

"Blaze and Daemon sitting in a slip..." Aden starts singing.

"Okay, shut up!" I scold, holding back a minor laugh. "We're going through some serious shit here, can we please focus!" There's a loud bang against the floor of the vent. "Shit, I think they found us. Aden, we go with your plan, move!" Aden hurries down the ventilation shaft to his right and I start scurrying down the left. "Okay, so Kelly, I take it you're are on board with the whole 'no genocide' thing?"

"I was never on board with their idea to begin with, I don't think the captain was either. It was mostly Mackelson and Red" Kelly says. "We'll make them see reason."

"Okay, then we'll deal with Hoffman and Red when we get back. Kelly, make contact with Blaze and Aphrodite and have Alexander warn them about the incoming soldiers. They know him, they'll trust him." I reference the ship's security plans and turn down another shaft toward the core.

"Daemon, I can't make contact with Aphrodite or Blaze. I tried traditional comms and back channels, but it seems like something's been tampered within their suits. It's weird though, I'm still getting a normal reading on their biosignatures and I can listen in on their chatter, but I can't make contact."

I open a secure feed to Alexander. "Alexander, what are the chances of Aphrodite and Blaze's comms malfunctioning in such a manner that we can hear them but they can't hear us?"

"Hold on, let me take a look at the readings." There's another loud sound beneath the vent behind me. "Based off of what I'm seeing here, something was disabled in their suits."

"Could they do it themselves?"

"No, they don't have the know-how, or the access for that matter. It would have to have been a High Scientist."

"You're certain? The Thyr couldn't do it?"

"Positive."

"Any clue who did it?"

"No, but give me a few minutes with Vali, we can probably find out."

"Good, get on it." I close the channel and turn my attention back to Kelly. "Help him find out who did this and see if you can find a way, any way, to communicate with them. We need to..." I'm tossed against the top of the ventilation shaft after an explosion blows a hole in the bottom of the shaft beneath me. I glance up to see Aden rocked by a similar situation in his video feed and scream, "Shit!" as I fall down into the room below.

I'm on my back and the proximity sensor in my visor starts going crazy as I can hear multiple Thyr closing on my position. "Aden, report!" I demand, hopping to my feet and spinning to get an idea of what I'm up against. The corridor is about twice as large as the ones on the Patriarch to accommodate for the Thyr's large size. There's smoke all around from the explosion and before I have a chance to change optics, a Thyr charges me from the darkness. I dodge to the left and as his fist sails past my face, I bring my foot down on his knee, collapsing it backward with a spine-tingling crack. Bringing my left hand up to the back of his neck, I grab the hilt of my Ka, pull it off of my thigh, and with one quick motion activate the Ka and shove it through the Thyr's face as he's falling forward.

"Gimme me a minute, kind of busy," Aden fires back over the comm. The proximity sensor takes priority and closes out our video feed, but I can hear Aden on the other end grunting and cursing under his breath as he fights off the massive beasts. I rotate around the corpse in front of me and pull my Ka from the front of his skull. Blood sprays against the wall and floor as I spin around and use his kneeling carcass to block my back for a second. The smoke is starting to clear and as I switch my optics, I see a long, thick, glimmering chain whip out of the darkness and wrap around my wrist and coil back around itself. Without thinking, my right hand shoots to the air and as I'm about to bring the blade down on the metallic leash, another chain appears from the corridor's abyss and wraps around my other wrist.

"Activate your kinetic barrier, Aden!" The chains pull and I lurch forward, losing my Ka to the floor as my arms straighten. The Thyr are strong, but the strength amplified by my suit can overpower them.

"What the hell?" Aden screams as he struggles on the other end. He didn't get the kinetic barrier up in time. I rotate my wrists so the chains lay across the palms of my hands, then clench down on the silvery agents of bondage, tense my muscles, and pull with all my might. At first it's no use, but then I start to gain a little ground, which allows me to put more of my back into it. As my hands get closer to my chest, the smoke clears and I can see ten Thyr about twenty feet in front of me, five on each one of the chains, trying to pull me back. Just as I think I'm about to break free, I see the chains glisten in the darkness and it hits me. They're the same kind of chains that Alexander used to hold the Mini K down on the Patriarch. The glistening is the electricity surging through the osmium; there's no chance of breaking free, I have to lurch forward and fight them.

"Aden, the chains. Don't..." The proximity warning is flashing again and my neck is jerked backward after another chain wraps around my neck. "Fuck!" I'm staring at the ceiling, unable move and I can hear a Thyr approach from behind. It wraps a chain around my feet, connects it to the one attached to my neck, then growls as he walks around the front of me and chains my wrists together. I can feel the original chains that were wrapped around my wrists loosen as the Thyr in front of me smacks his large hand against the back of my head, causing me to fall face first onto the floor. Then he proceeds to pick me up by the chain that's connecting my neck to my feet and carry me down the corridor past the ten Thyr that I played tug of war with.

It's a little hard to speak in this position, but I'm able to reactivate the video feed and squeeze out, "Aden, I've got a problem," in a fairly raspy voice.

Aden's eyes are wide and he seems to be struggling. "I think we both have a problem, Sir," he replies in an equally scratchy tone. Well this isn't good, getting captured is definitely going to put a kink in our plans. At least we still have our comms. "Should we contact Kelly?" he asks.

"Not yet. Let's see where they take us first. Hell, maybe we'll find out who betrayed us." After being carried around the ship for twenty minutes like some kind of slaughtered animal, the Thyr bring me to a small rectangular room where Aden is suspended two feet above the floor. They've attached chains to his wrists and ankles that go into the ceiling and floor and have his limbs pulled out to form an X.

"Fancy meeting you here," Aden chuckles nervously as the Thyr hooks up the new chains to my limbs, then undoes the old ones and walks over to the wall, activating a retraction and lifting me off the ground.

I look to my left at Aden and focus on his video feed in the upper right. My head shoots back as my entire body tenses up. I'm not in pain, but I can't control the suit.

"What's going on?" Aden yells. "Are you okay?"

"For the time being." My muscles loosen and my head drops forward. A bunch of readings start popping up in my visor about the condition of my kinetic barrier's energy reserve. "They just sent a massive electrical shock through the chains, which then shot through my suit, but I didn't feel anything." Okay, we need to pull Kelly and Alexander into this. I open a dual channel to both of them.

"We haven't figured out who messed with Aphrodite and Blaze's suits yet, but we're getting close," Alexander assures.

"That's great, but uh, in the meantime, we've got a little problem."

"What kind of a problem?" Kelly asks, concerned.

"After splitting up, the Thyr were able to overpower us using a small version of the osmium chains that Alexander used to keep the Mini K secure in the Patriarch. We're now in what very well may be an interrogation room, suspended by said chains."

"That's not a little problem!" Kelly screams. "Why the hell didn't you call us earlier?"

"I was hoping that they'd lead us to the Hemo they're working with, but instead they're sending massive electrical surges through the chains and my suit. Alexander, I don't have the kinetic barrier activated, but my visor keeps showing me a readout of its energy levels." I get shocked again and even though I can't feel it, the suit tenses and the energy level goes down. "How much trouble are we in?"

Alexander sighs, "Well, if you take off the suits voluntarily, I assume they'll just torture you anyways. The energy reserves in the kinetic barrier are taking the electricity and spreading it throughout the surface of the suit so you don't feel it, but that won't last long." Another surge.

"Shit," I say under my breath.

"After the kinetic barrier drains, your suit will be able to stay intact using its radioactive energy, but it will probably end up shutting down all unnecessary functions to do so, like the comms. It also won't be able to provide any protection from the electrical surges." There's a slight pause as he sighs again. "In order to get the barrier to work the way we intended it to, we had to make sure that the nanomaterial that your suit is constructed from would be able to conduct electricity."

Another surge. Based off of the readings, the energy reserves for my kinetic barrier won't last more than two more hits. "What does that mean?" Aden asks desperately. As I stare into

Aden's eyes I can tell that he already knows the answer, but he's too afraid of what's going to happen to me to believe it. The suits are hard-wired into our bodies, the back end of the scales have microscopic needles that burrow into our muscle fibers. "Alexander," Aden demands in a firm tone, "What's going to happen when his energy reserve drains?"

Another surge hits and my attention is drawn away from Aden's video as a large red emergency message flashes across my visor: *Warning, kinetic energy reserves dangerously low, shield failure imminent.*

"LT, listen to me. It's not going to kill you. It's going to be extremely painful, but it won't kill you. You have to hold on and figure out a way to escape. If you can get free, any type of movement will immediately begin to fill your reserves back up. Your systems will boot up, administer medical attention, and you can make contact with us again."

"I'm getting Red!" Kelly shouts. "We're going to find a way to get you guys out of there, just hold on!"

I clench my jaw and begin to breathe heavily through my nose in anticipation of what I'm about to experience. Staring through the warning message, I look at Aden with a mixed look of fear, desperation and anger that he's never seen in my eyes before. My breathing increases to the beat of my overworked heart as a look of hopelessness and emotional pain takes over my brother's eyes. They hit me again.

"Hold on, Daemon! We'll get out of this, just..." The electricity breaks the kinetic barrier and surges through my muscle fibers as my blood-curdling scream drowns out Aden's desperate plea for strength.

Chapter 40: Successful Failure

01.22 - 2465 - 212.921 - The Void

I slam into the ground and roll backward, flipping over my head twice before coming to an abrupt stop on my stomach in the coarse, tan sand. Bill grabs my left arm and helps me to my feet as the entire chamber of Almathe soldiers cheer on The Bull.

"Well, that went well," I squeeze out between coughs.

"He looks really weird without all his hair," Bill observes. I chuckle in between cracking my neck and trying to push my tweaked shoulder back into place. Bill turns to me and abruptly shoves his palm into the front of my shoulder and there's a loud crack.

"Son of a bitch," I mutter, stretching out my jaw. "Okay, so close quarters might not be the best of ideas." The Bull is relishing in the praise of his people. Our people are known for their brutality and prowess in battle, especially us Alphas. Making a public display of our death is going to win some huge respect from his soldiers. Not to mention any creatures that could be residing on the surrounding planets as well. I'm not saying that it's going to put the Almathe on the map, but it'll definitely make the High Order think twice about the benefits of controlling Peagle. Granted, it won't stop them, they'll just kick up the ordnance and manpower when they come to take it by force.

"Think our deaths will do 'em any good?" Bill asks.

"It won't do shit," I snap back. "Our reports indicated that the subsurface mineral deposits are rich in Muutahtion and you know that the High Scientists have been pushing to get their hands on large deposits for some new military defense application." The Bull finally stops waving his hands to the crowd and with a face of stone, turns his attention back to us. "It just means we get a worthy death."

The Bull charges us at full speed and I leap to the left at the last moment, avoiding his massive shoulder. Bill rotates to the right, then gets behind The Bull at the last second and manages to trip his legs up while doing so. The Almathe may be stronger than we are, but we've got a little edge on speed. It's the only thing keeping us alive right now.

The Bull tumbles forward into the dirt, rolling over once before locking his legs out and digging his heels into the sand, sliding to a stop with his back to us. Bill shrugs and smirks. "Well, can we at least have a little fun with him before we get killed?"

I tilt my head back and stare up at the dim yellow sky for a moment to see a red streak across the otherwise clear atmosphere. "Bill," I point to the streak.

"Think they'll watch for a bit?" he asks snidely with a hint of excitement. With that, The Bull makes contact with Bill's chest, tossing him some forty feet away. Hopefully not.

The Bull runs over to Bill and grabs him by the neck, raising him off the ground. I take the opportunity to run up behind The Bull and dive between his legs with my arms out to either side in the shape of an L, collapsing the back of his knees with my biceps. Bill has enough sense to spread his feet upon hitting the ground, so he doesn't land on my back, and falls forward on top of The Bull making him tumble backward onto the ground and my legs.

Bill pushes himself off of The Bull's chest and knees him in between the legs, but The Bull just smiles sadistically. I'm pretty sure the Almathe don't have the same reproductive organs that we do, or maybe they're retractable, hell if I know. The Bull starts to laugh and unsure of what else to do, Bill grabs his tongue and tries to pull it out of his mouth with all his might. I wriggle free from underneath them to see The Bull caught off guard and trying to bite down on Bill's hand. While it may hurt, it's not doing much damage since the Almathe only eat plants and have fairly flat teeth.

The Bull snaps out of his momentarily shocked stupor and leans his shoulders off the ground in preparation to hit Bill in the face. As he does, I slide my groin under The Bull's head, wrap my legs up over his shoulders, then my feet back under, and grab onto my ankles from behind, locking his arms to the ground. "What now?" Bill asks, genuinely confused about what the plan is.

The Bull mumbles "er adems r utile."

"I think he's trying to say *your attempts are futile*," Bill corrects with a smile. The Bull bucks his hips off of the ground and Bill pops up in the air, but it only gives Bill the chance to wrap his legs around The Bull's waist and lock his ankles into place behind his back while still holding onto the tongue. The Bull tries to squirm his way out of our grips as Bill sits on his stomach.

"He is right, though," I say, straining to hold his arms in place. "It won't be long before he breaks our hold."

"Well yeah, but it doesn't matter, LT." Bill glances up to the sky.

The Bull makes a curious grunt. "Oh, you're right. Here I was thinking we might have to wake up Nox." I smack The Bull in the cheek and point to the massive open hole above the chamber.

A thunderous noise from above silences the Almathe crowd as a SWIFT tears through the sky and two Alphas drop down through the opening, slamming into the ground on either side of us and shooting sand twenty feet into the air. The Alpha to our right draws her rifle and starts scanning the crowd, while the one to our left pulls out her side arm and points it at The Bull's midsection. She taps the side of her helmet and it retracts down into the collar. It's Aphrodite. "Well gentlemen, this a quite a compromising situation we've caught you in."

The distorted voice coming from the other Alpha's helmet is Blaze. "If I knew you boys liked it rough, I would have spent more R and R with you." Blaze's helmet scans the crowd, making the slightest stop on my direction before continuing its course. She's been getting more blatant with her comments lately.

"Mr. Bull. What do you think would happen if I shot you in the heart and you didn't happen to have your protective fur?"

Bill finally lets go of his tongue. "This means nothing!" he spits up from between my legs. "The second you kill me, my soldiers will overpower you." I'm not quite sure what their exit strategy is yet, so I keep my legs locked around his chest and Bill does the same at his waist.

Aphrodite nods her head toward Blaze while continuing to stare at the Bull. "What do you think, hun? Think he's right? I mean there are several thousand of them and only four of us, hell only two of us have weapons."

"I think the Almathe should learn simple bait and switch tactics," Blaze fires back over her shoulder, then simply commands. "Close the net."

Several more SWIFTs stream by the open sky above, dropping a total of twenty Beta soldiers down onto the chamber floor and they join Blaze in sweeping the entire collection of Almathe soldiers with their rifles. Roughly a hundred or so soldiers jump up from the outer edge of the stadium seating at the top of the chamber, surrounding the entire arena from top to bottom.

"You see, Mr. Bull," Aphrodite says calmly, kneeling down beside us and pressing her barrel into his chest. "These soldiers around us are all hoping to get into the Alpha program at some point in the future, but our captain is extremely selective. To boot, our combat technicians just armed them with a new superheated high density round that tears through the air at such a high velocity, that not even your people's impressively dense, naturally defensive fur could stop at a distance of at least a thousand feet. Every one of those soldiers has something to prove." She looks at me, then Bill. We both loosen our grips around The Bull and get to our feet. The Bull takes a second, then stands and sneers at Aphrodite. "Tell them to surrender," she demands.

Without warning, The Bull tries to head-butt Aphrodite in the face, but she side steps and shoves the barrel of her gun into his mouth, firing without hesitation. The Almathe cry out in fury and some even start to attack, but it's too late. Aphrodite doesn't have to give the order, the Betas know the score.

It doesn't take long and only a few Betas are taken down in the ensuing battle, but in the end, all the threats are eliminated. Five Almathe are taken into custody for questioning and experimentation by the High Scientists. Bill and I are able to retrieve our armor and suit up as Aphrodite and Blaze call in the skirmish to the Patriarch and coordinate the exfil.

"You know," Blaze says as we're approaching, "we could probably have Alexander hold on to one of the prisoners, in case you felt like having another naked tussle."

Bill scoffs, "Pfsh, need a little jump start for later?" He says the comment under his breath but makes sure she hears it. There's no question he knows what's going on. Shit Aphrodite probably knows as well. Normally Bill has no problem making snide comments to someone's face, but he knows saying it like that will piss off Blaze. That's more fun to him.

Blaze fires back, "What was that, you little piece of shit?"

Bill chuckles, "Calm down, doll. Wouldn't want your sass to be confused with fraternization." Blaze hates being called 'doll'. Leave it to Bill to find everyone's hot button nickname. Her anger flares up and she lurches forward, but Aphrodite slams her forearm across Blaze's clavicles.

"Stow it, Sergeant...s," she emphasizes the second 's' and looks Blaze in the eyes, then Bill. Before I have a chance to tell Bill to stop fooling around, Aphrodite turns her attention to me. "Captain Otto is demanding that you jump back up to the Patriarch. He wants to debrief you immediately. Wouldn't want to add insubordination to being caught."

"He's probably not the only one that wants to debrief LT." Bill says with a smile at Blaze.

This time I act before Blaze has a chance to attack again. Bill is no stranger to my right hook. It hits him clean across the jaw, with less force than it should due to the battle and fatigue from the last two weeks.

"Get on the fucking SWIFT!" I say pointing to the slip behind him.

Bill's smile fades and he regains his composure, then starts walking toward the SWIFT. "Mike will take you," Aphrodite says half squinting at me, no doubt analyzing Bill's comment and my response. "we're going to stay and clean up a bit."

"Yes, ma'am," I say, saluting her, even though we're the same rank. She nods, then turns to the Betas and starts barking orders. I chance a quick glance at Blaze, catch her eyes, and bathe in their beauty. It's only a moment, a fraction of a second, but in the moment I feel revitalized. She nods as well, before I turn and run up behind Bill and grab him by the back of the neck.

"Insubordinate pain-in-my-ass! Let's go, Sergeant."

For a moment I don't say anything, but it's clear there's no point in hiding it anymore. Not from Bill at least. "Think she bought it?" I ask quietly out of the side of my mouth.

"No, your acting is for shit, and Aphrodite isn't stupid, even if Blaze didn't tell her."

I push Bill forward and let go of his neck. "How long have you known?" Bill looks back at me like I asked if he knew how to fire a rifle. That look that just screams 'really dumbass?'

"The first time. Shit I knew before you two did. Both of you are so transparent. And follow through next time, the cross was weak."

Leave it to Bill to criticize my fake punch. Maybe we both put more weight on this than it needed. Well, me probably more than her. She never seemed to care whether or not people knew, not with all the comments she's made in recent years. There's nothing against two soldiers fraternizing, even at different ranks, I just didn't want to deal with all the bullshit questions from other soldiers. 'What's she like man?' 'Is she as feisty in the sack as she is on the battlefield?' 'Who's in charge in the rack?' I know how soldiers can get. Just seemed easier keeping it quiet.

"You didn't say anything."

This time Bill does shake his head. "That's not us. It wasn't my place."

"Yeah well, it's not a big deal, we're just screwing around, besides," Bill's chuckling cuts me off. "What?"

"You just keep telling yourself that."

Before I have a chance to reply, we're at the slip and Mike is waiting for us. Better off saving this conversation for another day. Besides right now, I'm more concerned with how pissed the captain's going to be.

* * *

Surprisingly, it's hard to tell whether or not the captain's angry with us. He doesn't tolerate failure, but then again our situation with The Bull did present several opportunities to test some of Alexander's equipment in the field.

First off, the distress beacons, called the Icarus Initiative, that are built into our suits. It's very rare that an Alpha is captured to the point of needing backup and/or retrieval, but after an incident a few years back, the captain wanted something outside of the normal comm channels to alert the Patriarch if something went wrong. In the event that our suits are removed, an internal distress beacon must be deactivated within twenty seconds. The beacon, which is so small that it's sewn into the fibers, is undetectable by scans and can only be disarmed by the user's biosignature. A small invisible scanner on the inside of the collar will read the user's fingerprint and activate micro needles that take samples. If this isn't done, the beacon activates and immediately sends a signal to the

Patriarch command room and the captain's office. They'll try to make contact with the Alphas and if contact can't be made, then it's assumed that we've fallen and the Icarus Initiative is activated.

Once the Icarus Initiative is activated, the most senior Alpha team available is called in to assess the situation. To aid in the recovery of information, there are five mini SWIFTs, pill-sized robotic drones that are imperceptibly built into our suits, that can be brought online by the newly activated Alphas. Aphrodite and Blaze were able to gain enough information from the drones to know exactly what they were walking into and the size of the Almathe force holding us. They assembled a company of Beta soldiers to aid in the recovery and, if need be, eliminate the threat.

Captain Otto is looking over Aphrodite's report on his desk's screen as we walk in. He motions to the chairs without looking up. "Sir," I offer, but he holds up his palm, signaling for me to wait.

After five minutes, he raises his head to look at us and sets his arms on the table. "Well gentlemen, I read Aphrodite's and your reports about the situation on Peagle. Is there anything you'd like to add?"

Actually, yes. "Sir, we're front lines for experimental tech going into the field. Why weren't we armed with the new rounds that the recovery team used to take down the Almathe threat?"

He nods as if to approve of my question. "Ah yes, well we weren't fully aware of the Almathe's defensive capabilities when you started your mission. It was a recon mission after all. We received a broken transmission before your capture about the laser fire being ineffective. The rounds the recovery team was supplied with were old tech that was tweaked by Alexander after we received your transmission and the secondary transmission from your suit's beacon. That's why it took us so long to recover you."

"Wait, so you didn't know if the new rounds would work on the Almathe?" Bill asks, leaning forward in his chair.

"Alexander was confident, as always, but no we did not know for sure." The captain looks down at his desk for a second, then turns his attention back to us. "As angry as I'd like to be with you for getting into a situation where you're captured to begin with, it supplied us with invaluable information and you did technically complete your mission."

"Sir?" I ask, surprised.

"Your mission was to assess the size of the Almathe force on Peagle, determine the best way to eliminate them, and report back. Although it took longer than we expected and required the use of a secondary Alpha team and a company of Betas, you did succeed. The sentries you killed with the laser rifles were headshots, as expected, and thus did not clue you in to their biological armor. Early reports that the science team sent in claim that the armor only activates while the Almathe are still living, so the corpse that you were required to bring back for analysis wouldn't have revealed the full extent of the armor. If you weren't discovered, we would have sent a force in with laser rifles, only to find out about their armor at a later date, which would have caused further casualties and frustrations. The mini SWIFTs we activated prior to launching the recovery effort provided us with invaluable data of their base's size and inner workings. Also, the distress beacons in your suits had not been field tested until you were caught."

"Well that's comforting," Bill mutters.

"All things considered, the mission was a success despite your failure." Bill and I sigh at the same time and look at each other with a weak smile of relief. "Still, you failed and there are consequences," and there goes the relief.

I look back at the captain with a raised eyebrow and hesitantly ask, "What consequences, sir?"

He intertwines his fingers before proceeding. "You boys have been under a lot of pressure to perform for quite some time. Decades in fact. With the Almathe handled, we have a very rare window of low activity. I'm sending you back to The Outer Shores for two years."

"Shit," Bill says, shaking his head and slouching back into his chair.

"Captain, with all due respect, there's plenty of work that we can do on the Patriarch; we can lend Red a hand in training, help Alexander with equipment testing..." He raises a hand to stop me.

"I understand. But I think you both need some time away from the Patriarch and Major Erislad personally requested you for this posting."

"Great, like he didn't have enough fun with us last time," Bill whines.

"Actually, the major offered nothing but compliments. The Outer Shores is upgrading its security due to the surprising amount of new, hostile species that we've discovered in the last few decades. They're settling into the final stages of activating the security forces over the next two years and the major requested you two to train his men."

"So not only do we get to babysit, but we get to train a bunch of green soldiers who couldn't make it in the Red Army?"

"Bill," I say, trying to get him to calm down. Given the events that transpired on Peagle, I'm just glad that we're not in more trouble. Getting stationed on The Outer Shores for an indefinite amount of time because the major hates us is one thing, being requested to train his security force for two years because he holds us in such high regard is something else.

"It's okay, LT," the captain says to me before turning to Bill. "Look, I know you boys don't like The Outer Shores, or the major." He looks back to me. "I don't blame you. I don't either, but this isn't like the last time. The major holds you in the highest regard for saving his wife and daughter and capturing the Revenant. He has some strong ties in the High Order, so doing a favor here and there could be beneficial to the Patriarch in the long run."

Bill sighs, thinking about what the captain said for a second. He has a point, friends in high places could come in handy someday given how intense everything has become in the known universe. "Well, I still don't like it," Bill groans.

"You don't have to. Just do the two-year stint, try to unwind a little, and get back here. That's an order."

"Yes, sir," we say at the same time.

"I'll make sure you have your choice of missions when you do."

"Thank you, sir," I say before getting up and saluting. Bill follows suit and we leave.

Once we're out of earshot from the captain's office, I shove my elbow into Bill's arm and say, "Hey, look at the bright side, the women, right?"

He shakes his head and smiles, "At least there's that. You gonna say goodbye?"

"Guess it depends on when the captain wants us to head out."

Bill turns the corner to head back to his bunk and without turning around say, "For what it's worth, you should."

Chapter 41: The One Who Returns

??.?? - ???? - ???.???

"We were once known as the Medicarious," the Revenant explains as I look up at her eagerly from the couch. "It meant 'healer' in the old tongue." She's looking at the ground and almost seems afraid to make eye contact while explaining the truth behind her people. Taking a seat in the chair to the right of the couch, she begins to rub her hands together while continuing.

"Our people are not invincible—as you saw with your own eyes—but without interference we will not die. Once we reach the age of peak physical performance, our bodies stop producing growth hormones and the cells stop deteriorating. This allows us to retain any and all information that we collect over time, and even though our regeneration isn't as quick as you Hemosapiens, we still heal faster than any other species in the universe."

"Not to question your intelligence, but that's quite a bold statement to make." She stops rubbing her hands together and looks up at me in offense. "I'm just saying, like, the universe is infinite, so..."

"The universe is not infinite," she fumes in a matter-of-fact tone. Okay, if she didn't have my attention before, she does now. She scoffs, "You Hemosapiens, such a young and ignorant species. So egotistical and confident that what you know is truth." Closing her eyes, the Revenant takes a moment to breathe and calm herself. Opening them again, she tilts her head back and looks at the ceiling.

"There was a time when the universe was at peace. A time when a greedy species such as your own," she lowers her head and looks at me, "wasn't in such a rush to kill and conquer every world it came across. For how small this universe truly is, you make it seem so large. It's hard to comprehend how much life is out there until someone goes around trying to silence it all. With so few of us left, it's such a daunting task."

"What is?" I ask.

"Cleaning up the mess we've made," she whispers, shaking her head. "Though it may be hard to fathom, your universe does indeed have an end. There is space and life beyond this universe you know."

I look down at the floor then rub my forehead, trying to wrap myself around what she's saying. "Wait, so our entire universe isn't infinite and there's in fact other...well...universes beyond our own? Like in the grand scheme of things, our universe is representative of one planet in an entire galaxy?"

She nods. "This is a very crude comparison, but yes. Essentially that is correct."

I look back up at her and shake my head. "How is that possible?"

"Your mind could not comprehend the reasoning."

Her overly superior mindset angers me as I growl, "Try me."

She widens her eyes for a second, equally surprised by my response and the apparently exhaustive task of describing how the universe or universes really operate. She breathes in deeply and contemplates how she's going to explain the unexplainable. After a moment, she leans forward and grabs my hand, placing it on the middle of her thigh. "You can see me, yes? You can feel me in this moment, can you not?"

Uneasy about the placement of my hand, I stutter, "Yes. Yes, I... of course."

"In this universe, your perceptions are the source of your reality. In my own it is different, just as it's different in others. If there were a way for you to cross into my universe, which there is not, then you could not see, hear, touch, taste, or smell what you perceive as me at this time."

"Wait, if I can't cross into your universe then how can you be here? And what are you there?"

"Describing it with your language would be," she looks back down to the ground and shakes her head as she talks, "Difficult at best. The word *consciousness,* could offer some enlightenment." She stops shaking her head and looks at my hand on her thigh. I jerk it back to my lap and look away nervously. "Though that would be like comparing a planet with metallurgical deposits to your sword."

Oh wow, okay, so that doesn't really explain much of anything. She can see the confusion painted across my face and uses it as a reason to continue. "As far as traveling to my universe, let's just say that you are not compatible. I'm able to be here due to the nature of my true existence and your perceptive universe. Although, technically speaking, I'm not truly here, since this physical form only represents what I am back there. Much like a hologram, but more...physical."

"Does that mean that your people who died in this universe revert back to your own?"

"No," she says solemnly.

We sit there in silence and I try my best to understand or even believe everything she's telling me as she focuses on the memory of her lost people. I have so many questions running through my mind, but if all of her answers are as cryptic and vague as what she's already told me, then I fear that I'll be asking them in vain. Like how did they teleport in the ballroom? Why can't she teleport out of here? Why did they want to kill everyone? Why doesn't she just return to her own universe and what did she mean by *cleaning up the mess we've made*? I don't know why, but I feel an overwhelming sense of calmness and practicality in listening to her explain what she can. None of it makes sense, or should be regarded as true, but something in her eyes makes me trust her.

Before I have a chance to continue, the door to the confinement room opens and Major Erislad walks into the room with a scientist and two Beta soldiers. I look past them into the hall to see eight more Betas that make up the transfer team.

"Lieutenant," he cocks his head to the side. "You've been given your leave, I didn't expect to find you here," the major says with an honest sounding sense of surprise.

I look deep into the eyes of the Revenant one last time. My own eyes contain sorrow, regret, confusion, and frustration before standing up and turning to the major. "Sir, I don't think…"

He raises a hand to stop me. "I'm sorry Lieutenant, I'm very grateful for what you've done, but the fate of this creature has already been decided. General Vietus has expressed a great deal of interest in her." He looks down at the back of her head and his lips curl. "I'd rather she just be killed and be done with it," then looks back at me. "Still, orders are orders. Please, Lieutenant." He steps to the side and motions to the door.

Fighting with the major isn't going to get me anywhere. He's right, orders are orders. With a slight nod, I throw one more brief glance at the Revenant before leaving.

As Bill and I are walking up the ramp to our slip, I turn around to see the Beta team escorting the Revenant to a transport ship in a deep sleep container. "What'd she say?" Bill asks from behind me. His voice is muted and sounds like an echo as I focus on the Revenant's beautiful, unconscious face underneath the clear walls of the container.

"She, uh, she said we're a mess," I say quietly.

Bill laughs, "Isn't thaaaaat the truuuuuthhhhh." Time slows, stretching out Bills voice and distorting his words.

"We're a mess." I hear my own voice repeat in normal time.

"A mess."

"Mess. Mess."

"We're, we're, we're..."

The words keep repeating, and the speed at which they're delivered changes drastically with every syllable.

"We're, we are. A mess."

Without warning I'm back on the Patriarch. I have no clue how I got here, but I know exactly where I am. It's the details that give it away, before the unmistakably obvious clue. Blaze carved a small notch into the support frame of her bunk after each mission. I remember each time so vividly. I'd lay there staring at the ceiling, her naked, sweating body next to mine, running my left fingers up and down the cool metallic frame, while my right ones stroked her arm.

With that thought, I'm in bed, naked, and next to her.

"It just blows," she says with a bit of pain in her voice. She's trying her best to hide it, but I've known her for too long.

"I know," I say without thinking. My body is acting out a script from my mind, long since written. I have no control, I'm just along for the ride. This isn't real. The Revenant, and now this, they're both memories.

"Maybe it'll be good, sometime away."

She rotates onto her side and looks at me. "Is that what you want?"

"I don't," I sigh, turn to meet her eyes and put my hands behind my head. "Not from you." I look back to the ceiling, it's easier than dealing with the pain in her eyes. When this all started, we were both just looking for a little fun. A little companionship between missions to fill the void created by our lives, our dedication to our people. It took centuries, but eventually it became more than that. Something beyond harmless, well, mostly harmless physical fun.

Without warning, she shoves me off the bunk. I roll off the edge and land on the floor four feet below on my back with a thud. Not more than a second later, she's straddling my waist.

"Well there's only one option isn't there? Time to retire," she says with a sarcastic smirk.

"Oh is that so?" I ask playfully. Hey, it may not be an option, but it doesn't hurt to dream.

"Yup, only one condition though," she raises her pointer finger, then pokes me in the stomach. "Discharged or not, you can't let yourself go." She winks.

"As long as you keep that fucking attitude." I say while grabbing her arms and swinging her around underneath me. Her back is against the floor now and I'm using my waist to keep her pinned down while my forearms rest on her shoulders. She juts her head up to score a kiss, but I move back just out of reach.

"The attitude is free of charge and I've got a lifetime supply. A public service really." She looks at my arms, my muscles tensed just holding her in place. "What's with the gun show?"

"Jealous?"

She flashes a smirk before wrestling an arm free, smacking the inside of my forearm and grabbing the back of my neck as I crumble. She pulls me in close against her cheek and I can feel her icy cold skin against mine. It's making my blood race.

"Careful Sergeant, don't make me call your CO," I whisper before biting her earlobe. It drives her crazy, makes the blood boil and awakens the insatiable beast within. She wrestles her other arm free and shoves my shoulder, forcing me back against the base of the bunk. Our eyes meet and lock into place. She's tensed, holding me into place and I'm returning just enough force to make her work for it.

To my surprise she asks, "What do you love about me?"

The questions throws me harder than she ever could, but even so, I don't hesitate to answer. "About you?" I've never actually said 'I love you' to her. "Your body," I grab her ass and pull her close. "Your tone, the way you move, your..."

"Intelligence?" she licks her lips.

"Among a great many other things. Not to mention the fact that you're..."

"Fucking unbelievable." We both say the phrase at the same time. The sexual tension fades away, the desire, the lust, the clawing need to meld my soul with hers. The moment is gone, replaced by and pungent sense of déjà vu, the likes of which I've never felt. Judging from the horrified look on Blaze's face, she felt it too.

"What was that?" she asks,

"I don't know," I respond almost incapacitated by the sensation.

Without warning a bright white light burns the center of my eyes, causing immense pain before I clamp them shut. Even through closed lids, the searing sensation won't go away. My temples start to throb as I try to open my eyes only to end up blinking furiously at strange light causing me so much pain. Everything is a blur, but after a few moments, shapes begin to focus and I realize that I'm still in the interrogation room of the Thyr warship. I turn my head to the right and Aden's still hanging in the same place, but his head is slumped forward and he's not moving.

My head shoots back as my muscles stiffen and electricity travels into and through my muscle fibers, the pain of which continues to be the most horrific experience I've ever had. Everything blurs again and the light fades as my eyelids collapse and my head falls forward too.

Chapter 42: The Mess

03.10 - 2467 - 938.224 - Outer Shores Common

What about your sergeant? - V. Vali's concerned about the information and access I requested. He has good reason to be. In the last two years, Bill and I have overseen the installation of a large amount of high tech, military grade facility equipment and have trained a pretty badass security team. Given the social atmosphere of The Outer Shores, I don't see why they needed an upgrade of this magnitude. Should they have beefed up security a bit? Sure, there's a lot of rich and powerful people who reside here, but now this place has more security than the Patriarch and I'm dying to know why.

He's overseeing our last security detail before heading out tomorrow. I told him I was reaching out to Blaze. - LT

So gullible - V. I throw my head up to the ceiling stifling a laugh then look back at the ICE unit in my arm to see, *Are you sure you want to go through with this? - V*

I have to know, V. - LT

Then you're all set. - V

One of the new installations includes a maximum security holding cell that was until last night, empty. I got a glimpse at the deep sleep container that was transporting the prisoner and swear that I had seen the impossible. I have to know for sure. It may be my only chance to right one of my many wrongs.

I push off from the wall I'm leaning on and round the corner to see six of the security guards that I trained in the last two years. There are three on either side standing at attention and staring at each other like statues. Bill and I did a damn good job training them. It's not uncommon to see men from a security detail like this shooting the shit when it's boring, but our men are stone. As I approach, a young soldier by the name of Kandera salutes me without changing his stance.

"Sir. Major Erislad told us that you and your partner would be supervising the ball for your last night. He also said that the supervision part would be pretty lax." After working with the kid for two years, I can tell that it's taking everything in him to hold back a smile. He was quite a partier before coming under my command.

"Indeed. The sergeant is already there, graciously testing out the refreshments for the patrons, I'm sure." There it is, the slightest smirk out of the left corner of his lip. "As this is the first time the containment unit is being used, I'm just going to have a look around and make sure that everything is in order."

Kandera still doesn't break his stance, but he's definitely questioning my motives. After a few seconds he says, "Sir, I don't mean to object, but we have strict orders from the major himself. No one gets in but him."

I'd be pretty upset if Kandera didn't need a little convincing. He's doing his job, which means that Bill and I did ours. Still, a little attitude from a superior officer goes a long way. "Private, did you forget who my C.O. is?"

"Well, no sir." Good, he's nervous, time to turn up the heat a little.

"Because it sounds like you're insinuating that I'm trying to access this room illegally and without permission from my C.O."

His eyes go wide, but he remains in formation. "Oh, no sir," he's fumbling his words, "no, not at all, I just, I need to see that the major has signed off on it."

"So, you're saying that I'd lie to you?"

"I, sir, I..." Perpendicular to the left of his face, I lean in nice and close and stare into the side of his eyes. My nose is only an inch away from his cheek. "No sir, I'm just trying to follow orders, sir."

I increase my breathing, allowing the exhaled breath to brush against his cheek as it exits my nose, then slow down and move back. Looking at each one of the other soldiers, I finally end back at Kandera and say in a jovial tone. "Of course, soldier. You've been trained well, I wouldn't expect anything less." Complimenting soldiers in a way that compliments yourself is par for the course with officers, especially when trying to intimidate one of a lower rank.

"Thank you, sir," he replies nervously, unsure of whether or not the fake test is over.

"At ease, check your ICE unit, Private. The major has already forwarded everything to you."

Kandera doesn't move for fear that he's breaking some unknown protocol by checking his ICE unit on duty. After a moment his stance loosens and he raises his right arm to check the documents that Vali sent to him. His eyes dart over the documents as quickly as possible, like he doesn't want to take too long, but also wants to make sure he's thorough enough. I have faith in Vali's forgery, this isn't the first time that I've had to rely on his skills.

Finally he returns to his stiffened formation and says, "Everything appears to be in order, sir. Please proceed."

"Thank you, Private." I salute and walk past the other men to the door.

As I'm inputting the code that Vali acquired and awaiting my biosignature to be approved, Kandera calls out from behind me. "Sir!" *Great, what did Vali miss?* Stiff and on guard, I rotate on one foot to face the private who's still in formation but saluting. "It was an honor to serve under you." The rest of the men snap up a salute and I return the gesture without saying anything, then turn and walk through the now open door.

The door behind me slides shut as I take in the small confinement room. It's nowhere near as comfy as that apartment they kept the Revenant in all those years ago. It's a solid metal box that's only about fifteen feet wide by fifteen feet deep. The ceiling is high enough to accompany a Thyr if need be and there are large electromagnetic shackles coming out of the ground and hanging from the ceiling. They look like the same shackles that were used to hold the Mini K in Alexander's lab.

There's an individual who's several feet shorter than I am, in an all-black outfit, and matching hood, facing the back wall and hanging from the ceiling with their limbs stretched out in an X formation from the ceiling. I cautiously walk around the side of the individual, equally positive and unsure of who I'm going to find underneath the dark hood. As I approach from the front, the hood rotates up an inch as my feet come into the prisoner's view.

"You're not the major," says a familiar female voice. "Who are you?"

Upon hearing her voice, my throat sinks into my chest and the anxiety makes it difficult to speak. It took everything I had to push her out of my mind these last two centuries, but the information she gave me all those years ago never stopped forming questions in my mind. Our little conversation forced me to scrutinize every little detail about life as I knew it and my thirst for knowledge hasn't been the same since. The scary part is that after two centuries of searching, there are more than enough inconsistencies in our own 'historical fact' to make me believe everything she had said. Documented evidence aside, I'd never seen anyone with such an honest and painfully burdened look in their eyes. "Someone willing to listen," I finally say.

The Revenant lifts her head to reveal the beautiful, pale face that's served as a representation of truth in my dreams since last we spoke. I feel awoken by this guardian of light who only exists in the universe to ensure that darkness will not fall upon us. She looks exactly the same as the last time I saw her, smooth skin, striking blue eyes; hell even her hair is the same. There's a mixture of sorrow and joy in those deep blue eyes as she tries to understand why I've come to see her. "What are you..."

"Ask me again," I say cutting her off.

"What?" she asks confused.

"Ask me again."

Hope flashes across her face for what can't even be described as a second and is quickly replaced with more confusion. We're both taken back to the day we met and after what feels like hours, she finally whispers. "Free me."

I nod. She nods back. "Is there any way that you can teleport again?"

"Teleport," she scoffs, "Such an ignorant species." She laughs and smiles. "To answer your question though, yes, but it requires some work on your end." I wait for her to continue. "Your

High Scientists, if ones so crude and brutal could be called that, spent the last two hundred years extracting the ability from my body and cultivating a nano serum that can be injected directly into the brain and create similar effects for the user."

"My partner and I field test equipment before it's ready for mass production and use, why haven't I heard of this?"

"It's nowhere near ready. When you shocked me in the ballroom two centuries ago, it delivered just the right amount of electricity to my microscopic internal unit to disable it. They've spent decades trying to piece together the tech that's no longer there, but they're close. Unfortunately, their design is infinitely more dangerous."

"How so?"

"We could only jump to pre-mapped locations with our unit, but they've found a way to control the new unit off of the user's thought patterns. No surprise in a universe based on perceptions. The idea being that you could look and think of a location, then jump to it."

By the High Order, that kind of tech would be useful in the field. The Revenant shakes her head at my mental musing. "You can't use it. They haven't finished figuring out a way to make it compatible with your biology, but I think it will work in my body."

"You *think*?" That's not very reassuring. The whole point of breaking her out is so that she can leave and make contact with her people. If there's any chance of setting things straight in our universe, then I have to take it. I've seen enough in the last two centuries to not only accept, but fully believe what she's said. I know there's more to the universe than what we've discovered and can only imagine what the universes beyond our own are like. Our people have strayed so far from what we once were, it's not only sad, it's ridiculous. It's far enough to make a seasoned vet like me commit treason, but I have no intention of getting caught in the process. I truly believe that she's the only one who can help us evolve past what we've become. Whatever that may mean.

"It's that or I die. I'm confident that I can make it work. You just need to get me to the lab where they're holding it."

"How do you know it's here?" I ask while I type away to Vali on my ICE.

"I overheard one of the scientists talking to the major." I guess it's possible. They just installed a state of the art lab near the major's office, all part of the base's upgrades. "But how do you plan on..." The lower shackles loosen as her legs dangle free, then the ones around her wrist unlock, dropping her to the ground. She looks up at me in shock.

I smile and shrug. "I know people." Rubbing her wrists, she smiles back. "Can you fight?"

"I can," she says with excitement.

"Okay, I'm getting the security feed disabled. There are six guards outside that you'll have to put down; don't kill them unless you have to. They're just following orders."

"My whole life has been spent stopping species who *just follow orders*." I stare her down until she agrees. "Fine. Not unless necessary." I move over to the door but before opening it, turn around and look at her.

"What do I call you?"

She stops and contemplates the question. As I begin to think that she's confused by what I'm asking, she finally says, "I have been called many things in my time here. My favorite was Ellie. It was given to me by a human a long time ago. He told me that it was representative of the brightest possible light."

I nod and press myself against the wall next to the door. "Ready?"

Getting through Kandera and his men was fairly easy for Ellie. Of course, I had the advantage of knowing how they'd react since I trained them, but still, Ellie didn't need any guidance. Holding true to her word, she didn't kill any of the guards, though I was very surprised at her speed and overall awareness during the fight. I guess you can take the time to learn a great deal about combat when you stay in peak physical condition and never age.

Since everyone else was at the celebratory ball commemorating the new security team and upgrades, it was easy enough to get over to the other side of the base where the new lab is located. Vali took care of all the security feeds along the way and made sure the lab door would open the second we showed up.

I ran over to one of the scientist's terminals which is to the left of a metal gurney with holes in it and sit down to see Vali already sorting through the information and looking for where they stored the serum. *Bingo - V.* Appears on my wrist and I turn around to the sound of a sealed chamber opening behind me.

"Wow, they aren't taking any chances, are they?" I say as we walk over to the small chamber that was seamlessly hidden in the wall.

"If they figure out how to get the serum working for your people, it could change the course of the universe in a very bad way." She pulls the five vials out of the chamber and rushes back over to the terminal that I was previously sitting at. "We must destroy whatever we don't use. We can burn these samples in the incinerator, can your people erase the data from their systems?" I nod and tell Vali to destroy every digital trace once we're done. Grabbing a metal probe that's a tenth of the width of my finger at it's widest point, she jabs the sharpened end into her chest. "Jaah!" she cries out in pain, inhaling and holding her breath.

"What the hell are you doing?" I yell over her shoulder, looking at the long probe sticking out of her chest. There's a thick flexible metal tube at the end of it that disappears into the top of the desk to the right of the terminal at the head of the gurney.

She winces while the screen starts recording a bunch of data about her biology and genetic makeup that I can't even begin to understand. "I need to get a reading of my biosignature and sync the serum with my body." She squeals as the tube attached to the probe flexes and contracts, and more information shows up on the screen.

"Couldn't you have just stuck it in your arm?"

Her face relaxes and she opens her eyes. "Blood flows through the heart faster than any other part of the body, it's the quickest way to get the first piece of information we need." She rips the needle out her chest and deeply breathes in and out a few times before returning to a normal rhythm.

"You just stabbed yourself in the heart?"

"Yes. I will be fine. Though I need your help with second point. It will be more...difficult. I can't do it myself."

Oh great. I'm a soldier, I'm trained to kill people, not shove needles into vital organs without doing damage. "I can try my best." She offers the probe up and I reach over her shoulder and grab it with my right hand. "Where are we talking about?"

"I need you to shove the probe into my spine to get a sample of cerebrospinal fluid." She gets up from the chair and rotates the back around to her chest, then sits down, pulls her shirt up over her head, and leans forward while calibrating the probe on the computer.

"I'm sorry, did you say from inside your spine?"

"Yes, specifically from the subarachnoid space, between the third and fourth lumbar vertebra. I've calibrated the probe to the proper size and the laser guidance will line up with where you need to puncture the skin. Once you're through you just have to push and the needle will find its way into the space and take the sample."

The front of the probe shrinks in size and emits a laser that points to a position on Ellie's lower back. I move the probe from side to side, but the laser dot stays in the same position. "Okay that doesn't seem too hard."

She stops typing and wraps her arms around the back of the chair. "It will be painful, but you must make sure that I move as little as possible." I reach down and set my left hand on the back of her neck and she nods, then looks down at the desk. "Do it."

Before she finishes, I tighten my grip and stab the probe into her back where the laser dot is. I may not be much of a scientist or medic, but I do have precision, accuracy and strength; all of which are coming in handy right now. Ellie tries to arch her back and head as the probe painfully burrows to its target, but I force her back into the chair as the hilt of the probe keeps her back in place. I can see her squinting and gritting her teeth as I watch a digital representation of the probe on the monitor in front of her.

After five seconds, the probe retracts into itself and the message, *Biometric Sampling Complete*, flashes across the monitor in bright green letters. Ellie's entire body loosens as she tries to stand, and she almost falls to the floor before I catch her. "Hey, take it easy for a second."

She stands up and pushes my hands away. "I'm fine." It takes a moment, but she composes herself. Turning the chair back around and sitting down at the terminal, she starts typing away then grabs one of the vials and inserts it into the handle of the probe as if to be chambering an ancient cartridge pistol.

"How long is it going to take for the computer to calibrate the serum to your body?" I ask. The monitor flashes *Calibration Complete, Proceed With Subject Injection*.

"Not long," she says, glancing over her shoulder at me with a half-smile and handing me the probe. "I need your help again. The serum needs to be injected into my choroid plexus."

"Okay, where's that?"

"It's the lower back portion of my brain behind the cerebellum."

I look Ellie in the eyes. "I don't...what happens if I miss? More importantly, what if the serum doesn't work?" It's clear that she knows the answer to both of the questions, but given the gravity of the situation, is hesitant to tell me.

"The answer to either question is the same, it could paralyze or kill me." I swallow and then let out a long exhale. "If this doesn't work it won't matter. With the technological advances that your species has made, this is the only chance I have of getting away and rebuilding. Please."

My entire life revolves around ending the lives of other species, the thought of accidentally ending one that I'm trying to save is pretty hard to bear. Ellie looks back at the desk and leans forward as the probe pinpoints where I need to stab the back of her head. I close my eyes and take a deep breath, momentarily expelling any doubt or emotions from my mind, then open them and drive the probe into the back of her head.

Clear. - V

Thank you...for everything. - LT

After the serum successfully took hold in Ellie's body, I asked Vali to give her a hand with security and make sure that she got out safe. There's no trace that I was involved in helping her escape and when the guards awake and alert the captain as to what happened, I'll explain how green soldiers have a habit of making up stories to cover their own asses. There's no footage left to corroborate their story and some fake footage, courtesy of Vali, to corroborate my own.

I walk into the ballroom with a smile on my face and scan the room for Bill. I'm sure he's taking advantage of the fact that Major Erislad said that this ball could be overseen by the men that we've trained and he didn't see any reason why we couldn't cut loose a little.

I spot Bill to the left of me about the same time that I'm close enough to hear him trying to pick up some young, beautiful, high society type who looks more amused than interested, until she hears him say, "Seriously though, you could suck me bone dry any day," and with his wink, her eyes go wide with disgust. I can't help but slap my hand over my mouth to muddle the 'shit' that I say out loud.

A couple of other women around him start shaking their heads in disgust and commenting on what a vile comment that was. I rush over and grab Bill by the arm, jerking him away from the woman and the increasingly large crowd of offended patrons surrounding her. "What the hell is the matter with you?" I growl in his ear.

"Lieutenant?" I hear from behind me. I turn around to see Private Gorson with an apologetic look on his face and nod while raising my eyebrows, signaling him to continue. "Captain Erislad would like a word with you and the sergeant."

"Of course he would," I confirm frustrated. We had one more night to go without getting in trouble; I just helped an extremely rare species break out of the most secure facility in the universe, and Bill's mouth gets us in trouble.

"Tell the captain I'm busy with this lovely," Bill's comment is replaced by a groan as I rotate and drive my elbow into the side of his mouth as hard as I can. What's a few more gasps at this point? Bill grumbles and spits blood on the floor.

"We'll go straight to his office, Private. Thank you."

Chapter 43: Hello Boys

3.23 - 2468 - 1124.032 Red Galaxy Standard

I slowly, but painfully, open my eyes to see the dark, empty interrogation room. For some reason they've stopped torturing me, and turned off the lights for the time being. My entire body is sore in a way that I've never experienced and even the act of lifting my head to look at Aden on my right is exhausting. He's still hanging in the same position with his head to the ground. There's no movement.

I drop my head back down and stare at the floor, cycling through the different menu options on my visor. Alexander was right, there isn't much working other than the menu itself and the suit staying active. A few diagnostic programs are still running, but there's not even enough energy for the medical administrative program, which explains why I'm in so much pain. The electricity isn't enough to kill me, but it's more than enough to hinder my biological regenerative abilities and force the suit to use most of its power protecting itself.

I want to move, break free, fight, do anything other than just hang here like a helpless puppet saved and confined by the very same thing that's allowed me to be such an efficient, elusive killer, but the truth is I don't even have enough energy to care. Maybe this is what Aden and I deserve after destroying so many lives for such a long time. A slow, bitter, painful exit from this cold and relentless world. Is this our fate?

The shackles next to me begin to make noise and I turn to see Aden slowly raising his head and flexing his fingers into and out of fists.

"Are you okay?" I squeeze out in a raspy voice that doesn't even sound like my own, but quickly realize that even our local comms are down now. I press my right thumb and pointer finger together creating an 'okay' signal for him to see. I get a thumbs up in return before he starts looking around the room and casually pulling on the chains.

Seeing my brother move, even uselessly and feebly has given me some energy to process the situation. I have to think. There's always a way out, there always has been, we just need to find it.

The lights in the room power on and I see Aden jerk his head from side to side in pain just before I do the same thing. You'd think closing my eyes would help to some degree, but it doesn't. As my eyes adjust I can see a dark figure blocking out the blinding light. I close my eyes tightly, then blink a few times to be sure I'm seeing what's in front of me. I can't see their face, but their build is way too small for a Thyr, about half the size and...oh shit.

"Gentlemen, it's great to see you again," Major Erislad sneers through a wicked grin. He's wearing some sort of clear visor over his eyes, it looks like a portable version of the ones built into our suits. I look to Aden who looks back at me and points to himself with his left hand, then me, then throws up his middle finger. "Ah yes, your comms are down no doubt. I'd say that's about the size of it though, Sergeant, you are indeed fucked." The major takes a few meticulous steps forward and stops three feet in front of us. "Let's see if we can change that for a few minutes, hmm?" He brings his left hand above his shoulder, palm facing us and waves two Thyr guards into the room without turning around. "I know you won't remove those suits willingly and there's no way for us to forcibly remove them, but it doesn't take much to power them up."

The chains above the ceiling suddenly loosen and we both collapse onto the floor, unable to stand with our own energy. The chains are still attached to our wrists and ankles, but we've been given slack for mobility. The Thyr to my left picks me up by the waist and begins to shake my body violently from side to side. As my limbs flail around, I can see a small amber light in the upper right hand corner of my visor, followed by a similarly colored text that says, *Kinetic reserves recharging, at current rate of movement, reserves will reach full power in five minutes.* Means aside, it's hard not to be impressed. That's a quick recharge time given what our suits are capable of at full power.

After about thirty seconds of shaking, the Thyr throws me to the ground and Aden lands next to me with a thud. There's more than enough power for us to turn on the internal and external communicators. I immediately patch in a feed to Aden.

"Are you okay?"

"Yeah. I'm a little shaken up," he chuckles at the wordplay, "but I'm okay."

"We need to get Kelly on the," before I can finish the sentence, the major's voice blares through our speakers.

"Now now, no secrets among friends." A video of the major's eyes pop up on my screen. The visor he has on has the same communication functions as ours. "We're all friends here aren't we?" A video of Kelly appears next to the major and she's got a cut on her lip and one of her eyes is bruised. Her shoulders are pulled back and it seems like she's restrained. "Aren't we...*Kelly*?"

"YOU SON OF A BITCH!" Aden screams, jolting up from the floor at Major Erislad. The Thyr next to him grabs the back of his neck before he has a chance to reach the end of the now loose chains.

"Sergeant, I think this is the first time I've seen you angry. No more jokes?"

Aden struggles underneath the Thyr's grasp even though it's pointless. "I'll fucking kill you! You think these chains can hold me? YOU THINK THEY'LL HOLD ME? " I've never seen Aden this angry. The fury in his voice reminds me of when Nox gets uncontrollable, but Aden's has never show any signs of turning like mine does. It sends a chill down my spine. The major doesn't know Aden like I do, if he isn't scared, even with Aden chained up, then it's out of sheer ignorance. "I don't care where you slink off to, you slimy piece of shit, I'll hunt you down no matter what dark crevice of the universe you hide in! DO YOU FUCKING HEAR ME?"

"The tough guy routine is amusing, but played out, Sergeant." The major taps a few buttons on the ICE unit built into his right arm and Aden's chains recede back into the ceiling and floor, forcefully pulling his limbs taught again. "Besides, I had expected a little more curiosity."

"Kelly, are you okay?" I ask as calmly as possible, trying my best not to alarm her further. Anger won't get us out of this situation and it's pretty clear that Aden can't think right now.

"I'm fine," she says with a stoic look, followed by a closed fist slamming into her eye socket. Aden wails and struggles in the chains.

"Oh, she's fine for now Daemon, but that's going to change real soon." The major's mouth curls into a sadistic smile and he turns to look at Aden. "How did you phrase it, Aden? She can show her appreciation in my chamber? Granted, she's much more attractive than my daughter, so there'll be no need to turn the lights off."

Aden's rage is getting the better of him and I can barely hear anything over his screams. I don't think he even realized that the major just used our real names. The major taps something into his ICE unit again and electricity surges through Aden's chains, causing him to tense and seize for few seconds before falling limp.

"Huh, guess we didn't charge those shields as much as we thought. That was getting a little annoying wasn't it?" the major asks the Thyr next to Aden. He offers a slight nod in agreement.

"You called me Daemon," I whisper.

"Hmm, what's that? Oh yes, and him, Aden. Your true names. Your *human* names."

I guess in a position like this there's no point in denying it, he clearly knows more than we ever expected. "How do you know that?" I ask cautiously; curious of the answer, but also fearful.

"Well that's the big question isn't it?" Kelly stares at her screen intently, also waiting for the answer. "Did you really think that you could get by after all this time without a little help? Huh?" The major looks at Aden's limp body, spits on it, then starts to circle the room. "Your first point of contact was who? Red? Yes, and he had a neuro chip in his head at the time that kept him from doing certain things, making it quite difficult I'm sure, to share information. But after his valiant and ultimately fool-hearted decision to *help* the human race, he needed to find a way to turn it off."

"You."

"Well, not me specifically. But I was aware of Red's actions and needed to make sure he didn't succeed, so I made sure the right people approached him and gained his trust. At the same time, our High Scientists had been looking for uniquely strong willed human test subjects for a genetics project." The major's back is to me, but he turns and offers both palms to the ceiling as he points. "Enter, you boys." He starts pacing again. "Kelly, Lieutenant Mackelson and Captain Hoffman were all icing on the cake, as you humans used to say. I occasionally sent teams to harass Red over the years and made sure that his *trusted associates* informed him of the incoming attacks, only to solidify his trust in them further. I believe one of those teams was present at your awakening in fact."

There's a flash of fire in my mind, followed by random imagery and I clamp my eyes shut in an attempt to ease the pain. The soldier that leaned against my glass tube and the subsequent ones that Red and I killed together that first day. My first day as a Hemo. A previously lost memory that I would have never expected to come back. What else can I remember, given the proper trigger?

"Why? Why go through all the trouble?"

"Why? We needed a way for our race to advance. It wouldn't be too long before we met other, stronger species out in the universe and we needed to look at every available option to combat them. Our High Scientists had high hopes for splicing you humans with our genes and activating the best attributes of both races. Then we discovered the Thyr." The Captain reaches up and pats the one next to me on its massive forearm. "Your experiment was already underway, you were under, but the Thyr had a much more impressive physiological structure for us to work with. But some of the scientists were still convinced that you and your brother were too significant an investment to dispose of. So once you thawed, we let Red and his little band of misfits keep up the ruse." He removes his hand from the Thyr's forearm.

"When the Thyr tried to take the remains of Earth by force, we responded in kind while I kept you and your brother holed up in The Outer Shores. We used them as slaves to build GHC, allowing their anger and lust for revenge to grow. They realized that for all their strength and honor, they'd need to advance in order to stay alive, and that's when I struck a deal."

"If that's the truth, then why were we sent back to Earth a few months ago to search for a Thyr threat? With the Revenant escaping, you had enough of an excuse and security risk to keep us holed up in The Outer Shores."

The major scowls. "Captain Otto, or should I say Hoffman, has his support in the High Order as well and not everyone is privy to his secret, nor mine. He pulled some major strings to get you reassigned to Earth. Luckily, I was in contact with the Thyr force down there. It was a blessing in disguise, until you survived the attack. It was clear that you were asking too many questions and getting too strong."

I scoff. "You told the Thyr to go into hiding and protect their positions. You made sure that they stayed under the radar until their force was significant enough and you gave them the cloaking tech, the weapons, and the ships."

The major, or the sack of shit standing in front of me who's no longer fit for that title, leans back against the small security console in the center of the room. "Well, once again, it wasn't all me," he smiles. "But yes."

I turn and look at the Thyr to my left, "Do they know that you're a backstabbing bastard?" Then to the one on my right, "And that you have every intention of killing them once you figure out how to splice their DNA with ours?" My focus lands back on Erislad.

"They know the truth!" Erislad snaps, jutting forward. "We'll need a significant force to help with security while the transition is made. They know that while they may no longer be at the top of the food chain, at least they'll be in the good favor of those who are."

This is ridiculously ambitious, even for the major and his well-placed cronies. The million soldiers being activated to fight the Thyr threat only represent a fraction of our total forces spread across the universe, and don't even include the civilian population. There's no way in hell they can convince all of the Hemosapiens that this 'conversion' is a good idea for our people. There are too many purists like Alexander out there, it would be all out civil war.

"Even if you kill us, the Hemosapiens will never go for this. They won't take this conversion lying down."

Erislad lets out a deep laugh. "Oh, that's where you're wrong. You see the data from your deep sleep during the Bloodwar, and the neural implants you've been using have provided us with some amazing information regarding neural genetics and communication. The soldiers will be put into a deep sleep in order to receive a new *combat implant* to tackle the *Thyr threat*. While they're under, we'll wipe their minds in a similar, but accelerated fashion and convert them in the process. They'll wake up with implanted training; stronger, faster, and none the wiser to their previous form. The Thyr will supply security and the civilians will be easy to handle after we control the military. Those that cause issues will be dealt with. Permanently."

I shake my head. "You're insane."

"I'm a visionary who sees the future." He turns back to the security console and types something into the touchscreen. A large holographic video screen appears behind him. "I'd like you to see something."

Erislad steps to the right so I can see the entire screen as a feed flickers to life. Aphrodite and Blaze are strung up like us, by the same chains, on the blue sandy surface of Saudade, surrounded by Thyr. With their combat suits removed, they've been stripped down to their undergarments and beaten badly, way past the torture of the electrified chains. It's clear that they don't have much time. Aphrodite slowly lifts her head and looks at the camera. A Thyr to the right of Blaze jabs his rifle into her gut and she coughs while summoning all her strength, head quivering as she looks up at the camera as well. Their faces are so battered I can barely recognize them.

There's never been a woman in my life that's made me think of anything beyond the next mission. My life as a solider is straight forward. Follow orders, don't fail, but Blaze managed to break through that. She took my engrained nature to follow orders and fight, and forced it into the background. She knows what it's like to be used like a tool, time and time again with total disregard to your own desires. She understands the mental and physical abuse of going on a six-month mission and barely sleeping the whole time. Our common connection over what our lives are has caused us to create something wholly new. Our love is something that I never expected, but now I can't see living without it. I can't see living without her. As I look at her, helplessly hanging there, the anger growing inside is near uncontrollable, but I manage to quell it for the time being. If I'm going to have any chance of making it out of here, I need to keep it under control.

"Looks like failure to me." I say flatly.

"We're not through yet," Erislad sneers.

"Failure on their part." I correct. "They got caught, they deal with the consequences. That's the life of an Alpha."

Erislad stares at my emotionless face through his visor, unsure of whether I'm bluffing, or seriously don't care for their wellbeing.

I stare deep into his eyes and clench my jaw to prevent from exploding. Instead, I just say, "Contrary, I don't think you've considered them."

"Considered what?" he asks unconcerned.

"The consequences of pissing off the four deadliest people in the universe."

Erislad's brow furrows as his eyes lock on to me, but before he has a chance to question me further, a communication comes through his ICE unit. I can't hear the other end as it's rerouted to his neural interface, but I'm assuming it's from the command deck. "What do you mean? No, no!" he shouts with clenched fists. "Don't do anything until I get there." He turns to the Thyr in front of Aden, "Watch them." As he storms out of the room, he continues to shout orders. "Activate security protocol 113, lock down the whole fucking ship, and get everyone to their posts." The holographic video feed of Aphrodite and Blaze disappears.

I don't know what's going on, but this may be the only chance I'll have to escape. I have to do something. Aden's still locked up tight and possibly out cold. I wouldn't put it past him to be awake this whole time, but Erislad had access to our comms, so I can't risk talking to him. My chains are still loose though and I've still got some reserve power.

The Thyr who was next to me turns to watch Erislad leave. I lurch forward and drive my fists into the back of his knees, causing his legs to collapse and him to tumble down to the floor. There's just enough slack for me to wrap one of the wrist chains around its neck and yank it tight. He tries to lean forward and pull me over his head, but the chain tightens behind me as he does, preventing him from doing so. The Thyr in front of Aden rushes over to the security console. I try to grab the Thyr's side arm with my free hand, but can't quite reach it. Looking up at the security console, the other Thyr sneers and I prepare for the electrical jolt to come, but instead, his head explodes into a vaporous cloud of black blood. The Thyr beneath me stops struggling for a brief second out of shock and the lack of tension gives me just enough time to snap his neck.

  Letting the body fall to the floor, I look up to see someone in a combat suit damn near identical to our own holstering their side arm. The facial potion peals way to reveals Red's face. "Heard you boys needed some help." I disengage my helmet as he wipes the dark blood off of the security terminal and releases the chains.

  "How the hell did you get here so quickly? Is that...I thought our suits were the only two?" I shout over my shoulder after shrugging the chains off and rushing over to Aden on the floor. Red comes up behind me and leans down, jabbing a small cylindrical device into Aden's arm. Surprisingly, the scales on the suit peel back to allow the device access to his skin. "And what the hell is that?"

  He smacks Aden's helmet a few times. "Your questions have the same answer." Aden begins to stir. "Alexander. He fitted multiple attack SWIFTs with the same propulsion tech that allowed you to get here so quickly. Captain Hoffman and I were monitoring your transmissions to Kelly, I left the second you had been caught. The suit was made for me after Kelly first turned Alexander." I'm too grateful at the moment to be angry about the eavesdropping. "And I injected your brother with a concentrated dose of adrenaline, blood, and radioactive nanomachines. They will boost his reserve tank up to twenty-five percent. Alexander's design." Alexander is proving to be more useful than I could have imagined.

"Kelly!" Aden screams with a jolt as the upper half of his body launches up from the floor.

Red grabs Aden's arms just below his shoulders and forcefully pins him against the wall, presumably for our safety as well as his. "She is safe," he says clearly and absolutely. Aden looks at Red, then me, then back to Red again before his helmet disengages to reveal the look of shock on his face.

"What the hell happened?"

"We do not really have time," Red starts to explain.

"Short version, Red was eavesdropping and left the second we got caught, Alexander gave him a suit, and a SWIFT that had our slip's capabilities, and as far as Kelly," I offer a hand to Red since he hasn't explained that yet.

"Hoffman knew that Erislad was sending men his way and intervened."

After a brief second of processing, Aden says, "We have to get out of here. I have to see her."

Red jumps up and rushes over to the security console, pulling the holographic screen back up and tapping into Kelly's feed. She's standing sideways and has a Ka in her hand closest to the camera. With a look of disgust and anger, she drives the sword down to the ground, off camera, with her whole body. I can hear blade meet flesh, then metal and she raises back up, firing at the ground twice with a laser pistol in her other hand. "Fuck you!" she screams at the ground.

There's blood all over the front of her shirt and face. Captain Hoffman rushes into the screen behind her and sets a hand on her shoulder in support, then turns and sits in front of the camera. "Red, report."

"Kelly!" Aden screams, jumping up from the floor.

"I'm okay," she says turning to the screen. Captain Hoffman is covered in just as much blood and they both have bruises and cuts all over their bodies. They look like shit, but it's good to know that they can hold their own.

"Package secured," Red replies like we're just another mission. "My diversion is in place, but we should leave now."

"Good. Return to the Patriarch immediately. Thanks to the nanomachines you delivered Red, Kelly can hack into the controls for the ship and can take it down from here. We seem to have the Patriarch under control, but there's no telling how many men Erislad has under his thumb."

"No!" I blurt out. "We have to get to the surface of Saudade and save Blaze and Aphrodite. There's still time." Everyone turns to look at me.

The captain takes a breath. "They're not part of the mission. We can't risk you three, especially when we'd just be delaying the inevitable."

"Fuck the mission," I fume. "We can't kill everyone. The High Order is to blame for the mess that we're in, but there are some good soldiers out there who would never want to be a part of what they've become. Look at Red, Alexander, I know Blaze and Aphrodite are beginning to question the High Order already and that's without even knowing their plans about the Thyr."

After a moment of Hoffman contemplating my words, Aden says, "I agree," followed by Kelly's consensus.

The captain turns to look at Kelly, then Red who says nothing, but merely nods once. "Okay Lieutenant, you've made your point, but we can't risk losing you three, or the Patriarch, if we're to have any chance of defeating the High Order. I need you back here."

"Blaze and Aphrodite are just as beneficial as us, they're practically as skilled, and with the four of us together, we can influence and turn the entire Alpha program in our favor. Alexander can engineer more suits and imagine what twenty Alpha teams like us could do. We need them."

Captain Hoffman puts his left hand up to his mouth and covers it while looking down at the desk. Something red blinks on the desk and is reflected against the bottom of his hand. He glances at whatever it is, then looks back up at the screen. "Okay. Get down there, pull them out and get back here. No theatrics, just get it done and get back. Understood?" I nod.

The captain gets up from the chair and rushes off to the right. Kelly sits down. "Aden." He gently pushes past me. "Be safe."

"I love you," he says quietly with a slight waver in his voice. In all the years I've known my brother, I never expected to hear those words come out of his mouth. Red rushes over to the doorway and peeks down either corridor.

"I love you, too," Kelly says with a luminescent smile that almost makes her disheveled look melt away. The video hologram disappears as Aden and I both reactivate our helmets.

"We must go," Red says looking back.

A smile spreads across my face under the helmet as we rush out of the interrogation room. Maybe it's because we're free. Maybe it's because everyone seems on board with salvaging all the good that's left in the Hemo race. Or maybe it's because I know that Blaze is strong. I know she can hold on and when we find her, I'm going to tell her what I've wanted to all these years, but just didn't realize. It only took three centuries, but I've finally found someone who can quell the increasing storm within and nothing's going to stop me from saving her.

Chapter 44: The Forgotten Planet

8.31 - 2467 - 321.651 Red Galaxy Standard

Bill and I walk through Captain Otto's door on the Patriarch and the captain is sitting behind his old wooden desk looking down at his screen, presumable going over Major Erislad's report of our performance. Without looking up, he motions for us to sit and, after a few more minutes, swipes off the screen to say. "Okay, let's hear it."

"Sir?" I ask, knowing full well that it doesn't have anything to do with Ellie. After Bill's little stunt with the attractive High Priestess in the ballroom, the major pulled us into his office for a scolding. Ellie covered her tracks well. Vali had a big hand in that.

"I've had five months to let the major's tongue lashing settle after Sergeant Tate's tasteless little stunt during your last night on The Outer Shores. So even though I'm infuriated by the fact that some of our new project funding has been rerouted to the major's facility for their upgrades as punishment for *his* behavior," he glares at Bill, "I figured I'd give you a chance to offer up some bullshit excuse."

I could tell by the way that Major Erislad overreacted to Bill's antics in the ballroom that he suspected I had a hand in helping Ellie escape. We've never come in contact with any other Revenants in the time that she was being held, at least to my knowledge, which was amplified due to having Vali search the universe for any signs. None of the new soldiers would risk helping her and I was the last person outside of the High Scientists and possibly the major himself to actually have contact with her. Even if it was two centuries ago. Still, the whole Revenant project, if you could call it that, was classified black. Not even Captain Otto knew the extent of the attack all those years ago, he just knew that there was an attack and we stopped it.

"Well, sir," Bill starts.

"I don't fucking care," the captain screams while slamming his clenched fists down on the table with a loud thud. He looks down at his desk and takes a deep breath. "What did I tell you before you left?"

"That's an order?" Bill asks holding back his usual chuckle.

"It was a rhetorical question, shut your damn mouth, Sergeant." Captain Otto sighs. He looks back up at us.

"Sir, this is bullshit if you don't mind me saying. Since when do Alphas get in trouble for something this trivial?" I ask since Bill can't take anything seriously.

"War is getting more political by the day, gentlemen. The major is one of the many reasons that the expansion of our people continues to be much more difficult than it should. There was a time when the warriors made the decisions and the brass was made of hardened veterans." Captain Otto shakes his head, "I don't know when that changed, but it hasn't been the same ever since. I'll find a way to get the funding back and hopefully you won't have to deal with the major anytime soon, but I need you boys to lock it *down*."

We both nod.

"I'm sending you to Earth."

"You may as well send us back to The Outer Shores." Bill whines. The captain slams a single fist on his table. "Sorry."

"Sir, the Earth is empty. It's a wasteland, everyone knows that. We've recovered everything we need from it and until it recoups from the scorching, which could be hundreds of years yet, it just serves as a giant flag."

The captain sits back in his chair and flicks forward on his desk's screen sending files to our VOK and ICE units. "New intel suggests that a group of Thyr have amassed somewhere in the old Americas. This is a simple recon mission. I want you boys to see if the Thyr are there and report back on the size of their camp if they are. Any extra intel that can be observed without engaging any camps should be gathered. We don't want you to interfere until we know what's going on."

I quickly scan the information while Bill makes a point to rolls his eyes in an exaggerated fashion for the captain. "Sir, this intel is several weeks old, if it's important enough to warrant our attention, why haven't Lieutenant Nyla and Sergeant Utha already been sent?" A valid question, and a way of figuring out whether or not I'll get a chance to see Blaze before leaving. I wasn't able to reach her through my VOK on the way back from The Outer Shores.

"India-November-Foxtrot is verifying Thyr presence at a different location, as are several other Alpha teams."

That doesn't make any sense. They've been all but extinct since the uprising of 2252, now there's enough to warrant several Alpha teams to do recon missions when we have the Plaguers to content with?

"This is bullshit," Bill mutters. While I'm not stupid enough to make insubordinate comments in front of the captain, he has a point. We've been gone for two years playing boot camp and the Plaguers have been spreading throughout the universe wreaking havoc. Sure at first they were just seen as nothing more than a nuisance, but now they pose a significant threat. A threat much greater to some small settlement on a distant rock that holds no significant value, strategic or otherwise. The last time the Thyr tried to take a foothold in the universe, Alphas and Betas crushed them with one swift blow. We didn't even have to pull in the regular military. Hell, we were even pulled away from The Outer Shores.

"I thought you would have been happy, Sergeant, seeing as you missed your chance last time." Bill shakes his head and shrugs off the captain's comment.

We would be happy, if there was any reason to believe that this threat was real before traveling to the other end of the known universe

I answer for Bill. "Sir, I've been following the reports throughout the universe during our time in The Outer Shores. Don't the Plaguers hold a greater threat than some back-alley whisper that the Thyr have returned? Not to mention the fact that last time they took a stand against us the fighting ended pretty quickly."

"Look, there are skeptics about the Thyr presence on Earth, but I've seen the intel and I'm concerned. Concerned enough to send you two." Captain Otto takes a minute before continuing as if he's trying to figure out a way to explain the situation without presenting all the facts. "This isn't a slap on the wrist. You boys were stranded on The Outer Shores during the last Thyr attack and even though it was over fairly quickly, we underestimated their abilities. This plague business," he waves his left hand up and behind his shoulders, "doesn't hold a candle to what a sizeable force of Thyr could do to our society. The High Scientists will find a cure soon enough." He leans forward in his chair, setting his forearms on the desk. "I've collected intel from reliable sources outside of the Red Military that the Thyr are there. I can't say anymore at this time, but if it's true, we need to know what we're up against."

It all sounds a little flimsy, but I've known the Captain long enough to know that the look in his eyes is serious. He believes that there's a legitimate threat on Earth, contrary to what we may have been led to believe in the past. "If there are Thyr on Earth, we'll find them, sir."

Captain Otto relaxes back into his chair with a metaphorical weight lifted from his chest. "I have no doubt that you boys will. You have a few days to rest, I've already directed the Patriarch to the Milky Way galaxy, if things go south, I want there to be back up readily available." He waves his left hand toward us. "Now get the hell out of here. Check in with Alexander for an upgrade on your neural links, get some chow and rest and," he pauses, "do whatever it is you do in your downtime."

"Mostly train, sir." He smiles at the thought. What use is a blade if it's not sharpened?

"Kiss ass," Bill says under his breath. I elbow him in the arm and we both get up, salute the captain, then turn and exit his office. We don't get ten feet out the door before Bill grabs my shoulder and spins me around. "You don't think there's actually Thyr on Earth do you? I mean this is all some kind of stupid punishment for what happened on The Outer Shores, right?"

I smirk, "What's wrong, Bill? Last time you were dying to face off against the Thyr."

He blushes, "No nothing. I just, I don't like being jerked around."

Yeah, that's what it is. "Honestly I don't know, but what I do know is that the captain doesn't move the Patriarch unless he has a reason, or he's ordered too."

"Erislad?"

"I don't think so. Not this time." I start walking back down the corridor and can hear Bill close behind.

"Blaze could have some intel, she squared up against them during the uprising right?"

He's giving me a reason to contact her, instead of pulling my chain for asking the captain where she was. Is he actually happy about my feelings for her? Seems fishy for Bill, but hell I'll take it, I'm not in the mood to stir shit up.

"That's what I was thinking. I'll reach out."

"Again," Bill adds with an audible smile.

"Yes," I laugh. "I'll reach out again."

Contacting Vali via my ICE unit I ask, *Can you get me a line to Blaze? I haven't been able to reach her. - LT*

I'll make it happen. - V

How reliable is the captain's Thyr info? - LT

Very - V

Where'd he get it? - LT

Me - V

Chapter 45: How Romantic

3.23 - 2468 - 1240.982 Red Galaxy Standard

Aden's face pops up in its normal position on the right hand side of my visor.

"Daemon."

I don't answer. There's too much rage flowing through my veins right now, any sense of calm I had was wasted on Erislad. At first it was relief. Relief in the fact that we were still alive, that Red had saved us, but it didn't take long for reality to set in. I'm not talking about the reality that we had come to believe either.

"Daemon." he says again. His voice sounds so far away, like an echo in my mind that can't seem to find its end and has no source. For a brief moment I can taste a stale, salty essence in the air even though my suit's sealed and filtered. It's not the first time this has happened. It's possible that it has something to do with my memories returning, my mind recalibrating to the old me, but I don't have time to think about that.

I activate my video feed on his visor and he asks, "Is this going to work?"

"I don't know." It's true too. I don't know. All I know is everything was so much simpler a few days ago when we were just trying to turn a bloodthirsty group of Plaguers in our favor so we could hunt down and kill every last member of the infectious Hemo race. Hoffman wanted to rid the universe of their greedy and murderous actions which were directly or indirectly created via the ignorance of their bloated, selfish existence. Part of me understands that, even though it's not, nor ever was, a viable or logical option. Even though I know there is plenty worth saving.

Nothing can come close to describing the hatred I feel toward Erislad. He destroyed the humans, and manipulated us from the very beginning, raising us as an experiment for his own twisted, personal enjoyment. There are two goals that fuel my tortured body through the atmosphere of Saudade; one of them is making sure that Erislad pays for what he's done to the humans, to me and my brother, and for what he has planned for his own people.

"We're going to get to her in time," Aden says with a half-sincere, half-worried expression on his face. There's the other goal.

"Daemon, she's strong. I swear on my life that we'll save her." Given the circumstances of the last few days, that's not saying much, even though my brother's life means more to me than my own.

"Contact," I say coldly in reference to the fifty Thyr below surrounding Blaze and Aphrodite's chained platforms on the blue sand surface.

I can see it in his eyes. Aden's worried that I'm losing my cool, he's worried that my rage is controlling my actions. He's right. But he has nothing to worry about. He doesn't know how powerful my anger makes me.

"Confirm," Aden replies professionally. He realizes that my emotions have glazed over and the business of killing is the only way to get through. "Fifty hostiles spread out below, possibly more in the nearby structures. Communications array creating feedback. Can't penetrate interior." Ten seconds until impact. "What's the plan?"

Plan? I don't have any plans left. Everything went out the window when I learned how evil Erislad truly is, how corrupt the High Order truly is. Leaders meant to protect the Hemosapiens were making back alley deals with the enemy and planning on maliciously converting every last soul into a vicious monster. Revenge for the humans makes sense, but it's hard for me to connect with that idea given the gaps in my memory, but the betrayal of Erislad and the High Order is fresh. It's an open wound that must be seared shut.

I don't know why I'm surprised, even after everything that Red and Hoffman told us. I guess I just never thought that the High Order would stoop so low to keep cleansing the universe. Maybe this is the first time that I've actually accepted the gravity of the situation. I understand Ellie's hatred so much more now. I need to focus that hate and rage into a beam of insufferable, undeniable light that'll burn through the heart of the corrupt High Order. That intent has taken over all that I am now and is focused on anything associated with Erislad

"Fucking kill them. Kill them all."

Our suits are specifically built to dampen exterior noise to a non-existent level and as Aden's face is currently twisted in a mess of shock and fear, I can only surmise that the deep-seeded animalistic screams I hear are resonating from my own core. The suits also have a way of dampening the external noise around us as we move, making it all but impossible to hear movement we make. Maybe it's the faint sound of Red's SWIFT streaming high above the sky, maybe it's chance or instinct, but a few of the outlying Thyr decide to look up a second before we hit the ground. Whatever it is, I'm glad I can see the fear in their faces before we land. It's an emotion I previously thought the Thyr were incapable of having.

Red let us out of the SWIFT twenty miles above Saudade and due to the increased gravity and the weight of our suits we hit the deep blue sands of the planet's surface at a speed of 1,362 miles per hour. Needless to say, the resulting touch down provides a little bit of a bang. In fact, the activated setule feature on the bottom of our feet and hands has a hard time figuring out what it can lock onto given the speed that we slam into the ground. To add to the confusion, the finely ground sand creates a blinding, blue cloud of dust around us for hundreds of yards, making it easy for us to dispatch of the remaining guards.

Still, we have to land fairly far away from Blaze and Aphrodite as to not harm them in the aftershock. This means fighting through the remaining Thyr as fast as possible and securing the two captured woman.

Red's laser blasts illuminate the sapphire cloud in a purple haze as I switch my optics to see through the confusion and dust. The Thyr closest to us were killed by our impact; a group behind them were knocked down by the shockwave of our landing, and a group farther back decided to charge our position. The first Thyr to attack me is uncharacteristically ambitious and makes contact a few seconds before the others. I grab the hilt of my Ka and lock the deadly end into place before rotating around the side of its body and sweeping the blade across the back of its knees. The Thyr falls painfully forward into the ground and I leap, planting my knees on the back of its shoulders while driving my Ka into the rear of its skull. I turn and the advancing troops hesitate and glare at their fallen comrade. It doesn't take long for them to join their friend in the afterlife.

With methodical precision, they fall. One by one, until I stare down at a lone soldier standing in front of the two Alpha mobile crucifixions who's fully intent on trying to accomplish the impossible task of preventing me from saving the one woman I've come to love. My chest heaves up and down with adrenaline as I rush forward with unmatched fury in my eyes. It's a gamble as to how I'll attack, but the Thyr assumes high and I slide between its legs digging my Ka into its right knee. It falls to the ground and I take to my feet, pivot and drive my Ka through the back of its left knee. It begins to slump forward, and I toss my Ka into the sand. Aden walks up as I do and tilts his head in confusion. I come up from behind the Thyr and using the augmented strength of my suit, clamp my hands onto either sides of its head. Then with all the pent up anger toward Erislad and love meant for Blaze, I twist and pull, disconnecting the head from the spine and tearing the surrounding flesh in the process.

    Aden's hand tenderly falls on my shoulder as I toss the Thyr's head off to the right, watching it roll ten feet into a small ditch. I didn't even notice Aden walk over to me. Shrugging his hand off, I rush over to the outstretched Blaze who's strung up by the Osmium chains that I know all too well. They may be unbreakable when electrified, but are quite brittle on their own. Erislad and the Thyr were overconfident, using the women as a show piece for how strong they had become. The cables providing the constricting electrical current are clearly visible on the ground, next to the women's gear. I bring my Ka down, severing the line of lethargic pain from the Thyr's temporary compound to our right. The chains are next. Sweeping my Ka through the lower chains restricting Blaze, I allow her legs to swing free, then position myself to catch her, while slicing through the ones wrapped around her wrists.

    With one smooth, simultaneous motion, I drop to my knees and cushion her fall into my arms. I navigate through the menus of my visor to the external adrenaline blood cocktail and a syringe manifests on the front of my nanobelt. Less than a second after I drive the life blood into Blaze's heart, she jolts awake driving her head into the air, stopping just before smacking her forehead into my helmet. Her drug-filled, widened eyes stare at my visor as she tries her best to accept the fact that she's been rescued by the man who's come to love her. Seeing her eyes allows me to relax as I retract my helmet and smile down at her in pure, unadulterated joy. "Hey."

"Hey." she replies with a weak voice and smile. I help her to her feet then briefly glance over at Aden who's already administered the shot to Aphrodite and filling her in on the situation. Blaze takes a second to gain her bearings and balance, shakes her head, then turns to me and asks, "How'd you escape?"

"It's a long story, but..."

Time stops. Literally stops. I want to continue telling Blaze what happened but everything is frozen. The weak smile on her face, the glint of joy in her eyes, the blue sand cloud settling down around us. I don't know if it's the adrenaline or the sheer ecstasy of seeing her beautiful face, but my mind has done some weird things to me lately, so I don't question the odd phenomenon, I just take in as much of her as I can, while I can. Then I understand why that moment in time seems frozen.

It's not a sound that most people would notice, laser rifle fire. Our personal rifles are modified to make noise, to screw with our enemies during a battle, but standard issue Hemo rifles barely make a noise. Without the suit's amplification feature, I wouldn't have heard it either. I wish I hadn't.

That moment...that one absolutely perfect moment, frozen in time, shatters in instant. It's obliterated to pieces, much like Blaze's chest as the laser round hits from behind and explodes on impact. It sears through her heart, the front of her chest turning into chunks of burnt flesh that bounce harmlessly off of my suit. She's forced forward by the blast and falls into my arms as her legs give out. Her suit doesn't have the protection or medical advancements that ours do. Time returns to normal and there's a short barrage of blasts from behind me as Aden takes out the sniper.

"NO!" I catch her and even though I'm not injured, my legs give out, causing me to fall straight down on my ass with her in my arms. "No, no, no, no... you can't...I... no." Our regenerative ability is quick, but a shot to the heart takes too long to repair without a Lazarus tank. The explosion from the laser round seared the edges of the hole shut, but without the heart her body has no way of pumping blood through her veins. She'll slip into a coma-like state and could be revived at a later time, but the lack of blood in her brain will cause irreparable damage. With how long it would take us to get back to the Patriarch, the resulting brain damage would be too severe to recover from. Our own minds recovered due to Red's ingenuity, but they died in pieces and we were regenerated quickly, she doesn't have that chance. Her entire brain would die, and even if we could get her to a tank, she'd be a mindless sack of living flesh.

Nothing feels more painful than watching the one you love slowly torn from your arms. Her eyes switch from shock, to horror, to pain, then finally to fear. "This can't be...hold on," I squeeze out frantically. Her breathing increases drastically as I speak.

"Don't let go," I plead. Our eyes begin to well up at the same time and the tears start to stream down my face.

"Please, please," I press as though she has a choice in the matter. "Please don't let go." Her body relaxes and the fear dissipates as she displays a look that can only be described as peace.

"Fight for me," she says with a weak smile.

"I am. I am! You just have to hold on."

"Oh. No, not like that, dear. It's too late for that." We both know that she's going to die in a few seconds and she's come to terms with it. I haven't, and I won't. "Oh, Daemon." She raises a hand to my cheek. "Did you really think you and your brother were the only ones?"

She used my real name. She used my human name. "Why?"

"I wanted you to choose me. Not my history, not our species, but *me*."

Before I have a chance to respond, her body starts to jerk from the convulsions. It's not getting the blood or air that it needs to perform the most basic functions.

"No! No! Not now, not now!" She's already dead, but much like me, her body continues to refuse that it's the end.

"I love you. I said it, I said it!" As if to answer my plea, her convulsions stop. Her body lies limp in my hands, but it can't be the end.

"You can't, not now! I won't let you," I whisper. Then without control over my actions, I slap her face. Her lifeless body reacts to the hit, then stops moving once again. "That's an order, Sergeant!"

"You told me you wouldn't go anywhere," I shout hoarsely, my throat dry from screaming at her. "You promised!"

Aden comes up from behind and sets his right hand on my left shoulder in support.

I reactivate my helmet, and release Blaze's body to the dirt. My hand clamps down on my brother's as I spin and stand at the same time, striking his face with my free fist. Letting go of his hand,

I grab his throat and proceed to pummel his armored face with my equally armored fist.

"She's not gone!" I scream while continuing to hit his face. After a few more hits, I push him back into Aphrodite, and draw my side arm pointing it directly at his head. It's pointless, his barrier would deflect the blast, but I'm not exactly thinking clearly at the moment. The gesture is more symbolic than anything, I've never pointed a weapon at Aden and he doesn't take it lightly either.

"Whoa, whoa…okay," he says in a soothing voice. He steps in front of Aphrodite and shows me both of his empty palms. "I'm not going to tell you calm down, I can't even begin to understand what you're going through right now, if that," his voice starts to crack. "If that was Kelly…I don't know what I'd do, but I wouldn't be long for this world. You're stronger than I am." His voice cracks again, "I need you here, I need you back with us, I can't do this on my own." The last sentence is almost cut short by the emotion in his words. If his video feed was activated, there's no doubt in my mind I'd see tears forming in his eyes.

My throat is dry from screaming and I try to swallow but all I feel is a burning sensation. A quick glance at the diagnostics menu shows that the suit is functioning normally, but my skin is on fire. I look at Aden, then Aphrodite, the pain clear on her face. My eyes dart between them before I turn around to Blaze's cold, dead body on the sand in front of me.

"She's not gone," I manage to squeeze out.

"Maybe not," Aden says, placating my stubborn insanity. I turn to look at him and he points to her body. "But she is *not* in there anymore, and we can't stay here. You know what we need to do."

An Alpha's suit has a self-combustion feature for when one of us falls in combat. We'd never want the tech to get in an enemy's hand and if one of us falls, it's unlikely that the body will be recovered. We're not taken out lightly. If Blaze's suit wasn't violently peeled from her body, she'd still be alive…but she's not. She's not here.

Aden's right. She's gone.

It all hits me at once as my legs give out again and I fall to my knees. I close my eyes and two deep breaths feel like a lifetime as I pull in the recycled air of my combat suit and expel carbon dioxide back out.

"Daemon, words cannot describe my sorrow right now, but we have to move, those buildings are full of Thyr and we're exposed." Aden presses with as much sincerity as he can muster. There's a desperation in his voice that momentarily pulls me back to the present. I can recognize the danger we're in, I just don't know that I care anymore. I believe that Aden cared about Blaze, but his distance from her gives him the clarity to assess our current situation without the burden of lost love on his hands.

"Daemon, Daemon!" There's a female voice screaming in my ear, but I'm still disoriented. "Aden, Daemon, come in!"

"Kelly?" Aden replies running up to my side and grabbing my right arm. He motions to Aphrodite who grabs the left one as they both lift me to my feet. "What's wrong?" he asks.

"The Patriarch is compromised. Hoffman and I can't hold the ship." An explosion sounds out in the background. I shake free from Aden and Aphrodite's grasp, then stumble forward and kneel next to Blaze. I tilt her head toward me and press my palm against her cheek. She looks unreal, fake, like her skin is made from some kind of synthetic compound. Aphrodite kneels on the other side of

Blaze, with her combat suit in hand. We silently redress her and then Aphrodite activates the combustion feature from her VOK unit. Three button sequences. That's all it takes to erase her from this world. I pull her tight against my chest and there's a flash of white. Her body is gone, the sand beneath her feet burned to glass and my visor flashing a variety of warnings due to the close proximity of the combustion.

"Erislad had some men undercover and now the Thyr," another explosion, "Look it doesn't matter. I didn't have time to overload the core of the Thyr ship you escaped from, but I was able to set it on a crash course." She pauses and there's several laser blasts. "Fucking asshole! Look, it's coming down on your position."

"What?" Aden yells back.

"The ship is coming down on your position, something with the navigation locking onto their base on Saudade, I'm trying to change the course so it hits farther away but," I can hear Captain Hoffman shouting 'let's go' in the background. "I'll do what I can."

"Kelly, just get out of there. Get out of there!" Aden screams. A final laser blast cuts out the transmission. Aphrodite walks over to her gear, puts her suit and helmet back on, then secures her weapons to her back.

"We're going to take the compound," Aphrodite says, standing and pointing toward the only buildings within thousands of miles.

"That's insane, we need to get Red to swing back around and get us the hell out of here," Aden exclaims.

"And go where?" she asks coldly staring at the buildings. "Erislad has the Patriarch, Thyr are taking up positions in the galaxy, he'll have us branded as traitors and hunted down."

Aden grabs my arm and jerks up from the ground. "Daemon, you have to tell her this is insane, Kelly is still on the Patriarch, we have to go back."

Aphrodite marches up to us and shoves my rifle into my hands. "It would take us over an hour to get back on Red's SWIFT. The only reason Erislad kept us alive was to torture us. She either gets out, or she doesn't." My eyes dart around the dirt below and Blaze's body. "I'm sorry," Aphrodite says firmly.

She's right, we really don't have any other options. Given the chance between fighting or running to the darkest corners of the universe to try and hide from Erislad, there's no choice.

"Go to assault mode." I say in a raspy voice while strategically placing my trigger and middle finger just below the scope of my rifle. The barrel separates halfway and the nanomachines that make up the rifle peal backward over the body building a more agile design with a compensator around the shorter barrel. The stock reduces in length and develops into a bulkier design which stays tucked between my shoulder and chest for greater stability. Finally, the scope breaks down from a long distance one to a close quarters red sight with built-in density calculations.

"We need to get out of here," Aden presses.

"No." I say firmly. "She's right."

Aphrodite turns to Aden, "There's nothing else we can do for anyone on the Patriarch and this compound is Red Military tech, there's gotta be a bunker beneath it. All our colonization compounds include bombardment bunkers. We can ride out the crash inside. Besides, what's left for us hybrids?" She offers, confirming what Blaze insinuated.

Aden lets go of my arm and looks at Aphrodite while my gaze remains fixed on the compound in front of us. Kelly's voice comes through our speakers with a variety of chaos going on in the background. It's hard to hear what she's saying but it sounds like, "Rerouting...you'll never believe..." then it goes silent again.

Without saying another word, I charge forward as fast as I can, raising the rifle and firing off rounds at the Thyr beginning to pour from the buildings. If this really is the end, I'll take as many of these bastards with me as I can. Hold on Blaze, I'll see you soon.

Chapter 46: Prerequisite Bullshit

8.31 - 2467 - 653.011 Red Galaxy Standard

"No, come on," I press. "There's no fucking way."

"I'm telling you," Alexander assures holding back a smug smile.

"Okay, I could take the fucking time at The Outer Shores," Bill says pacing around the lab. The volume of his voice increases with each word. "I could take the stupid ass assignment on Earth even though it's a whole other galaxy over from ours, shit I could even take the idea of testing out new tech on an alien species that we've never fucking encountered before, but *THIS*?"

"Hey I," Alexander stops to chuckle, I think he's enjoying this a little too much. I'm pretty positive I've never seen him laugh in all the time I've known him. "I didn't make the decision. This came from high up on the High Order. All senior members of active duty operators are to receive the neural upgrade. Alpha members were specifically pointed out, what do you want me to do?"

"Well you could stop fucking laughing for one!" Bill yells.

Alexander pretends to rub his chin and turns around to fiddle with the implants on his lab table.

"Why don't you just shove a leash up our ass, or better yet, a fucking camera!"

"Bill, come on,"

"No, no seriously. That way the High Order could get a nice glimpse of my,"

"Sergeant!" I scold.

"Oh come on, you're okay with this?" Bill groans.

Alexanders is preparing the implants at his desk, but at least he's had the courtesy to stop laughing. His assistant Brent enters the lab from a side door and cautiously approaches the desk, nervously glancing up at Bill as he does. I get the feeling that we weren't the first ones to get this upgrade, and if I know the other teams, not the only ones to act this way.

I could care less if he bitches, this whole thing is totally asinine, I'm just tired of hearing him incessantly whine. It starts off being funny, which to be fair, lasts for a while. If he keeps pressing though, it gets annoying. That's usually when we're in front of some superior officer; we get yelled at and he stops. Occasionally though it becomes like a grating audible force that just sheers away pieces of my soul. It's the last thing I need right now. Based off of Vali's intel, not only are we about to get into the shit with a sizable Thyr force, who we still haven't had the chance of fighting for real, but I haven't see Blaze in over two years. Now, between her mission and ours, it doesn't look like I'll be seeing her anytime soon. That fact pushes what would normally be annoying, well into the range of soul grating yada yada yada.

"NO!" I shout, throwing my hands in the air. I jut toward him, bumping my chest against his, hard. "I'm not fucking okay with it! But guess what, we don't have much of a fucking choice do we?"

"What's up your ass?" he says pushing me back toward Alexander. He relaxes as a smile spreads across his face. "Ohhhh, I see what it is now."

"Don't fucking say it," I clench one fist and use the other to thrust my pointer finger toward him.

"Yeah, I get that way too when I haven't had any ass in a while," he says, pleased to have figured out what's got me so tightly wound.

"Fuck you, and when's the last time you got any, huh? Not counting that meat beater you call a hand." I turn to Alexander and the lab table.

"Well there was,"

"Bullshit," I counter.

"And the time,"

"Bullshit."

"Well,"

I turn back around to face Bill. "Bullshit, bullshit bullshit."

"At least I'm not," Bill begins to yell, but Alexander cuts him off.

"Gentlemen!"

"Shut up!" we both shoot back in unison. With that, Alexander is on both of us. He presses a small tube against our necks and I hear a quick, sharp hiss, followed by a biting sensation on my neck.

"Ow," Bill groans rubbing his neck

"Pussy," I say out of the side of my mouth. "So that's it?" I direct at Alexander taking a moment to rub my own neck as well.

"Yes. So gentlemen, I'd watch what you say or think from here on out." He turns back to the lab table and throws the disposable tubes used to inject the new neural chips, into a small incinerator near the floor. There a beep, and the faint whiff of burning chemicals.

"Ugh," Bill shrugs. "High Order just made super creeper status. Watching everything we think and do through neural implants? Talk about twisted fucks."

"Not yet, but to be honest, it isn't far off. This is mostly to help with the integration of neural activated hardware that we have coming down the pipeline. But, theoretically speaking, if someone knew what they were doing, they could figure out a way to record brain impulses." Alexander mentions as he points something out to Brent. Whatever it was, Brent must have screwed it up, because Alexander smacks his hand, before pushing him out of the way and taking over his terminal.

"Recording too?" Bill moans. "What the hell are they thinking, no one wants to be in here," he knocks on the side of his head.

"Isn't that the truth? I feel sorry for whoever gets the detail to decipher Bill's thoughts. Alexander we done? There's prep work I need to get on."

"Pfsh, prep work," Bill scoffs.

Alexander types something into the terminal. "Yesss," he says slowly, his attention focused on whatever's he's working on. "Everything seems to be in order. Try not to worry about this too much. Every member of the High Order was once an Operator, they know you're loyal and there's nothing you could think that would shock them."

"Challenge accepted!" Bill shouts thrusting his fist into the air. I turn away from Alexander and grab Bill by the arm, dragging him toward the door.

"Let's go numb nuts. Alexander, until next time."

"Try not to die," he pauses. "LT."

"Awww, Alexee…" Bill says with feigned pain.

As we're walking down the hall, the ice unit under my skin goes off.

"Do you think that Vali could, you know…do something for us with this implant?"

"I thought you didn't like Vali?" I ask while ironically reading an update from Vali.

"Yeah well, lesser of two evils yeah know?"

"Uh huh," I nod. He's already on top of it. Vali knew this program was coming down the pipeline well before we did. Hell, he knew well before the captain or even Alexander knew this was going to be a thing. Apparently it's been in the works for quite a while. I'm not quite sure who's responsible for it or why, but I don't like it.

"It's taken care of," I assure, paying attention to one line in particular in Vali's message that has nothing to do with the implants.

"What really? Already?" Bill stops in the middle of the hall. "I mean, I knew he was good but,"

"Hey, I uh,"

"Go," he says without hesitation. I give him a thankful nod before running down the hall as nonchalantly as possible toward my room. Vali was finally able to secure a connection with Blaze and she just so happened to have the rare opportunity to talk while on mission. That won't last long. Normal recon missions were one thing, but I have a bad feeling about the Thyr popping up again.

The military is already stretched thin as it is with the Plague War going on.

    The door slides shut behind me and not two seconds later I make the connection to Blaze's helmet feed which is now projected on the wall of my room. Vali set it up so that we could talk through our new neural implants without having anyone else drop in. As the High Order becomes more obtrusive, Vali becomes more valuable than ever.

    The feed flickers to life, a soft blue, hazy holographic image of Blaze's face covers my wall. For a moment my blood runs hot and my heartbeat quickens, but I stifle that shit immediately. It's just a holographic image, and I won't get to see her for a while as is, no point in getting too excited. Still the sight of her face is soothing.

    "Liam! How did you get this connection?" She asks amazed. Vali must have done a hard transfer. I don't know who he works with and Blaze has never mentioned him before. No point in bringing it up now. "We've been having problems with our comms, connection to the Patriarch is spotty at best. Rumor has it Otto is sending you to Earth?" The holographic image flickers and the audio cracks as she speaks, which distorts her voice.

    "Don't worry about the connection, it's closed. No third parties and yeah, Bill and I are headed out in a few hours. Supposedly a Thyr presence in western US region." That name still sounds so odd. The humans were a weird bunch.

    "Listen Liam, I don't know how long this connection will last," the image flickers, and dims, and for a second it looks like the feed is going to cut, but her face comes back. "The Thyr are strong, stronger than the training drones we fought. Smarter too. The idea, the basic principles are all there, but," the feed flickers again. "So much different in real combat."

"Sergeant, it sounds like you care about what happens to us," I say with a smirk.

"No shit, Lieutenant," the feed flickers. "Be..." the audio distorts and her voice gets distance. "Careful."

I sigh as the projection disappears completely and any hint of her voice trails from my head.

"You too," I say to the blank wall. "You too."

Chapter 47: The Final Mission

3.23 - 2468 - 1821.987 Red Galaxy Standard

I stoically walk down the corridor beneath the temporary command center on Saudade, and a laser blast strikes my chest. It explodes on impact as I walk through the remaining reddish orange cloud of fire. My visor makes sure I'm aware of the impact and the negligible damage that's done to the suit. The last Thyr guarding the underground bunker roars in reply.

Smacking his chest with the oversized rifle that the traitorous major supplied them, he tosses it into the wall like toy and reaches over his shoulder to unveil a massive double sided axe with a forged handle. I toss my rifle into the air and it collapses into its compact form, shoots over my shoulder, and snaps to the back of my suit.

I expect another customary roar to emerge from the soldier, but their nomadic warrior mentality must be diminishing with their other traditions. Without warning, it whips the axe forward from his shoulder and releases the handle at chest height. The double-headed blade topples over itself with ease as the momentum launches it toward my upper body at an increasingly impressive speed. Given the size of the Thyr, the axe itself is large enough to encompass most of my body, something that's easier to see as it rotates closer. Still, the speed and strength at which it was thrown is no match for my augmented abilities.

I rotate out of the way, grabbing the handle as it sails past my face and swing it around, launching the ridiculously large blade right back to its owner. The Thyr didn't expect me to do that, and by the time its little brain has a chance to register what's happening, the blade tears through his skull and upper chest. I can hear Aden land at the bottom of the lift shaft behind me.

"Eww," he says in reference to the half-split Thyr corpse stuck to the far door. I threw the axe hard enough to wedge the sharp end in between the metal blast doors. He walks up next to me.

"Topside secure. Aphrodite is just doing one last sweep and we're good."

I don't say anything.

"Kelly was able to get another transmission through. She and Hoffman were able to occupy a SWIFT that Alexander was working on and make it off of the Patriarch."

I grunt in reply.

"You don't sound too excited."

I spin around and pin Aden to the wall. "I just watched Blaze die in my arms. And you," I take a breath and decide not to blame my brother for still having what I couldn't hold on to. I know it's not his fault, but I can't help feeling some animosity toward him. "This conversation will not take place. This conversation will never take place. Do you understand?" He doesn't reply. I pull him forward then slam him back into the wall before shouting, "Do you understand?"

"Yes," he says absolutely.

I release him and turn to walk away.

Aphrodite lands in the open lift shaft behind us. She rushes over and nods at the Thyr. "Cool. Okay, topside is secure, not a soul remaining. How much time do we have?"

We both look at Aden. "Last communique from Kelly was five minutes ago and she said we had ten till the ship crashed. I haven't been able to reach her since. Transmission was spotty, which is why I'm the only one who got it. She said Erislad had his own tech guys trying to hack her signal and it was fucking everything up."

"Let's get into the bunker," Aphrodite says as she walks past us. She rips the axe out of the door, then pushes the corpse aside. The Thyr's physiology is a little different than ours and even though it's dead, the heart and basic internal functions are still continuing to pump away. That'll continue for another few minutes or so, which works out well for us, because it means that we can still use its biosignature. I grab one of its hands and set it on the scanner to the right of the door. The microneedles activate, read its signature, and the door opens without a hitch.

The room is about the size of the mess hall on the Patriarch and includes enough space for most of the Thyr occupying the base. It also has a cache of weapons, food, and its own energy source. I jog over to the security terminal on the right wall. "What about getting out?" Aden asks.

I close the doors on the terminal, then reopen them, and close them once more.

"They're worried about people getting in, not out." Aphrodite explains. "Once the signature is confirmed at the door, anyone can operate the controls from the inside. Failsafe for those trapped inside. Not everyone has access."

He nods. Aphrodite walks over to the weapons cache and starts looking for anything that we can use. "There's something else I need to tell you." Aden says. I turn to face him and retract my helmet, unsure of whether or not this is good news. He also retracts his helmet. "Kelly got a transmission before we attacked the compound." I shrug and shake my head waiting for him to continue. "It was Mackelson."

I stare at him for a moment, then look away contemplating what this means. If it means what I think it means, then it could be a huge benefit to the coming battle. Problem is, I'm still not sure that I want that. Dying in battle sounds very appealing right now.

"Who's Mackelson?" Aphrodite asks while walking back over and removing her helmet.

"He was human, too." Aden explains. "He was working with us and Hoffman."

"Hoffman?"

"Captain Otto."

"Holy shit, Captain Otto was human, too?" she exclaims shaking her head.

If Mackelson managed to win over the favor of the Plaguers and Kelly thought to bring it up, then they'd have to be close. She wouldn't have wasted her breath if they were even a planet away from us. They must be here on Saudade.

"Wait, you didn't know Captain Otto used to be human?" Aden asks.

"No," she says shaking her head in honest disbelief.

There's four of us, who for all intents and purpose are at full capacity. The suits and the combat cocktails we took will see to that. Red is still circling above in the SWIFT, but it doesn't have a full combat load. Saudade is pretty desolate, sand, rocks and mountain. We can only fight for so long before having to leap out of the area. Plaguers, even thousands of them, and us versus five hundred thousand troops. Maybe I'll get to see Blaze sooner than I thought.

Aden and Aphrodite are still talking. Aphrodite seems pretty oblivious to the fact that I'm so quiet, but Aden isn't. He keeps glancing at me as he talks. "So, do you remember being human?" he asks.

Her eyes go wide as she looks at the ceiling and recalls what happened. "No. There were the nightmares that helped piece it all together, but that was all more recent. We were, me and..." She doesn't say Blaze's name, but looks at me and continues. "We were contacted by some hacker called Vali years, hell, decades ago."

"Holy shit." Aden mutters.

"What?"

"Did you ever meet Captain Otto's niece?" he asks.

"What, you mean the pretty one, the High Priestess? Yeah, once on..." We're both nodding at her. "Holy shit no way! Really? Was she human, too? So wait, you guys don't remember anything either?"

I wish giving up was an option, just running into the ranks without my gear or suit. I could let some opportunistic sniper take me out before the battle, or get bludgeoned to death within seconds. Problem is, it's not in my DNA, very possibly literally not considering our past. I want to give up, but it's just not in me, not who I am, and she wouldn't want that. In the end, that's all that's pushing me forward. I'd like to say that keeping Aden safe would do it, or the thought of getting revenge, but I can't. Not a hundred percent. Letting down Blaze though, even if she's not here, that I just can't do.

Now Aden is full on staring at me as he answers Aphrodite. He just wants me to be me, but I can't. We both deal with things differently, only I don't have the option to just shut down right now. He's never been comfortable with my approach. "No. Fragments here and there occasionally, but nothing solid. Supposedly Kelly, the captain, and Mackelson do though, and Red fills in the gaps. Before you ask, no he wasn't human. He just didn't agree with the Hemos slaughtering the humans and helped us fight the Bloodwar as a sleeper agent, so to speak."

I turn back to Aden and let Aphrodite process all that information. Maybe, I can start with something small, if for nothing other than to quench his silent judgement. "Mackelson?"

He jolts back to life as if he forgot what he was going to tell me during our little spinoff conversation with Aphrodite. "Oh, yeah! So Mackelson, that son of a bitch, he did it."

"Uh, did what guys?" Aphrodite interjects.

"And even better. He's here on Saudade. Ten miles south of our position on the other side of that small mountain ridge. Turns out they've been hiding under the planet for years."

I run a hand through my hair at the prospect of having a very large ally in the coming fight. The Thyr probably scanned the planet and found out they were there and assumed they were black ops or something.

"I don't know how the hell he did it, but Kelly's filled him in, and they're on their way."

Frustrated Aphrodite shouts, "Who's on their way?"

I nod to Aden to explain, then turn away from them to check the weapons cache. "Mackelson was Mike, our SWIFT pilot, prior to all this going down. He was also human, working with Otto-slash-Hoffman for centuries to exact revenge on the Hemo race for what they had done to Earth. We had no memory of it, but he, Red, Otto, and Kelly got us up to speed on their plans. Apparently we played a big role in fighting off the initial wave of Hemos on Earth, thanks to Red."

"Kelly is Vali?" Aphrodite asks trying to keep up.

Aden nods and continues, "Yes, exactly. Their original plan was ludicrous. They were going to slowly but surely eliminate all of the Hemos due to our penchant for spreading and killing like a disease. My guess is Kelly and Hoffman were close to pulling you two in, but just didn't get the chance. But we needed more help. Mackelson purposely exposed himself to the plague in order to try and get them to become allies with us."

"And he pulled it off?" she asks in amazement.

I pull the rifle off my back and force it onto the table. As Aden continues I fiddle with nothing in particular. Changing settings then changing them back. Participating in anything other than breathing sounds exhausting, even thinking is taking its toll right now. "Apparently, that's what Kelly tells me. He was quiet for so long, I'm still having a hard time believing that he's alive, let alone that he's coming here with a shit ton of Plaguers who won't kill us. He's a royal dick, fucked up Daemon pretty good, but he's for the cause, there's no question there."

"He cheated," I mutter. Aden doesn't say anything, but I'm positive he's smirking.

"This is a lot to process." Aphrodite says in an exhausted tone.

"Understood, but we need to get ready." Aden walks over to me. "We've got about thirty seconds before the ship crashes into the surface."

"What's the plan once we get up there?" Aphrodite asks. We don't have much time, so Aden quickly lays out a ridiculous plan that's two steps past bat-shit crazy. Luckily that's pretty much where we reside on a good day. Erislad will likely send out a throng of Thyr the second the ship comes to a stop. There's no way he'd take a chance on losing us a second time. I'll admit, the idea of killing his soldiers until I can no longer stand is about the most appealing thing I can think of right now. Outside of pummeling his face until it's just a red smear in the sand that is.

There's a monstrous noise as the ship slams into the planet and the entire bunker shakes for thirty seconds. Luckily, we're fifty floors underground. Once everything settles, Aden finishes explaining the plan and Aphrodite's response is, "You're insane."

"It's kept us alive this long." Aden chimes in with a smile, but it doesn't change the fact that she's right.

"Well," I say with a sigh, "at the very least it'll be interesting." I walk over to the security terminal that controls the blast door and a gust of hot air shoots into the room along with a cloud of blue gray dust as it slides open. I activate my helmet before the cloud reaches us and scan the hallway beyond. No signs of Thyr yet, understandably, but I can already tell the crash has made a ridiculous mess. I turn to look at Aden and Aphrodite who both have their helmets up.

Getting back up to the surface is a mess. The elevator shaft we came down is riddled with debris, but luckily with the strength our suits provide and all the tech we've got, it doesn't take too long.

I toss a mini SWIFT out of the opening above and pilot it into the cloud of dust on the surface. I have control over the unit, but the feed is patched into both Aden's and Aphrodite's helmets.

"Shit," Aden exclaims long and loud.

Shit is right. The ship obliterated the compound and gouged a trench in the surface of the planet that is probably too wide for Aphrodite to leap across in her older model suit. The drone scans the area for life but doesn't find anything. After switching the optics to cut through the sea of blue dust and panning the drone, the downed ship comes into view. It's a good distance to the west of our position, leaning against the base of a large mountain. The drone feed cuts and the mini SWIFT guides itself back to my suit.

I turn to Aden, "Let's do it." he gives me a slight nod as I look at Aphrodite to his left. "If we fail, get the hell out of here before..."

"Fuck you."

I just stare at her. Saying the words was enough work on its own, I wasn't exactly expecting a response like that.

Aphrodite activates a video feed and her face appears in front of where she's standing. A second later, Aden's face appears on my left. "I said, *fuck you!*" She's sure to emphasize the second part, her teeth clenched, head quivering as she does. Tears begin to well up in her eyes.

"You think you're the only one who loved Blaze? That her death didn't have as much if not more of an impact on me than it did you? You haven't been through a tenth of the shit that I have with her. What if he died?" she yells pointing at Aden. "Huh? You going to stand there and tell me that you wouldn't take as many of those bastards out as you could before going down in a *Blaze* of glory and following him into the afterlife?"

I stare at Aphrodite, half in shock, half accepting of everything she says. It all makes sense, I just, I feel like the recent events have blinded me to the emotions of those around me. How could I be so stupid to think that she was okay with Blaze's death regardless of how quickly she seemed to shake off the shock? Aden, just averts his eyes, he never was one for the emotional parts of life. I broke down while Aphrodite held it together, but the emotions are still there.

"I don't remember much about my human life outside of the flashbacks, but Blaze," she stops herself, "Callie…"

Her name was Callie. What a beautiful name.

Aphrodite's voice started to break. "She was my sister. Maybe not true sisters, I don't know, but as far as I was concerned we were blood nonetheless."

"You remember her name?" Aden asks meekly.

Aphrodite chuckles through the tears that are streaming down her cheeks. "Callie claimed to remember them from the flashbacks. Said she remembered spelling it C-A-L-I for short because she was from southern California. Some place called San Diego."

My senses dull, sounds disappear, replaced by a faint ringing in my ears. Aphrodite is still talking but I can't hear her. A sharp, painful sensation strikes the back of my head, near the tip of my spine. If it wasn't for how casual the other two look and our remote location, I could swear that someone snuck up behind me and drove a spear up through the back of my head. Aphrodite drives her finger at me and the episode dissipates.

"So don't you *dare* tell me to run, you selfish bastard. Shit goes wrong and I'm following you assholes into the afterlife are we clear?"

I nod, and without another word Aphrodite closes the feed then jumps through a hole in the rubble below to find a more secure position. I leap up through the open area above us and land just outside of the shaft. The massive cloud of blue sand is finally starting to settle. Aden jumps out of the hole and lands to my left. His name appears in blue on the upper left side of my visor, signaling a closed channel.

"You felt it didn't you?" I turn to face him. "You did."

Shaking my head, I say, "I felt something, I don't what the hell it was."

"San Diego, something about that place, it triggered something in our heads. It was the same feeling I got on the Thyr ship when I had the flashbacks, I thought it was just residual pain from the electrocution but..."

"Wait," I say holding up a hand. "You had flashbacks on the ship?"

"Yeah, and so did you."

"How could you know that?"

Aden cocks his head, "Come on, it's me." I drop my hand and lower my shoulders, tilting my head forward so he can see that I'm frustrated with the bullshit answer. "All right! There were times when you weren't really conscious. In between the torture, you'd move a bit and gain a small bit of power in the suit. I'd do the same and your comms were on. You were rambling about the past. I could hear you, not well granted, I was struggling to stay conscious myself, but still."

We're both struggling with memories that, according to Red, should no longer exist. Aphrodite had flashbacks, Bla...Callie had flashbacks, and we have them too. It seems like the part of us that was supposed to have been erased is trying to reach out and say something, but what? What do we need to know that we can't access?

"So San Diego? What do you got?" Aden asks.

I look away and shake my head, "Nothing." It's like, it's just outside of my conscious thought. I know it's important for some reason, it feels familiar to me, but I can't piece the memories together.

"If," Aden pauses as I look at him. It takes a second, but I realize why he stopped and silently thank him for not saying her name. "*She* was from San Diego and Aphrodite feels connected to her, could we have known them as humans?"

"Seems logical." My suits blinking a warning across my visor in bright red letters. LIFE FORMS DETECTED. "But we can't worry about that now. We've got work to do."

"Daemon," he says quickly grabbing my arm. I look at him but don't say anything. "I uh..."

He wants to say something about the fact that I'm retreating into myself. He wants to ask me to try and act normal, by whatever means possible at this point, so he can process the situation. He's scared, but he also knows that asking is selfish and is unsure if it's over the line.

"I'm trying," I say. It's all I can offer at this point.

"Yeah," he nods.

Chapter 48: The Firestorm

3.23 - 2468 - 1925.109 Red Galaxy Standard

"So this is it, huh?" Aden asks as we stare out at the blue sandy surface of Saudade. My visor currently reads twenty-five thousand Thyr charging toward our position. It'll take less than two minutes for them to reach us. I turn around and look at the barren wasteland behind us, just to check, before turning back to the oncoming storm.

Seems like it. An odd thought enters my head, I'm amazed at what these suits have been through in the short amount of time that we've had them. I turn to Aden and retract my helmet. He does the same and we look each other in the eyes as I set a hand on his shoulder. "It's been one hell of a crazy life." I'm trying to hold back the emotion but a tear rolls down my cheek. "I'm proud to be standing here with you. Brother."

He grabs my hand and squeezes, "As am I."

It takes a moment, but I'm able to muster up the words, "I'm sorry about falling apart, I..."

"Shut up," Aden says through a snort. "Not needed and you know it."

The Thyr are closing fast and at this point will be on our position in thirty seconds. I reactivate my helmet, extend my Ka locking it into place, and drive it through the sand and into the dense ground underneath. Aden does the same and the Thyr are only fifteen seconds out. I open my comm to all frequencies and close my eyes. "Red Alpha...reign death."

As the counter on my visor gets closer to zero, audible ticks start to go off in my ear. The Thyr are almost on top of us. I fight the urge, but at one second left, I open my eyes to see a Thyr so close that I can reach out and touch it, but before it has a chance to hit me, the surrounding area explodes into a fiery blaze. The Thyr disappear. The suit informs me that the napalm-like substance is burning at a ridiculous five thousand degrees and increasing. The kinetic barrier is holding, but it won't for long.

It didn't take long for the Thyr to make their way out of the downed ship. No doubt Erislad was tracking us, and is more than pissed off about the crash. Time and time again, we've escaped situations where the odds were stacked against us, so the former major wasn't taking any chances. Twenty-five thousand Thyr poured out of the ship and charged forward with rage and lust for the fabled blood of an Alpha. Too bad they missed Red circling the area in his SWIFT.

Just before the Thyr made contact with us, the bait, Red unleashed a payload of thermite napalm on our heads. It won't kill them all and hopefully our kinetic barriers will last long enough for us to survive the blast, but it should take out at least half their current force and more importantly, buy us some time.

Switching my optics, I can see through the ocean of flames as hundreds of Thyr appear at a distance, flailing about as their skin and muscle literally melt off their bones. There's no signs of the ones that were closest to us before it started. It's unfortunate that the SWIFT isn't packed with a full payload of weapons, it would have definitely come in handy, but we don't have to fight them all. We just have to hold out providing Kelly's intel is correct.

Aden's video appears to the right and he looks worried. I'm sure seeing my widened eyes and clenched teeth at the increasing atmospheric temperature around us doesn't help. The barrier is holding yes, and we have temperature control within the suits, but the intensity of the heat surrounding us is starting to affect our systems and bleed through. The microneedles are beginning to heat up, which leads to an odd feeling of increased warmth from inside my muscles and outside my body. It's a tingling sensation at first, but that changes as the inferno rages on.

Tingling turns to heat, heat turns to fire, and fire turns into a searing that rapes our bodies from the inside out. All of my strength is focused on clenching the hilt of my sword as the hellfire creates gusts that threaten to rip us off the ground and fling us across the landscape like a grain of the blue sand below our feet, now glazing over into glass. The strength that I'm pouring into my grasp is only matched by my locked jaw and clamped eyelids. This feeble attempt to will away the pain is quickly replaced by the opposite uncontrollable approach of screaming at the top of my lungs. I'm sure Aden is doing the same, but I can't hear him over my own demonic purge which has barely begun to drown out the sound of the fiery hurricane around us.

The discharge of agony in vocal form finally gives way as I inhale hard and deep to repeat the process. This only allows for the burning to reach my lungs, the one place that was previously untouched, even though I just realized it. My chest stops; my lungs empty, I begin to suffocate and choke on the epic stalemate of battling expulsion and inhalation. All I want to do is move my eyes to the right to see how Aden's holding up, but there's no strength left for even the most simplistic physical maneuvers. As my grip loosens on the hilt, all I can do is hope, beyond all hope, that the insanity of a current situation will subside.

Slipping down the hilt of my sword, my hands fall to the smooth blue surface below, but with the exception of my slumping shoulders and head, the rest of my body doesn't move. My eyes slowly close as the illuminated exterior around me fades to darkness.

Death is not a comfortable event.

The swelling fire slows and dissipates, molding itself into one solid curtain of red. Something slams into my ribs and I can feel sand spray across my body. I open my eyes to see a woman in green cargo shorts and a black bikini top tumble over me to the left. Turning to the right, then back to the left where the woman is in the sand, I take a moment to gather my surroundings. I'm on Coronado beach. It's the Fourth of July. I didn't want to come, but Aden bugged me until I said yes.

The woman is getting to her feet and reaches over to grab a football to her left. "You missed," I say with a smirk.

She turns back to me with a partial scowl, "I didn't miss, I tripped over your fat ass and fumbled."

"Heh, I've heard my ass described a lot of ways and fat was never one of them."

She points off to my right and whips the football back to one of her buddies. Looking down, she nods at the pack I'm currently using as a pillow. "Army huh? That explains it. Discharged or not, marines don't let themselves go."

With the exception of my bad habits, there's nothing about my body that's been let go. I'm still in top physical shape, I have to be working with the Park Ranger service. This is just her way of flirting. It's a good thing Aden isn't around, I doubt he'd catch on.

"Ah, and that explains the fucking attitude," I say back with a smirk.

She nods at someone down the beach, then looks down at me, her beautiful smile spreading as I stare back at her. "The attitude is free of charge, a public service really. Just to let you know that your sad gun show isn't doing much to pull in the ladies. You should head down near the hotel, probably plenty of pretty bimbos on vacation that'll be impressed."

"You have me confused with my brother," I point back behind me at Aden who is currently getting slapped in the face by Kelly, which only makes him smile. "I'm just here because he dragged me down and promised to pay for the booze."

"Yeah well, try not get in the way of my foot again," she says hopping over me.

"I can sleep through damn near anything," I say putting my hands behind me head and closing my eyes again. "But if it happens again, Sergeant," with that I can hear her stop a few feet to my right. I take a second, turn my head and open my eyes to look at her puzzled face. "I might have to call your CO, a name would be nice."

She turns around for a second to yell at the guys in her group who are hassling her for not being back in the game yet, then looks at me and takes a step closer. "Who says I'm a sergeant?"

"Your body does, your tone, the way you move. I notice things that most people don't."

She licks her lips, "Huh, Intelligence?"

"Not something I can discuss," I turn back to the sky and close my eyes. "Besides, it's all in my past. Have a good day, Sergeant."

For a moment she just stands there. I can feel her gaze, until her buddies up the beach start heckling some more and she starts back. "Blaze!" she yells. "They call me Blaze."

"Good name for a sapper," I yell at the sky.

"Fucking unbelievable," I hear her mutter as she starts jogging through the sand.

I can feel the beach around me melt away as decades of memories shoot through my mind. My eyes jolt open to a massive thud in front of me. A familiar looking man with dark red eyes approaches a glass barrier inches from my face and stares at me before pressing a button to my right. "Hello, Daemon,"

Another massive thud sounds, causing me to clap my eyes shut. The memories come again, fast and harsh, but clear. This is followed by what feels like a massive Thyr war hammer slamming into my chest as life shoots back into my heart and my head launches back into the air. Oxygen is forced into my lungs as my body reacts to the suit's lifesaving procedure and medicine. The visor displays my vital statistics in front of the orange and blue sky above. Once my chest is full of life, I lower my head and turn to look at Aden on my right who's already staring back at me. The statistics disappear and his face takes their place.

"What the fuck was that?" he asks.

"The heat made us pass out. I couldn't breath and my heart stopped, the suit shocked me back to life."

"Yeah no shit," I don't respond. He waits, then squints before asking, "You mean, you didn't have a flashback?"

I did. I knew it felt like more than a dream or vision, but didn't want to accept it. We were told that our memories were gone and would never return. Either way, it doesn't matter right now, there are more pressing issues at hand. There's a roar in the distance. "We don't have time." I reach forward and push off the hilt of my sword to get back on my feet. Aden follows suit, stumbling on his way up. I close out Aden's video, but keep the channel open and can already see thousands of Thyr in the distance regrouping and preparing to attack. They don't know that Red only had one payload to drop, but it won't take them long to figure it out. "Administer additional pain medication and adrenaline, we're going to need it."

Aden's slumped shoulders shoot up as his back straightens from the suit tightening and pumping his body full of chemicals that will allow him to fight for the next few hours without feeling much pain. I do the same and call out to Aphrodite on the open channel. "Aden, see if you can get a hold of Kelly and find out if she's heard anything from Mackelson. Aphrodite?"

"Go ahead, LT."

"They're regrouping, but it won't take long before the second wave closes in."

"Understood."

"Red, find a place to park the SWIFT..."

My rear proximity sensor goes off and I turn around to see him land just behind us in combat gear as his boots shatter the now glass surface of the surrounding area. "It is safe behind a small range to the east. In the very unlikely event that we survive, we will have transport."

"Thanks for the vote of confidence," Aden chimes in.

"Confidence does not change fact," Red explains.

"LT. LT, come in." It's Alexander. What the hell is he doing calling us? I thought he was going to stay low and try to avoid Erislad's men.

"Alexander? What's going on? I thought you were going to stay quiet for the time being."

"I was able to create a secure channel, but don't have much time. I've been monitoring you as best I can. You have incoming, I wanted to let you know."

Aden laughs and I shake my head. "Yeah thanks, we just survived the bombing run of a lifetime while thousands of Thyr burned around us, but we'll be sure to keep an eye out for the other twenty thousand looking to charge us."

"No, not them." I walk over to Aden and offer my forearm up. He bumps it with his own and even though I can't see his face, I can tell that he's just as excited about the news as I am. Alexander must be talking about the Plaguers, it looks like we have a chance of getting out of this battle after all. "Mini K. To the north."

My heart sinks. I can feel a lump in my throat as I turn to my right to see a thin black line on the horizon. "Since when the fuck have there been Mini K on Saudade?"

"Roughly ten years. The High Order commissioned a breeding facility to be built, they wanted to use the Mini K as weapons."

"Weapons? Shit they're animals! You can't freaking train them," Aden shouts. Nobody replies. "Wait, I mean, you can't train them...can you?" he genuinely asks Alexander.

"No, you can't train them," he snaps. "But you're all wearing combat suits aren't you?"

"Yeah," I reply dryly. Where's he going with this?

"Well then, let them do what they've been bred to do, what they instinctively do; trample everything in their path," he says optimistically.

"Holy shit...you let them loose," I say still trying to process what's about to happen. Alexander just gave us an asset not a complication. He's right, Aden and I could get knocked around with our kinetic barriers and have no problem surviving the wave of massive beasts. Red and Aphrodite have older suits, but they can still launch into the air, bypassing the stampede altogether, or at least strategically bouncing once or twice to avoid getting trampled.

"You're welcome," he says with a smile. I don't have a video feed, but I can hear it in his voice. "I have to go," he says with a rush.

"Our chances of survival have just increased greatly," Red says.

"Thanks for the update," Aden quips.

All I can hope is that with the blanket of Mini K making their way across the blue sands of Saudade, I can kill as many of these fucking Thyr as possible. We can bide our time until an army of Plaguers being led by Mackelson show up. Maybe Blaze won't have died in complete vain.

No! Fuck! I immediately force that thought from my head. I'd give anything to have her standing by my side. I'd have snuffed out the entire universe for another minute with her. Now I'm trying to assuage her death by trying to say that it meant something? No.

I have one goal. It may not have been what Blaze would have wanted, but she not here. She was ripped out of my fucking life by Erislad. First, I'm going to find that bastard and feed him his own heart before crushing his fucking throat and watching the life slowly drain from his eyes. Then, I'm going to hunt down his master, Vietus, and get really creative. The pain of losing Blaze is indescribable and it has finally shaped me into the monster that I was meant to be all along. Anyone that gets caught in my path will come to understand this, in what brief moments they have left.

Chapter 49: The Fall

3.23 - 2468 - 1985.239 Red Galaxy Standard

There's so much that I've come to experience in the four hundred and eighty-nine years that I've been alive. Some of it, well some of it would just sound down right crazy if I had the chance to go back and tell my younger self. It would seem damn near impossible, yet all of it has come to pass.

I should be focusing on the fight at hand and the heavy sword that just took down my kinetic barrier by fifteen percent before knocking me to my knees, but I find my mind wandering back. Besides, a maneuver like spinning on one knee while sliding my own Ka into the kidney of the Thyr behind me, then standing and rotating the blade around the outside of its stomach causing guts to spill onto the ground has really become second nature at this point. I've seen planets on fire with frozen subterranean surfaces, I've seen giant mammalian-like creatures that glide through space the size of a class two chariot. I've seen two-legged creatures that are three feet high, but strong enough to put a Thyr to shame, and eight-legged creatures that crawl through the moon of Actihan, which is made entirely of trees and their roots, even at the core. There was one time when we discovered a colony of aliens the size of my thumb and they were vicious as hell. Given all the rage and darkness flowing through my system, it makes me think that part of this musing, part of this internal dialogue is my inner self trying to fight off Nox. He's taken on a whole new meaning and killing no longer satisfies him, he needs more blood, more carnage. The old me, maybe the human me, is trying to fight that. Which brings me back to it, I never, ever, thought I would see a wave of Mini K slamming into ten thousand Thyr.

The Thyr don't even notice the Mini K on the north horizon and to my knowledge have never seen one. It only took minutes for the Thyr to realize that there wasn't going to be a second round of bombing and when that fact took hold they charged. My visor shows thirty seconds until the Thyr wave hits and when I look north it shows two minutes for the Mini K. Holding the Thyr for a minute and a half won't be a problem.

We keep to a tight group as they descend and rely off of each other's speed and situational awareness to stay alive. It's basic hit and run tactics; we strike, injuring a Thyr enough to slow them down, then move on to the next within a specific perimeter. By keeping the action close and the attacks swift, a Thyr falls every three seconds and gets hit by all four of us before going down for good. They're so preoccupied with trying to catch us, that they don't even see the Mini K until it's too late.

I leap and drive my sword into the rear shoulder of an already injured Thyr, then reach for my rifle which is still in assault mode, ride its back down as it falls forward, and fire a few rounds into the chest of another Thyr that means to bring an axe down on my head. The laser blasts tear through his body and Aden stops the axe with his sword as Aphrodite sails across the Thyr's shoulders, taking the head off with one fell swoop. Aden kicks the body back and dodges off to the right following Aphrodite while I leap to my feet.

I can hear the Mini K make contact with the outside wall of Thyr a hundred yards in front of us. Between the un-expectant roar of the Thyr, the wails of the Mini K, and the sound of all those massive bodies slamming together, I half expect a shock wave to knock me back. Instead, all I see is a wall of dark limbs barreling toward us. "LAUNCH!" I shout, hoping that everyone can hear me over the commotion.

I'm in the air. Aden flies above the fighting, Red follows closely behind, but Aphrodite is nowhere to be seen. The Mini K have slowed due to being bogged down, but they're still plowing through the Thyr with ease and will be on her last position in fifteen seconds. I activate the gravity field on the bottom of my boots and shoot back down to the cracked glass surface. "Aphrodite, talk to me!" I turn around trying to get my visor to pick up her suit.

"Twenty feet west," she says nervously. I dodge three Thyr who are too occupied with firing lasers and throwing weapons at the oncoming wall of beasts to attack me. She's pinned, stomach down by the hilt of an axe that's been driven into the ground. There are two corpses on either side and the odd position she's laying in, makes it impossible for her to reach back and remove the axe. I run over and yank at it with all my might then toss it aside. She's on her feet, but the Mini K are on us before we have a chance to launch. Wrapping my arms around her, I yell, "Hold on!" then activate my kinetic barrier with a two-foot insulation field.

We're instantly knocked to the left by a Mini K with an overly large, oblong head and slam into the leg of another one, getting flung forward some thirty feet. This jarring, dizzying activity lasts for another twenty seconds, wearing down the energy in my kinetic barrier until I finally have a chance to plant my feet on solid ground and launch into the air with Aphrodite still in my arms. Red and Aden are both on their way back down as we're going up. "Head east," Aden points behind us. "The stampede is deep, but just less than a mile wide. We can get off to the side of it in one jump. Maybe two for the others."

We continue to climb and watch as Aden and Red touch down in between the chaos, then leap back out a second later, shooting off to the east. I turn off my kinetic barrier and release Aphrodite. "Line up and launch as soon as you hit."

"I've got it," she says.

"Give it all you've got and you should be able to make it in one jump." She nods in confirmation as we begin pick up speed in our decent. Luckily we both touch down and launch without a problem and cover the stretch at our first go. Aden and Red are keeping their distance from the edge of the stampeding chaos, which extends much further than the front lines of the Thyr attack. If we keep out of the way, then we'll have some time to collect ourselves and formulate the next move. Based off of what I could see from the air, we have a few minutes before the wave passes.

"Aden, any word from Kelly?" I ask, walking over to him.

He holds a hand up to my face and nods, then looks up at me. "Mackelson and the Plaguers will be here in minutes, but we've got another problem." A thunderous explosion radiates down from above and we all look up to see two more warships breaking through the edge of the atmosphere. "The Thyr rerouted two of their ships, we're about to have a lot of company."

No matter what we do, how much we fight or push back, there's always another fucking problem. "Did Kelly say how many Plaguers Mackelson has in tow?"

Aden shakes his head then seems to go back to his private conversation with Kelly. Life would be a little easier if she could open a secure, all comms channel for us, but if it comes at the cost of Erislad's men listening in, I'd rather not take the chance. "Wait, Kelly? Kelly, come in." Aden begins to pace. "Shit! The line is dead, it sounds like something hit their ship prior to the transmission going down. Fuck!"

I walk over to Aden and grasp his left shoulder with my right hand. "Calm down, she's a tough soldier. So is Hoffman." He's not listening. "I need you here," I say. He stops, looks at me and nods. "We've got our own problems to worry about, keep your head."

"Right, shit!" Aden exclaims as the warships leap to the front of his mind. "That's another two hundred thousand troops at least, on top of whatever survives the stampede and is in the wreck."

"Mackelson better have one hell of a force behind him," I mutter under my breath. At that moment, there's a high-pitched screech from the south, which causes Aphrodite to almost jump out of her suit. We all turn to our right, looking for the source of the noise. Red, Aden, and I know the sound all too well, but it's the first time that any of us have actually welcomed it.

Perfect timing, too. The stampede of Mini K is finishing up and passing to the south, just west of the Plaguers who are coming into the area. Some of the Plaguers begin to leap into the air, blocking out part of the Redantus's sun while the rest sweep across the blue sands like a high-pitched sea of darkness.

Mackelson falls from the sky, landing fifteen feet in front of us on his left foot and right knee. He's wearing one of the combat suits that was previously stolen from GHC and lifts his head to look at us. The skin from his face is peeling and pale, exposing the swelling muscle tissue underneath. His eyes are glazed over in a ghostly two toned, light gray and all of the hair has fallen out from his head. "Ready for another round?" he asks me with a smirk. His men press forward into battle against the remaining Thyr on the ground as the warships make their way toward the surface. It won't take more than a few minutes for them to touch down and join the fight.

"With you or the Thyr?" I throw back.

"Why don't we leave our personal bullshit till after the war, or at the very least the battle." He's clearly changed, anyone could tell by looking at him, but at least he's still got that 'business first' mentality. "Shithead," he says, nodding at Aden.

"Asshole," Aden nods back.

"How many fighters do you have?" I ask, walking up to him.

"Seventy thousand strong," he says with a hint of pride. "They should make easy work of the Thyr. They're matched in strength, but more agile and much quicker."

"Maybe the ones on the ground right now." I point up to the two warships descending. "Those carry two hundred and fifty thousand troops each."

"They're fighting for their homes," he snaps. "They'll complete the mission." With that Mackelson leaps into the air, disappearing into the massive crowd of Plaguers making their way toward the Thyr.

"I think that went well," Aden says.

"I think they underestimate the Thyr," I shoot back. Ten to one, not exactly the odds that I was hoping for. Especially since I can see SWIFTs streaming out of the two warships above. It's almost guaranteed that they're going to be performing bombing runs before dropping their soldiers. "We need to do something about those SWIFTs or the Plaguers are going to get slaughtered."

As one closes on our position, a Plaguer launches above the battlefield fray, and slams onto the outside of its cockpit. Four more follow behind him and latch on to different sections of the ship. Despite the pilot's attempt to shake them from the hull, they hang on and breach the interior within seconds. To my surprise, the

SWIFT whips around and begins firing on the others behind it. Fuck me. Plaguers can pilot.

"Looks like you underestimated the Plaguers," Aden says equally shocked.

"Time for us to get back into the fight," I say, launching back toward the Thyr before anyone has a chance to reply. Aden may be right, but I still have my doubts of our ability to turn the tide and unfortunately it doesn't take long for them to be confirmed. The Thyr continue to fall at a rapid pace, thanks to our four-man formation and the Plaguers overtaking some of their air power, but it isn't enough. The SWIFTs start turning on their Plaguer-occupied counterparts and soon there's weaponized debris in the form of metal fireballs raining down on the battle field. Lucky for us, at least as lucky as we can get right now, the payloads are only pinpoint situational piercers instead of the incendiary rounds that Red dropped earlier. The resulting blasts are only taking out several hundred men instead of several thousand.

Our numbers are dwindling and even though the Thyr are dropping much faster than us, it's not enough. The warships begin to send down troop transports that dump five hundred Thyr onto the surface per trip. Aphrodite takes down another Thyr in front of me, but I can see her movements are becoming slightly less precise. I can't tell if it's from stress brought on by the chaos of battle or if she's injured in some way. My proximity sensor goes off, alerting me to an abnormally large object closing fast on our position. "Move!" I shout, realizing that a burning SWIFT is spiraling out of control toward us.

Aden turns and grabs Aphrodite while leaping out of the area. I offset the balance of the Thyr I'm fighting, then push off just in time to look up and see Red's arms locked in combat. The Thyr he's battling stares back at me with a wicked grin. I don't have the chance to scream before the flaming scrap of metal that was once a SWIFT smashes them into the ground, igniting the ordinance attached and exploding into a fifty yard fireball. Our suits barely survive the impact and subsequent blast. Red had no chance.

While Blaze's death drained me emotionally, watching Red sweeps over my entire body in the form of shock-based muscle atrophy. I want to move upon landing, but can't. Red was always this indestructible father figure to Aden and me, and now in the time it takes me to blink, he's gone. Aden didn't have the personal connection that I did with Blaze and while he felt bad for my loss, it didn't compare to realizing that his lifelong mentor is now fused with the newly glassed surface of the planet. His reaction to Red's death is similar to my reaction to Blaze, minus begging the universe to reconsider.

Reading his body language, I can see doubt, followed by blinding anger that takes over within an instant. The surrounding Thyr close on him and Aphrodite as he drops his Ka, which causes it to retract and snap into place on his thigh. He leaps forward, clamping his left hand down on an advancing Thyr's clavicle, wraps his legs around its upper abdomen, then drives his right arm into its chest, pulling out a heart. Aden shrieks in tormented pain as his emotions leak through, then tosses the vital organ to his right, blinding an advancing Thyr with the blood splatter and leaping to attack another on his left. Aphrodite, though shocked by his barbarism, has her hands full and I've got Thyr advancing all around. Hopefully Aden's rage and ferocity will help him stay alive; I've never seen him this brutal. I'm ashamed to say that the sight also makes me happy, gleeful in fact. That fact worries me.

My body reactivates and my visor throws various warnings at my eyes while the muscle memory kicks in, causing me to dodge a laser blast, then leap backward away from an incoming sword. Any hold that we have on this fight is rapidly declining. The field of battle is overly saturated with a purple haze due to laser blasts cutting through clouds of kicked up blue sand. My eyes dart between the chaos to see glistening swords and axes. The Thyr may have adopted our weapons, but aren't quite ready to give up their old ways just yet. We have our Kas for close combat and they have theirs. SWIFTs fall from the sky at a rapid rate causing random explosions to ring out in every direction. As I continue to fight and keep my eyes on the surrounding battle, it gets harder and harder for me to get a location on the Plaguers or even Aden or Aphrodite. Everything is falling apart.

     Multiple Thyr to my right roar out in unison and I'm able to offer a short-lived glance in that direction to see Aphrodite's body impaled by a sword and held into the air above the crowd of savages. Her limbs are twitching and the width of the sword extends from her stomach to just below her neck. She's become another fallen soldier in the lost battle for Saudade. I should care, I should feel something, but I don't have any emotions left to offer. I think my brother and the fact that we're physically here are the only reasons that I'm still fighting. My survival instincts kick in and there's a moment of short-lived clarity. I need to find him. I need to get him out of here before they overwhelm us. Kelly must have escaped and they still have a chance at happiness together. We need to retreat from the battle and find Red's SWIFT to the east. Once he's secure, I can continue my bloody quest for vengeance and my downward spiral into psychotic barbarism.

     I dodge and weave, flip, rotate, and slide under Thyr, slicing and firing along the way to look for my brother. Just follow the bloody carnage, I tell myself, that's all I have to do. Blade cuts are clean, lasers sear and burn, but the brute strength of Aden and his augmented suit is leaving a crimson trail of torn body parts fit for a horror story from the Void. As I make my way through the carnage, there's a small clearing from the fighting and an arm that's slowing raising up from the bodies and shattered blue sand from my right. Recognizing the armor, I dash over to help the owner up.

Mackelson is torn to pieces, and looks even worse than before. He's missing a hand, has various stab wounds in his chest and no longer has legs. I grab an overdose of pain medication from my belt and prepare to jab it into his arm. There's no saving him, but there's also no need for him to lay here in agony. He grabs my hand with the one he has left. "No. No," he says in a calm voice. "Let me feel the pain. It's almost over now," he laughs weakly and coughs blood onto my suit. "History repeats itself. My men lay down their lives for you and your brother." Before I have a chance to respond he grabs the back of my neck and jerks me in close. "I'd do it all over again." I'm not sure what to say. He closes his eyes and rests his head back on the ground. "Gonna die now," he says quietly, trailing off toward the end.

It seems wrong to just leave Lieutenant Mackelson's body lying there among the dead Thyr given everything he's sacrificed for us, but I don't have much of a choice. "Thank you," I say with a slight nod before jumping to my feet and continuing on Aden's trail.

"Vali and Hoffman's slip was shot down," Alexander's voice comes through the comm like a megaphone, echoing through my helmet. I stop dead in my tracks. Tell me you didn't open the channel to Aden as well, please for love of whatever I have left, tell me it's a private channel.

There's a pause, then Aden's horrified voice asks "What?" as if he doesn't believe or understand what Alexander just said. I start running again, frantically hoping to catch up to Aden. The transmission was clear, no hint of movement in his voice, hopefully he's stopped.

"I'm sorry," Alexander apologizes as though it's his fault. "Erislad's men were able to trace their last communication to you.

He sent two SWIFTs to follow their slip." No, no no, why the fuck are you telling Aden this right now, Alexander? It could not be a worse time! Aden was unstable after Red's death, there's no telling what he'll do now that Kelly's gone.

"Alexander, shut up and close the channel!" I shout, bolting across a section of barren battlefield toward Aden. Most of the fighting has moved west, there aren't many Plaguers left, but I can see them making one hell of a last stand in the distance.

"I just thought..."

"CLOSE THE FUCKING CHANNEL!"

The comm goes silent. I run over the crest of a small hill and on the other side is a large crater from a downed SWIFT, with Aden kneeling on the ground in the center. There are corpses all around, Thyr and Plaguer alike. A majority of it is Aden's most recent handy work, I can tell by the damage done to the corpses. The rest was a result of the downed craft that caused the crater. Aden's helmet is retracted along with the abdominal portion of his suit. His shoulders are slumped over and it looks like there's something in his right hand, but I can't tell what it is from this angle.

I survey the area and upon seeing no immediate threats, slowly walk down the hill toward my brother fifty yards away. "Hey, brother," I say through the comm, retracting my helmet. I figure if he turns and sees my face, it might help more than the black, cold exterior of the armor. The audio comes through our neural chips and the microphone is tapped into our vocal chords, so even though our helmets are retracted, we can still hear and speak like normal. "I'm at your eight o'clock, forty yards out."

He turns his head slightly to see me through his peripheral vision, then looks back at the ground in front of his knees. "She's dead, Daemon."

"I heard Alexander."

"There's nothing left for me now."

"You've still got me," I say only slightly hurt by his statement as I know how painful this is for him. Thirty yards out, I continue to scanning the area for threats; we are very exposed at the moment.

"And what do you have?" he asks.

"I've got you," I reassure.

"Do you remember when we were human?"

"I do. I saw it, just after passing out from the hellfire payload."

"I did, too," he confirms. "We can't ever forget that. Forget who we once were." Twenty yards out. He sighs. "The universe doesn't want us anymore, Daemon. We've lived too long."

Aden lifts the object in his right hand from the ground and sets it on his lap. It's his sidearm. "Come on, brother, let's get the hell out of here and make those bastards pay. We've still got work to do."

"Not this time," he says quietly, lifting the gun. "No more bullshit." He presses the barrel to his chest, pointing it at his heart.

"Aden!" Fuck the perimeter, I start running toward him. "ADEN!"

"I'm sorry, Daemon, I swore," his voice cracks. "I told you that you were stronger than me." He whispers, "I'm coming Kelly."

"NO!"

There's a flash. The laser round explodes on impact blowing a hole through his back so large that I could fit my arm through it. The action I've just witnessed cuts out all communication from my brain, causing my body to fail. I want to scream but nothing comes out. My mouth won't move. I want to continue to run, to scoop up his body and cradle it in my arms until the Thyr find me, but my legs give out and I fall face first onto the ground.

My mind fires a single impulse, allowing me to open my mouth and wail into the shattered glass, sand, and blood beneath me. The resulting noise is sure to be heard by any Thyr within a mile radius. That wail gives way to nearly five hundred years of compounded emotional interest. I lay, helpless, crying, crippled by the loss of the one true thing in this world that defined who I am. Aden was everything that was best in me, I was his older brother and it was my job to protect him at all costs. I failed. First I failed the humans, then the Hemos, then Blaze, and finally my brother. There's only one thing left to do.

I must have clawed the remaining distance to Aden, though I don't remember doing so. I'm sitting up, ass buried in blood from the Thyr corpses all around, one of which I'm leaning against, with my brother's limp body in my arms, slowly rocking back and forth. Tears are streaming down my face, snot is leaking from my nose like a faucet, though I'm not crying with my body. I'm just staring at Aden's carnage throughout the crater and holding his body. All my emotions are gone, expelled by the harsh realities of the battlefield like an exorcised demon. The physical is just trying to catch up; taking its toll by rendering certain functions useless. In the event that I can will my arms to move before the Thyr find me, I have every intention of following my brother. Something moves to my left and sharp, stinging pain pierces my temple as the world goes dark.

* * *

My eyes slowly open to reveal Aden's body on my lap. I don't know how long I was out, but it couldn't have been too long as I'm still in the same place. Probably minutes. Darkness again. It's almost painful to open my eyes; lifting my groggy, wobbling head, I see Thyr all around the crater. They must have heard my scream and come to investigate. Judging by how many are here and how far away from the bulk of the battle we are, I'm guessing the fight is over. They've won.

"Whhh," My mouth isn't working too well, much like the rest of my body. No surprise there seeing as how the mere action of keeping my eyelids open is a daunting task right now. "Whhh. Well. You've won," I say slowly, looking at the feet of a particularly large Thyr approaching from the center of the pack. It stops five feet in front of me and as I look up, it seems to extend to the outer atmosphere of the planet. My eyelids shut for a few seconds of glorious darkness and upon opening, it's staring back down at me with a snide grin. The mouth has long scars on either side of it that extend up to its ears. A rifle butt to the temple doesn't provide for good memory recollection, but after a few seconds it comes to me. It's the same Thyr that climbed over the cliff wall and threw a sword at the blood tree on Earth before we launched and subsequently discovered their cloaking tech. I remember those scars and that snide grin.

"Small universe," I say under my breath. "Well come onnnn!" I shout, spit and blood spraying from my mouth. "What are you waiting for?" I blurt out in a surprisingly loud and frustrated tone. My voice echoes around the crater. The Thyr steps to the side of me and raises his axe into the air. I lower my head and stare at the lifeless body of my brother. "Aden." My eyelids feel heavy and drag the world around me into darkness, I figure it's be the last time.

To my surprise, I open them to the sound of my executioner's head hitting the ground in front of me. Using what little energy I have left, I lift my head to see the Thyr around me beginning to panic. Doing my best to keep my eyes open, I see random, severed limbs fall to the ground followed by the Thyr themselves, dead, as if killed by some invisible force or ghost. My eyes close for a few moments and when I open them, a third of the surrounding force is dead and the rest are freaking out, randomly shooting at thin air in an attempt to quell their invisible killer.

Then I see it. An armored soldier; a female, armored soldier wearing a gray and black combat suit with a gray hood. The armor and the mask is like nothing I've ever seen before, smooth and hard, confirming to the body, yet flexible and fast. Oh, so fast. She disappears from the view to my right, then reappears in my left peripheral, stabs a Thyr in the back with amazing speed and precision, then disappears again. Five more Thyr are dead before the one who was stabbed in the back slumps to his knees. Darkness once again. The suit's chemicals that are keeping my body awake and operating are beginning to burn out.

When I wake this time, two thirds of the surrounding force are dead. The mysterious assassin is hiding less and swings her blade in an arc, separating it into smaller sections like our own. However unlike ours, she releases the sections unto the world, using the momentum of the swing to hurl them at seven different Thyr who reel back in disorienting pain. The hilt rebuilds another solid blade from thin air and she disappears. She dispatches all seven before they have a chance to recover from the hits. I lower my head to the ground, unable to lift it anymore as my remaining energy is reserved for keeping my eyes open.

Less than a minute passes and I can no longer hear any Thyr in the area. I'm staring at my brother's body, then look up at the executioner's head on the ground as a grey boot kicks it off to the left. The assassin crouches down and pushes my forehead back so that I'm sitting up, leaning back a bit on the Thyr corpse behind me. "Who are you?" I manage to squeeze out weakly.

"Someone willing to listen," says a mechanical, robotic voice.

My eyes go wide as the assassin's helmet deconstructs, revealing her face.

"Ellie," my voice cracks.

"Hey, soldier."

I squint and zero in on her stark blue eyes. "Free me." She cocks her head in confusion and I'm so afraid to say the words that my lips quiver as I quietly demand. "Kill me." A tear rolls down my cheek and she shakes her head slightly. "Kill me," I say louder, almost shouting through flood of wet depression.

"Oh, Daemon." She shakes her head more purposefully and puts her right hand on my left cheek. "I can't."

"I want..." I try to explain, but stop. She called me Daemon.

"I'm sorry," she cuts me off. "This universe still needs you."

I gasp at the sudden warmth on my cheek beneath her hand. My consciousness starts to fade and my eyelids feel heavy. I know what this feeling is. My body isn't giving up, I'm not passing out from the stress, or pain, or shock. She dosed me with an extremely potent drug meant to knock me out. My bodily functions are normalizing, slowing, and I no longer have control. She offers a weak smile before the entire world goes black for one last time.

Epilogue: The Myth

6.25 - 2570 - 0123.1734 Grecillian High Command Mark

It took over a century for Major Erislad and General Vietus to hunt down every last Hemosapien that needed to be converted to the genetic Thyr mixture, but it was finally done. Major Erislad operated the Patriarch with a special team of loyal men scouring the universe to make sure the whole of the race was in fact converted. Now, after all this time, he and his men underwent the conversion as well. For their efforts, his men were rewarded with a new ship and a new captain, while the major was awarded control over the newly rebuilt Grecillian High Command.

Part of the reason for the new GHC was appreciation from the High Order. Its technological updates were unmatched in the known universe, but part of it was just the acceptance of simple fact. The new bodies they inhabited were larger than old ones and therefore new ships and structures needed to be built. The Thyr played their part in the construction and with the new gene pool of loyal, unflinching warriors, were easily dispatched once the job was done. Erislad was still getting used to the body and more specifically the ingestion of food and liquid beyond blood. It would take time. He was also getting used to his most recent promotion. With all his work over the last century, a few moves up was all but assured. Still, he didn't expect a Blood General promotion.

General Erislad's assistant, Private Rinowas, entered his office with a holographic display of the previous day's operational statistics. "Sir, the new facility is now operating at optimal levels since it's been brought up to full staff." The major sometimes envied the soldiers who had their memories wiped. His mind often wandered as other spoke and explained the mundane day to day operations of the base. He longed to command a crew that knew of battle, a crew that remembered what they were fighting for, but now, only a few remembered the truth. The general, as well as a few high placed individuals, maintained their memories in the conversion, along with a selected group of his best soldiers in the event that the impossible would arise. It just so happened that today, the so-called impossible would seem much less so.

Lieutenant Pomo stormed into the office with purpose and pushed Private Rinowas to the side. "Sir," he offered a salute. The general responded with a nod. "We've found him."

The general's eyes went wide and after some hesitation, he raised and flicked his right hand at the private. "Leave us. Now." The private saluted, then without waiting for a response, retreated from the room.

"How solid is the intel?" the general asked.

"I'd bet my life on it, sir. We've found Apor."

The general scoffed. "You very well may lose that bet." He looked down at his desk and a holographic screen appeared in front of him with a feed to Lieutenant Ofovos whose stone cold face stared back. *

"Sir?"

"Ready your men. We've found Daemon Athanos."

It was a long time since General Erislad had referred to him by that name. Daemon was the only reason that the major and his men had to retain their old memories. He looked forward to erasing the last shred of evidence that the old universe ever existed and moving forward with their new lives, without the ghosts of the past. Once Daemon was gone, they too would have their ancient memories wiped.

"It's time to end this."

About the Author

Jason grew up in PA and always enjoyed writing various poems or stories as a kid. He felt comfortable with writing, but there was never much thought or time put into it.

After going to Florida in 2006 to study 3D animation/film, he discovered a passion for the creative process. Years later, he moved out to California to pursue a career in animation, but eventually discovered that his heart just wasn't in it. Unsure of what to do next, he decided to create a bucket list and subsequently started writing.

Jason fell in love with writing and became intoxicated by the process involved in world and character creation. He took to Facebook and Wattpad to interact with other writers and polish his skills. He posted the first chapter of his second book, VOK, on Wattpad, an internationally renowned website that at the time saw 40 million users monthly and boasted over 80 million stories. While the main intent was to get feedback, he became inundated with requests to continue VOK. Weekly updates, led to updating twice a week. It reached the top five for Sci-Fi within four months and at seven months peaked at the #1 spot in Sci-Fi and #2 spot in Fantasy. The high rankings continued for the next four months until the book was finished and at the time of this printing the unedited version of VOK has just under one million views.

Jason currently works as a Wireless Consultant, and lives in Pennsylvania, but is looking to write full-time in the future. VOK is his first self-published book, and he is working on several other books in and out of the VOK universe, examples of which can be found on his Wattpad. He also has a short story published in Brave New Girls, an anthology of stories centered around strong, intelligent, tech-savvy young females. The book is available for purchase on Amazon and proceeds for the anthology are donated to a scholarship fund through the Society of Women Engineers.

Made in the USA
Middletown, DE
24 May 2016